Shavings
A Novel

by
Joseph Crosby Lincoln

Shavings
A Novel
by Joseph Crosby Lincoln

Copyright © 2024

All Rights reserved.

No part of this publication may be reproduced, stored in a retrieval system, or transmitted in any form or by any means, electronic, mechanical, photocopying or Otherwise, without the written permission of the publisher.
The author/editor asserts the moral right to be identified as the author/editor of this work.

ISBN: 978-93-67145-94-4

Published by
DOUBLE 9 BOOKS
2/13-B, Ansari Road
Daryaganj, New Delhi – 110002
info@double9books.com
www.double9books.com
Tel. 011-40042856

This book is under public domain

ABOUT THE AUTHOR

Joseph Crosby Lincoln was an American novelist, poet, and short story writer, with many of his works situated on a fictional Cape Cod. Lincoln was born in 1870 in Brewster, Massachusetts, on Cape Cod, and after his father died, his mother relocated the family to Chelsea, Massachusetts, an industrial community outside of Boston. Lincoln's writing career extolling "old Cape Cod" can be viewed as an attempt to return to an Eden that he had fled due to familial sorrow. Lincoln's work was frequently featured in renowned journals like The Saturday Evening Post and The Delineator. Lincoln was aware of contemporary naturalist writers like Frank Norris and Theodore Dreiser, who utilized American literature to delve into the depths of human nature, but he rejected the creative exercise. Lincoln stated that he was content "spinning yarns" that made readers feel good about themselves and their neighbors. His work served as the basis for six films and a short.

CONTENTS

- CHAPTER I 7
- CHAPTER II 16
- CHAPTER III 29
- CHAPTER IV 48
- CHAPTER V 55
- CHAPTER VI 71
- CHAPTER VII 91
- CHAPTER VIII 103
- CHAPTER IX 109
- CHAPTER X 124
- CHAPTER XI 134
- CHAPTER XII 148
- CHAPTER XIII 166
- CHAPTER XIV 177
- CHAPTER XV 188
- CHAPTER XVI 199
- CHAPTER XVII 210
- CHAPTER XVIII 226
- CHAPTER XIX 241
- CHAPTER XX 254
- CHAPTER XXI 271
- CHAPTER XXII 281

CHAPTER I

Mr. Gabriel Bearse was happy. The prominence given to this statement is not meant to imply that Gabriel was, as a general rule, unhappy. Quite the contrary; Mr. Bearse's disposition was a cheerful one and the cares of this world had not rounded his plump shoulders. But Captain Sam Hunniwell had once said, and Orham public opinion agreed with him, that Gabe Bearse was never happy unless he was talking. Now here was Gabriel, not talking, but walking briskly along the Orham main road, and yet so distinctly happy that the happiness showed in his gait, his manner and in the excited glitter of his watery eye. Truly an astonishing condition of things and tending, one would say, to prove that Captain Sam's didactic remark, so long locally accepted and quoted as gospel truth, had a flaw in its wisdom somewhere.

And yet the flaw was but a small one and the explanation simple. Gabriel was not talking at that moment, it is true, but he was expecting to talk very soon, to talk a great deal. He had just come into possession of an item of news which would furnish his vocal machine gun with ammunition sufficient for wordy volley after volley. Gabriel was joyfully contemplating peppering all Orham with that bit of gossip. No wonder he was happy; no wonder he hurried along the main road like a battery galloping eagerly into action.

He was on his way to the post office, always the gossip-sharpshooters' first line trench, when, turning the corner where Nickerson's Lane enters the main road, he saw something which caused him to pause, alter his battle-mad walk to a slower one, then to a saunter, and finally to a halt altogether. This something was a toy windmill fastened to a white picket fence and clattering cheerfully as its arms spun in the brisk, pleasant summer breeze.

The little windmill was one of a dozen, all fastened to the top rail of that fence and all whirling. Behind the fence, on posts, were other and larger windmills; behind these, others larger still. Interspersed among the mills were little wooden sailors swinging paddles; weather vanes in the shapes of wooden whales, swordfish, ducks, crows, seagulls; circles of little wooden profile sailboats, made to chase each other 'round and 'round a central post.

All of these were painted in gay colors, or in black and white, and all were in motion. The mills spun, the boats sailed 'round and 'round, the sailors did vigorous Indian club exercises with their paddles. The grass in the little yard and the tall hollyhocks in the beds at its sides swayed and bowed and nodded. Beyond, seen over the edge of the bluff and stretching to the horizon, the blue and white waves leaped and danced and sparkled. As a picture of movement and color and joyful bustle the scene was inspiring; children, viewing it for the first time, almost invariably danced and waved their arms in sympathy. Summer visitors, loitering idly by, suddenly became fired with the desire to set about doing something, something energetic.

Gabriel Bearse was not a summer visitor, but a "native," that is, an all-the-year-round resident of Orham, and, as his fellow natives would have cheerfully testified, it took much more than windmills to arouse HIS energy. He had not halted to look at the mills. He had stopped because the sight of them recalled to his mind the fact that the maker of these mills was a friend of one of the men most concerned in his brand new news item. It was possible, barely possible, that here was an opportunity to learn just a little more, to obtain an additional clip of cartridges before opening fire on the crowd at the post office. Certainly it might be worth trying, particularly as the afternoon mail would not be ready for another hour, even if the train was on time.

At the rear of the little yard, and situated perhaps fifty feet from the edge of the high sand bluff leading down precipitously to the beach, was a shingled building, whitewashed, and with a door, painted green, and four windows on the side toward the road. A clamshell walk led from the gate to the doors. Over the door was a sign, very neatly lettered, as follows: "J. EDGAR W. WINSLOW. MILLS FOR SALE." In the lot next to that, where the little shop stood, was a small, old-fashioned story-and-a-half Cape Cod house, painted a speckless white, with vivid green blinds. The blinds were shut now, for the house was unoccupied. House and shop and both yards were neat and clean as a New England kitchen.

Gabriel Bearse, after a moment's reflection, opened the gate in the picket fence and walked along the clamshell walk to the shop door. Opening the door, he entered, a bell attached to the top of the door jingling as he did so. The room which Mr. Bearse entered was crowded from floor to ceiling, save for a narrow passage, with hit- or-miss stacks of the wooden toys evidently finished and ready for shipment. Threading his way between the heaps of sailors, mills, vanes and boats, Gabriel came to a door evidently leading to another room. There was a sign tacked to this door, which read, "PRIVATE," but Mr. Bearse did not let that trouble him. He pushed the door open.

The second room was evidently the work-shop. There were a circular saw and a turning lathe, with the needful belts, and a small electric motor to furnish power. Also there were piles of lumber, shelves of paint pots and brushes, many shavings and much sawdust. And, standing beside a dilapidated chair from which he had evidently risen at the sound of the door bell, with a dripping paint brush in one hand and a wooden sailor in the other, there was a man. When he saw who his visitor was he sat down again.

He was a tall man and, as the chair he sat in was a low one and the heels of his large shoes were hooked over its lower rounds, his knees and shoulders were close together when he bent over his work. He was a thin man and his trousers hung about his ankles like a loose sail on a yard. His hair was thick and plentiful, a brown sprinkled with gray at the temples. His face was smooth-shaven, with wrinkles at the corners of the eyes and mouth. He wore spectacles perched at the very end of his nose, and looked down over rather than through them as he dipped the brush in the can of paint beside him on the floor.

"Hello, Shavin's," hailed Mr. Bearse, blithely.

The tall man applied the brush to the nude pine legs of the wooden sailor. One side of those legs were modestly covered forthwith by a pair of sky-blue breeches. The artist regarded the breeches dreamily. Then he said:

"Hello, Gab."

His voice was a drawl, very deliberate, very quiet, rather soft and pleasant. But Mr. Bearse was not pleased.

"Don't call me that," he snapped.

The brush was again dipped in the paint pot and the rear elevation of the pine sailor became sky-blue like the other side of him. Then the tall man asked:

"Call you what?"

"Gab. That's a divil of a name to call anybody. Last time I was in here Cap'n Sam Hunniwell heard you call me that and I cal'lated he'd die laughin'. Seemed to cal'late there was somethin' specially dum funny about it. I don't call it funny. Say, speakin' of Cap'n Sam, have you heard the news about him?"

He asked the question eagerly, because it was a part of what he came there to ask. His eagerness was not contagious. The man on the chair put down the blue brush, took up a fresh one, dipped it in another paint pot and proceeded to garb another section of his sailor in a spotless white shirt. Mr. Bearse grew impatient.

"Have you heard the news about Cap'n Sam?" he repeated. "Say, Shavin's, have you?"

The painting went serenely on, but the painter answered.

"Well, Gab," he drawled, "I—"

"Don't call me Gab, I tell you. 'Tain't my name."

"Sho! Ain't it?"

"You know well enough 'tain't. My name's Gabriel. Call me that— or Gabe. I don't like to be called out of my name. But say, Shavin's—"

"Well, Gab, say it."

"Look here, Jed Winslow, do you hear me?"

"Yes, hear you fust rate, Gabe—now."

Mr. Bearse's understanding was not easily penetrated; a hint usually glanced from it like a piece of soap from a slanting cellar door, but this time the speaker's tone and the emphasis on the "now" made a slight dent. Gabriel's eyes opened.

"Huh?" he grunted in astonishment, as if the possibility had never until that moment occured to him. "Why, say, Jed, don't you like to be called 'Shavin's'?"

No answer. A blue collar was added to the white shirt of the sailor.

"Don't you, Jed?" repeated Gabe.

Mr. Winslow's gaze was lifted from his work and his eyes turned momentarily in the direction of his caller.

"Gabe," he drawled, "did you ever hear about the feller that was born stone deef and the Doxology?"

"Eh? What— No, I never heard it."

The eyes turned back to the wooden sailor and Mr. Winslow chose another brush.

"Neither did he," he observed, and began to whistle what sounded like a dirge.

Mr. Bearse stared at him for at least a minute. Then he shook his head.

10 | Shavings: A Novel

"Well, by Judas!" he exclaimed. "I—I—I snum if I don't think you BE crazy, same as some folks say you are! What in the nation has— has your name got to do with a deef man and the Doxology?"

"Eh? . . . Oh, nothin'."

"Then what did you bust loose and tell me about 'em for? They wan't any of MY business, was they?"

"No-o. That's why I spoke of 'em."

"What? You spoke of 'em 'cause they wan't any of my business?"

"Ye-es . . . I thought maybe—" He paused, turned the sailor over in his hand, whistled a few more bars of the dirge and then finished his sentence. "I thought maybe you might like to ask questions about 'em," he concluded.

Mr. Bearse stared suspiciously at his companion, swallowed several times and, between swallows, started to speak, but each time gave it up. Mr. Winslow appeared quite oblivious of the stare. His brushes gave the wooden sailor black hair, eyes and brows, and an engaging crimson smile. When Gabriel did speak it was not concerning names.

"Say, Jed," he cried, "HAVE you heard about Cap'n Sam Hunniwell? 'Bout his bein' put on the Exemption Board?"

His companion went on whistling, but he nodded.

"Um-hm," grunted Gabe, grudgingly. "I presumed likely you would hear; he told you himself, I cal'late. Seth Baker said he see him come in here night afore last and I suppose that's when he told you. Didn't say nothin' else, did he?" he added, eagerly.

Again Mr. Winslow nodded.

"Did he? Did he? What else did he say?"

The tall man seemed to consider.

"Well," he drawled, at length, "seems to me I remember him sayin'—sayin'—"

"Yes? Yes? What did he say?"

"Well—er—seems to me he said good night just afore he went home."

The disappointed Gabriel lost patience. "Oh, you DIVILISH fool head!" he exclaimed, disgustedly. "Look here, Jed Winslow, talk sense for a minute, if you can, won't you? I've just heard somethin' that's goin' to make a big row in this town and it's got to do with Cap'n Sam's bein' app'inted on that Gov'ment Exemption Board for drafted folks. If you'd heard Phineas Babbitt goin' on the way I done, I guess likely you'd have been interested."

It was plain that, for the first time since his caller intruded upon his privacy, the maker of mills and sailors WAS interested. He did not put down his brush, but he turned his head to look and listen. Bearse, pleased with this symptom of attention, went on.

"I was just into Phineas' store," he said, "and he was there, so I had a chance to talk with him. He's been up to Boston and never got back till this afternoon, so I cal'lated maybe he hadn't heard about Cap'n Sam's app'intment. And I knew, too, how he does hate the Cap'n; ain't had nothin' but cuss words and such names for him ever since Sam done him out of gettin' the postmaster's job. Pretty mean trick, some folks call it, but—"

Mr. Winslow interrupted; his drawl was a trifle less evident.

"Congressman Taylor asked Sam for the truth regardin' Phineas and a certain matter," he said. "Sam told the truth, that's all."

"Well, maybe that's so, but does tellin' the truth about folks make 'em love you? I don't know as it does."

Winslow appeared to meditate.

"No-o," he observed, thoughtfully, "I don't suppose you do."

"No, I... Eh? What do you mean by that? Look here, Jed Winslow, if—"

Jed held up a big hand. "There, there, Gabe," he suggested, mildly. "Let's hear about Sam and Phin Babbitt. What was Phineas goin' on about when you was in his store?"

Mr. Bearse forgot personal grievance in his eagerness to tell the story.

"Why," he began, "you see, 'twas like this: 'Twas all on account of Leander. Leander's been drafted. You know that, of course?"

Jed nodded. Leander Babbitt was the son of Phineas Babbitt, Orham's dealer in hardware and lumber and a leading political boss. Between Babbitt, Senior, and Captain Sam Hunniwell, the latter President of the Orham National Bank and also a vigorous politician, the dislike had always been strong. Since the affair of the postmastership it had become, on Babbitt's part, an intense hatred. During the week just past young Babbitt's name had been drawn as one of Orham's quota for the new National Army. The village was still talking of the draft when the news came that Captain Hunniwell had been selected as a member of the Exemption Board for the district, the Board which was to hold its sessions at Ostable and listen to the pleas of those desiring to be excused from service. Not all of Orham knew this as yet. Jed Winslow had heard it, from Captain Sam himself. Gabe Bearse had heard it because he made it his business to hear everything, whether it concerned him or not—preferably not.

The war had come to Orham with the unbelievable unreality with which it had come to the great mass of the country. Ever since the news of the descent of von Kluck's hordes upon devoted Belgium, in the fall of 1914, the death grapple in Europe had, of course, been the principal topic of discussion at the post office and around the whist tables at the Setuckit Club, where ancient and retired mariners met and pounded their own and each other's knees while they expressed sulphurous opinions concerning the attitude of the President and Congress. These opinions were, as a usual thing, guided by the fact of their holders' allegiance to one or the other of the great political parties. Captain Sam Hunniwell, a lifelong and ardent Republican, with a temper as peppery as the chile con carne upon which, when commander of a steam freighter trading with Mexico, he had feasted so often—Captain Sam would have hoisted the Stars and Stripes to the masthead the day the Lusitania sank and put to sea in a dory, if need be, and armed only with a shotgun, to avenge that outrage. To hear Captain Sam orate concerning the neglect of duty of which he considered the United States government guilty was an experience, interesting or shocking, according to the drift of one's political or religious creed.

Phineas Babbitt, on the contrary, had at first upheld the policy of strict neutrality. "What business is it of ours if them furriners take to slaughterin' themselves?" he wanted to know. He hotly declared the Lusitania victims plaguey fools who knew what they were riskin' when they sailed and had got just what was comin' to 'em—that is, he was proclaiming it when Captain Sam heard him; after that the captain issued a proclamation of his own and was proceeding to follow words with deeds. The affair ended by mutual acquaintances leading Captain Sam from the Babbitt Hardware Company's store, the captain rumbling like a volcano and, to follow up the simile, still emitting verbal brimstone and molten lava, while Mr. Babbitt, entrenched behind his counter, with a monkey wrench in his hand, dared his adversary to lay hands on a law- abiding citizen.

When the Kaiser and von Tirpitz issued their final ultimatum, however, and the President called America to arms, Phineas, in company with others of his breed, appeared to have experienced a change of heart. At all events he kept his anti-war opinions to himself and, except that his hatred for the captain was more virulent than ever since the affair of the postmastership, he found little fault with the war preparations in the village, the organizing of a Home Guard, the raising of funds for a new flag and flagpole and the recruiting meeting in the town hall.

At that meeting a half dozen of Orham's best young fellows had expressed their desire to fight for Uncle Sam. The Orham band— minus its first cornet, who was himself one of the volunteers—had serenaded them at the railway station and the Congregational minister and Lawyer Poundberry of the Board of Selectmen had made speeches. Captain Sam Hunniwell, being called upon to say a few words, had said a few—perhaps, considering the feelings of the minister and the feminine members of his flock present, it is well they were not more numerous.

"Good luck to you, boys," said Captain Sam. "I wish to the Almighty I was young enough to go with you. And say, if you see that Kaiser anywheres afloat or ashore give him particular merry hell for me, will you?"

And then, a little later, came the news that the conscription bill had become a law and that the draft was to be a reality. And with that news the war itself became a little more real. And, suddenly, Phineas Babbitt, realizing that his son, Leander, was twenty-five years old and, therefore, within the limits of the draft age, became once more an ardent, if a little more careful, conscientious objector.

He discovered that the war was a profiteering enterprise engineered by capital and greed for the exploiting of labor and the common people. Whenever he thought it safe to do so he aired these opinions and, as there were a few of what Captain Hunniwell called "yellow-backed swabs" in Orham or its neighborhood, he occasionally had sympathetic listeners. Phineas, it is only fair to say, had never heretofore shown any marked interest in labor except to get as much of it for as little money as possible. If his son, Leander, shared his father's opinions, he did not express them. In fact he said very little, working steadily in the store all day and appearing to have something on his mind. Most people liked Leander.

Then came the draft and Leander was drafted. He said very little about it, but his father said a great deal. The boy should not go; the affair was an outrage. Leander wasn't strong, anyway; besides, wasn't he his father's principal support? He couldn't be spared, that's all there was about it, and he shouldn't be. There was going to be an Exemption Board, wasn't there? All right—just wait until he, Phineas, went before that board. He hadn't been in politics all these years for nothin'. Sam Hunniwell hadn't got all the pull there was in the county.

And then Captain Sam was appointed a member of that very board. He had dropped in at the windmill shop the very evening when he decided to accept and told Jed Winslow all about it. There never were two people more unlike than Sam Hunniwell and Jed Winslow, but they had been fast friends since boyhood. Jed knew that Phineas Babbitt had been on a trip to Boston and, therefore, had not heard of the captain's appointment. Now, according to Gabriel Bearse, he had returned and had heard of it, and according to Bearse's excited statement he had "gone on" about it.

"Leander's been drafted," repeated Gabe. "And that was bad enough for Phineas, he bein' down on the war, anyhow. But he's been cal'latin', I cal'late, to use his political pull to get Leander exempted off. Nine boards out of ten, if they'd had a man from Orham on 'em, would have gone by what that man said in a case like Leander's. And Phineas, he was movin' heavens and earth to get one of his friends put on as the right Orham man. And now—NOW, by godfreys domino, they've put on the ONE man that Phin can't influence, that hates Phin worse than a cat hates a swim. Oh, you ought to heard Phineas go on when I told him. He'd just got off the train, as you might say, so nobody'd had a chance to tell him. I was the fust one, you see. So—"

"Was Leander there?"

"No, he wan't. There wan't nobody in the store but Susie Ellis, that keeps the books there now, and Abner Burgess's boy, that runs errands and waits on folks when everybody else is busy. That was a funny thing, too—that about Leander's not bein' there. Susie said she hadn't seen him since just after breakfast time, half past seven o'clock or so, and when she telephoned the Babbitt house it turned out he hadn't been there, neither. Had his breakfast and went out, he did, and that's all his step-ma knew about him. But Phineas, he. . . . Eh? Ain't that the bell? Customer, I presume likely. Want me to go see who 'tis, Shavin's—Jed, I mean?"

CHAPTER II

But the person who had entered the outer shop saved Mr. Bearse the trouble. He, too, disregarded the "Private" sign on the door of the inner room. Before Gabriel could reach it that door was thrown open and the newcomer entered. He was a big man, gray-mustached, with hair a grizzled red, and with blue eyes set in a florid face. The hand which had opened the door looked big and powerful enough to have knocked a hole in it, if such a procedure had been necessary. And its owner looked quite capable of doing it, if he deemed it necessary, in fact he looked as if he would rather have enjoyed it. He swept into the room like a northwest breeze, and two bundles of wooden strips, cut to the size of mill arms, clattered to the floor as he did so.

"Hello, Jed!" he hailed, in a voice which measured up to the rest of him. Then, noticing Mr. Bearse for the first time, he added: "Hello, Gabe, what are you doin' here?"

Gabriel hastened to explain. His habitual desire to please and humor each person he met—each person of consequence, that is; very poor people or village eccentrics like Jed Winslow did not much matter, of course—was in this case augmented by a particular desire to please Captain Sam Hunniwell. Captain Sam, being one of Orham's most influential men, was not, in Mr. Bearse's estimation, at all the sort of person whom it was advisable to displease. He might—and did—talk disparagingly of him behind his back, as he did behind the back of every one else, but he smiled humbly and spoke softly in his presence. The consciousness of having just been talking of him, however, of having visited that shop for the express purpose of talking about him, made the explaining process a trifle embarrassing.

"Oh, howd'ye do, howd'ye do, Cap'n Hunniwell?" stammered Gabriel. "Nice day, ain't it, sir? Yes, sir, 'tis a nice day. I was just— er—that is, I just run in to see Shavin's here; to make a little call, you know. We was just settin' here talkin', wan't we, Shavin's—Jed, I mean?"

Mr. Winslow stood his completed sailor man in a rack to dry.

"Ya-as," he drawled, solemnly, "that was about it, I guess. Have a chair, Sam, won't you? . . . That was about it, we was sittin' and talkin' . . . I was sittin' and Gab—Gabe, I mean—was talkin'."

Captain Sam chuckled. As Winslow and Mr. Bearse were occupying the only two chairs in the room he accepted the invitation in its broad sense and, turning an empty box upon end, sat down on that.

"So Gabe was talkin', eh?" he repeated. "Well, that's singular. How'd that happen, Gabe?"

Mr. Bearse looked rather foolish. "Oh, we was just—just talkin' about—er—this and that," he said, hastily. "Just this and that, nothin' partic'lar. Cal'late I'll have to be runnin' along now, Jed."

Jed Winslow selected a new and unpainted sailor from the pile near him. He eyed it dreamily.

"Well, Gabe," he observed, "if you must, you must, I suppose. Seems to me you're leavin' at the most interestin' time. We've been talkin' about this and that, same as you say, and now you're leavin' just as 'this' has got here. Maybe if you wait—wait—a—"

The sentence died away into nothingness. He had taken up the brush which he used for the blue paint. There was a loose bristle in it. He pulled this out and one or two more came with it.

"Hu-um!" he mused, absently.

Captain Sam was tired of waiting.

"Come, finish her out, Jed—finish her out," he urged. "What's the rest of it?"

"I cal'late I'll run along now," said Mr. Bearse, nervously moving toward the door.

"Hold on a minute," commanded the captain. "Jed hadn't finished what he was sayin' to you. He generally talks like one of those continued-in-our-next yarns in the magazines. Give us the September installment, Jed—come."

Mr. Winslow smiled, a slow, whimsical smile that lit up his lean, brown face and then passed away as slowly as it had come, lingering for an instant at one corner of his mouth.

"Oh, I was just tellin' Gabe that the 'this' he was talkin' about was here now," he said, "and that maybe if he waited a space the 'that' would come, too. Seems to me if I was you, Gabe, I'd—"

But Mr. Bearse had gone.

Captain Hunniwell snorted. "Humph!" he said; "I judge likely I'm the 'this' you and that gas bag have been talkin' about. Who's the 'that'?"

His companion was gazing absently at the door through which Gabriel had made his hurried departure. After gazing at it in silence for a moment, he rose from the chair, unfolding section by section like a pocket rule, and, crossing the room, opened the door and took from its other side the lettered sign "Private" which had hung there. Then, with tacks and a hammer, he proceeded to affix the placard to the inner side of the door, that facing the room where he and Captain Sam were. The captain regarded this operation with huge astonishment.

"Gracious king!" he exclaimed. "What in thunder are you doin' that for? This is the private room in here, ain't it?"

Mr. Winslow, returning to his chair, nodded.

"Ya-as," he admitted, "that's why I'm puttin' the 'Private' sign on this side of the door."

"Yes, but— Why, confound it, anybody who sees it there will think it is the other room that's private, won't they?"

Jed nodded. "I'm in hopes they will," he said.

"You're in hopes they will! Why?"

"'Cause if Gabe Bearse thinks that room's private and that he don't belong there he'll be sartin sure to go there; then maybe he'll give me a rest."

He selected a new brush and went on with his painting. Captain Hunniwell laughed heartily. Then, all at once, his laughter ceased and his face assumed a troubled expression.

"Jed," he ordered, "leave off daubin' at that wooden doll baby for a minute, will you? I want to talk to you. I want to ask you what you think I'd better do. I know what Gab Bearse— Much obliged for that name, Jed; 'Gab's' the best name on earth for that critter—I know what Gab came in here to talk about. 'Twas about me and my bein' put on the Exemption Board, of course. That was it, wan't it? Um-hm, I knew 'twas. I was the 'this' in his 'this and that.' And Phin Babbitt was the 'that'; I'll bet on it. Am I right?"

Winslow nodded.

"Sure thing!" continued the captain. "Well, there 'tis. What am I goin' to do? When they wanted me to take the job in the first place I kind of hesitated. You know I did. 'Twas bound to be one of those thankless sort of jobs that get a feller into trouble, bound to be. And yet—and yet—well, SOMEBODY has to take those kind of jobs. And a man hadn't ought to talk all the time about how he wishes he could do somethin' to help his country, and then lay down and quit on the first chance that comes his way, just 'cause that chance ain't—ain't eatin' up all the pie in the state so the Germans can't get it, or somethin' like that. Ain't that so?"

"Seems so to me, Sam."

"Yes. Well, so I said I'd take my Exemption Board job. But when I said I'd accept it, it didn't run across my mind that Leander Babbitt was liable to be drafted, first crack out of the box. Now he IS drafted, and, if I know Phin Babbitt, the old man will be down on us Board fellers the first thing to get the boy exempted. AND, I bein' on the Board and hailin' from his own town, Orham here, it would naturally be to me that he'd come first. Eh? That's what he'd naturally do, ain't it?"

His friend nodded once more. Captain Sam lost patience.

"Gracious king!" he exclaimed. "Jed Winslow, for thunder sakes say somethin'! Don't set there bobbin' your head up and down like one of those wound-up images in a Christmas-time store window. I ask you if that ain't what Phin Babbitt would do? What would you do if you was in his shoes?"

Jed rubbed his chin.

"Step out of 'em, I guess likely," he drawled.

"Humph! Yes—well, any self-respectin' person would do that, even if he had to go barefooted the rest of his life. But, what I'm gettin' at is this: Babbitt'll come to me orderin' me to get Leander exempted. And what'll I say?"

Winslow turned and looked at him.

"Seems to me, Sam," he answered, "that if that thing happened there'd be only one thing to say. You'd just have to tell him that you'd listen to his reasons and if they seemed good enough to let the boy off, for your part you'd vote to let him off. If they didn't seem good enough—why—"

"Well—what?"

"Why, then Leander'd have to go to war and his dad could go to—"

"Eh? Go on. I want to hear you say it. Where could he go?"

Jed wiped the surplus paint from his brush on the edge of the can.

"To sellin' hardware," he concluded, gravely, but with a twinkle in his eye.

Captain Sam sniffed, perhaps in disappointment. "His hardware'd melt where I'D tell him to go," he declared. "What you say is all right, Ed. It's an easy doctrine to preach, but, like lots of other preacher's doctrines, it's hard to live up to. Phin loves me like a step-brother and I love him the same way.

Well, now here he comes to ask me to do a favor for him. If I don't do it, he'll say, and the whole town'll say, that I'm ventin' my spite on him, keepin' on with my grudge, bein' nasty, cussed, everything that's mean. If I do do it, if I let Leander off, all hands'll say that I did it because I was afraid of Phineas and the rest would say the other thing. It puts me in a devil of a position. It's all right to say, 'Do your duty,' 'Stand up in your shoes,' 'Do what you think's right, never mind whose boy 'tis,' and all that, but I wouldn't have that old skunk goin' around sayin' I took advantage of my position to rob him of his son for anything on earth. I despise him too much to give him that much satisfaction. And yet there I am, and the case'll come up afore me. What'll I do, Jed? Shall I resign? Help me out. I'm about crazy. Shall I heave up the job? Shall I quit?"

Jed put down the brush and the sailor man. He rubbed his chin.

"No-o," he drawled, after a moment.

"Oh, I shan't, eh? Why not?"

"'Cause you don't know how, Sam. It always seemed to me that it took a lot of practice to be a quitter. You never practiced."

"Thanks. All right, then, I'm to hang on, I suppose, and take my medicine. If that's all the advice you've got to give me, I might as well have stayed at home. But I tell you this, Jed Winslow: If I'd realized—if I'd thought about the Leander Babbitt case comin' up afore me on that Board I never would have accepted the appointment. When you and I were talkin' here the other night it's queer that neither of us thought of it. . . . Eh? What are you lookin at me like that for? You don't mean to tell me that YOU DID think of it? Did you?"

Winslow nodded.

"Yes," he said. "I thought of it."

"You DID! Well, I swear! Then why in thunder didn't you—"

He was interrupted. The bell attached to the door of the outer shop rang. The maker of windmills rose jerkily to his feet. Captain Sam made a gesture of impatience.

"Get rid of your customer and come back here soon as you can," he ordered. Having commanded a steamer before he left the sea and become a banker, the captain usually ordered rather than requested. "Hurry all you can. I ain't half through talkin' with you. For the land sakes, MOVE! Of all the deliberate, slow travelin'—"

He did not finish his sentence, nor did Winslow, who had started toward the door, have time to reach it. The door was opened and a short, thickset man, with a leathery face and a bristling yellow-white chin beard, burst into the room. At the sight of its occupants he uttered a grunt of satisfaction and his bushy brows were drawn together above his little eyes, the latter a washed-out gray and set very close together.

"Humph!" he snarled, vindictively. "So you BE here. Gabe Bearse said you was, but I thought probably he was lyin', as usual. Did he lie about the other thing, that's what I've come here to find out? Sam Hunniwell, have you been put on that Draft Exemption Board?"

"Yes," he said, curtly, "I have."

The man trembled all over.

"You have?" he cried, raising his voice almost to a scream.

"Yes, I have. What's it matter to you, Phin Babbitt? Seems to have het you up some, that or somethin' else."

"Het me up! By—" Mr. Phineas Babbitt swore steadily for a full minute. When he stopped for breath Jed Winslow, who had stepped over and was looking out of the window, uttered an observation.

"I'm afraid I made a mistake, changin' that sign," he said, musingly. "I cal'late I'll make another: 'Prayer meetin's must be held outside.'"

"By—," began Mr. Babbitt again, but this time it was Captain Sam who interrupted. The captain occasionally swore at other people, but he was not accustomed to be sworn at. He, too, began to "heat up." He rose to his feet.

"That'll do, Babbitt," he commanded. "What's the matter with you? Is it me you're cussin'? Because if it is—"

The little Babbitt eyes snapped defiance.

"If it is, what?" he demanded. But before the captain could reply Winslow, turning away from the window, did so for him.

"If it is, I should say 'twas a pretty complete job," he drawled. "I don't know when I've heard fewer things left out. You have reason to be proud, both of you. And now, Phineas," he went on, "what's it all about? What's the matter?"

Mr. Babbitt waved his fists again, preparatory to another outburst. Jed laid a big hand on his shoulder.

"Don't seem to me time for the benediction yet, Phineas," he said. "Ought to preach your sermon or sing a hymn first, seems so. What did you come here for?"

Phineas Babbitt's hard gray eyes looked up into the big brown ones gazing mildly down upon him. His gaze shifted and his tone when he next spoke was a trifle less savage.

"He knows well enough what I came here for," he growled, indicating Hunniwell with a jerk of his thumb. "He knows that just as well as he knows why he had himself put on that Exemption Board."

"I didn't have myself put there," declared the captain. "The job was wished on me. Lord knows I didn't want it. I was just tellin' Jed here that very thing."

"Wished on you nothin'! You planned to get it and you worked to get it and I know why you did it, too. 'Twas to get another crack at me. 'Twas to play another dirty trick on me like the one you played that cheated me out of the post office. You knew they'd drafted my boy and you wanted to make sure he didn't get clear. You—"

"That'll do!" Captain Hunniwell seized him by the shoulder. "That's enough," cried the captain. "Your boy had nothin' to do with it. I never thought of his name bein' drawn when I said I'd accept the job."

"You lie!"

"WHAT? Why, you little sawed-off, dried-up, sassy son of a sea cook! I'll—"

Winslow's lanky form was interposed between the pair; and his slow, gentle drawl made itself heard.

"I'm sorry to interrupt the experience meetin'," he said, "but I'VE got a call to testify and I feel the spirit aworkin'. Set down again, Sam, will you please. Phineas, you set down over there. Please set down, both of you. Sam, as a favor to me—"

But the captain was not in a favor-extending mood. He glowered at his adversary and remained standing.

"Phin—" begged Winslow. But Mr. Babbitt, although a trifle paler than when he entered the shop, was not more yielding.

"I'm particular who I set down along of," he declared. "I'd as soon set down with a—a rattlesnake as I would with some humans."

Captain Sam was not pale, far from it.

"Skunks are always afraid of snakes, they tell me," he observed, tartly. "A rattlesnake's honest, anyhow, and he ain't afraid to bite. He ain't all bad smell and nothin' else."

Babbitt's bristling chin beard quivered with inarticulate hatred. Winslow sighed resignedly.

"Well," he asked, "you don't mind the other—er—critter in the menagerie sittin', do you? Now—now—now, just a minute," he pleaded, as his two companions showed symptoms of speaking simultaneously. "Just a minute; let me say a word. Phineas, I judge the only reason you have for objectin' to the captain's bein' on the Exemption Board is on account of your son, ain't it? It's just on Leander's account?"

But before the furious Mr. Babbitt could answer there came another interruption. The bell attached to the door of the outer shop rang once more. Jed, who had accepted his own invitation to sit, rose again with a groan.

"Now I wonder who THAT is?" he drawled, in mild surprise.

Captain Hunniwell's frayed patience, never noted for long endurance, snapped again. "Gracious king! go and find out," he roared. "Whoever 'tis 'll die of old age before you get there."

The slow smile drifted over Mr. Winslow's face. "Probably if I wait and give 'em a chance they'll come in here and have apoplexy instead," he said. "That seems to be the fashionable disease this afternoon. They won't stay out there and be lonesome; they'll come in here where it's private and there's a crowd. Eh? Yes, here they come."

But the newest visitor did not come, like the others, uninvited into the "private" room. Instead he knocked on its door. When Winslow opened it he saw a small boy with a yellow envelope in his hand.

"Hello, Josiah," hailed Jed, genially. "How's the president of the Western Union these days?"

The boy grinned bashfully and opined the magnate just mentioned was "all right." Then he added:

"Is Mr. Babbitt here? Mr. Bearse—Mr. Gabe Bearse—is over at the office and he said he saw Mr. Babbitt come in here."

"Yes, he's here. Want to see him, do you?"

"I've got a telegram for him."

Mr. Babbitt himself came forward and took the yellow envelope. After absently turning it over several times, as so many people do when they receive an unexpected letter or message, he tore it open.

Winslow and Captain Sam, watching him, saw his face, to which the color had returned in the last few minutes, grow white again. He staggered a little. Jed stepped toward him.

"What is it, Phin?" he asked. "Somebody dead or—"

Babbitt waved him away. "No," he gasped, chokingly. "No, let me be. I'm—I'm all right."

Captain Sam, a little conscience-stricken, came forward. "Are you sick, Phin?" he asked. "Is there anything I can do?"

Phineas glowered at him. "Yes," he snarled between his clenched teeth, "you can mind your own darned business."

Then, turning to the boy who had brought the message, he ordered: "You get out of here."

The frightened youngster scuttled away and Babbitt, the telegram rattling in his shaking hand, followed him. The captain, hurrying to the window, saw him go down the walk and along the road in the direction of his store. He walked like a man stricken.

Captain Sam turned back again. "Now what in time was in that telegram?" he demanded. Jed, standing with his back toward him and looking out of the window on the side of the shop toward the sea, did not answer.

"Do you hear me?" asked the captain. "That telegram struck him like a shock of paralysis. He went all to pieces. What on earth do you suppose was in it? Eh? Why don't you say somethin'? YOU don't know what was in it, do you?"

Winslow shook his head. "No," he answered. "I don't know's I do."

"You don't know as you do? Well, do you GUESS you do? Jed Winslow, what have you got up your sleeve?"

The proprietor of the windmill shop slowly turned and faced him. "I don't know's there's anything there, Sam," he answered, "but— but I shouldn't be much surprised if that telegram was from Leander."

"Leander? Leander Babbitt? What . . . Eh? What in thunder do YOU want?"

The last question was directed toward the window on the street side of the shop. Mr. Gabriel Bearse was standing on the outside of that window, energetically thumping on the glass.

"Open her up! Open her up!" commanded Gabe. "I've got somethin' to tell you."

Captain Sam opened the window. Gabriel's face was aglow with excitement. "Say! Say!" he cried. "Did he tell you? Did he tell you?"

"Did who tell what?" demanded the captain.

"Did Phin Babbitt tell you what was in that telegram he just got? What did he say when he read it? Did he swear? I bet he did! If that telegram wan't some surprise to old Babbitt, then—"

"Do you know what 'twas—what the telegram was?"

"Do I? You bet you I do! And I'm the only one in this town except Phin and Jim Bailey that does know. I was in the telegraph office when Jim took it over the wire. I see Jim was pretty excited. 'Well,' says he, 'if this won't be some jolt to old Phin!' he says. 'What will?' says I. 'Why,' says he—"

"What was it?" demanded Captain Sam. "You're dyin' to tell us, a blind man could see that. Get it off your chest and save your life. What was it?"

Mr. Bearse leaned forward and whispered. There was no real reason why he should whisper, but doing so added a mysterious, confidential tang, so to speak, to the value of his news.

"'Twas from Leander—from Phin's own boy, Leander Babbitt, 'twas. 'Twas from him, up in Boston and it went somethin' like this: 'Have enlisted in the infantry. Made up my mind best thing to do. Will not be back. Have written particulars.' That was it, or pretty nigh it. Leander's enlisted. Never waited for no Exemption Board nor nothin', but went up and enlisted on his own hook without tellin' a soul he was goin' to. That's the way Bailey and me figger it up. Say, ain't that some news? Godfreys, I must hustle back to the post office and tell the gang afore anybody else gets ahead of me. So long!"

He hurried away on his joyful errand. Captain Hunniwell closed the window and turned to face his friend.

"Do you suppose that's true, Jed?" he asked. "Do you suppose it CAN be true?"

Jed nodded. "Shouldn't be surprised," he said.

"Good gracious king! Do you mean the boy went off up to Boston on his own hook, as that what's-his-name—Gab—says, and volunteered and got himself enlisted into the army?"

"Shouldn't wonder, Sam."

"Well, my gracious king! Why—why—no wonder old Babbitt looked as if the main topsail yard had fell on him. Tut, tut, tut! Well, I declare! Now what do you suppose put him up to doin' that?"

Winslow sat down in his low chair again and picked up the wooden sailor and the paint brush.

"Well, Sam," he said, slowly, "Leander's a pretty good boy."

"Yes, I suppose he is, but he's Phin Babbitt's son."

"I know, but don't it seem to you as if some sorts of fathers was like birthmarks and bow legs; they come early in life and a feller ain't to blame for havin' 'em? Sam, you ain't sorry the boy's volunteered, are you?"

"Sorry! I should say not! For one thing his doin' it makes my job on the Exemption Board a mighty sight easier. There won't be any row there with Phineas now."

"No-o, I thought 'twould help that. But that wan't the whole reason, Sam."

"Reason for what? What do you mean?"

"I mean that wan't my whole reason for tellin' Leander he'd better volunteer, better go up to Boston and enlist, same as he did. That was part, but 'twan't all."

Captain Sam's eyes and mouth opened. He stared at the speaker in amazement.

"You told him to volunteer?" he repeated. "You told him to go to Boston and— YOU did? What on earth?"

Jed's brush moved slowly down the wooden legs of his sailor man.

"Leander and I are pretty good friends," he explained. "I like him and he—er—hum—I'm afraid that paint's kind of thick. Cal'late I'll have to thin it a little."

Captain Sam condemned the paint to an eternal blister.

"Go on! go on!" he commanded. "What about you and Leander? Finish her out. Can't you see you've got my head whirlin' like one of those windmills of yours? Finish her OUT!"

Jed looked over his spectacles.

"Oh!" he said. "Well, Leander's been comin' in here pretty frequent and we've talked about his affairs a good deal. He's always wanted to enlist ever since the war broke out."

"He HAS?"

"Why, sartin. Just the same as you would, or—or I hope I would, if I was young and—and," with a wistful smile, "different, and likely to be any good to Uncle Sam. Yes, Leander's been anxious to go to war, but his dad was so set against it all and kept hollerin' so about the boy's bein' needed in the store, that Leander didn't hardly know what to do. But then when he was drawn on the draft list he came in here and he and I had a long talk. 'Twas yesterday, after you'd told me about bein' put on the Board, you know. I could see the trouble there'd be between you and Phineas and—and—well, you see, Sam, I just kind of wanted that boy to volunteer. I—I don't know why, but—" He looked up from his work and stared dreamily out of the window. "I guess maybe 'twas because I've been wishin' so that I could go myself—or—do SOMETHIN' that was some good. So Leander and I talked and finally he said, 'Well, by George, I WILL go.' And—and—well, I guess that's all; he went, you see."

The captain drew a long breath.

"He went," he repeated. "And you knew he'd gone?"

"No, I didn't know, but I kind of guessed."

"You guessed, and yet all the time I've been here you haven't said a word about it till this minute."

"Well, I didn't think 'twas much use sayin' until I knew."

"Well, my gracious king, Jed Winslow, you beat all my goin' to sea! But you've helped Uncle Sam to a good soldier and you've helped me out of a nasty row. For my part I'm everlastin' obliged to you, I am so."

Jed looked pleased but very much embarrassed.

"Sho, sho," he exclaimed, hastily, "'twan't anything. Oh, say," hastily changing the subject, "I've got some money 'round here somewheres I thought maybe you'd take to the bank and deposit for me next time you went, if 'twan't too much trouble."

"Trouble? Course 'tain't any trouble. Where is it?"

Winslow put down his work and began to hunt. From one drawer of his work bench, amid nails, tools and huddles of papers, he produced a small bundle of banknotes; from another drawer another bundle. These, however, did not seem to satisfy him entirely. At last, after a good deal of very deliberate search, he unearthed more paper currency from the pocket of a dirty pair of overalls hanging on a nail, and emptied a heap of silver and coppers from a battered can on the shelf. Captain Hunniwell, muttering to himself, watched the collecting process. When it was completed, he asked:

"Is this all?"

"Eh? Yes, I guess 'tis. I can't seem to find any more just now. Maybe another batch'll turn up later. If it does I'll keep it till next time."

The captain, suppressing his emotions, hastily counted the money.

"Have you any idea how much there is here?" he asked.

"No, I don't know's I have. There's been quite consider'ble comin' in last fortni't or so. Summer folks been payin' bills and one thing or 'nother. Might be forty or fifty dollars, I presume likely."

"Forty or fifty! Nearer a hundred and fifty! And you keep it stuffed around in every junk hole from the roof to the cellar. Wonder to me you don't light your pipe with it. I shouldn't wonder if you did. How many times have I told you to deposit your money every three days anyhow? How many times?"

Mr. Winslow seemed to reflect.

"Don't know, Sam," he admitted. "Good many, I will give in. But— but, you see, Sam, if—if I take it to the bank I'm liable to forget I've got it. Long's it's round here somewheres I—why, I know where 'tis and—and it's handy. See, don't you?"

The captain shook his head.

"Jed Winslow," he declared, "as I said to you just now you beat all my goin' to sea. I can't make you out. When I see how you act with money and business, and how you let folks take advantage of you, then I think you're a plain dum fool. And yet when you bob up and do somethin' like gettin' Leander Babbitt to volunteer and gettin' me out of that row with his father, then—well, then, I'm ready to swear you're as wise as King Solomon ever was. You're a puzzle to me, Jed. What are you, anyway—the dum fool or King Solomon?"

Jed looked meditatively over his spectacles. The slow smile twitched the corners of his lips.

"Well, Sam," he drawled, "if you put it to vote at town meetin' I cal'late the majority'd be all one way. But, I don't know"—; he paused, and then added, "I don't know, Sam, but it's just as well as 'tis. A King Solomon down here in Orham would be an awful lonesome cuss."

CHAPTER III

Upon a late September day forty-nine years and some months before that upon which Gabe Bearse came to Jed Winslow's windmill shop in Orham with the news of Leander Babbitt's enlistment, Miss Floretta Thompson came to that village to teach the "downstairs" school. Miss Thompson was an orphan. Her father had kept a small drug store in a town in western Massachusetts. Her mother had been a clergyman's daughter. Both had died when she was in her 'teens. Now, at twenty, she came to Cape Cod, pale, slim, with a wealth of light brown hair and a pair of large, dreamy brown eyes. Her taste in dress was peculiar, even eccentric, and Orham soon discovered that she, herself, was also somewhat eccentric.

As a schoolteacher she was not an unqualified success. The "downstairs" curriculum was not extensive nor very exacting, but it was supposed to impart to the boys and girls of from seven to twelve a rudimentary knowledge of the three R's and of geography. In the first two R's, "readin' and 'ritin'," Miss Thompson was proficient. She wrote a flowery Spencerian, which was beautifully "shaded" and looked well on the blackboard, and reading was the dissipation of her spare moments. The third "R," 'rithmetic, she loathed.

Youth, even at the ages of from seven to twelve, is only too proficient in learning to evade hard work. The fact that Teacher took no delight in traveling the prosaic highways of addition, multiplication and division, but could be easily lured to wander the flowery lanes of romantic fiction, was soon grasped by the downstairs pupils. The hour set for recitation by the first class in arithmetic was often and often monopolized by a holdover of the first class in reading, while Miss Floretta, artfully spurred by questions asked by the older scholars, rhapsodized on the beauties of James Fenimore Cooper's "Uncas," or Dickens' "Little Nell," or Scott's "Ellen." Some of us antiques, then tow-headed little shavers in the front seats, can still remember Miss Floretta's rendition of the lines:

"And Saxon—I am Roderick Dhu!"

The extremely genteel, not to say ladylike, elocution of the Highland chief and the indescribable rising inflection and emphasis on the "I."

These literary rambles had their inevitable effect, an effect noted, after a time, and called to the attention of the school committee by old Captain Lycurgus Batcheldor, whose two grandchildren were among the ramblers.

"Say," demanded Captain Lycurgus, "how old does a young-one have to be afore it's supposed to know how much four times eight is? My Sarah's Nathan is pretty nigh ten and HE don't know it. Gave me three answers he did; first that 'twas forty-eight, then that 'twas eighty-four and then that he'd forgot what 'twas. But I noticed he could tell me a whole string about some feller called Lockintar or Lochinvar or some such outlandish name, and not only his name but where he came from, which was out west somewheres. A poetry piece 'twas; Nate said the teacher'd been speakin' it to 'em. I ain't got no objection to speakin' pieces, but I do object to bein' told that four times eight is eighty-four, 'specially when I'm buyin' codfish at eight cents a pound. I ain't on the school committee, but if I was—"

So the committee investigated and when Miss Thompson's year was up and the question arose as to her re-engagement, there was considerable hesitancy. But the situation was relieved in a most unexpected fashion. Thaddeus Winslow, first mate on the clipper ship, "Owner's Favorite," at home from a voyage to the Dutch East Indies, fell in love with Miss Floretta, proposed, was accepted and married her.

It was an odd match: Floretta, pale, polite, impractical and intensely romantic; Thad, florid, rough and to the point. Yet the married pair seemed to be happy together. Winslow went to sea on several voyages and, four years after the marriage, remained at home for what, for him, was a long time. During that time a child, a boy, was born.

The story of the christening of that child is one of Orham's pet yarns even to this day. It seems that there was a marked disagreement concerning the name to be given him. Captain Thad had had an Uncle Edgar, who had been very kind to him when a boy. The captain wished to name his own youngster after this uncle. But Floretta's heart was set upon "Wilfred," her favorite hero of romance being Wilfred of Ivanhoe. The story is that the parents being no nearer an agreement on the great question, Floretta made a proposal of compromise. She proposed that her husband take up his stand by the bedroom window and the first male person he saw passing on the sidewalk below, the name of that person should be given to their offspring; a sporting proposition certainly. But the story goes on to detract a bit from the sporting element by explaining that Mrs. Winslow was expecting a call at that hour from the Baptist minister, and the Baptist minister's Christian name was "Clarence," which, if not quite as romantic as Wilfred, is by no means common and prosaic. Captain Thad, who had not been informed of the expected ministerial call and was something of a sport himself, assented to the arrangement. It was solemnly agreed that the name of the first male passer-by should be the name of the new Winslow. The captain took up his post of observation at the window and waited.

He did not have to wait long. Unfortunately for romance, the Reverend Clarence was detained at the home of another parishioner a trifle longer than he had planned and the first masculine to pass the Winslow home was old Jedidah Wingate, the fish peddler. Mrs. Diadama Busteed, who was acting as nurse in the family and had been sworn in as witness to the agreement between husband and wife, declared to the day of her death that that death was hastened by the shock to her nervous and moral system caused by Captain Thad's language when old Jedidah hove in sight. He vowed over and over again that he would be everlastingly condemned if he would label a young-one of his with such a crashety-blank-blanked outrage of a name as "Jedidah." "Jedidiah" was bad enough, but there WERE a few Jedidiahs in Ostable County, whereas there was but one Jedidah. Mrs. Winslow, who did not fancy Jedidah any more than her husband did, wept; Captain Thad's profanity impregnated the air with brimstone. But they had solemnly sworn to the agreement and Mrs. Busteed had witnessed it, and an oath is an oath. Besides, Mrs. Winslow was inclined to think the whole matter guided by Fate, and, being superstitious as well as romantic, feared dire calamity if Fate was interfered with. It ended in a compromise and, a fortnight later, the Reverend Clarence, keeping his countenance with difficulty, christened a red-faced and protesting infant "Jedidah Edgar Wilfred Winslow."

Jedidah Edgar Wilfred grew up. At first he was called "Edgar" by his father and "Wilfred" by his mother. His teachers, day school and Sunday school, called him one or the other as suited their individual fancies. But his schoolmates and playfellows, knowing that he hated the name above all else on earth, gleefully hailed him as "Jedidah." By the time he was ten he was "Jed" Winslow beyond hope of recovery. Also it was settled locally that he was "queer"—not "cracked" or "lacking," which would have implied that his brain was affected—but just "queer," which meant that his ways of thinking and acting were different from those of Orham in general.

His father, Captain Thaddeus, died when Jed was fifteen, just through the grammar school and ready to enter the high. He did not enter; instead, the need of money being pressing, he went to work in one of the local stores, selling behind the counter. If his father had lived he would, probably, have gone away after finishing high school and perhaps, if by that time the mechanical ability which he possessed had shown itself, he might even have gone to some technical school or college. In that case Jed Winslow's career might have been very, very different. But instead he went to selling groceries, boots, shoes, dry goods and notions for Mr. Seth Wingate, old Jedidah's younger brother.

As a grocery clerk Jed was not a success, neither did he shine as a clerk in the post office, nor as an assistant to the local expressman. In desperation he began to learn the carpenter's trade and, because he liked to handle tools, did pretty well at it. But he continued to be "queer" and his absent-minded dreaminess was in evidence even then.

"I snum I don't know what to make of him," declared Mr. Abijah Mullett, who was the youth's "boss." "Never know just what he's goin' to do or just what he's goin' to say. I says to him yesterday: 'Jed,' says I, 'you do pretty well with tools and wood, considerin' what little experience you've had. Did Cap'n Thad teach you some or did you pick it up yourself?' He never answered for a minute or so, seemed to be way off dreamin' in the next county somewheres. Then he looked at me with them big eyes of his and he drawled out: 'Comes natural to me, Mr. Mullett, I guess,' he says. 'There seems to be a sort of family feelin' between my head and a chunk of wood.' Now what kind of an answer was that, I want to know!"

Jed worked at carpentering for a number of years, sometimes going as far away as Ostable to obtain employment. And then his mother was seized with the illness from which, so she said, she never recovered. It is true that Doctor Parker, the Orham physician, declared that she had recovered, or might recover if she cared to. Which of the pair was right does not really matter. At all events Mrs. Winslow, whether she recovered or not, never walked abroad again. She was "up and about," as they say in Orham, and did some housework, after a fashion, but she never again set foot across the granite doorstep of the Winslow cottage. Probably the poor woman's mind was slightly affected; it is charitable to hope that it was. It seems the only reasonable excuse for the oddity of her behavior during the last twenty years of her life, for her growing querulousness and selfishness and for the exacting slavery in which she kept her only son.

During those twenty years whatever ambition Jedidah Edgar Wilfred may once have had was thoroughly crushed. His mother would not hear of his leaving her to find better work or to obtain promotion. She needed him, she wailed; he was her life, her all; she should die if he left her. Some hard-hearted townspeople, Captain Hunniwell among them, disgustedly opined that, in view of such a result, Jed should be forcibly kidnaped forthwith for the general betterment of the community. But Jed himself never rebelled. He cheerfully gave up his youth and early middle age to his mother and waited upon her, ran her errands, sat beside her practically every evening and read romance after romance aloud for her benefit. And his "queerness" developed, as under such circumstances it was bound to do.

Money had to be earned and, as the invalid would not permit him to leave her to earn it, it was necessary to find ways of earning it at home. Jed did odd jobs of carpentering and cabinet making, went fishing sometimes, worked in gardens between times, did almost anything, in fact, to bring in the needed dollars. And when he was thirty-eight years old he made and sold his first "Cape Cod Winslow windmill," the forerunner of the thousands to follow. That mill, made in some of his rare idle moments and given to the child of a wealthy summer visitor, made a hit. The child liked it and other children wanted mills just like it. Then "grown-ups" among the summer folk took up the craze. "Winslow mills" became the fad. Jed built his little shop, or the first installment of it.

Mrs. Floretta Winslow died when her son was forty. A merciful release, Captain Sam and the rest called it, but to Jed it was a stunning shock. He had no one to take care of now except himself and he did not know what to do. He moped about like a deserted cat. Finally he decided that he could not live in the old house where he was born and had lived all his life. He expressed his feelings concerning that house to his nearest friend, practically his sole confidant, Captain Sam.

"I can't somehow seem to stand it, Sam," he said, solemnly. "I can't stay in that house alone any longer, it's—it's too sociable."

The captain, who had expected almost anything but that, stared at him.

"Sociable!" he repeated. "You're sailin' stern first, Jed. Lonesome's what you mean, of course."

Jed shook his head.

"No-o," he drawled, "I mean sociable. There's too many boys in there, for one thing."

"Boys!" Captain Sam was beginning to be really alarmed now. "Boys! Say—say, Jed Winslow, you come along home to dinner with me. I bet you've forgot to eat anything for the last day or so— been inventin' some new kind of whirlagig or other—and your empty stomach's gone to your head and made it dizzy. Boys! Gracious king! Come on home with me."

Jed smiled his slow smile. "I don't mean real boys, Sam," he explained. "I mean me—I'm the boys. Nights now when I'm walkin' around in that house alone I meet myself comin' round every corner. Me when I was five, comin' out of the buttery with a cooky in each fist; and me when I was ten sittin' studyin' my lesson book in the corner; and me when I was fifteen, just afore Father died, sittin' all alone thinkin' what I'd do when I went to Boston Tech same as he said he was cal'latin' to send me. Then—"

He paused and lapsed into one of his fits of musing. His friend drew a breath of relief.

"Oh!" he exclaimed. "Well, I don't mind your meetin' yourself. I thought first you'd gone off your head, blessed if I didn't. You're a queer critter, Jed. Get those funny notions from readin' so many books, I guess likely. Meetin' yourself! What an idea that is! I suppose you mean that, bein' alone in that house where you've lived since you was born, you naturally get to thinkin' about what used to be."

Jed stared wistfully at the back of a chair.

"Um-hm," he murmured, "and what might have been—and—and ain't."

The captain nodded. Of all the people in Orham he, he prided himself, was the only one who thoroughly understood Jed Winslow. And sometimes he did partially understand him; this was one of the times.

"Now—now—now," he said, hastily, "don't you get to frettin' yourself about your not amountin' to anything and all that. You've got a nice little trade of your own buildin' up here. What more do you want? We can't all be—er—Know-it-alls like Shakespeare, or— or rich as Standard Oil Companies, can we? Look here, what do you waste your time goin' back twenty-five years and meetin' yourself for? Why don't you look ahead ten or fifteen and try to meet yourself then? You may be a millionaire, a—er—windmill trust or somethin' of that kind, by that time. Eh? Ha, ha!"

Jed rubbed his chin.

"When I meet myself lookin' like a millionaire," he observed, gravely, "I'll have to do the way you do at your bank, Sam—call in somebody to identify me."

Captain Sam laughed. "Well, anyhow," he said, "don't talk any more foolishness about not livin' in your own house. If I was you—"

Mr. Winslow interrupted. "Sam," he said, "the way to find out what you would do if you was me is to make sure WHAT you'd do—and then do t'other thing, or somethin' worse."

"Oh, Jed, be reasonable."

Jed looked over his spectacles. "Sam," he drawled, "if I was reasonable I wouldn't be me."

And he lived no longer in the old house. Having made up his mind, he built a small two-room addition to his workshop and lived in that. Later he added a sleeping room—a sort of loft—and a little covered porch on the side toward the sea. Here, in pleasant summer twilights or on moonlight nights, he sat and smoked. He had a good many callers and but few real friends. Most of the townspeople liked him, but almost all considered him a joke, an oddity, a specimen to be pointed out to those of the summer people who were looking for "types." A few, like Mr. Gabriel Bearse, who distinctly did NOT understand him and who found his solemn suggestions and pointed repartee irritating at times, were inclined to refer to him in these moments of irritation as "town crank." But they did not really mean it when they said it. And some others, like Leander Babbitt or Captain Hunniwell, came to ask his advice on personal matters, although even they patronized him just a little. He had various nicknames, "Shavings" being the most popular.

His peculiar business, the making of wooden mills, toys and weather vanes, had grown steadily. Now he shipped many boxes of these to other seashore and mountain resorts. He might have doubled his output had he chosen to employ help or to enlarge his plant, but he would not do so. He had rented the old Winslow house furnished once to a summer tenant, but he never did so again, although he had many opportunities. He lived alone in the addition to the little workshop, cooking his own meals, making his own bed, and sewing on his own buttons.

And on the day following that upon which Leander Babbitt enrolled to fight for Uncle Sam, Jedidah Edgar Wilfred Winslow was forty- five years old.

He was conscious of that fact when he arose. It was a pleasant morning, the sun was rising over the notched horizon of the tumbling ocean, the breeze was blowing, the surf on the bar was frothing and roaring cheerily — and it was his birthday. The morning, the sunrise, the surf and all the rest were pleasant to contemplate — his age was not. So he decided not to contemplate it. Instead he went out and hoisted at the top of the short pole on the edge of the bluff the flag he had set there on the day when the United States declared war against the Hun. He hoisted it every fine morning and he took it in every night.

He stood for a moment, watching the red, white and blue flapping bravely in the morning sunshine, then he went back into his little kitchen at the rear of the workshop and set about cooking his breakfast. The kitchen was about as big as a good-sized packing box and Jed, standing over the oilstove, could reach any shelf in sight without moving. He cooked his oatmeal porridge, boiled his egg and then sat down at the table in the next room — his combined living and dining-room and not very much bigger than the kitchen— to eat. When he had finished, he washed the dishes, walked up to the post office for the mail and then, entering the workshop, took up the paint brush and the top sailor-man of the pile beside him and began work. This, except on Sundays, was his usual morning routine. It varied little, except that he occasionally sawed or whittled instead of painted, or, less occasionally still, boxed some of his wares for shipment.

During the forenoon he had some visitors. A group of summer people from the hotel came in and, after pawing over and displacing about half of the movable stock, bought ten or fifteen dollars' worth and departed. Mr.

Winslow had the satisfaction of hearing them burst into a shout of laughter as they emerged into the yard and the shrill voice of one of the females in the party rose above the hilarity with: "Isn't he the WEIRDEST thing!" And an accompanying male voice appraised him as "Some guy, believe me! S-o-o-me guy!" Jed winced a little, but he went on with his painting. On one's forty-fifth birthday one has acquired or should have acquired a certain measure of philosophical resignation.

Other customers or lookers came and went. Maud Hunniwell, Captain Sam's daughter, dropped in on her way to the post office. The captain was a widower and Maud was his only child. She was, therefore, more than the apple of his eye, she was a whole orchard of apples. She was eighteen, pretty and vivacious, and her father made a thorough job of spoiling her. Not that the spoiling had injured her to any great extent, it had not as yet, but that was Captain Sam's good luck. Maud was wearing a new dress—she had a new one every week or so—and she came into the windmill shop to show it. Of course she would have denied that that was the reason for her coming, but the statement stands, nevertheless. She and Jed were great chums and had been since she could walk. She liked him, took his part when she heard him criticized or made fun of, and was always prettily confidential and friendly when they were alone together. Of course there was a touch of superiority and patronage in her friendship. She should not be blamed for this; all Orham, consciously or unconsciously, patronized Jed Winslow.

She came into the inner shop and sat down upon the same upturned box upon which her father had sat the afternoon before. Her first remark, after "good mornings" had been exchanged, was concerning the "Private" sign on the inner side of the door.

"What in the world have you put that sign inside here for?" she demanded.

Mr. Winslow explained, taking his own deliberate time in making the explanation. Miss Hunniwell wrinkled her dainty upturned nose and burst into a trill of laughter.

"Oh, that's lovely," she declared, "and just like you, besides. And do you think Gabe Bearse will go back into the other room when he sees it?"

Jed looked dreamily over his spectacles at the sign. "I don't know," he drawled. "If I thought he'd go wherever that sign was I ain't sure but I'd tack it on the cover of the well out in the yard yonder."

His fair visitor laughed again. "Why, Jed," she exclaimed. "You wouldn't want to drown him, would you?"

Jed seemed to reflect. "No-o," he answered, slowly, "don't know's I would—not in my well, anyhow."

Miss Hunniwell declared that that was all nonsense. "You wouldn't drown a kitten," she said. "I know that because when Mrs. Nathaniel Rogers' old white cat brought all her kittens over here the first of this summer you wouldn't even put them out in the yard at night, to say nothing of drowning them. All six and the mother cat stayed here and fairly swarmed over you and ate you out of house and home. Father said he believed they fed at the first table and you were taking what was left. It was a mercy the old cat decided to lead them back to the Rogers' again or I don't know WHAT might have become of you by this time."

Jed seemed to be thinking; there was a reminiscent twinkle in his eye.

"The old cat didn't lead 'em back," he said. "Nathaniel took 'em back. Didn't I ever tell you about that?"

"No, you didn't. You KNOW you didn't. Mr. Rogers took them back? I can't believe it. He told everywhere about town that he was glad to get rid of the whole family and, as you and the cats seemed to be mutually happy together, he wasn't going to disturb you. He thought it was a great joke on you. And he took them back himself? Why?"

Mr. Winslow rubbed his chin. "I don't know's I'd ought to say anything about it," he said. "I haven't afore. I wouldn't interfere with Nate's sales for anything."

"Sales? Sales of what? Oh, you mean thing! Don't be so provoking! Tell me the whole story this minute."

Jed painted a moment or two. Then he said: "We-ell, Maud, you see those kittens got to be kind of a nuisance. They was cunnin' and cute and all that, but they was so everlastin' lively and hungry that they didn't give me much of a chance. I was only one, you see, and they had a majority vote every time on who should have the bed and the chairs and the table and one thing or 'nother. If I sat down I sat on a cat. If I went to bed I laid down on cats, and when I turned them out and turned in myself they came and laid down on ME. I slept under fur blankets most of June. And as for eatin'— Well, every time I cooked meat or fish they sat down in a circle and whooped for some. When I took it off the fire and put it in a plate on the table, I had to put another plate and a—a plane or somethin' heavy on top of it or they'd have had it sartin sure. Then when I sat down to eat it they formed a circle again like a reg'lar band and tuned up and hollered. Lord a-mercy, HOW they did holler! And if one of the kittens stopped, run out of wind or got a sore throat or anything, the old cat would bite it to set it goin' again. She wan't goin' to have any shirkin' in HER orchestra. I ate to music, as you might say, same as I've read they do up to Boston restaurants. And about everything I did eat was stuffed with cats' hairs. Seemed sometimes as if those kittens was solid fur all the way through; they never could have shed all that hair from the outside. Somebody told me that kittens never shed hair, 'twas only full grown cats did that. I don't believe it. Nate Rogers' old maltee never shed all that alone; allowin' her a half barrel, there was all of another barrel spread around the premises. No-o, those cats was a good deal of a nuisance. Um-hm.... Yes, they was...."

He paused and, apparently having forgotten that he was in the middle of a story, began to whistle lugubriously and to bend all his other energies to painting. Miss Hunniwell, who had laughed until her eyes were misty, wiped them with her handkerchief and commanded him to go on.

"Tell me the rest of it," she insisted. "How did you get rid of them? How did Mr. Rogers come to take them back?"

"Eh?... Oh, why, you see, I went over to Nate's three or four times and told him his cat and kittens were here and I didn't feel right to deprive him of 'em any longer. He said never mind, I could keep 'em long as I wanted to. I said that was about as long as I had kept 'em. Then he said he didn't know's he cared about ever havin' 'em again; said he and his wife had kind of lost their taste for cats, seemed so. I—well, I hinted that, long as the tribe was at my house I wan't likely to have a chance to taste much of anything, but it didn't seem to have much effect. Then—"

"Yes, yes; go on! go on!"

"Oh.... Then one day Nate he happened to be in here—come to borrow somethin', some tool seems to me 'twas—and the cats was climbin' round promiscuous same as usual. And one of the summer women came in while he was here, wanted a mill for her little niece or somethin'. And she saw one of the animals and she dropped everything else and sang out: 'Oh, what a beautiful kitten! What unusual coloring! May I see it?' Course she was seein' it already, but I judged she meant could she handle it, so I tried to haul the critter loose from my leg—there was generally one or more of 'em shinnin' over me somewhere. It squalled when I took hold of it and she says: 'Oh, it doesn't want to come, does it! It must have a very affectionate disposition to be so attached to you.' Seemed to me 'twas attached by its claws more'n its disposition, but I pried it loose and handed it to her. Then she says again, 'What unusual colorin'! Will you sell this one to me? I'll give you five dollars for it.'"

He stopped again. Another reminder from Miss Hunniwell was necessary to make him continue.

"And you sold one of those kittens for five dollars?" she cried.

"No-o."

"You didn't? Why, you foolish man! Why not?"

"I never had a chance. Afore I could say a word Nate Rogers spoke up and said the kittens belonged to him. Then she saw another one that she hadn't seen afore and she says: 'Oh, that one has more unusual colorin's even than this. I never saw such color in a cat.' Course she meant ON a cat but we understood what she meant. 'Are they a very rare breed?' she asked. Nate said they was and—"

Miss Hunniwell interrupted. "But they weren't, were they?" she cried. "I never knew they were anything more than plain tabby."

Jed shook his head. "Nate said they was," he went on solemnly. "He said they were awful rare. Then she wanted to know would he sell one for five dollars. He said no, he couldn't think of it."

"Why, the greedy old thing!"

"And so he and she had it back and forth and finally they struck a bargain at seven dollars for the one that looked most like a crazy quilt."

"Seven dollars for a CAT? What color was it, for goodness' sake?"

"Oh, all kinds, seemed so. Black and white and maltee and blue and red and green—"

"Green! What ARE you talking about? Who ever saw a green cat?"

"This woman saw one that was part green and she bought it. Then she said she'd take it right along in her car. Said she had a friend that was as loony about cats as she was and she was goin' to fetch her right down the very next day. And a couple of hours after she'd gone Nate and his boy came back with a clothes basket with a board over the top and loaded in the balance of the family and went off with 'em. I ain't seen a hair of 'em since—no, I won't say that quite, but I ain't seen THEM."

"And didn't he give you any of the seven dollars?"

"No-o."

"But you had been feeding those kittens and their mother for weeks."

"Ye-es."

"But didn't you ASK for anything?"

"We-ll, I told Nate he might maybe leave one of the kittens, so's I could have a—er—souvenir of the visit, but he wouldn't do it. Said those kittens was rare and—er—precious, or words to that effect. He didn't intend to let another go as cheap as he had that one."

"Oh. . . . I see. I remember now; I heard some one saying something, early in July, about the sign on the Rogers' front fence. 'Rare Cats for Sale' they said it was. I think. Of course, I never thought of THOSE kittens. He must have sold them all, for the sign isn't there now."

Jed whistled a few bars. "I don't hardly think he's sold 'em," he said. "I presume likely he's just gone out of the business."

"I don't see why he shouldn't sell them. Green cats ought to sell quickly enough, I should think. Were they green, honest and truly, Jed?"

Mr. Winslow nodded.

"They were that mornin'," he drawled, solemnly.

"That morning? What do you mean?"

"We-ll, you see, Maud, those kittens were into everything and over everything most of the time. Four of 'em had got in here early afore I came downstairs that day and had been playin' hide and hoot amongst my paint pots. They was green in spots, sure enough, but I had my doubts as to its bein' fast color."

Maud laughed joyfully over the secret of the green pussies.

"I wish I might have seen that woman's face after the colors began to wear off her 'rare' kitten," she said.

Jed smiled slightly. "Nathan saw it," he said. "I understood he had to take back the kitten and give up the seven dollars. He don't hardly speak to me nowadays. Seems to think 'twas my fault. I don't hardly think 'twas, do you?"

Miss Hunniwell's call lasted almost an hour. Besides a general chat concerning Leander Babbit's voluntary enlistment, the subject which all Orham had discussed since the previous afternoon, she had a fresh bit of news. The government had leased a large section of land along the bay at East Harniss, the next village to Orham and seven or eight miles distant, and there was to be a military aviation camp there.

"Oh, it's true!" she declared, emphatically. "Father has known that the Army people have been thinking of it for some time, but it was really decided and the leases signed only last Saturday. They will begin building the barracks and the buildings—the—oh, what do they call those big sheds they keep the aeroplanes in?"

"The hangars," said Winslow, promptly.

"Yes, that's it. They will begin building those right away." She paused and looked at him curiously. "How did you know they called them hangars, Jed?" she asked.

"Eh? . . . Oh, I've read about 'em in the newspapers, that's all. . . . H-u-u-m. . . . So we'll have aeroplanes flyin' around here pretty soon, I suppose. Well, well!"

"Yes. And there'll be lots and lots of the flying men—the what-do-you-call-'ems—aviators, and officers in uniform—and all sorts. What fun! I'm just crazy about uniforms!"

Her eyes snapped. Jed, in his quiet way, seemed excited, too. He was gazing absently out of the window as if he saw, in fancy, a procession of aircraft flying over Orham flats.

"They'll be flyin' up out there," he said, musingly. "And I'll see 'em—I will. Sho!"

"Jed," she asked, "would you like to be an aviator?"

Miss Hunniwell regarded him mischievously. "Jed," she asked, "would you like to be an aviator?"

Jed's answer was solemnly given. "I'm afraid I shouldn't be much good at the job," he drawled.

His visitor burst into another laugh. He looked at her over his glasses.

"What is it?" he asked.

"Oh, nothing; I—I was just thinking of you in a uniform, that's all."

Jed smiled his slow, fleeting smile.

"I guess likely I would be pretty funny," he admitted. "Any Germans I met would probably die laughin' and that might help along some."

But after Miss Hunniwell had gone he sat for some minutes gazing out of the window, the wistful, dreamy look on his lean, homely face. Then he sighed, and resumed his painting.

That afternoon, about half past five, he was still at his task when, hearing the doorbell ring, he rose and went into the front shop. To his astonishment the shop was empty. He looked about for the expected customer or caller, whoever he or she might be, and saw no one. He stepped to the window and looked out, but there was no one on the steps or in the yard. He made up his mind that he must have dreamed of the bell-ringing and was turning back to the inner room, when a voice said:

"Please, are you the windmill man?"

Jed started, turned again, and stared about him.

"Please, sir, here I am," said the voice.

Jed, looking down, instead of up or on a level, saw his visitor then. That is, he saw a tumbled shock of curls and a pair of big round eyes looking up at him over a stock of weather vanes.

"Hello!" he exclaimed, in surprise.

The curls and eyes came out from behind the stack of vanes. They were parts of a little girl, and the little girl made him a demure little courtesy.

"How do you do?" she said.

Jed regarded her in silence for a moment. Then, "Why, I'm fair to middlin' smart just at present," he drawled. "How do YOU find yourself to-day?"

The young lady's answer was prompt and to the point. "I'm nicely, thank you," she replied, and added: "I was sick at my stomach yesterday, though."

This bit of personal information being quite unexpected, Mr. Winslow scarcely knew what comment to make in reply to it.

"Sho!" he exclaimed. "Was you, though?"

"Yes. Mamma says she is 'clined to think it was the two whole bananas and the choc'late creams, but I think it was the fried potatoes. I was sick twice—no, three times. Please, I asked you something. Are you the windmill man?"

Jed, by this time very much amused, looked her over once more. She was a pretty little thing, although just at this time it is doubtful if any of her family or those closely associated with her would have admitted it. Her face was not too clean, her frock was soiled and mussed, her curls had been blown into a tangle and there were smooches, Jed guessed them to be blackberry stains, on her hands, around her mouth and even across her small nose. She had a doll, its raiment in about the same condition as her own, tucked under one arm. Hat she had none.

Mr. Winslow inspected her in his accustomed deliberate fashion.

"Guess you've been havin' a pretty good time, haven't you?" he inquired.

The small visitor's answer was given with dignity.

"Yes," she said. "Will you please tell me if you are the windmill man?"

Jed accepted the snub with outward humility and inward appreciation.

"Why, yes," he admitted; "I presume likely I'm the windmill man. Is there anything I can do for you this evenin'?"

Apparently there was, for the child, untucking the doll from beneath her right arm and tucking it under the left, pointed her right hand at a wooden weather-vane in the shape of a sperm whale and asked:

"Please, does that fish go 'round?"

"Go 'round? Go 'round where?"

"I mean does it go 'round and 'round on a stick?"

"Cal'late it does when it has a chance."

"And does it make the wind blow no'theast by no'th and—and like that?"

"Eh? Make the wind blow—how?"

"I mean does it make the wind blow different ways, no'theast by no'th and cantin' 'round to the sou-east and—and those ways? Captain Hedge has got a fish up on his barn that used to do that, but now it won't 'cause he cal'lates it's rusted fast. He said he guessed he would have to be getting a new one. When I saw the fishes out in your yard I thought about it and I thought I would come in and see if you had the right kind. Is this one a—a gunfish?"

"A WHICH fish?"

"A gunfish. No, that isn't it. A—a swordfish, that's it. Captain Hedge's is a swordfish."

"We-ll, that particular one got a wrong start and ended up by bein' a whale, but I shouldn't wonder if we could find a swordfish if we looked. Yes, here's one. Think that would do?"

The child looked it over very carefully.

"Yes," she said, "I think it would. If you're sure it would make the wind go right."

"We-ll, I guess likely I could guarantee that fish would go 'most any way the wind did, unless it should take a notion to blow straight up and down, which don't happen often. So you know Cap'n Hedge, do you? Relation of his, are you? Visitin' there?"

"No. Mamma and I are boarding at Mrs. Smalley's, but I go over to call on Captain Hedge 'most every day."

"Sho! Want to know! Well, that's nice and sociable. So you're boardin' at Luretta Smalley's. My! you're consider'ble ways from home, ain't you? Is your mamma with you?"

For the first time the youthful caller's poise seemed a trifle shaken.

"No-o . . . no," she stammered, and added, hastily: "How much is this fish, please?"

"I generally sell that sort of fish for about two dollars." He looked out of the window, hummed a tune, and then added: "Let's see, what did you say your name was?"

"I didn't, but it's Barbara Armstrong. HOW much did you say the fish was?"

"Eh? . . . Oh, two dollars."

Miss Armstrong looked very much disappointed.

"Oh, dear," she sighed. "I didn't know it would be as much as that. I—I'm 'fraid I can't get it."

"So? That's too bad. What was you cal'latin' to do with it, if you did get it?"

"I was going to give it to Captain Hedge. He misses his, now that it's rusted so fast that it won't go. But I can't get it. I haven't got but fourteen cents, ten that Mamma gave me this morning for being a good girl and taking my medicine nice yesterday, and four that Mrs. Smalley gave me for getting the eggs last week. And two dollars is EVER so much more than fourteen cents, isn't it?"

"Hum. . . . 'Tis a little more, that's right. It's considered more by the—um—er—best authorities. Hum . . . er . . . h-u-u-m. Sometimes, though, I do take off a little somethin' for spot cash. You'd pay spot cash, I presume likely, wouldn't you?"

"I—I don't know what spot cash is. I'd pay fourteen cents."

Jed rubbed his chin. "We-e-ll," he drawled, gravely, "I'm afraid I couldn't hardly knock off all that that comes to. But," taking another and much smaller vane from a shelf, "there's an article, not quite so big, that I usually get fifty cents for. What do you think of that?"

The child took the miniature swordfish and inspected it carefully.

"It's a baby one, isn't it," she observed. "Will it tell wind just as good as the big one?"

"Tell wind? Hum! . . . Don't know's I ever heard it put just that way afore. But a clock tells time, so I suppose there's no reason why a vane shouldn't tell wind. Yes, I guess 'twill tell wind all right."

"Then I think it might do." She seemed a little doubtful. "Only," she added, "fifty cents is lots more than fourteen, isn't it?"

Mr. Winslow admitted that it was. "But I tell you," he said, after another period of reflection, "seein' as it's you I'll make a proposal to you. Cap'n Eri Hedge is a pretty good friend of mine, same as he is of yours. Suppose you and I go in partners. You put in your fourteen cents and I'll put in the rest of the swordfish. Then you can take it to Cap'n Eri and tell him that we're givin' it to him together. You just consider that plan for a minute now, will you?"

Miss Armstrong looked doubtful.

"I—I don't know as I know what you mean," she said. "What did you want me to do?"

"Why, consider the plan. You know what 'consider' means, don't you?"

"I know a Mother Goose with it in. That one about the piper and the cow:

> 'He took up his pipes and he played her a tune,
>
> Consider, old cow, consider.'

But I don't know as I SURELY know what he wanted the cow to do? Does 'consider' mean see if you like it?"

"That's the idea. Think it over and see if you'd like to go halves with me givin' the fish to Cap'n Hedge."

The curls moved vigorously up and down.

"I think I should," she decided.

"Good! Now you wait and I'll do it up."

He wrapped the toy vane in a piece of paper and handed it to his small patron. She gravely produced a miniature velvet purse with the remnants of some bead fringe hanging to its lower edge and laid a dime and four pennies on the top of a packing case between them. It was growing dark in the shop and Jed lighted one of the bracket lamps. Returning, he found the coins laid in a row and Miss Armstrong regarding them somewhat soberly.

"There isn't any MORE than fourteen, is there?" she asked. "I mean—I mean fourteen cents takes all of it, doesn't it?"

Jed looked at her face. His eye twinkled.

"Well, suppose it didn't?" he asked. "What then?"

She hesitated. "Why," she stammered, "if—if there was ONE left over I—maybe I could buy something tomorrow at the candy store. Not to-day, 'cause I told Mamma I wouldn't to-day 'cause I was sick at my stomach yesterday—but to-morrow I could."

Mr. Winslow carefully counted the coins and then, spreading them out on his big palm, showed them to her.

"There!" he said. "Now you've given me the fourteen cents. I've got 'em, haven't I?"

Miss Barbara solemnly nodded.

"Yes," continued Jed. "Now I'll put 'em back in your wallet again. There they are, shut up in the wallet. Now you put the wallet in your pocket. Now take your fish bundle under your arm. There! now everything's settled. You've got the fish, haven't you? Sartin'. Yes, and I've been paid for it, haven't I?"

The child stared at him.

"But—but—" she began.

"Now—now don't let's argue about it," pleaded Jed, plaintively. "Argum always gives me the—er—epizootic or somethin'. You saw me have the money right in my hand. It's all settled; think it over and see if it ain't. You've got the fish and I've HAD the fourteen cents. Now run right along home and don't get lost. Good-night."

He led her gently to the door and closed it behind her. Then, smiling and shaking his head, he returned to the inner shop, where he lit the lamps and sat down for another bit of painting before supper. But that bit was destined not to be done that night. He had scarcely picked up his brush before the doorbell rang once more. Returning to the outer room, he found his recent visitor, the swordfish under one arm and the doll under the other, standing in the aisle between the stacked mills and vanes and looking, so it seemed to him, considerably perturbed.

"Well, well!" he exclaimed. "Back again so soon? What's the matter; forget somethin', did you?"

Miss Armstrong shook her head.

"No-o," she said. "But—but—"

"Yes? But what?"

"Don't you think—don't you think it is pretty dark for little girls to be out?"

Jed looked at her, stepped to the door, opened it and looked out, and then turned back again.

"Why," he admitted, "it is gettin' a little shadowy in the corners, maybe. It will be darker in an hour or so. But you think it's too dark for little girls already, eh?"

She nodded. "I don't think Mamma would like me to be out when it's so awful dark," she said.

"Hum! . . . Hum. . . . Does your mamma know where you are?"

The young lady's toe marked a circle on the shop floor.

"No-o," she confessed, "I—I guess she doesn't, not just exactly."

"I shouldn't be surprised. And so you've come back because you was afraid, eh?"

She swallowed hard and edged a little nearer to him.

"No-o," she declared, stoutly, "I—I wasn't afraid, not very; but— but I thought the—the swordfish was pretty heavy to carry all alone and—and so—"

Jed laughed aloud, something that he rarely did.

"Good for you, sis!" he exclaimed. "Now you just wait until I get my hat and we'll carry that heavy fish home together."

Miss Armstrong looked decidedly happier.

"Thank you very much," she said. "And—and, if you please, my name is Barbara."

CHAPTER IV

The Smalley residence, where Mrs. Luretta Smalley, relict of the late Zenas T., accommodated a few "paying guests," was nearly a mile from the windmill shop and on the Orham "lower road." Mr. Winslow and his new acquaintance took the short cuts, through by-paths and across fields, and the young lady appeared to have thoroughly recovered from her misgivings concerning the dark—in reality it was scarcely dusk—and her doubts concerning her ability to carry the "heavy" swordfish without help. At all events she insisted upon carrying it alone, telling her companion that she thought perhaps he had better not touch it as it was so very, very brittle and might get broken, and consoling him by offering to permit him to carry Petunia, which fragrant appellation, it appeared, was the name of the doll.

"I named her Petunia after a flower," she explained. "I think she looks like a flower, don't you?"

If she did it was a wilted one. However, Miss Armstrong did not wait for comment on the part of her escort, but chatted straight on. Jed learned that her mother's name was Mrs. Ruth Phillips Armstrong. "It used to be Mrs. Seymour Armstrong, but it isn't now, because Papa's name was Doctor Seymour Armstrong and he died, you know." And they lived in a central Connecticut city, but perhaps they weren't going to live there any more because Mamma had sold the house and didn't know exactly WHAT to do. And they had been in Orham ever since before the Fourth of July, and they liked it EVER so much, it was so quaint and—and "franteek"—

Jed interrupted here. "So quaint and what?" he demanded.

"Franteek." Miss Barbara herself seemed a little doubtful of the word. At any rate Mamma said it was something like that, and it meant they liked it anyway. So Mr. Winslow was left to ponder whether "antique" or "unique" was intended and to follow his train of thought wherever it chanced to lead him, while the child prattled on. They came in sight of the Smalley front gate and Jed came out of his walking trance to hear her say:

"Anyway, we like it all but the sal'ratus biscuits and the coffee and THEY are dreadful. Mamma thinks it's made of chickenry—the coffee, I mean."

At the gate Jed's "queerness," or shyness, came upon him. The idea of meeting Mrs. Armstrong or even the members of the Smalley family he shrank from. Barbara invited him to come in, but he refused even to accompany her to the door.

"I'll just run along now," he said, hurriedly. "Good night."

The child put out her hand. "Good night," she said. "Thank you very much for helping me carry the fish home. I'm coming to see you again some day."

She scampered up the walk. Jed, waiting in the shadow of the lilac bushes by the fence, saw her rattle the latch of the door, saw the door open and the child caught up in the arms of a woman, who cried: "Oh, Babbie, dear, where HAVE you been? Mamma was SO frightened!"

He smiled over the memory of the little girl's visit more than once that evening. He was very fond of children and their society did not embarrass or annoy him as did the company of most grown-ups— strangers, that is. He remembered portions of Miss Barbara's conversation and determined to repeat them to Captain Sam Hunniwell, the next time the latter called.

And that next time was the following forenoon. Captain Sam, on the way to his office at the bank, stopped his car at the edge of the sidewalk and came into the shop. Jed, having finished painting wooden sailors for the present, was boxing an assorted collection of mills and vanes to be sent South, for a certain demand for "Winslow mills" was developing at the winter as well as the summer resorts. It was far from winter yet, but this purchaser was forehanded.

"Hello, Jed," hailed the captain, "busy as usual. You've got the busy bee a mile astern so far as real hustlin' is concerned."

Jed took a nail from the half dozen held between his lips and applied its point to the box top. His sentences for the next few minutes were mumbled between nails and punctuated with blows of the hammer.

"The busy bee," he mumbled, "can sting other folks. He don't get stung much himself. Collectin' honey's easier, I cal'late, than collectin' money."

Captain Sam grunted. "Are you stung again?" he demanded. "Who did it this time?"

Jed pointed with the hammer to an envelope lying on a pile of wooden crows. The captain took up the envelope and inspected its contents.

"'We regret to inform you,' he read aloud, 'that the Funny Novelty Company of this town went into bankruptcy a month ago.

"'JOHN HOLWAY.'"

"Humph!" he sniffed. "That's short and sweet. Owed you somethin', I presume likely?"

Jed nodded. "Seventeen dollars and three cents," he admitted, between the remaining nails.

"Sho! Well, if you could get the seventeen dollars you'd throw off the three cents, wouldn't you?"

"No-o."

"You wouldn't? Why not?"

Jed pried a crookedly driven nail out again and substituted a fresh one.

"Can't afford to," he drawled. "That's the part I'll probably get."

"Guess you're right. Who's this John Holway?"

"Eh. . . . Why, when he ordered the mills of me last summer he was president of the Funny Novelty Company up there to Manchester."

"Good Lord! Well, I admire his nerve. How did you come to sell these—er—Funny folks, in the first place?"

Mr. Winslow looked surprised.

"Why, they wrote and sent an order," he replied.

"Did, eh? And you didn't think of lookin' 'em up to see whether they was good for anything or good for nothin'? Just sailed in and hurried off the stuff, I presume likely?"

Jed nodded. "Why—why, yes, of course," he said. "You see, they said they wanted it right away."

His friend groaned. "Gracious king!" he exclaimed. "How many times have I told you to let me look up credits for you when you get an order from a stranger? Well, there's no use talkin' to you. Give me this letter. I'll see what I can squeeze out of your Funny friend. . . . But, say," he added, "I can't stop but a minute, and I ran in to ask you if you'd changed your mind about rentin' the old house here. If you have, I believe I've got a good tenant for you."

Jed looked troubled. He laid down the hammer and took the last nail from his mouth.

"Now—now, Sam," he began, "you know—"

"Oh, I know you've set your thick head dead against rentin' it at all, but that's silly, as I've told you a thousand times. The house is empty and it doesn't do any house good to stay empty. Course if 'twas anybody but you,

Jed Winslow, you'd live in it yourself instead of campin' out in this shack here."

Jed sat down on the box he had just nailed and, taking one long leg between his big hands, pulled its knee up until he could have rested his chin upon it without much inconvenience.

"I know, Sam," he drawled gravely, "but that's the trouble—I ain't been anybody but me for forty-five years."

The captain smiled, in spite of his impatience. "And you won't be anybody else for the next forty-five," he said, "I know that. But all the same, bein' a practical, more or less sane man myself, it makes me nervous to see a nice, attractive, comfortable little house standin' idle while the feller that owns it eats and sleeps in a two-by-four sawmill, so to speak. And, not only that, but won't let anybody else live in the house, either. I call that a dog in the manger business, and crazy besides."

The big foot at the end of the long leg swung slowly back and forth. Mr. Winslow looked absently at the roof.

"DON'T look like that!" snapped Captain Sam. "Come out of it! Wake up! It always gives me the fidgets to see you settin' gapin' at nothin'. What are you daydreamin' about now, eh?"

Jed turned and gazed over his spectacles.

"I was thinkin'," he observed, "that most likely that dog himself was crazy. If he wasn't he wouldn't have got into the manger. I never saw a dog that wanted to climb into a manger, did you, Sam?"

"Oh, confound the manger and the dog, too! Look here, Jed; if I found you a good tenant would you rent 'em that house of yours?"

Jed looked more troubled than ever.

"Sam," he began, "you know I'd do 'most anything to oblige you, but—"

"Oblige me! This ain't to oblige me. It's to oblige you."

"Oh, then I won't do it."

"Well, then, 'tis to oblige me. It'll oblige me to have you show some sense. Come on, Jed. These people I've got in mind are nice people. They want to find a little house and they've come to me at the bank for advice about findin' it. It's a chance for you, a real chance."

Jed rocked back and forth. He looked genuinely worried.

"Who are they?" he asked, after a moment

"Can't name any names yet."

Another period of reflection. Then: "City folks or Orham folks?" inquired Mr. Winslow.

"City folks."

Some of the worried look disappeared. Jed was plainly relieved and more hopeful.

"Oh, then they won't want it," he declared. "City folks want to hire houses in the spring, not along as late in the summer as this."

"These people do. They're thinkin' of livin' here in Orham all the year round. It's a first-rate chance for you, Jed. Course, I know you don't really need the money, perhaps, but—well, to be real honest, I want these folks to stay in Orham—they're the kind of folks the town needs—and I want 'em contented. I think they would be contented in your house. You let those Davidsons from Chicago have the place that summer, but you've never let anybody so much as consider it since. What's the real reason? You've told me as much as a dozen, but I'll bet anything you've never told me the real one. 'Twas somethin' the Davidsons did you didn't like—but what?"

Jed's rocking back and forth on the box became almost energetic and his troubled expression more than ever apparent.

"Now—now, Sam," he begged, "I've told you all about that ever and ever so many times. There wasn't anything, really."

"There was, too. What was it?"

Jed suffered in silence for two or three minutes.

"What was the real reason? Out with it," persisted Captain Hunniwell.

"Well—well, 'twas—'twas—" desperately, "'twas the squeakin' and—and squealin'."

"Squeakin' and squealin'? Gracious king! What are you talkin' about?"

"Why—the—the mills, you know. The mills and vanes outside on—on the posts and the fence. They squeaked and—and sometimes they squealed awful. And he didn't like it."

"Who didn't?"

"Colonel Davidson. He said they'd got to stop makin' that noise and I said I'd oil 'em every day. And—and I forgot it."

"Yes—well, I ain't surprised to death, exactly. What then?"

"Well—well, you see, they were squealin' worse than usual one mornin' and Colonel Davidson he came in here and—and I remembered I hadn't oiled 'em for three days. And I—I said how horrible the squealin' was and that I'd oil 'em right away and—and—"

"Well, go on! go on!"

"And when I went out to do it there wasn't any wind and the mills wasn't goin' at all. You see, 'twas his oldest daughter takin' her singin' lessons in the house with the window open."

Captain Sam put back his head and shouted. Jed looked sadly at the floor. When the captain could speak he asked:

"And you mean to tell me that was the reason you wouldn't let the house again?"

"Er—why, yes."

"I know better. You didn't have any row with the Davidsons. You couldn't row with anybody, anyhow; and besides the Colonel himself told me they would have taken the house the very next summer but you wouldn't rent it to 'em. And you mean to say that yarn you've just spun was the reason?"

"Why—yes."

"Rubbish! You've told me a dozen reasons afore, but I'm bound to say this is the most foolish yet. All right, keep the real reason to yourself, then. But I tell you what I'm goin' to do to get even with you: I'm goin' to send these folks down to look at your house and I shan't tell you who they are or when they're comin'."

The knee slipped down from Mr. Winslow's grasp and his foot struck the floor with a crash. He made a frantic clutch at his friend's arm.

"Oh, now, Sam," he cried, in horror, "don't do that! Don't talk so! You don't mean it! Come here! . . . Sam!"

But the captain was at the door. "You bet I mean it!" he declared. "Keep your weather eye peeled, Jed. They'll be comin' 'most any time now. And if you have ANY sense you'll let 'em the house. So long!"

He drove away in his little car. Jed Winslow, left standing in the shop doorway, staring after him, groaned in anxious foreboding.

He groaned a good many times during the next few hours. Each time the bell rang announcing the arrival of a visitor he rose to answer it perfectly sure that here were the would-be tenants whom his friend, in the mistaken kindness of his heart, was sending to him. Not that he had the slightest idea of renting his old home, but he dreaded the ordeal of refusing. In fact he was not sure that he could refuse, not sure that he could invent a believable excuse for doing so. Another person would not have sought excuses, would have declared simply that the property was not for rent, but Jed Winslow was not that other person; he was himself, and ordinary methods of procedure were not his.

Two or three groups of customers came in, purchased and departed. Captain Jerry Burgess dropped in to bring the Winslow mail, which in this case consisted of an order, a bill and a circular setting forth the transcendent healing qualities of African Balm, the Foe of Rheumatism. Mr. Bearse happened in to discuss the great news of the proposed aviation camp and to tell with gusto and detail how Phineas Babbitt had met Captain Hunniwell "right square in front of the bank" and had not spoken to him. "No, sir, never said a word to him no more'n if he wan't there. What do you think of that? And they say Leander wrote his dad that he thought he was goin' to like soldierin' fust-rate, and Mrs. Sarah Mary Babbitt she told Melissa Busteed that her husband's language when he read that was somethin' sinful. She said she never was more thankful that they had lightnin' rods on the roof, 'cause such talk as that was enough to fetch down fire from heaven."

CHAPTER V

It was nearly noon when Jed, entering the front shop in answer to the bell, found there the couple the sight of which caused his heart to sink. Here they were, the house hunters—there was no doubt of it in his mind. The man was short and broad and protuberant and pompous. The woman possessed all the last three qualities, besides being tall. He shone with prosperity and sunburn, she reeked of riches and talcum. They were just the sort of people who would insist upon hiring a house that was not in the market; its not being in the market would, in their eyes, make it all the more desirable.

Jed had seen them before, knew they were staying at the hotel and that their names were Powless. He remembered now, with a thrill of alarm, that Mr. Bearse had recently spoken of them as liking Orham very much and considering getting a place of their own. And of course Captain Sam, hearing this, had told them of the Winslow place, had sent them to him. "Oh, Lord! Oh, Lord!" thought Jed, although what he said was: "Good mornin'."

He might as well have said nothing. Mrs. Powless, looming large between the piles of mills and vanes, like a battleship in a narrow channel, was loftily inspecting the stock through her lorgnette. Her husband, his walking stick under his arm and his hands in his pockets, was not even making the pretense of being interested; he was staring through the seaward window toward the yard and the old house.

"These are really quite extraordinary," the lady announced, after a moment. "George, you really should see these extraordinary things."

George was, evidently, not interested. He continued to look out of the window.

"What are they?" he asked, without turning.

"Oh, I don't know. All sorts of queer dolls and boats—and creatures, made of wood. Like those outside, you know—er— teetotums, windmills. Do come and look at them."

Mr. Powless did not comply. He said "Umph" and that was all.

"George," repeated Mrs. Powless, "do you hear me? Come and look at them."

And George came. One might have inferred that, when his wife spoke like that, he usually came. He treated a wooden porpoise to a thoroughly wooden stare and repeated his remark of "Umph!"

"Aren't they extraordinary!" exclaimed his wife. "Does this man make them himself, I wonder?"

She seemed to be addressing her husband, so Jed did not answer.

"Do you?" demanded Mr. Powless.

"Yes," replied Jed.

Mrs. Powless said "Fancy!" Mr. Powless strolled back to the window.

"This view is all right, Mollie," he observed. "Better even than it is from the street. Come and see."

Mrs. Powless went and saw. Jed stood still and stared miserably.

"Rather attractive, on the whole, don't you think, dear?" inquired the gentleman. "Must be very decent in the yard there."

The lady did not reply, but she opened the door and went out, around the corner of the shop and into the back yard. Her husband trotted after her. The owner of the property, gazing pathetically through the window, saw them wandering about the premises, looking off at the view, up into the trees, and finally trying the door of the old house and peeping in between the slats of the closed blinds. Then they came strolling back to the shop. Jed, drawing a long breath, prepared to face the ordeal.

Mrs. Powless entered the shop. Mr. Powless remained by the door. He spoke first.

"You own all this?" he asked, indicating the surrounding country with a wave of his cane. Jed nodded.

"That house, too?" waving the point of the cane toward the Winslow cottage.

"Yes."

"How old is it?"

Jed stammered that he guessed likely it was about a hundred years old or such matter.

"Umph! Furniture old, too?"

"Yes, I cal'late most of it is."

"Nobody living in it?"

"No-o."

"Got the key to it?"

Here was the question direct. If he answered in the affirmative the next utterance of the Powless man would be a command to be shown the interior of the house. Jed was certain of it, he could see it in the man's eye. What was infinitely more important, he could see it in the lady's eye. He hesitated.

"Got the key to it?" repeated Mr. Powless.

Jed swallowed.

"No-o," he faltered, "I—I guess not."

"You GUESS not. Don't you know whether you've got it or not?"

"No. I mean yes. I know I ain't."

"Where is it; lost?"

The key was usually lost, that is to say, Jed was accustomed to hunt for fifteen minutes before finding it, so, his conscience backing his inclination, he replied that he cal'lated it must be.

"Umph!" grunted Powless. "How do you get into the house without a key?"

Jed rubbed his chin, swallowed hard, and drawled that he didn't very often.

"You do sometimes, don't you?"

The best answer that the harassed windmill maker could summon was that he didn't know. The red-faced gentleman stared at him in indignant amazement.

"You don't KNOW?" he repeated. "Which don't you know, whether you go into the house at all, or how you get in without a key?"

"Yes,—er—er—that's it."

Mr. Powless breathed deeply. "Well, I'll be damned!" he declared, with conviction.

His wife did not contradict his assertion, but she made one of her own.

"George," she commanded majestically, "can't you see the man has been drinking. Probably he doesn't own the place at all. Don't waste another moment on him. We will come back later, when the real owner is in. Come!"

George came and they both went. Mr. Winslow wiped his perspiring forehead on a piece of wrapping paper and sat down upon a box to recover. Recovery, however, was by no means rapid or complete. They had gone, but they were coming back again; and what should he say to them then?

Very likely Captain Sam, who had sent them in the first place, would return with them. And Captain Sam knew that the key was not really lost. Jed's satisfaction in the fact that he had escaped tenantless so far was nullified by the fear that his freedom was but temporary.

He cooked his dinner, but ate little. After washing the dishes he crossed the road to the telephone and telegraph office and called up the Orham Bank. He meant to get Captain Hunniwell on the wire, tell him that the house hunters had paid him a visit, that he did not like them, and beg the captain to call them off the scent. But Captain Sam had motored to Ostable to attend a preliminary session of the Exemption Board. Jed sauntered gloomily back to the shop. When he opened the door and entered he was greeted by a familiar voice, which said:

"Here he is, Mamma. Good afternoon, Mr. Winslow."

Jed started, turned, and found Miss Barbara Armstrong beaming up at him. The young lady's attire and general appearance were in marked contrast to those of the previous evening. Petunia also was in calling costume; save for the trifling lack of one eye and a chip from the end of her nose, she would have been an ornament to doll society anywhere.

"This is my mamma," announced Barbara. "She's come to see you."

"How do you do, Mr. Winslow?" said Mrs. Armstrong.

Jed looked up to find her standing beside him, her hand extended. Beside a general impression that she was young and that her gown and hat and shoes were white, he was at that moment too greatly embarrassed to notice much concerning her appearance. Probably he did not notice even this until later. However, he took her hand, moved it up and down, dropped it again and said: "I—I'm pleased to meet you, ma'am."

She smiled. "And I am very glad to meet you," she said. "It was very kind of you to bring my little girl home last night and she and I have come to thank you for doing it."

Jed was more embarrassed than ever.

"Sho, sho!" he protested; "'twasn't anything."

"Oh, yes, it was; it was a great deal. I was getting very worried, almost frightened. She had been gone ever since luncheon—dinner, I mean—and I had no idea where. She's a pretty good little girl, generally speaking," drawing the child close and smiling down upon her, "but sometimes she is heedless and forgets. Yesterday she forgot, didn't you, dear?"

Barbara shook her head.

"I didn't forget," she said. "I mean I only forgot a little. Petunia forgot almost EVERYTHING. I forgot and went as far as the bridge, but she forgot all the way to the clam field."

Jed rubbed his chin.

"The which field?" he drawled.

"The clam field. The place where Mrs. Smalley's fish man unplants the clams she makes the chowder of. He does it with a sort of hoe thing and puts them in a pail. He was doing it yesterday; I saw him."

Jed's eyes twinkled at the word "unplants," but another thought occurred to him.

"You wasn't out on those clam flats alone, was you?" he asked, addressing Barbara.

She nodded. "Petunia and I went all alone," she said. "It was kind of wet so we took off our shoes and stockings and paddled. I—I don't know's I remembered to tell you that part, Mamma," she added, hastily. "I—I guess it must have slipped my mind."

But Mrs. Armstrong was watching Jed's face.

"Was there any danger?" she asked, quickly.

Jed hesitated before answering. "Why," he drawled, "I—I don't know as there was, but—well, the tide comes in kind of slow off ON the flats, but it's liable to fill up the channels between them and the beach some faster. Course if you know the wadin' places it's all right, but if you don't it's—well, it's sort of uncomfortable, that's all."

The lady's cheeks paled a bit, but she did not exclaim, nor as Jed would have said "make a fuss." She said, simply, "Thank you, I will remember," and that was the only reference she made to the subject of the "clam field."

Miss Barbara, to whom the events of dead yesterdays were of no particular concern compared to those of the vital and living to- day, was rummaging among the stock.

"Mamma," she cried, excitedly, "here is a whale fish like the one I was going to buy for Captain Hedge. Come and see it."

Mrs. Armstrong came and was much interested. She asked Jed questions concerning the "whale fish" and others of his creations. At first his replies were brief and monosyllabic, but gradually they became more lengthy, until, without being aware of it, he was carrying on his share of a real conversation. Of course, he hesitated and paused and drawled, but he always did that, even when talking with Captain Sam Hunniwell.

He took down and exhibited his wares one by one. Barbara asked numberless questions concerning each and chattered like a red squirrel. Her mother showed such a genuine interest in his work and was so pleasant and quiet and friendly, was, in short, such a marked contrast to Mrs. George Powless, that he found himself actually beginning to enjoy the visit. Usually he was glad when summer folks finished their looking and buying and went away; but now, when Mrs. Armstrong glanced at the clock on the shelf, he was secretly glad that that clock had not gone for over four months and had providentially stopped going at a quarter after three.

He took them into the inner shop, his workroom, and showed them the band saw and the lathe and the rest of his manufacturing outfit. Barbara asked if he lived there all alone and he said he did.

"I live out there," he explained, pointing toward the shop extension. "Got a sittin'-room and a kitchen out there, and a little upstairs, where I sleep."

Mrs. Armstrong seemed surprised. "Why!" she exclaimed, "I thought you lived in that dear little old house next door here. I was told that you owned it."

Jed nodded. "Yes, ma'am," he said, "I do own it, but I don't live in it. I used to live there, but I ain't for quite a spell now."

"I don't see how you could bear to give it up. It looks so quaint and homey, and if the inside is as delightful as the outside it must be quite wonderful. And the view is the best in town, isn't it?"

Jed was pleased. "Why, yes, ma'am, 'tis pretty good," he admitted. "Anyhow, most folks seem to cal'late 'tis. Wouldn't you like to come out and look at it?"

Barbara clapped her hands. "Oh, yes, Mamma, do!" she cried.

Her mother hesitated. "I don't know that we ought to trouble Mr. Winslow," she said. "He is busy, you know."

Jed protested. "It won't be a mite of trouble," he declared. "Besides, it ain't healthy to work too long at a stretch. That is," he drawled, "folks say 'tain't, so I never take the risk."

Mrs. Armstrong smiled and followed him out into the yard, where Miss Barbara had already preceded them. The view over the edge of the bluff was glorious and the grass in the yard was green, the flowers bright and pretty and the shadows of the tall lilac bushes by the back door of the little white house cool and inviting.

Barbara danced along the bluff edge, looking down at the dories and nets on the beach below. Her mother sighed softly.

"It is lovely!" she said. Then, turning to look at the little house, she added, "And it was your old home, I suppose."

Jed nodded. "Yes, ma'am," he replied. "I was born in that house and lived there all my life up to five years ago."

"And then you gave it up. Why? . . . Please forgive me. I didn't mean to be curious."

"Oh, that's all right, ma'am. Nothin' secret about it. My mother died and I didn't seem to care about livin' there alone, that's all."

"I see. I understand."

She looked as if she did understand, and Jed, the seldom understood, experienced an unusual pleasure. The sensation produced an unusual result.

"It's a kind of cute and old-fashioned house inside," he observed. "Maybe you'd like to go in and look around; would you?"

She looked very much pleased. "Oh, I should, indeed!" she exclaimed. "May I?"

Now, the moment after he issued the invitation he was sorry. It had been quite unpremeditated and had been given he could not have told why. His visitor had seemed so genuinely interested, and, above all, had treated him like a rational human being instead of a freak. Under this unaccustomed treatment Jed Winslow had been caught off his guard—hypnotized, so to speak. And now, when it was too late, he realized the possible danger. Only a few hours ago he had told Mr. and Mrs. George Powless that the key to that house had been lost.

He paused and hesitated. Mrs. Armstrong noticed his hesitation.

"Please don't think any more about it," she said. "It is delightful here in the yard. Babbie and I will stay here a few minutes, if we may, and you must go back to your work, Mr. Winslow."

But Jed, having put his foot in it, was ashamed to withdraw. He hastened to disclaim any intention of withdrawal.

"No, no," he protested. "I don't need to go to work, not yet anyhow. I should be real pleased to show you the house, ma'am. You wait now and I'll fetch the key."

Some five minutes later he reappeared with triumph in his eye and the "lost" key in his hand.

"Sorry to keep you waitin', ma'am," he explained. "The key had— er— stole its nest, as you might say. Got it now, though."

His visitors looked at the key, which was attached by a cord to a slab of wood about the size of half a shingle. Upon one side of the slab were lettered in black paint the words HERE IT IS. Barbara's curiosity was aroused.

"What have you got those letters on there for, Mr. Winslow?" she asked. "What does it say?"

Jed solemnly read the inscription. "I printed that on there," he explained, "so I'd be able to find the key when I wanted it."

Mrs. Armstrong smiled. "I should think it might help," she observed, evidently much amused.

Mr. Winslow nodded. "You would think so," he said, "wouldn't you? Maybe 'twould, too, only 'twas such a plaguey nuisance, towin' that half a cord of wood around, that I left it to home last time. Untied the string, you know, and just took the key. The wood and the string was hangin' up in the right place, but the key wan't among those present, as they say in the newspapers."

"Where was it?" demanded Barbara.

"Hush, dear," cautioned her mother. "You mustn't ask so many questions."

"That's all right, ma'am; I don't mind a mite. Where was it? We-ll, 'twas in my pants pocket here, just where I put it last time I used it. Naturally enough I shouldn't have thought of lookin' there and I don't know's I'd have found it yet, but I happened to shove my hands in my pockets to help me think, and there 'twas."

This explanation should have been satisfying, doubtless, but Barbara did not seem to find it wholly so.

"Please may I ask one more question, Mamma?" she pleaded. "Just only one?"

She asked it before her mother could reply.

"How does putting your hands in your pockets help you think, Mr. Winslow?" she asked. "I don't see how it would help a bit?"

Jed's eye twinkled, but his reply was solemnly given.

"Why, you see," he drawled, "I'm built a good deal like the old steam launch Tobias Wixon used to own. Every time Tobias blew the whistle it used up all the steam and the engine stopped. I've got a head about like that engine; when I want to use it I have to give all the rest of me a layoff. . . . Here we are, ma'am. Walk right in, won't you."

He showed them through room after room of the little house, opening the closed shutters so that the afternoon sunlight might stream in and brighten their progress. The rooms were small, but they were attractive and cosy. The furniture was almost all old mahogany and in remarkably good condition. The rugs were home-made; even the coverlets of the beds were of the old-fashioned blue and white, woven on the hand looms of our great-grandmothers. Mrs. Armstrong was enthusiastic.

"It is like a miniature museum of antiques," she declared. "And such wonderful antiques, too. You must have been besieged by people who wanted to buy them."

Jed nodded. "Ye-es," he admitted, "I cal'late there's been no less'n a million antiquers here in the last four or five year. I don't mean here in the house—I never let 'em in the house—but 'round the premises. Got so they kind of swarmed first of every summer, like June bugs. I got rid of 'em, though, for a spell."

"Did you; how?"

He rubbed his chin. "Put up a sign by the front door that said: 'Beware of Leprosy.' That kept 'em away while it lasted."

Mrs. Armstrong laughed merrily. "I should think so," she said. "But why leprosy, pray?"

"Oh, I was goin' to make it smallpox, but I asked Doctor Parker if there was anything worse than smallpox and he said he cal'lated leprosy was about as bad as any disease goin'. It worked fine while it lasted, but the Board of Health made me take it down; said there wan't any leprosy on the premises. I told 'em no, but 'twas a good idea to beware of it anyhow, and I'd put up the sign just on general principles. No use; they hadn't much use for principles, general or otherwise, seemed so."

The lady commented on the neatness and order in the little rooms. They were in marked contrast to the workshop. "I suppose you have a woman come here to clean and sweep," she said.

Jed shook his head.

"No-o," he answered. "I generally cal'late to come in every little while and clean up. Mother was always a great one for keepin' things slicked up," he added, apologetically, "and I—I kind of like to think 'twould please her. Foolish, I presume likely, but— well, foolish things seem to come natural to me. Got a kind of a gift for 'em, as you might say. I . . ."

He lapsed into silence, his sentence only begun. Mrs. Armstrong, looking up, found him gazing at her with the absent, far-off look that his closest associates knew so well. She had not met it before and found it rather embarrassing, especially as it kept on and on.

"Well?" she asked, after a time. He started and awoke to realities.

"I was just thinkin'," he explained, "that you was the only woman that has been in this house since the summer I let it to the Davidson folks. And Mrs. Davidson wan't a mite like you."

That was true enough. Mrs. Davidson had been a plump elderly matron with gray hair, a rather rasping voice and a somewhat aggressive manner. Mrs. Armstrong was young and slim, her hair and eyes were dark, her manner refined and her voice low and gentle. And, if Jed had been in the habit of noticing such things, he might have noticed that she was pleasant to look at. Perhaps he was conscious of this fact, but, if so, it was only in a vague, general way.

His gaze wandered to Barbara, who, with Petunia, was curled up in a big old-fashioned rocker.

"And a child, too," he mused. "I don't know when there's been a child in here. Not since I was one, I guess likely, and that's too long ago for anybody to remember single-handed."

But Mrs. Armstrong was interested in his previous remark.

"You have let others occupy this house then?" she asked.

"Yes, ma'am, one summer I did. Let it furnished to some folks name of Davidson, from Chicago."

"And you haven't rented it since?"

"No, ma'am, not but that once."

She was silent for a moment. Then she said: "I am surprised that it hasn't been occupied always. Do you ask such a VERY high rent, Mr. Winslow?"

Jed looked doubtful. "Why, no, ma'am," he answered. "I didn't cal'late 'twas so very high, considerin' that 'twas just for 'summer and furnished and all. The Davidsons paid forty dollars a month, but—"

"FORTY dollars! A month? And furnished like that? You mean a week, don't you?"

Mr. Winslow looked at her. The slow smile wandered across his face. He evidently suspected a joke.

"Why, no, ma'am," he drawled. "You see, they was rentin' the place, not buyin' it."

"But forty dollars a month is VERY cheap."

"Is it? Sho! Now you speak of it I remember that Captain Sam seemed to cal'late 'twas. He said I ought to have asked a hundred, or some such foolishness. I told him he must have the notion that I was left out of the sweet ile when they pickled the other thirty- nine thieves. Perhaps you've read the story, ma'am," he suggested.

His visitor laughed. "I have read it," she said. Then she added, plainly more to herself than to him: "But even forty is far too much, of course."

Jed was surprised and a little hurt.

"Yes—er—yes, ma'am," he faltered. "Well, I—I was kind of 'fraid 'twas, but Colonel Davidson seemed to think 'twas about fair, so—"

"Oh, you misunderstand me. I didn't mean that forty dollars was too high a rent. It isn't, it is a very low one. I meant that it was more than I ought to think of paying. You see, Mr. Winslow, I have been thinking that we might live here in Orham, Barbara and I. I like the town; and the people, most of those I have met, have been very pleasant and kind. And it is necessary—that is, it seems to me preferable—that we live, for some years at least, away from the city. This little house of yours is perfect. I fell in love with the outside of it at first sight. Now I find the inside even more delightful. I"—she hesitated, and then added—"I don't suppose you would care to let it unfurnished at—at a lower rate?"

Jed was very much embarrassed. The idea that his caller would make such a proposition as this had not occurred to him for a moment. If it had the lost key would almost certainly have remained lost. He liked Mrs. Armstrong even on such short acquaintance, and he had taken a real fancy to Barbara; but his prejudice against tenants remained. He rubbed his chin.

"Why—why, now, ma'am," he stammered, "you—you wouldn't like livin' in Orham all the year 'round, would you?"

"I hope I should. I know I should like it better than living— elsewhere," with, so it seemed to him, a little shudder. "And I cannot afford to live otherwise than very simply anywhere. I have been boarding in Orham for almost three months now and I feel that I have given it a trial."

"Yes—yes, ma'am, but summer's considerable more lively than winter here on the Cape."

"I have no desire for society. I expect to be quiet and I wish to be. Mr. Winslow, would you consider letting me occupy this house— unfurnished, of course? I should dearly love to take it just as it is—this furniture is far more fitting for it than mine—but I cannot afford forty dollars a month. Provided you were willing to let me hire the house of you at all, not for the summer alone but for all the year, what rent do you think you should charge?"

Jed's embarrassment increased. "Well, now, ma'am," he faltered, "I—I hope you won't mind my sayin' it, but—but I don't know's I want to let this house at all. I—I've had consider'ble many chances to rent it, but—but—"

He could not seem to find a satisfactory ending to the sentence and so left it unfinished. Mrs. Armstrong was evidently much disappointed, but she did not give up completely.

"I see," she said. "Well, in a way I think I understand. You prefer the privacy. I think I could promise you that Barbara and I would disturb you very little. As to the rent, that would be paid promptly."

"Sartin, ma'am, sartin; I know 'twould, but—"

"Won't you think it over? We might even live here for a month, with your furniture undisturbed and at the regular rental. You could call it a trial month, if you liked. You could see how you liked us, you know. At the end of that time," with a smile, "you might tell us we wouldn't do at all, or, perhaps, then you might consider making a more permanent arrangement. Barbara would like it here, wouldn't you, dear?"

Barbara, who had been listening, nodded excitedly from the big rocker. "Ever and ever so much," she declared; "and Petunia would just adore it."

Poor Jed was greatly perturbed. "Don't talk so, Mrs. Armstrong," he blurted. "Please don't. I—I don't want you to. You—you make me feel bad."

"Do I? I'm so sorry. I didn't mean to say anything to hurt your feelings. I beg your pardon."

"No, you don't. I—I mean you hadn't ought to. You don't hurt my feelin's; I mean you make me feel bad—wicked—cussed mean—all that and some more. I know I ought to let you have this house. Any common, decent man with common decent feelin's and sense would let you have it. But, you see, I ain't that kind. I—I'm selfish and—and wicked and—" He waved a big hand in desperation.

She laughed. "Nonsense!" she exclaimed. "Besides, it isn't so desperate as all that. You certainly are not obliged to rent the house unless you want to."

"But I do want to; that is, I don't, but I know I'd ought to want to. And if I was goin' to let anybody have it I'd rather 'twould be you—honest,

I would. And it's the right thing for me to do, I know that. That's what bothers me; the trouble's with ME. I don't want to do the right thing." He broke off, seemed to reflect and then asked suddenly:

"Ma'am, do you want to go to heaven when you die?"

The lady was naturally somewhat surprised at the question. "Why, yes," she replied, "I— Why, of course I do."

"There, that's it! Any decent, sensible person would. But I don't."

Barbara, startled into forgetting that children should be seen and not heard, uttered a shocked "Oh!"

Jed waved his hand. "You see," he said, "even that child's morals are upset by me. I know I ought to want to go to heaven. But when I see the crowd that KNOW they're goin' there, are sartin of it, the ones from this town, a good many of 'em anyhow; when I hear how they talk in prayer-meetin' and then see how they act outside of it, I— Well," with a deep sigh, "I want to go where they ain't, that's all." He paused, and then drawled solemnly, but with a suspicion of the twinkle in his eye: "The general opinion seems to be that that's where I'll go, so's I don't know's I need to worry."

Mrs. Armstrong made no comment on this confession. He did not seem to expect any.

"Ma'am," he continued, "you see what I mean. The trouble's with me, I ain't made right. I ought to let that house; Sam Hunniwell told me so this mornin'. But I—I don't want to. Nothin' personal to you, you understand; but... Eh? Who's that?"

A step sounded on the walk outside and voices were heard. Jed turned to the door.

"Customers, I cal'late," he said. "Make yourselves right to home, ma'am, you and the little girl. I'll be right back."

He went out through the dining-room into the little hall. Barbara, in the big rocker, looked up over Petunia's head at her mother.

"Isn't he a funny man, Mamma?" she said.

Mrs. Armstrong nodded. "Yes, he certainly is," she admitted.

"Yes," the child nodded reflectively. "But I don't believe he's wicked at all. I believe he's real nice, don't you?"

"I'm sure he is, dear."

"Yes. Petunia and I like him. I think he's what you said our Bridget was, a rough damson."

"Not damson; diamond, dear."

"Oh, yes. It was damson preserve Mrs. Smalley had for supper last night. I forgot. Petunia told me to say damson; she makes so many mistakes."

They heard the "rough diamond" returning. He seemed to be in a hurry. When he re-entered the little sitting-room he looked very much frightened.

"What is the matter?" demanded Mrs. Armstrong.

Jed gulped.

"They've come back," he whispered. "Godfreys, I forgot 'em, and they've come back. WHAT'LL I do now?"

"But who—who has come back?"

Mr. Winslow waved both hands.

"The Old Scratch and his wife," he declared. "I hope they didn't see me, but—Land of love, they're comin' in!"

A majestic tread sounded in the hall, in the dining-room. Mrs. George Powless appeared, severe, overwhelming, with Mr. George Powless in her wake. The former saw Mr. Winslow and fixed him with her glittering eye, as the Ancient Mariner fixed the wedding guest.

"Ah!" she observed, with majestic irony, "the lost key is found, it would seem."

Jed looked guilty.

"Yes, ma'am," he faltered. "Er—yes, ma'am."

"So? And now, I presume, as it is apparent that you do show the interior of this house to other interested persons," with a glance like a sharpened icicle in the direction of the Armstrongs, "perhaps you will show it to my husband and me."

Jed swallowed hard.

"Well, ma'am," he faltered, "I—I'd like to, but—but the fact is, I—"

"Well, what?"

"It ain't my house."

"Isn't your house? George," turning to Mr. Powless, "didn't I hear this man distinctly tell you that this house WAS his?"

George nodded. "Certainly, my dear," he declared. Then turning to Mr. Winslow, he demanded: "What do you mean by saying it is yours one moment and not yours the next; eh?"

Jed looked around. For one instant his gaze rested upon the face of Mrs. Armstrong. Then he drew himself up.

"Because," he declared, "I've rented it furnished to this lady here. And, that bein' the case, it ain't mine just now and I ain't got any right to be in it. And," his voice rising in desperation, "neither has anybody else."

Mrs. George Powless went a few moments later; before she went she expressed her opinion of Mr. Winslow's behavior. Mr. George Powless followed her, expressing his opinion as he went. The object of their adjuration sat down upon a rush-bottomed chair and rubbed his chin.

"Lord!" he exclaimed, with fervor. Mrs. Armstrong looked at him in amazement.

"Why, Mr. Winslow!" she exclaimed, and burst out laughing.

Jed groaned. "I know how Jonah felt after the whale unloaded him," he drawled. "That woman all but had me swallered. If you hadn't been here she would."

"Jed!" shouted a voice outside. "Jed, where are you?"

Mr. Winslow raised his head. "Eh?" he queried. "That's Sam hollerin', ain't it?"

It was Captain Hunniwell and a moment later he entered the little sitting-room. When he saw who his friend's companions were he seemed greatly surprised.

"Why, Mrs. Armstrong!" he exclaimed. "Are you here? Now that's a funny thing. The last time I saw Jed I warned him I was goin' to send you here to look at this house. And you came without bein' sent, after all; eh?"

Jed stared at him. Before the lady could reply he spoke. "What?" he cried. "Was she—Sam Hunniwell, was it HER you was goin' to send to see about hirin' this house?"

"Sure it was. Why not?"

Jed pointed toward the door. "Then—then who," he demanded, "sent those Powlesses here?"

"No one that I know of. And anyhow they don't want to rent any houses. They've bought land over at Harnissport and they're goin' to build a house of their own there."

"They are? They are? Then—then WHAT did that woman say I'd got to show her the inside of this house for?"

"I don't know. Did she? Oh, I tell you what she was after, probably. Some one had told her about your old furniture and things, Jed. She's the greatest antique hunter on earth, so they tell me. That's what she was after—antiques."

Jed, having paused until this had sunk in, groaned.

"Lord!" he said, again. "And I went and—"

Another groan finished the sentence.

Mrs. Armstrong came forward.

"Please don't worry about it, Mr. Winslow," she said. "I know you didn't mean it. Of course, knowing your feelings, I shouldn't think of taking the house."

But Jed slowly shook his head.

"I want you to," he declared. "Yes, I mean it. I want you to come and live in this house for a month, anyhow. If you don't, that Powless woman will come back and buy every stick and rag on the place. I don't want to sell 'em, but I couldn't say no to her any more than I could to the Old Harry. I called her the Old Scratch's wife, didn't I," he added. "Well, I won't take it back."

Captain Sam laughed uproariously.

"You ain't very complimentary to Mr. Powless," he observed.

Jed rubbed his chin.

"I would be if I was referrin' to him," he drawled, "but I judge he's her second husband."

CHAPTER VI

Of course Mrs. Armstrong still insisted that, knowing, as she did, Mr. Winslow's prejudice against occupying the position of landlord, she could not think of accepting his offer. "Of course I shall not," she declared. "I am flattered to know that you consider Barbara and me preferable to Mr. and Mrs. Powless; but even there you may be mistaken, and, beside, why should you feel you must endure the lesser evil. If I were in your place I shouldn't endure any evil at all. I should keep the house closed and empty, just as you have been doing."

Captain Sam shook his head impatiently. "If you was in his place," he observed, "you would have let it every year. Don't interfere with him, Mrs. Armstrong, for the land sakes. He's showed the first streak of common sense about that house that he's showed since the Davidsons went out. Don't ask him to take it back."

And Jed stubbornly refused to take it back. "I've let it to you for a month, ma'am," he insisted. "It's yours, furniture and all, for a month. You won't sell that Mrs. Powless any of it, will you?" he added, anxiously. "Any of the furniture, I mean."

Mrs. Armstrong scarcely knew whether to be amused or indignant.

"Of course I shouldn't sell it," she declared. "It wouldn't be mine to sell."

Jed looked frightened. "Yes, 'twould; yes, 'twould," he persisted. "That's why I'm lettin' it to you. Then I can't sell it to her; I CAN'T, don't you see?"

Captain Sam grinned. "Fur's that goes," he suggested, "I don't see's you've got to worry, Jed. You don't need to sell it, to her or anybody else, unless you want to."

But Jed looked dubious. "I suppose Jonah cal'lated he didn't need to be swallowed," he mused. "You take it, ma'am, for a month, as a favor to me."

"But how can I—like this? We haven't even settled the question of rent. And you know nothing whatever about me."

He seemed to reflect. Then he asked:

"Your daughter don't sing like a windmill, does she?"

Barbara's eyes and mouth opened. "Why, Mamma!" she exclaimed, indignantly.

"Hush, Babbie. Sing like a—what? I don't understand, Mr. Winslow."

The captain burst out laughing. "No wonder you don't, ma'am," he said. "It takes the seven wise men of Greece to understand him most of the time. You leave it to me, Mrs. Armstrong. He and I will talk it over together and then you and he can talk to-morrow. But I guess likely you'll have the house, if you want it; Jed doesn't go back on his word. I always say that for you, don't I, old sawdust?" turning to the gentleman thus nicknamed.

Jed, humming a mournful hymn, was apparently miles away in dreamland. Yet he returned to earth long enough to indulge in a mild bit of repartee. "You say 'most everything for me, Sam," he drawled, "except when I talk in my sleep."

Mrs. Armstrong and Barbara left a moment later, the lady saying that she and Mr. Winslow would have another interview next day. Barbara gravely shook hands with both men.

"I and Petunia hope awfully that we are going to live here, Mr. Winslow," she said, "'specially Petunia."

Jed regarded her gravely. "Oh, she wants to more'n you do, then, does she?" he asked.

The child looked doubtful. "No-o," she admitted, after a moment's reflection, "but she can't talk, you know, and so she has to hope twice as hard else I wouldn't know it. Good-by. Oh, I forgot; Captain Hedge liked his swordfish EVER so much. He said it was a— a—oh, yes, humdinger."

She trotted off after her mother. Captain Hunniwell, after a chuckle of appreciation over the "humdinger," began to tell his friend what little he had learned concerning the Armstrongs. This was, of course, merely what Mrs. Armstrong herself had told him and amounted to this: She was a widow whose husband had been a physician in Middleford, Connecticut. His name was Seymour Armstrong and he had now been dead four years. Mrs. Armstrong and Barbara, the latter an only child, had continued to occupy the house at Middleford, but recently the lady had come to feel that she could not afford to live there longer, but must find some less expensive quarters.

"She didn't say so," volunteered Captain Sam, "but I judge she lost a good deal of her money, bad investments or somethin' like that. If there's any bad investment anywheres in the neighborhood you can 'most generally trust a widow to hunt it up and put her insurance money into it. Anyhow, 'twas somethin' like that, for after livin' there a spell, just as she did when her husband was alive, she all at once decides to up anchor and find some cheaper moorin's. First off, though, she decided to spend the summer in a cool place and some friend, somebody with good, sound judgment, suggests Orham. So she lets her own place in Middleford, comes to Orham, falls in love with the place—same as any sensible person would naturally, of course—and, havin' spent 'most three months here, decides she wants to spend nine more anyhow. She comes to the bank to cash a check, she and I get talkin', she tells me what she's lookin' for, I tell her I cal'late I've got a place in my eye that I think might be just the thing, and—"

He paused to bite the end from a cigar. His friend finished the sentence for him.

"And then," he said, "you, knowin' that I didn't want to let this house any time to anybody, naturally sent her down to look at it."

"No such thing. Course I knew that you'd OUGHT to let the house and, likin' the looks and ways of these Armstrong folks first rate, I give in that I had made up my mind TO send her down to look at it. But, afore I could do it, the Almighty sent her on His own hook. Which proves," he added, with a grin, "that my judgment has pretty good backin' sometimes."

Jed rubbed his chin. "Careful, Sam," he drawled, "careful. The Kaiser'll be gettin' jealous of you if you don't look out. But what," he inquired, "made her and the little girl move out of Middleford, or wherever 'twas they lived? They could have found cheaper quarters there, couldn't they? Course I ain't never been there, but seems as if they could."

"Sartin they could, but the fact of their movin' is what makes me pretty sure the widow's investments had turned sour. It's a plaguey sight easier to begin to cut down and live economical in a place where nobody knows you than 'tis in one where everybody has known you for years. See that, don't you?"

Jed whistled sadly, breaking off in the middle of a bar to reply that he didn't know as he did.

"I've never cut up, so cuttin' down don't worry me much," he observed. "But I presume likely you're right, Sam; you generally are." He whistled a moment longer, his gaze apparently fixed upon a point in the middle of the white plastered ceiling. Then he said, dreamily: "Well, anyhow, 'twon't be but a month. They'll go somewheres else in a month."

Captain Sam sniffed. "Bet you a dollar they won't," he retorted. "Not unless you turn 'em out. And I see you turnin' anybody out."

But Mr. Winslow looked hopeful. "They'll go when the month's up," he reiterated. "Nobody could stand me more than a month. Mother used to say so, and she'd known me longer than anybody."

And so, in this curious fashion, did tenants come to the old Winslow house. They moved in on the following Monday. Jed saw the wagon with the trunks backing up to the door and he sighed. Then he went over to help carry the trunks into the house.

For the first week he found the situation rather uncomfortable; not as uncomfortable as he had feared, but a trifle embarrassing, nevertheless. His new neighbors were not too neighborly; they did not do what he would have termed "pester" him by running in and out of the shop at all hours, nor did they continually ask favors. On the other hand they did not, like his former tenants, the Davidsons, treat him as if he were some sort of odd wooden image, like one of his own weather vanes, a creature without feelings, to be displayed and "shown off" when it pleased them and ignored when it did not. Mrs. Armstrong was always quietly cheerful and friendly when they met in the yard or about the premises, but she neither intruded nor patronized. Jed's first impression of her, a favorable one, was strengthened daily.

"I like her first-rate," he told Captain Sam. "She ain't too folksy and she ain't too standoffish. Why, honest truth, Sam," he added, ingenuously, "she treats me just the same as if I was like the common run of folks."

The captain snorted. "Gracious king! Do stop runnin' yourself down," he commanded. "Suppose you are a little mite—er—different from the—well, from the heft of mackerel in the keg, what of it? That's your own private business, ain't it?"

Jed's lip twitched. "I suppose 'tis," he drawled. "If it wan't there wouldn't be so many folks interested in it."

At first he missed the freedom to which he had accustomed himself during his years of solitude, the liberty of preparing for bed with the doors and windows toward the sea wide open and the shades not drawn; of strolling out to the well at unearthly hours of the early morning singing at the top of his lungs; of washing face and hands in a tin basin on a bench by that well curb instead of within doors. There were some necessary concessions to convention to which his attention was called by Captain Hunniwell, who took it upon himself to act as a sort of social mentor.

"Do you always wash outdoors there?" asked the captain, after watching one set of ablutions.

"Why—er—yes, I 'most generally do in good weather. It's sort of— er—well, sort of cool and roomy, as you might say."

"Roomy, eh? Gracious king! Well, I should say you needed room. You splash into that basin like a kedge anchor goin' overboard and when you come out of it you puff like a grampus comin' up to blow. How do you cal'late Mrs. Armstrong enjoys seein' you do that?"

Jed looked startled and much disturbed. "Eh?" he exclaimed. "Why, I never thought about her, Sam. I declare I never did. I—I'll fetch the wash basin inside this very minute."

And he did. The inconvenience attached to the breaking off of a summer-time habit of years troubled him not half as much as the fear that he might have offended a fellow creature's sensibilities. Jed Winslow was far too sensitive himself and his own feelings had been hurt too many times to make hurting those of another a small offense in his eyes.

But these were minor inconveniences attached to his new position as landlord. There were recompenses. At work in his shop he could see through the window the white-clad, graceful figure of Mrs. Armstrong moving about the yard, sitting with Barbara on the bench by the edge of the bluff, or writing a letter at a table she had taken out under the shadow of the silver-leaf tree. Gradually Jed came to enjoy seeing her there, to see the windows of the old house open, to hear voices once more on that side of the shop, and to catch glimpses of Babbie dancing in and out over the shining mica slab at the door.

He liked the child when he first met her, but he had been a little fearful that, as a neighbor, she might trouble him by running in and out of the shop, interfering with his privacy and his work or making a small nuisance of herself when he was waiting on customers. But she did none of these things, in fact she did not come into the shop at all and, after the first week had passed, he began to wonder why. Late that afternoon, seeing her sitting on the bench by the bluff edge, her doll in her arms, he came out of the door of his little kitchen at the back of the shop and called her.

"Good evenin'," he hailed. "Takin' in the view, was you?"

She bobbed her head. "Yes, sir," she called in reply; "Petunia and I were looking at it."

"Sho! Well, what do you and-er—What's-her-name think of it?"

Barbara pondered. "We think it's very nice," she announced, after a moment. "Don't you like it, Mr. Winslow?"

"Eh? Oh, yes, I like it, I guess. I ain't really had time to look at it to-day; been too busy."

The child nodded, sympathetically. "That's too bad," she said. Jed had, for him, a curious impulse, and acted upon it.

"Maybe I might come and look at it now, if I was asked," he suggested. "Plenty of room on that bench, is there?"

"Oh, yes, sir, there's lots. I don't take much room and Petunia almost always sits on my lap. Please come."

So Jed came and, sitting down upon the bench, looked off at the inlet and the beach and the ocean beyond. It was the scene most familiar to him, one he had seen, under varying weather conditions, through many summers and winters. This very thought was in his mind as he looked at it now.

After a time he became aware that his companion was speaking.

"Eh?" he ejaculated, coming out of his reverie. "Did you say somethin'?"

"Yes, sir, three times. I guess you were thinking, weren't you?"

"Um-m—yes, I shouldn't be surprised. It's one of my bad habits, thinkin' is."

She looked hard to see if he was smiling, but he was not, and she accepted the statement as a serious one.

"Is thinking a bad habit?" she asked. "I didn't know it was."

"Cal'late it must be. If it wasn't, more folks would do it. Tell me, now," he added, changing the subject to avoid further cross-questioning, "do you and your ma like it here?"

The answer was enthusiastic. "Oh, yes!" she exclaimed, "we like it ever and ever so much. Mamma says it's—" Barbara hesitated, and then, after what was evidently a severe mental struggle, finished with, "she said once it was like paradise after category."

"After—which?"

The young lady frowned. "It doesn't seem to me," she observed, slowly, "as if 'category' was what she said. Does 'category' sound right to you, Mr. Winslow?"

Jed looked doubtful. "I shouldn't want to say that it did, right offhand like this," he drawled.

"No-o. I don't believe it was 'category.' But I'm almost sure it was something about a cat, something a cat eats—or does—or something.

Mew—mouse—milk—" she was wrinkling her forehead and repeating the words to herself when Mr. Winslow had an inspiration.

"'Twan't purgatory, was it?" he suggested.

Miss Barbara's head bobbed enthusiastically. "Purr-gatory, that was it," she declared. "And it was something a cat does—purr, you know; I knew it was. Mamma said living here was paradise after purr-gatory."

Jed rubbed his chin.

"I cal'late your ma didn't care much for the board at Luretta Smalley's," he observed. He couldn't help thinking the remark an odd one to make to a child.

"Oh, I don't think she meant Mrs. Smalley's," explained Barbara. "She liked Mrs. Smalley's pretty well, well as any one can like boarding, you know," this last plainly another quotation. "I think she meant she liked living here so much better than she did living in Middleford, where we used to be."

"Hum," was the only comment Jed made. He was surprised, nevertheless. Judged by what Captain Sam had told him, the Armstrong home at Middleford should have been a pleasant one. Barbara rattled on.

"I guess that was it," she observed. "She was sort of talking to herself when she said it. She was writing a letter—to Uncle Charlie, I think it was—and I and Petunia asked her if she liked it here and she sort of looked at me without looking, same as you do sometimes, Mr. Winslow, when you're thinking of something else, and then she said that about the catty—no, the purr-gatory. And when I asked her what purr-gatory meant she said, 'Never mind,' and. . . . Oh, I forgot!" in consternation; "she told me I mustn't tell anybody she said it, either. Oh, dear me!"

Jed hastened to reassure her. "Never mind," he declared, "I'll forget you ever did say it. I'll start in forgettin' now. In five minutes or so I'll have forgot two words of it already. By to-morrow mornin' I wouldn't remember it for money."

"Truly?"

"Truly bluely, lay me down and cut me in twoly. But what's this you're sayin' about your ma lookin' at things without seein' 'em, same as I do? She don't do that, does she?"

The young lady nodded. "Yes," she said; "course not as bad—I mean not as often as you do, but sometimes, 'specially since—" She hastily clapped her hand over her mouth. "Oh!" she exclaimed.

"What's the matter? Toothache?"

"No. Only I almost told another somethin' I mustn't."

"Sho! Well, I'm glad you put on the cover just in time."

"So am I. What else was I talking about? Oh, yes, Mamma's thinking so hard, same as you do, Mr. Winslow. You know," she added, earnestly, "she acts quite a lot like you sometimes."

Jed looked at her in horror. "Good Lord!" he exclaimed. Then, in his solemnest drawl, he added, "You tell her to take somethin' for it afore it's too late."

As he rose from the bench he observed: "Haven't seen you over to the shop since you moved in. I've been turnin' out another school of swordfish and whales, too. Why don't you run in and look 'em over?"

She clapped her hands. "Oh, may I?" she cried. "I've wanted to ever and ever so much, but Mamma said not to because it might annoy you. Wouldn't it annoy you, TRULY?"

"Not a bit."

"Oh, goody! And might Petunia come, too?"

"Um-hm. Only," gravely, "she'll have to promise not to talk too much. Think she'll promise that? All right; then fetch her along."

So, the very next morning, when Jed was busy at the bandsaw, he was not greatly surprised when the door opened and Miss Barbara appeared, with Petunia in her arms. He was surprised, however, and not a little embarrassed when Mrs. Armstrong followed.

"Good morning," said the lady, pleasantly. "I came over to make sure that there hadn't been a mistake. You really did ask Babby to come in and see you at work?"

"Yes, ma'am, I—I did. I did, sartin."

"And you don't mind having her here? She won't annoy you?"

"Not a mite. Real glad to have her."

"Very well, then she may stay—an hour, but no longer. Mind, Babby, dear, I am relying on you not to annoy Mr. Winslow."

So the juvenile visitor stayed her hour and then obediently went away, in spite of Jed's urgent invitation to stay longer. She had asked a good many questions and talked almost continuously, but Mr. Winslow, instead of being bored by her prattle, was surprised to find how empty and uninteresting the shop seemed after she had quitted it.

She came again the next day and the next. By the end of the week Jed had become sufficiently emboldened to ask her mother to permit her to come in the afternoon also. This request was the result of a conspiracy between Barbara and himself.

"You ask your ma," urged Jed. "Tell her I say I need you here afternoons."

Barbara looked troubled. "But that would be a wrong story, wouldn't it?" she asked. "You don't really need me, you know."

"Eh? Yes, I do; yes, I do."

"What for? What shall I tell her you need me for?"

Jed scratched his chin with the tail of a wooden whale.

"You tell her," he drawled, after considering for a minute or two, "that I need you to help carry lumber."

Even a child could not swallow this ridiculous excuse. Barbara burst out laughing.

"Why, Mr. Winslow!" she cried. "You don't, either. You know I couldn't carry lumber; I'm too little. I couldn't carry any but the littlest, tiny bit."

Jed nodded, gravely. "Yes, sartin," he agreed; "that's what I need you to carry. You run along and tell her so, that's a good girl."

But she shook her head vigorously. "No," she declared. "She would say it was silly, and it would be. Besides, you don't really need me at all. You just want Petunia and me for company, same as we want you. Isn't that it, truly?"

"Um-m. Well, I shouldn't wonder. You can tell her that, if you want to; I'd just as soon."

The young lady still hesitated. "No-o," she said, "because she'd think perhaps you didn't really want me, but was too polite to say so. If you asked her yourself, though, I think she'd let me come."

At first Jed's bashfulness was up in arms at the very idea, but at length he considered to ask Mrs. Armstrong for the permission. It was granted, as soon as the lady was convinced that the desire for more of her daughter's society was a genuine one, and thereafter Barbara visited the windmill shop afternoons as well as mornings. She sat, her doll in her arms, upon a box which she soon came to consider her own particular and private seat, watching her long-legged friend as he sawed or glued or jointed or painted. He had little waiting on customers to do now, for most of the summer people had gone. His small visitor and he had many long and, to them, interesting conversations.

Other visitors to the shop, those who knew him well, were surprised and amused to find him on such confidential and intimate terms with a child. Gabe Bearse, after one short call, reported about town that crazy Shavin's Winslow had taken up with a young-one just about as crazy as he was.

"There she set," declared Gabriel, "on a box, hugging a broken- nosed doll baby up to her and starin' at me and Shavin's as if we was some kind of curiosities, as you might say. Well, one of us was; eh? Haw, haw! She didn't say a word and Shavin's he never said nothin' and I felt as if I was preaching in a deef and dumb asylum. Finally, I happened to look at her and I see her lips movin'. 'Well,' says I, 'you CAN talk, can't you, sis, even if it's only to yourself. What was you talkin' to yourself about, eh?' She didn't seem to want to answer; just sort of reddened up, you know; but I kept right after her. Finally she owned up she was countin'. 'What was you countin'?' says I. Well, she didn't want to tell that, neither. Finally I dragged it out of her that she was countin' how many words I'd said since I started to tell about Melissy Busteed and what she said about Luther Small's wife's aunt, the one that's so wheezed up with asthma and Doctor Parker don't seem to be able to do nothin' to help. 'So you was countin' my words, was you?' says I. 'Well, that's good business, I must say! How many have I said?' She looked solemn and shook her head. 'I had to give it up,' says she. 'It makes my head ache to count fast very long. Doesn't it give you a headache to count fast, Mr. Winslow?' Jed, he mumbled some kind of foolishness about some things givin' him earache. I laughed at the two of 'em. 'Humph!' says I, 'the only kind of aches I have is them in my bones,' meanin' my rheumatiz, you understand. Shavin's he looked moony up at the roof for about a week and a half, same as he's liable to do, and then he drawled out: 'You see he DOES have headache, Babbie,' says he. Now did you ever hear such fool talk outside of an asylum? He and that Armstrong kid are well matched. No wonder she sits in there and gapes at him half the day."

Captain Sam Hunniwell and his daughter were hugely tickled.

"Jed's got a girl at last," crowed the captain. "I'd about given up hope, Jed. I was fearful that the bloom of your youth would pass away from you and you wouldn't keep company with anybody. You're so bashful that I know you'd never call on a young woman, but I never figured that one might begin callin' on you. Course she's kind of extra young, but she'll grow out of that, give her time."

Maud Hunniwell laughed merrily, enjoying Mr. Winslow's confusion. "Oh, the little girl is only the bait, Father," she declared. "It is the pretty widow that Jed is fishing for. She'll be calling here soon, or he'll be calling there. Isn't that true, Jed? Own up, now. Oh, see him blush, Father! Just see him!"

Jed, of course, denied that he was blushing. His fair tormentor had no mercy.

"You must be," she insisted. "At any rate your face is very, very red. I'll leave it to Father. Isn't his face red, Father?"

"Red as a flannel lung-protector," declared Captain Sam, who was never known to contradict his only daughter, nor, so report affirmed, deny a request of hers.

"Of course it is," triumphantly. "And it can't be the heat, because it isn't at all warm here."

Poor Jed, the long-suffering, was goaded into a mild retort.

"There's consider'ble hot air in here some spells," he drawled, mournfully. Miss Hunniwell went away reaffirming her belief that Mr. Winslow's friendship for the daughter was merely a strategical advance with the mother as the ultimate objective.

"You'll see, Father," she prophesied, mischievously. "We shall hear of his 'keeping company' with Mrs. Armstrong soon. Oh, he couldn't escape even if he wanted to. These young widows are perfectly irresistible."

When they were a safe distance from the windmill shop the captain cautioned his daughter.

"Maud," he said, "you'd better not tease Jed too much about that good-lookin' tenant of his. He's so queer and so bashful that I'm afraid if you do he'll take a notion to turn the Armstrongs out when this month's up."

Miss Hunniwell glanced at him from the corner of her eye.

"Suppose he does?" she asked. "What of it? She isn't a GREAT friend of yours, is she, Father?"

It was the captain's turn to look embarrassed.

"No, no, course she ain't," he declared, hastily. "All I've been thinkin' is that Jed ought to have a tenant in that house of his, because he needs the money. And from what I've been able to find out about this Mrs. Armstrong she's a real nice genteel sort of body, and—and—er—"

"And she's very sweet and very pretty and so, of course, naturally, all the men, especially the middle-aged men—"

Captain Sam interrupted explosively. "Don't be so foolish!" he ordered. "If you don't stop talkin' such nonsense I'll—I don't know what I'll do to you. What do you suppose her bein' sweet and good-lookin' has got to do with me? Gracious king! I've got one good-lookin'—er—that is to say, I've got one young female to take care of now and that's enough, in all conscience."

His daughter pinched his arm.

"Oh, ho!" she observed. "You were going to say she was good-looking and then you changed your mind. Don't you think this young female—WHAT a word! you ought to be ashamed of it—DON'T you think she is good-looking, Daddy, dear?"

She looked provokingly up into his face and he looked fondly down into hers.

"Don't you?" she repeated.

"We-ll, I—I don't know as I'd want to go so far as to say that. I presume likely her face might not stop a meetin'-house clock on a dark night, but—"

As they were in a secluded spot where a high hedge screened them from observation Miss Maud playfully boxed her parent's ears, a proceeding which he seemed to enjoy hugely.

But there was reason in the captain's caution, nevertheless. Miss Maud's "teasing" concerning the widow had set Jed to thinking. The "trial" month was almost up. In a little while he would have to give his decision as to whether the little Winslow house was to continue to be occupied by Barbara and her mother, or whether it was to be, as it had been for years, closed and shuttered tight. He had permitted them to occupy it for that month, on the spur of the moment, as the result of a promise made upon impulse, a characteristic Jed Winslow impulse. Now, however, he must decide in cold blood whether or not it should be theirs for another eleven months at least.

In his conversation with Captain Sam, the conversation which took place immediately after the Armstrongs came, he had stoutly maintained that the latter would not wish to stay longer than the month, that his own proximity as landlord and neighbor would be unbearable longer than that period. But if the widow found it so she had so far shown no evidence of her disgust. Apparently that means of breaking off the relationship could not be relied upon. Of course he did not know whether or not she wished to remain, but, if she did, did he wish her to do so? There was nothing personal in the matter; it was merely the question as to whether his prejudice of years against renting that house to any one was to rule or be overthrown. If she asked him for his decision what should he say? At night, when he went to bed, his mind was made up. In the morning when he arose it was unmade. As he told Captain Hunniwell: "I'm like that old clock I used to have, Sam.

The pendulum of that thing used to work fine, but the hands wouldn't move. Same way with me. I tick, tick, tick all day over this pesky business, but I don't get anywheres. It's always half- past nothin'."

Captain Sam was hugely disgusted. "It ain't more'n quarter past, if it is that," he declared, emphatically. "It's just nothin', if you ask me. And say, speakin' of askin', I'd like to ask you this: How are you goin' to get 'em out, provided you're fool enough to decide they've got to go? Are you goin' to tell Mrs. Armstrong right up and down and flat-footed that you can't stand any more of her? I'd like to hear you say it. Let me know when the show's goin' to come off. I want a seat in the front row."

Poor Jed looked aghast at the very idea. His friend laughed derisively and walked off and left him. And the days passed and the "trial month" drew closer and closer to its end until one morning he awoke to realize that that end had come; the month was up that very day.

He had not mentioned the subject to the widow, nor had she to him. His reasons for not speaking were obvious enough; one was that he did not know what to say, and the other that he was afraid to say it. But, as the time approached when the decision must be made, he had expected that she would speak. And she had not. He saw her daily, sometimes several times a day. She often came into the shop to find Barbara, who made the workroom a playhouse on rainy or cloudy days, and she talked with him on other topics, but she did not mention this one.

It was raining on this particular day, the last day in the "trial month," and Jed, working at his lathe, momentarily expected Barbara to appear, with Petunia under one arm and a bundle of dolls' clothes under the other, to announce casually that, as it was such bad weather, they had run in to keep him, Mr. Winslow, from getting lonesome. There was precious little opportunity to be lonesome where Babbie was.

But this morning the child did not come and Jed, wondering what the reason for her absence might be, began to feel vaguely uncomfortable. Just what was the matter he did not know, but that there was something wrong with him, Jed Winslow, was plain. He could not seem to keep his mind on his work; he found himself wandering to the window and looking out into the yard, where the lilac bushes whipped and thrashed in the gusts, the overflowing spouts splashed and gurgled, and the sea beyond the edge of the bluff was a troubled stretch of gray and white, seen through diagonal streaks of wind-driven rain. And always when he looked out of that window he glanced toward the little house next door, hoping to see a small figure, bundled under a big rain coat and sheltered by a big umbrella, dodge out of the door and race across the yard toward the shop.

But the door remained shut, the little figure did not appear and, except for the fact that the blinds were not closed and that there was smoke issuing from the chimney of the kitchen, the little house might have been as empty as it had been the month before.

Or as it might be next month. The thought came to Jed with a meaning and emphasis which it had not brought before. A stronger gust than usual howled around the eaves of the shop, the sashes rattled, the panes were beaten by the flung raindrops which pounded down in watery sheets to the sills, and Jed suddenly diagnosed his own case, he knew what was the matter with him—he was lonesome; he, who had lived alone for five years and had hoped to live alone for the rest of his life, was lonesome.

He would not admit it, even to himself; it was ridiculous. He was not lonesome, he was just a little "blue," that was all. It was the weather; he might have caught a slight cold, perhaps his breakfast had not agreed with him. He tried to remember what that breakfast had been. It had been eaten in a hurry, he had been thinking of something else as usual, and, except that it consisted of various odds and ends which he had happened to have on hand, he could not itemize it with exactness. There had been some cold fried potatoes, and some warmed-over pop-overs which had "slumped" in the cooking, and a doughnut or two and—oh, yes, a saucer of canned peaches which had been sitting around for a week and which he had eaten to get out of the way. These, with a cup of warmed- over coffee, made up the meal. Jed couldn't see why a breakfast of that kind should make him "blue." And yet he was blue—yes, and there was no use disguising the fact, he was lonesome. If that child would only come, as she generally did, her nonsense might cheer him up a bit. But she did not come. And if he decided not to permit her mother to occupy the house, she would not come much more. Eh? Why, it was the last day of the month! She might never come again!

Jed shut off the motor and turned away from the lathe. He sank down into his little chair, drew his knee up under his chin, and thought, long and seriously. When the knee slid down to its normal position once more his mind was made up. Mrs. Armstrong might remain in the little house—for a few months more, at any rate. Even if she insisted upon a year's lease it wouldn't do any great harm. He would wait until she spoke to him about it and then he would give his consent. And—and it would please Captain Sam, at any rate.

He rose and, going to the window, looked out once more across the yard. What he saw astonished him. The back door of the house was partially open and a man was just coming out. The man, in dripping oil-skins and a sou'wester, was Philander Hardy, the local expressman. Philander turned and spoke to some one in the house behind him. Jed opened the shop door a crack and listened.

"Yes, ma'am," he heard Hardy say. "I'll be back for 'em about four o'clock this afternoon. Rain may let up a little mite by that time, and anyhow, I'll have the covered wagon. Your trunks won't get wet, ma'am; I'll see to that."

A minute later Jed, an old sweater thrown over his head and shoulders, darted out of the front door of his shop. The express wagon with Hardy on the driver's seat was just moving off. Jed called after it.

"Hi, Philander!" he called, raising his voice only a little, for fear of being overheard at the Armstrong house. "Hi, Philander, come here a minute. I want to see you."

Mr. Hardy looked over his shoulder and then backed his equipage opposite the Winslow gate.

"Hello, Jedidah Shavin's," he observed, with a grin. "Didn't know you for a minute, with that shawl over your front crimps. What you got on your mind; anything except sawdust?"

Jed was too much perturbed even to resent the loathed name "Jedidah."

"Philander," he whispered, anxiously; "say, Philander, what does she want? Mrs. Armstrong, I mean? What is it you're comin' back for at four o'clock?"

Philander looked down at the earnest face under the ancient sweater. Then he winked, solemnly.

"Well, I tell you, Shavin's," he said. "You see, I don't know how 'tis, but woman folks always seem to take a terrible shine to me. Now this Mrs. Armstrong here— Say, she's some peach, ain't she!— she ain't seen me more'n half a dozen times, but here she is beggin' me to fetch her my photograph. 'It's rainin' pretty hard, to-day,' I says. 'Won't it do if I fetch it to-morrow?' But no, she—"

Jed held up a protesting hand. "I don't doubt she wants your photograph, Philander," he drawled. "Your kind of face is rare. But I heard you say somethin' about comin' for trunks. Whose trunks?"

"Whose? Why, hers and the young-one's, I presume likely. 'Twas them I fetched from Luretta Smalley's. Now she wants me to take 'em back there."

A tremendous gust, driven in from the sea, tore the sweater from the Winslow head and shoulders and wrapped it lovingly about one of the posts in the yard. Jed did not offer to recover it; he scarcely seemed to know that it was gone. Instead he stood staring at the express driver, while the rain ran down his nose and dripped from its tip to his chin.

"She—she's goin' back to Luretta Smalley's?" he repeated. "She—"

He did not finish the sentence. Instead he turned on his heel and walked slowly back to the shop. The sweater, wrapped about the post where, in summer, a wooden sailor brandished his paddles, flapped soggily in the wind. Hardy gazed after him.

"What in time—?" he exclaimed. Then, raising his voice, he called: "Hi, Jed! Jed! You crazy critter! What—Jed, hold on a minute, didn't you know she was goin'? Didn't she tell you? Jed!"

But Jed had entered the shop and closed the door. Philander drove off, shaking his head and chuckling to himself.

A few minutes later Mrs. Armstrong, hearing a knock at the rear door of the Winslow house, opened it to find her landlord standing on the threshold. He was bareheaded and he had no umbrella.

"Why, Mr. Winslow!" she exclaimed. It was the first time that he had come to that house of his own accord since she had occupied it. Now he stood there, in the rain, looking at her without speaking.

"Why, Mr. Winslow," she said again. "What is it? Come in, won't you? You're soaking wet. Come in!"

Jed looked down at the sleeves of his jacket. "Eh?" he drawled, slowly. "Wet? Why, I don't know's I ain't—a little. It's—it's rainin'."

"Raining! It's pouring. Come in."

She took him by the arm and led him through the woodshed and into the kitchen. She would have led him further, into the sitting-room, but he hung back.

"No, ma'am, no," he said. "I—I guess I'll stay here, if you don't mind."

There was a patter of feet from the sitting-room and Barbara came running, Petunia in her arms. At the sight of their visitor's lanky form the child's face brightened.

"Oh, Mr. Winslow!" she cried. "Did you come to see where Petunia and I were? Did you?"

Jed looked down at her. "Why—why, I don't know's I didn't," he admitted. "I—I kind of missed you, I guess."

"Yes, and we missed you. You see, Mamma said we mustn't go to the shop to-day because— Oh, Mamma, perhaps he has come to tell you we won't have to—"

Mrs. Armstrong interrupted. "Hush, Babbie," she said, quickly. "I told Barbara not to go to visit you to-day, Mr. Winslow. She has been helping me with the packing."

Jed swallowed hard. "Packin'?" he repeated. "You've been packin'? Then 'twas true, what Philander Hardy said about your goin' back to Luretta's?"

The lady nodded. "Yes," she replied. "Our month here ends to-day. Of course you knew that."

Jed sighed miserably. "Yes, ma'am," he said, "I knew it, but I only just realized it, as you might say. I . . . Hum! . . . Well . . ."

He turned away and walked slowly toward the kitchen door. Barbara would have followed but her mother laid a detaining hand upon her shoulder. On the threshold of the door between the dining-room and kitchen Jed paused.

"Ma'am," he said, hesitatingly, "you—you don't cal'late there's anything I can do to—to help, is there? Anything in the packin' or movin' or anything like that?"

"No, thank you, Mr. Winslow. The packing was very simple."

"Er—yes, ma'am. . . . Yes, ma'am."

He stopped, seemed about to speak again, but evidently changed his mind, for he opened the door and went out into the rain without another word. Barbara, very much surprised and hurt, looked up into her mother's face.

"Why, Mamma," she cried, "has—has he GONE? He didn't say good-by to us or—or anything. He didn't even say he was sorry we were going."

Mrs. Armstrong shook her head.

"I imagine that is because he isn't sorry, my dear," she replied. "You must remember that Mr. Winslow didn't really wish to let any one live in this house. We only came here by—well, by accident."

But Barbara was unconvinced.

"He ISN'T glad," she declared, stoutly. "He doesn't act that way when he is glad about things. You see," she added, with the air of a Mrs. Methusaleh, "Petunia and I know him better than you do, Mamma; we've had more chances to get—to get acquainted."

Perhaps an hour later there was another knock at the kitchen door. Mrs. Armstrong, when she opened it, found her landlord standing there, one of his largest windmills—a toy at least three feet high—in his arms. He bore it into the kitchen and stood it in the middle of the floor, holding the mammoth thing, its peaked roof high above his head, and peering solemnly out between one of its arms and its side.

"Why, Mr. Winslow!" exclaimed Mrs. Armstrong.

"Yes, ma'am," said Jed. "I—I fetched it for Babbie. I just kind of thought maybe she'd like it."

Barbara clasped her hands.

"Oh!" she exclaimed. "Oh, is it for me."

Jed answered.

"'Tis, if you want it," he said.

"Want it? Why, Mamma, it's one of the very best mills! It's a five dollar one, Mamma!"

Mrs. Armstrong protested. "Oh, I couldn't let you do that, Mr. Winslow," she declared. "It is much too expensive a present. And besides—"

She checked herself just in time. It had been on the tip of her tongue to say that she did not know what they could do with it. Their rooms at Mrs. Smalley's were not large. It was as if a dweller in a Harlem flat had been presented with a hippopotamus.

The maker of the mill looked about him, plainly seeking a place to deposit his burden.

"'Tisn't anything much," he said, hastily. "I—I'm real glad for you to have it."

He was about to put it on top of the cookstove, in which there was a roaring fire, but Mrs. Armstrong, by a startled exclamation and a frantic rush, prevented his doing so. So he put it on the table instead. Barbara thanked him profusely. She was overjoyed; there were no comparisons with hippopotami in HER mind. Jed seemed pleased at her appreciation, but he did not smile. Instead he sighed.

"I—I just thought I wanted her to have it, ma'am," he said, turning to Mrs. Armstrong. "'Twould keep her from—from forgettin' me altogether, maybe. . . . Not that there's any real reason why she should remember me, of course," he added.

Barbara was hurt and indignant.

"Of COURSE I shan't forget you, Mr. Winslow," she declared. "Neither will Petunia. And neither will Mamma, I know. She feels awful bad because you don't want us to live here any longer, and—"

"Hush, Babbie, hush!" commanded her mother. Barbara hushed, but she had said enough. Jed turned a wondering face in their direction. He stared without speaking.

Mrs. Armstrong felt that some one must say something.

"You mustn't mind what the child says, Mr. Winslow," she explained, hurriedly. "Of course I realize perfectly that this house is yours and you certainly have the right to do what you please with your own. And I have known all the time that we were here merely on trial."

Jed lifted a big hand.

"Er—er—just a minute, ma'am, please," he begged. "I—I guess my wooden head is beginnin' to splinter or somethin'. Please answer me just this—if—if you'd just as soon: Why are you movin' back to Luretta's?"

It was her turn to look wonderingly at him. "Why, Mr. Winslow," she said, after a moment's hesitation, "isn't that rather an unnecessary question? When Babbie and I came here it was with the understanding that we were to be on trial for a month. We had gone into no details at all, except that the rent for this one month should be forty dollars. You were, as I understood it, to consider the question of our staying and, if you liked us and liked the idea of renting the house at all, you were to come to me and discuss the matter. The month is up and you haven't said a word on the subject. And, knowing what your feelings HAD been, I of course realized that you did not wish us to remain, and so, of course, we are going. I am sorry, very sorry. Babbie and I love this little house, and we wish you might have cared to have us stay in it, but—"

"Hold on! hold on!" Jed was, for him, almost energetic. "Mrs. Armstrong, ma'am, do you mean to tell me you're goin' back to Luretta Smalley's because you think I don't want you to stay? Is that it, honest truth?"

"Why, of course, it is. What else?"

"And—and 'tain't because you can't stand me any longer, same as Mother used to say?"

"Can't stand you? Your mother used to say? What DO you mean, Mr. Winslow?"

"I mean—I mean you ain't goin' because I used to wash my face out in the yard, and—and holler and sing mornin's and look so everlastin' homely—and—and be what everybody calls a town crank— and—"

"Mr. Winslow! PLEASE!"

"And—and you and Babbie would stay right here if—if you thought I wanted you to?"

"Why, of course. But you don't, do you?"

Before Jed could answer the outside door was thrown open without knock or preliminary warning, and Captain Sam Hunniwell, dripping water like a long-haired dog after a bath, strode into the kitchen.

"Mornin', ma'am," he said, nodding to Mrs. Armstrong. Then, turning to the maker of windmills: "You're the feller I'm lookin' for," he declared. "Is what Philander Hardy told me just now true? Is it?"

Jed was dreamily staring out of the window. He was smiling, a seraphic smile. Receiving no reply, Captain Sam angrily repeated his question. "Is it true?" he demanded.

"No-o, no, I guess 'tisn't. I'd know better if I knew what he told you."

"He told me that Mrs. Armstrong here was movin' back to Luretta Smalley's to-day. Jed Winslow, have you been big enough fool—"

Jed held up the big hand.

"Yes," he said. "I always am."

"You always are—what?"

"A big enough fool. Sam, what is a lease?"

"What is a lease?"

"Yes. Never mind tellin' me; show me. Make out a lease of this house to Mrs. Armstrong here."

Mrs. Armstrong was, naturally, rather surprised.

"Why, Mr. Winslow," she cried; "what are you talking about? We haven't agreed upon rent or—"

"Yes, we have. We've agreed about everything. Er—Babbie, you get your things on and come on over to the shop. You and I mustn't be sittin' 'round here any longer. We've got to get to WORK."

CHAPTER VII

And so, in as sudden a fashion as he had granted the "month's trial," did Jed grant the permanent tenure of his property. The question of rent, which might easily have been, with the ordinary sort of landlord, a rock in the channel, turned out to be not even a pebble. Captain Hunniwell, who was handling the business details, including the making out of the lease, was somewhat troubled.

"But, Jed," he protested, "you've GOT to listen to me. She won't pay forty a month, although she agrees with me that for a furnished house in a location like this it's dirt cheap. Of course she's takin' it for all the year, which does make consider'ble difference, although from May to October, when the summer folks are here, I could get a hundred and forty a month just as easy as . . . Eh? I believe you ain't heard a word I've been sayin'. Gracious king! If you ain't enough to drive the mate of a cattle boat into gettin' religion! Do you hear me? I say she won't pay—"

Jed, who was sitting before the battered old desk in the corner of his workshop, did not look around, but he waved his right hand, the fingers of which held the stump of a pencil, over his shoulder.

"Ssh-h, sh-h, Sam!" he observed, mildly. "Don't bother me now; please don't, there's a good feller. I'm tryin' to work out somethin' important."

"Well, this is important. Or, if it ain't, there's plenty that is important waitin' for me up at the bank. I'm handlin' this house business as a favor to you. If you think I've got nothin' else to do you're mistaken."

Jed nodded, contritely, and turned to face his friend. "I know it, Sam," he said, "I know it. I haven't got the least mite of excuse for troublin' you."

"You ain't troublin' me—not that way. All I want of you is to say yes or no. I tell you Mrs. Armstrong thinks she can't afford to pay forty a month."

"Yes."

"And perhaps she can't. But you've got your own interests to think about. What shall I do?"

"Yes."

"YES! What in time are you sayin' yes for?"

"Hum? Eh? Oh, excuse me, Sam; I didn't mean yes, I mean no."

"Gracious king!"

"Well—er—er—," desperately, "you told me to say yes or no, so I—"

"See here, Jed Winslow, HAVE you heard what I've been sayin'?"

"Why, no, Sam; honest I ain't. I've run across an idea about makin' a different kind of mill—one like a gull, you know, that'll flap its wings up and down when the wind blows—and—er—I'm afraid my head is solid full of that and nothin' else. There generally ain't more'n room for one idea in my head," he added, apologetically. "Sometimes that one gets kind of cramped."

The captain snorted in disgust. Jed looked repentant and distressed.

"I'm awful sorry, Sam," he declared. "But if it's about that house of mine—rent or anything, you just do whatever Mrs. Armstrong says."

"Whatever SHE says? Haven't you got anything to say?"

"No, no-o, I don't know's I have. You see, I've settled that she and Babbie are to have the house for as long as they want it, so it's only fair to let them settle the rest, seems to me. Whatever Mrs. Armstrong wants to pay'll be all right. You just leave it to her."

Captain Sam rose to his feet.

"I've a dum good mind to," he declared "'Twould serve you right if she paid you ten cents a year." Then, with a glance of disgust at the mountain of old letters and papers piled upon the top of the desk where his friend was at work, he added: "What do you clean that desk of yours with—a shovel?"

The slow smile drifted across the Winslow face. "I cal'late that's what I should have to use, Sam," he drawled, "if I ever cleaned it."

The captain and the widow agreed upon thirty-five dollars a month. It developed that she owned their former house in Middleford and that the latter had been rented for a very much higher rent. "My furniture," she added, "that which I did not sell when we gave up housekeeping, is stored with a friend there. I know it is extravagant, my hiring a furnished house, but I'm sure Mr. Winslow wouldn't let this one unfurnished and, besides, it would be a crime to disturb furniture and rooms which fit each other as these do. And, after all, at the end of a year I may wish to leave Orham. Of course I hope I shall not, but I may."

Captain Sam would have asked questions concerning her life in Middleford, in fact he did ask a few, but the answers he received were unsatisfactory. Mrs. Armstrong evidently did not care to talk on the subject. The captain thought her attitude a little odd, but decided that the tragedy of her husband's death must be the cause of her reticence. Her parting remarks on this occasion furnished an explanation.

"If you please, Captain Hunniwell," she said, "I would rather you did not tell any one about my having lived in Middleford and my affairs there. I have told very few people in Orham and I think on the whole it is better not to. What is the use of having one's personal history discussed by strangers?"

She was evidently a trifle embarrassed and confused as she said this, for she blushed just a little. Captain Sam decided that the blush was becoming. Also, as he walked back to the bank, he reflected that Jed Winslow's tenant was likely to have her personal history and affairs discussed whether she wished it or not. Young women as attractive as she were bound to be discussed, especially in a community the size of Orham. And, besides, whoever else she may have told, she certainly had told him that Middleford had formerly been her home and he had told Maud and Jed. Of course they would say nothing if he asked them, but perhaps they had told it already. And why should Mrs. Armstrong care, anyway?

"Let folks talk," he said that evening, in conversation with his daughter. "Let 'em talk, that's my motto. When they're lyin' about me I know they ain't lyin' about anybody else, that's some comfort. But women folks, I cal'late, feel different."

Maud was interested and a little suspicious.

"You don't suppose, Pa," she said, "that this Mrs. Armstrong has a past, do you?"

"A past? What kind of a thing is a past, for thunder sakes?"

"Why, I mean a—a—well, has she done something she doesn't want other people to know; is she trying to hide something, like—well, as people do in stories?"

"Eh? Oh, in the books! I see. Well, young woman, I cal'late the first thing for your dad to do is to find out what sort of books you read. A past! Ho, ho! I guess likely Mrs. Armstrong is a plaguey sight more worried about the future than she is about the past. She has lived the past already, but she's got to live the future and pay the bills belongin' to it, and that's no triflin' job in futures like these days."

Needless to say Jed Winslow did no speculating concerning his tenant's "past." Having settled the question of that tenancy definitely and, as he figured it, forever, he put the matter entirely out of his mind and centered all his energies upon the new variety of mill, the gull which was to flap its wings when the wind blew. Barbara was, of course, much interested in the working out of this invention, and her questions were many. Occasionally Mrs. Armstrong came into the shop. She and Jed became better acquainted.

The acquaintanceship developed. Jed formed a daily habit of stopping at the Armstrong door to ask if there were any errands to be done downtown. "Goin' right along down on my own account, ma'am," was his invariable excuse. "Might just as well run your errands at the same time." Also, whenever he chopped a supply of kindling wood for his own use he chopped as much more and filled the oilcloth-covered box which stood by the stove in the Armstrong kitchen. He would not come in and sit down, however, in spite of Barbara's and her mother's urgent invitation; he was always too "busy" for that.

But the time came when he did come in, actually come in and sit down to a meal. Barbara, of course, was partially responsible for this amazing invitation, but it was Heman Taylor's old brindle tomcat which really brought it to pass. The cat in question was a disreputable old scalawag, with tattered ears and a scarred hide, souvenirs of fights innumerable, with no beauty and less morals, and named, with appropriate fitness, "Cherub."

It was a quarter to twelve on a Sunday morning and Jed was preparing his dinner. The piece de resistance of the dinner was, in this instance, to be a mackerel. Jed had bought the mackerel of the fish peddler the previous afternoon and it had been reposing on a plate in the little ancient ice-chest which stood by the back door of the Winslow kitchen. Barbara, just back from Sunday school and arrayed in her best, saw that back door open and decided to call. Jed, as always, was glad to see her.

"You're getting dinner, aren't you, Mr. Winslow?" she observed.

Jed looked at her over his spectacles. "Yes," he answered. "Unless somethin' happens I'm gettin' dinner."

His visitor looked puzzled.

"Why, whatever happened you would be getting dinner just the same, wouldn't you?" she said. "You might not have it, but you'd be getting it, you know."

Jed took the mackerel out of the ice-chest and put the plate containing it on the top of the latter. "We-ell," he drawled, "you can't always tell. I might take so long gettin' it that, first thing I knew, 'twould be supper."

Humming a hymn he took another dish from the ice-chest and placed it beside the mackerel plate.

"What's that?" inquired Barbara.

"That? Oh, that's my toppin'-off layer. That's a rice puddin', poor man's puddin', some folks call it. I cal'late your ma'd call it a man's poor puddin', but it makes good enough ballast for a craft like me." He began singing again.

> "'I know not, yea, I know not
> What bliss awaits me there.
> Di, doo de di di doo de—'"

Breaking off to suggest: "Better stay and eat along with me to-day, hadn't you, Babbie?"

Barbara tried hard not to seem superior.

"Thank you," she said, "but I guess I can't. We're going to have chicken and lemon jelly." Then, remembering her manners, she added: "We'd be awful glad if you'd have dinner with us, Mr. Winslow."

Jed shook his head.

"Much obliged," he drawled, "but if I didn't eat that mackerel, who would?"

The question was answered promptly. While Mr. Winslow and his small caller were chatting concerning the former's dinner, another eager personality was taking a marked interest in a portion of that dinner. Cherub, the Taylor cat, abroad on a foraging expedition, had scented from his perch upon a nearby fence a delicious and appetizing odor. Following his nose, literally, Cherub descended from the fence and advanced, sniffing as he came. The odor was fish, fresh fish. Cherub's green eyes blazed, his advance became crafty, strategical, determined. He crept to the Winslow back step, he looked up through the open door, he saw the mackerel upon its plate on the top of the ice-chest.

"If I didn't eat that mackerel," drawled Jed, "who would?"

There was a momentary glimpse of a brindle cat with a mackerel crosswise in its mouth

There was a swoop through the air, a scream from Barbara, a crash—two crashes, a momentary glimpse of a brindle cat with a mackerel crosswise in its mouth and the ends dragging on the ground, a rattle of claws on the fence. Then Jed and his visitor were left to gaze upon a broken plate on the floor, an overturned bowl on top of the ice-chest, and a lumpy rivulet of rice pudding trickling to the floor.

"Oh! Oh! Oh!" cried Barbara, wringing her hands in consternation.

Jed surveyed the ruin of the "poor man's pudding" and gazed thoughtfully at the top of the fence over which the marauder had disappeared.

"Hum," he mused. "H-u-u-m. . . . Well, I did cal'late I could get a meal out of sight pretty fast myself, but—but—I ain't in that critter's class."

"But your dinner!" wailed Barbara, almost in tears. "He's spoiled ALL your dinner! Oh, the BAD thing! I hate that Cherub cat! I HATE him!"

Mr. Winslow rubbed his chin. "We-e-ll," he drawled again. "He does seem to have done what you might call a finished job. H-u-u-m! ... 'Another offensive on the—er—no'theast'ard front; all objectives attained.' That's the way the newspapers tell such things nowadays, ain't it? ... However, there's no use cryin' over spilt—er—puddin'. Lucky there's eggs and milk aboard the ship. I shan't starve, anyhow."

Barbara was aghast. "Eggs and milk!" she repeated. "Is THAT all you've got for Sunday dinner, Mr. Winslow? Why, that's awful!"

Jed smiled and began picking up the fragments of the plate. He went to the closet to get a broom and when he came out again the young lady had vanished.

But she was back again in a few minutes, her eyes shining.

"Mr. Winslow," she said, "Mamma sent me to ask if you could please come right over to our house. She—she wants to see you."

Jed regarded her doubtfully. "Wants to see me?" he repeated. "What for?"

The child shook her head; her eyes sparkled more than ever. "I'm not sure," she said, "but I think there's something she wants you to do."

Wondering what the something might be, Jed promised to be over in a minute or two. Barbara danced away, apparently much excited. Mr. Winslow, remembering that it was Sunday, performed a hasty toilet at the sink, combed his hair, put on his coat and walked across the yard. Barbara met him at the side door of the house.

"Mamma's in the dining-room," she said. "Come right in, Mr. Winslow."

So Jed entered the dining-room, to find the table set and ready, with places laid for three instead of two, and Mrs. Armstrong drawing back one of three chairs. He looked at her.

"Good mornin', ma'am," he stammered. "Babbie, she said—er—she said there was somethin' you wanted me to do."

The lady smiled. "There is," she replied. "Babbie has told me what happened to your dinner, and she and I want you to sit right down and have dinner with us. We're expecting you, everything is ready, and we shall— yes, we shall be hurt if you don't stay. Shan't we, Babbie?"

Barbara nodded vigorously. "Awf'ly," she declared; "'specially Petunia. You will stay, won't you, Mr. Winslow—please?"

Poor Jed! His agitation was great, his embarrassment greater and his excuses for not accepting the invitation numerous if not convincing. But at last he yielded and sat reluctantly down to the first meal he had eaten in that house for five years.

Mrs. Armstrong, realizing his embarrassment, did not urge him to talk and Barbara, although she chattered continuously, did not seem to expect answers to her questions. So Jed ate a little, spoke a little, and thought a great deal. And by the time dinner was over some of his shyness and awkwardness had worn away. He insisted upon helping with the dishes and, because she saw that he would be hurt if she did not, his hostess permitted him to do so.

"You see, ma'am," he said, "I've been doin' dishes for a consider'ble spell, more years than I like to count. I ought to be able to do 'em fair to middlin' well. But," he added, as much to himself as to her, "I don't know as that's any sign. There's so many things I ought to be able to do like other folks—and can't. I'm afraid you may not be satisfied, after all, ma'am," he went on. "I suppose you're a kind of an expert, as you might say."

She shook her head. "I fear I'm no expert, Mr. Winslow," she answered, just a little sadly, so it seemed to him. "Barbara and I are learning, that is all."

"Nora used to do the dishes at home," put in Barbara. "Mamma hardly ever—"

"Hush, dear," interrupted her mother. "Mr. Winslow wouldn't be interested."

After considerable urging Jed consented to sit a while in the living-room. He was less reluctant to talk by this time and, the war creeping into the conversation, as it does into all conversations nowadays, they spoke of recent happenings at home and abroad. Mrs. Armstrong was surprised to find how well informed her landlord was concerning the world struggle, its causes and its progress.

"Why, no, ma'am," he said, in answer to a remark of hers; "I ain't read it up much, as I know of, except in the newspapers. I ain't an educated man. Maybe—" with his slow smile—"maybe you've guessed as much as that already."

"I know that you have talked more intelligently on this war than any one else I have heard since I came to this town," she declared, emphatically. "Even Captain Hunniwell has never, in my hearing, stated the case against Germany as clearly as you put it just now; and I have heard him talk a good deal."

Jed was evidently greatly pleased, but he characteristically tried not to show it. "Well, now, ma'am," he drawled, "I'm afraid you ain't been to the post office much mail times. If you'd just drop in there some evenin' and hear Gabe Bearse and Bluey Batcheldor raise hob with the Kaiser you'd understand why the confidence of the Allies is unshaken, as the Herald gave out this mornin'."

A little later he said, reflectively:

"You know, ma'am, it's an astonishin' thing to me, I can't get over it, my sittin' here in this house, eatin' with you folks and talkin' with you like this."

Mrs. Armstrong smiled. "I can't see anything so very astonishing about it," she said.

"Can't you?"

"Certainly not. Why shouldn't you do it—often? We are landlord and tenant, you and I, but that is no reason, so far as I can see, why we shouldn't be good neighbors."

He shook his head.

"I don't know's you quite understand, ma'am," he said. "It's your thinkin' of doin' it, your askin' me and—and WANTIN' to ask me that seems so kind of odd. Do you know," he added, in a burst of confidence, "I don't suppose that, leavin' Sam Hunniwell out, another soul has asked me to eat at their house for ten year. Course I'm far from blamin' 'em for that, you understand, but—"

"Wait. Mr. Winslow, you had tenants in this house before?"

"Yes'm. Davidson, their names was."

"And did THEY never invite you here?"

Jed looked at her, then away, out of the window. It was a moment or two before he answered. Then—

"Mrs. Armstrong," he said, "you knew, I cal'late, that I was—er— kind of prejudiced against rentin' anybody this house after the Davidsons left?"

The lady, trying not to smile, nodded.

"Yes," she replied, "I—well, I guessed as much."

"Yes'm, I was. They would have took it again, I'm pretty sartin, if I'd let 'em, but—but somehow I couldn't do it. No, I couldn't, and I never meant anybody else should be here. Seems funny to you, I don't doubt."

"Why, no, it was your property to do what you pleased with, and I am sure you had a reason for refusing."

"Yes'm. But I ain't ever told anybody what that reason was. I've told Sam a reason, but 'twan't the real one. I—I guess likely I'll tell it to you. I imagine 'twill sound foolish enough. 'Twas just somethin' I heard Colonel Davidson say, that's all."

He paused. Mrs. Armstrong did not speak. After an interval he continued:

"'Twas one day along the last of the season. The Davidsons had company and they'd been in to see the shop and the mills and vanes and one thing or 'nother. They seemed nice, pleasant enough folks; laughed a good deal, but I didn't mind that. I walked out into the yard along with 'em and then, after I left 'em, I stood for a minute on the front step of the shop, with the open door between me and this house here. A minute or so later I heard 'em come into this very room. They couldn't see me, 'count of the door, but I could hear them, 'count of the windows bein' open. And then . . . Huh . . . Oh, well."

He sighed and lapsed into one of his long fits of abstraction. At length Mrs. Armstrong ventured to remind him.

"And then—?" she asked.

"Eh? Oh, yes, ma'am! Well, then I heard one of the comp'ny say: 'I don't wonder you enjoy it here, Ed,' he says. 'That landlord of yours is worth all the rent you pay and more. 'Tain't everybody that has a dime museum right on the premises.' All hands laughed and then Colonel Davidson said: 'I thought you'd appreciate him,' he says. 'We'll have another session with him before you leave. Perhaps we can get him into the house here this evenin'. My wife is pretty good at that, she jollies him along. Oh, he swallows it all; the poor simpleton don't know when he's bein' shown off.'"

Mrs. Armstrong uttered an exclamation.

"Oh!" she cried. "The brute!"

"Yes'm," said Jed, quietly, "that was what he said. You see," with an apologetic twitch of the lip, "it came kind of sudden to me and— and it hurt. Fact is, I—I had noticed he and his wife was—er— well, nice and— er—folksy, as you might say, but I never once thought they did it for any reason but just because they—well, liked me, maybe. Course I'd ought to have known better. Fine ladies and gentlemen like them don't take much fancy to dime museum folks."

There was just a trace of bitterness in his tone, the first Mrs. Armstrong had ever noticed there. Involuntarily she leaned toward him.

"Don't, Mr. Winslow," she begged. "Don't think of it again. They must have been beasts, those people, and they don't deserve a moment's thought. And DON'T call them ladies and gentlemen. The only gentleman there was yourself."

Jed shook his head.

"If you said that around the village here," he drawled, "somebody might be for havin' you sent to the asylum up to Taunton. Course I'm much obliged to you, but, honest, you hadn't ought to take the risk."

Mrs. Armstrong smiled slightly, but hers was a forced smile. What she had just heard, told in her guest's quaint language as a statement of fact and so obviously with no thought of effect, had touched her more than any plea for sympathy could have done. She felt as if she had a glimpse into this man's simple, trusting, sensitive soul. And with that glimpse came a new feeling toward him, a feeling of pity—yes, and more than that, a feeling of genuine respect.

He sighed again and rose to go. "I declare," he said, apologetically, "I don't know what I've been botherin' you with all this for. As I said, I've never told that yarn to anybody afore and I never meant to tell it. I—"

But she interrupted him. "Please don't apologize," she said. "I'm very glad you told it to me."

"I cal'late you think it's a queer reason for lettin' this house stand empty all this time."

"No, I think it was a very good one, and Babbie and I are honored to know that your estimate of us is sufficiently high to overcome your prejudice."

"Well, ma'am, I—I guess it's goin' to be all right. If you feel you can get along with me for a landlord I'd ought sartin to be willin' to have you for tenants. Course I don't blame the Davidsons, in one way, you understand, but—"

"I do. I blame them in every way. They must have been unspeakable. Mr. Winslow, I hope you will consider Babbie and me not merely tenants and neighbors, but friends—real friends."

Jed did not reply for at least a minute. Then he said: "I'm afraid you'll be kind of lonesome; my friends are like corn sprouts in a henyard, few and scatterin'."

"So much the better; we shall feel that we belong to select company."

He did not thank her nor answer, but walked slowly on through the dining-room and kitchen, where he opened the door and stepped out upon the grass. There he stood for a moment, gazing at the sky, alternately puckering his lips and opening them, but without saying a word. Mrs. Armstrong and Barbara, who had followed him, watched these facial gymnastics, the lady with astonishment, her daughter with expectant interest.

"I know what he is doing that for, Mamma," she whispered. "It's because he's thinking and don't know whether to whistle or not. When he thinks AWFUL hard he's almost sure to whistle—or sing."

"Hush, hush, Babbie!"

"Oh, he won't hear us. He hardly ever hears any one when he's thinking like that. And see, Mamma, he IS going to whistle."

Sure enough, their guest whistled a few mournful bars, breaking off suddenly to observe:

"I hope there wan't any bones in it."

"Bones in what? What do you mean, Mr. Winslow?" queried Mrs. Armstrong, who was puzzled, to say the least.

"Eh? Oh, I hope there wan't any bones in that mackerel Heman's cat got away with. If there was it might choke or somethin'."

"Good gracious! I shouldn't worry over that possibility, if I were you. I should scarcely blame you for wishing it might choke, after stealing your dinner."

Mr. Winslow shook his head. "That wouldn't do," solemnly. "If it choked it couldn't ever steal another one."

"But you don't WANT it to steal another one, do you?"

"We-ll, if every one it stole meant my havin' as good an afternoon as this one's been, I'd—"

He stopped. Barbara ventured to spur him on.

"You'd what?" she asked.

"I'd give up whittlin' weather vanes and go mackerel-seinin' for the critter's benefit. Well—er—good day, ma'am."

"Good afternoon, Mr. Winslow. We shall expect you again soon. You must be neighborly, for, remember, we are friends now."

Jed was half way across the yard, but he stopped and turned.

"My—my FRIENDS generally call me 'Jed,'" he said. Then, his face a bright red, he hurried into the shop and closed the door.

CHAPTER VIII

After this, having broken the ice, Jed, as Captain Sam Hunniwell might have expressed it, "kept the channel clear." When he stopped at the kitchen door of his tenants' house he no longer invariably refused to come in and sit down. When he inquired if Mrs. Armstrong had any errands to be done he also asked if there were any chores he might help out with. When the old clock—a genuine Seth Willard—on the wall of the living-room refused to go, he came in, sat down, took the refractory timepiece in his arms and, after an hour of what he called "putterin' and jackleggin'," hung it up again apparently in as good order as ever. During the process he whistled a little, sang a hymn or two, and talked with Barbara, who found the conversation a trifle unsatisfactory.

"He hardly EVER finished what he was going to say," she confided to her mother afterward. "He'd start to tell me a story and just as he got to the most interesting part something about the clock would seem to—you know—trouble him and he'd stop and, when he began again, he'd be singing instead of talking. I asked him what made him do it and he said he cal'lated his works must be loose and every once in a while his speaking trumpet fell down into his music box. Isn't he a funny man, Mamma?"

"He is indeed, Babbie."

"Yes. Petunia and I think he's—he's perfectly scrushe-aking. 'Twas awful nice of him to fix our clock, wasn't it, Mamma."

"Yes, dear."

"Yes. And I know why he did it; he told me. 'Twas on Petunia's account. He said not to let her know it but he'd taken consider'ble of a shine to her. I think he's taken a shine to me, don't you, Mamma?"

"I'm sure of it."

"So am I. And I 'most guess he's taken one to you, too. Anyhow he watches you such a lot and notices so many things. He asked me to-day if you had been crying. I said no. You hadn't, had you, Mamma?"

Mrs. Armstrong evaded the question by changing the subject. She decided she must be more careful in hiding her feelings when her landlord was about. She had had no idea that he could be so observing; certainly he did not look it.

But her resolution was a little late. Jed had made up his mind that something was troubling his fair tenant. Again and again, now that he was coming to know her better and better, he had noticed the worn, anxious look on her face, and once before the day of the clock repairing he had seen her when it seemed to him that she had been crying. He did not mention his observations or inferences to any one, even Captain Sam, but he was sure he was right. Mrs. Armstrong was worried and anxious and he did not like the idea. He wished he might help her, but of course he could not. Another man, a normal man, one not looked upon by a portion of the community as "town crank," might have been able to help, might have known how to offer his services and perhaps have them accepted, but not he, not Jedidah Edgar Wilfred Winslow. But he wished he could. She had asked him to consider her a real friend, and to Jed, who had so few, a friend was a possession holy and precious.

Meanwhile the war was tightening its grip upon Orham as upon every city, town and hamlet in the land. At first it had been a thing to read about in the papers, to cheer for, to keep the flags flying. But it had been far off, unreal. Then came the volunteering, and after that the draft, and the reality drew a little nearer. Work upon the aviation camp at East Harniss had actually begun. The office buildings were up and the sheds for the workmen. They were erecting frames for the barracks, so Gabriel Bearse reported. The sight of a uniform in Orham streets was no longer such a novelty as to bring the population, old and young, to doors and windows. Miss Maud Hunniwell laughingly confided to Jed that she was beginning to have hopes, real hopes, of seeing genuine gold lace some day soon.

Captain Sam, her father, was busy. Sessions of the Exemption Board were not quite as frequent as at first, but the captain declared them frequent enough. And volunteering went on steadily here and there among young blood which, having drawn a low number in the draft, was too impatient for active service to wait its turn. Gustavus Howes, bookkeeper at the bank, was one example. Captain Sam told Jed about it on one of his calls.

"Yep," he said, "Gus has gone, cleared out yesterday afternoon. Goin' to one of the trainin' camps to try to learn to be an officer. Eh? What did I say to him? Why, I couldn't say nothin', could I, but 'Hurrah' and 'God bless you'? But it's leavin' a bad hole in the bank just the same."

Jed asked if the bank had any one in view to fill that hole. Captain Sam looked doubtful.

"Well," he replied, "we've got somebody in view that would like to try and fill it. Barzilla Small was in to see me yesterday afternoon and he's sartin that his boy Luther—Lute, everybody calls him—is just the one for the place. He's been to work up in Fall River in a bank, so Barzilla says; that would mean he must have had some experience. Whether he'll do or not I don't know, but he's about the only candidate in sight, these war times. What do you think of him, Jed?"

Jed rubbed his chin. "To fill Gus Howes' place?" he asked.

"Yes, of course. Didn't think I was figgerin' on makin' him President of the United States, did you?"

"Hum! . . . W-e-e-ll. . . . One time when I was a little shaver, Sam, down to the fishhouse, I tried on a pair of Cap'n Jabe Kelly's rubber boots. You remember Cap'n Jabe, Sam, of course. Do you remember his feet?"

The captain chuckled. "My dad used to say Jabe's feet reminded him of a couple of chicken-halibut."

"Um-hm. . . . Well, I tried on his boots and started to walk across the wharf in em. . . ."

"Well, what of it? Gracious king! hurry up. What happened?"

"Eh? . . . Oh, nothin' much, only seemed to me I'd had half of my walk afore those boots began to move."

Captain Hunniwell enjoyed the story hugely. It was not until his laugh had died away to a chuckle that its application to the bank situation dawned upon him.

"Umph!" he grunted. "I see. You cal'late that Lute Small will fill Gus Howes' job about the way you filled those boots, eh? You may be right, shouldn't wonder if you was, but we've got to have somebody and we've got to have him now. So I guess likely we'll let Lute sign on and wait till later to find out whether he's an able seaman or a—a—"

He hesitated, groping for a simile. Mr. Winslow supplied one.

"Or a leak," he suggested.

"Yes, that's it. Say, have you heard anything from Leander Babbitt lately?"

"No, nothin' more than Gab Bearse was reelin' off last time he was in here. How is Phin Babbitt? Does he speak to you yet?"

"Not a word. But the looks he gives me when we meet would sour milk. He's dead sartin that I had somethin' to do with his boy's volunteerin' and he'll never forgive me for it. He's the best hand at unforgivin' I ever saw.

No, no! Wonder what he'd say if he knew 'twas you, Jed, that was really responsible?"

Jed shook his head, but made no reply. His friend was at the door.

"Any money to take to the bank?" he inquired. "Oh, no, I took what you had yesterday, didn't I? Any errands you want done over to Harniss? Maud and I are goin' over there in the car this afternoon."

Jed seemed to reflect. "No-o," he said; "no, I guess not. . . . Why, yes, I don't know but there is, though. If you see one of those things the soldiers put on in the trenches I'd wish you'd buy it for me. You know what I mean—a gas mask."

"A gas mask! Gracious king! What on earth?"

Jed sighed. "'Twould be consider'ble protection when Gabe Bearse dropped in and started talkin'," he drawled, solemnly.

October came in clear and fine and on a Saturday in that month Jed and Barbara went on their long anticipated picnic to the aviation camp at East Harniss. The affair was one which they had planned together. Barbara, having heard much concerning aviation during her days of playing and listening in the windmill shop, had asked questions. She wished to know what an aviation was. Jed had explained, whereupon his young visitor expressed a wish to go and see for herself. "Couldn't you take Petunia and me some time, Mr. Winslow?" she asked.

"Guess maybe so," was the reply, "provided I don't forget it, same as you forget about not callin' me Mr. Winslow."

"Oh, I'm so sorry. Petunia ought to have reminded me. Can't you take me some time, Uncle Jed?"

He had insisted upon her dropping the "Mr." in addressing him. "Your ma's goin' to call me Jed," he told her; "that is to say, I hope she is, and you might just as well. I always answer fairly prompt whenever anybody says 'Jed,' 'cause I'm used to it. When they say 'Mr. Winslow' I have to stop and think a week afore I remember who they mean."

But Barbara, having consulted her mother, refused to address her friend as "Jed." "Mamma says it wouldn't be respect—respectaful," she said. "And I don't think it would myself. You see, you're older than I am," she added.

Jed nodded gravely. "I don't know but I am, a little, now you remind me of it," he admitted. "Well, I tell you—call me 'Uncle Jed.' That's got a handle to it but it ain't so much like the handle to an ice pitcher as Mister is. 'Uncle Jed' 'll do, won't it?"

Barbara pondered. "Why," she said, doubtfully, "you aren't my uncle, really. If you were you'd be Mamma's brother, like—like Uncle Charlie, you know."

It was the second time she had mentioned "Uncle Charlie." Jed had never heard Mrs. Armstrong speak of having a brother, and he wondered vaguely why. However, he did not wonder long on this particular occasion.

"Humph!" he grunted. "Well, let's see. I tell you: I'll be your step-uncle. That'll do, won't it? You've heard of step-fathers? Um-hm. Well, they ain't real fathers, and a step-uncle ain't a real uncle. Now you think that over and see if that won't fix it first-rate."

The child thought it over. "And shall I call you 'Step-Uncle Jed'?" she asked.

"Eh? . . . Um. . . . No-o, I guess I wouldn't. I'm only a back step-uncle, anyway—I always come to the back steps of your house, you know—so I wouldn't say anything about the step part. You ask your ma and see what she says."

So Barbara asked and reported as follows:

"She says I may call you 'Uncle Jed' when it's just you and I together," she said. "But when other people are around she thinks 'Mr. Winslow' would be more respectaful."

It was settled on that basis.

"Can't you take me to the aviation place sometime, Uncle Jed?" asked Barbara.

Jed thought he could, if he could borrow a boat somewhere and Mrs. Armstrong was willing that Barbara should go with him. Both permission and the boat were obtained, the former with little difficulty, after Mrs. Armstrong had made inquiries concerning Mr. Winslow's skill in handling a boat, the latter with more. At last Captain Perez Ryder, being diplomatically approached, told Jed he might use his eighteen foot power dory for a day, the only cost being that entailed by purchase of the necessary oil and gasoline.

It was a beautiful morning when they started on their six mile sail, or "chug," as Jed called it. Mrs. Armstrong had put up a lunch for them, and Jed had a bucket of clams, a kettle, a pail of milk, some crackers, onions and salt pork, the ingredients of a possible chowder.

"Little mite late for 'longshore chowder picnics, ma'am," he said, "but it's a westerly wind and I cal'late 'twill be pretty balmy in the lee of the pines. Soon's it gets any ways chilly we'll be startin' home. Wish you were goin' along, too."

Mrs. Armstrong smiled and said she wished it had been possible for her to go, but it was not. She looked pale that morning, so it seemed to Jed, and when she smiled it was with an obvious effort.

"You're not going without locking your kitchen door, are you, Mr. Jed?" she asked.

Jed looked at her and at the door.

"Why," he observed, "I ain't locked that door, have I! I locked the front one, the one to the shop, though. Did you see the sign I tacked on the outside of it?"

"No, I didn't."

"I didn't know but you might have. I put on it: 'Closed for the day. Inquire at Abijah Thompson's.' You see," he added, his eye twinkling ever so little, "'Bije Thompson lives in the last house in the village, two mile or more over to the west'ard."

"He does! Then why in the world did you tell people to inquire there?"

"Oh, if I didn't they'd be botherin' you, probably, and I didn't want 'em doin' that. If they want me enough to travel way over to 'Bije's they'll come back here to-morrow, I shouldn't wonder. I guess likely they'd have to; 'Bije don't know anything about me."

He rubbed his chin and then added:

"Maybe 'twould be a good notion to lock that kitchen door."

They were standing at the edge of the bluff. He sauntered over to the kitchen, closed the door, and then, opening the window beside it, reached in through that window and turned the key in the lock of the door. Leaving the key in that lock and the window still open, he came sauntering back again.

"There," he drawled, "I guess everything's safe enough now."

Mrs. Armstrong regarded him in amused wonder. "Do you usually lock your door on the inside in that way?" she asked.

"Eh? . . . Oh, yes'm. If I locked it on the outside I'd have to take the key with me, and I'm such an absent-minded dumb-head, I'd be pretty sure to lose it. Come on, Babbie. All aboard!"

CHAPTER IX

The "Araminta," which was the name of Captain Perez's power dory—a name, so the captain invariably explained, "wished onto her" before he bought her—chugged along steadily if not swiftly. The course was always in protected water, inside the outer beaches or through the narrow channels between the sand islands, and so there were no waves to contend with and no danger. Jed, in the course of his varied experience afloat and ashore, had picked up a working knowledge of gasoline engines and, anyhow, as he informed his small passenger, the "Araminta's" engine didn't need any expert handling. "She runs just like some folks' tongues; just get her started and she'll clack along all day," he observed, adding philosophically, "and that's a good thing—in an engine."

"I know whose tongue you're thinking about, Uncle Jed," declared Barbara. "It's Mr. Gabe Bearse's."

Jed was much amused; he actually laughed aloud. "Gabe and this engine are different in one way, though," he said. "It's within the bounds of human possibility to stop this engine."

They threaded the last winding channel and came out into the bay. Across, on the opposite shore, the new sheds and lumber piles of what was to be the aviation camp loomed raw and yellow in the sunlight. A brisk breeze ruffled the blue water and the pines on the hilltops shook their heads and shrugged their green shoulders. The "Araminta" chugged across the bay, rising and falling ever so little on the miniature rollers.

"What shall we do, Uncle Jed?" asked Barbara. "Shall we go to see the camp or shall we have our chowder and luncheon first and then go?"

Jed took out his watch, shook it and held it to his ear—a precautionary process rendered necessary because of his habit of forgetting to wind it—then after a look at the dial, announced that, as it was only half-past ten, perhaps they had better go to the camp first.

"You see," he observed, "if we eat now we shan't hardly know whether we're late to breakfast or early to dinner."

Barbara was surprised.

"Why, Uncle Jed!" she exclaimed, "I had breakfast ever so long ago! Didn't you?"

"I had it about the same time you did, I cal'late. But my appetite's older than yours and it don't take so much exercise; I guess that's the difference. We'll eat pretty soon. Let's go and look the place over first."

They landed in a little cove on the beach adjoining the Government reservation. Jed declared it a good place to make a fire, as it was sheltered from the wind. He anchored the boat at the edge of the channel and then, pulling up the tops of his long-legged rubber boots, carried his passenger ashore. Another trip or two landed the kettle, the materials for the chowder and the lunch baskets. Jed looked at the heap on the beach and then off at the boat.

"Now," he said, slowly, "the question is what have I left aboard that I ought to have fetched ashore and what have I fetched here that ought to be left there? . . . Hum. . . . I wonder."

"What makes you think you've done anything like that, Uncle Jed?" asked Barbara.

"Eh? . . . Oh, I don't think it, I know it. I've boarded with myself for forty-five year and I know if there's anything I can get cross-eyed I'll do it. Just as likely as not I've made the bucket of clams fast to that rope out yonder and hove it overboard, and pretty soon you'll see me tryin' to make chowder out of the anchor. . . . Ah hum. . . well. . . .

> 'As numberless as the sands on the seashore,
> As numberless as the sands on the shore,
> Oh, what a sight 'twill be, when the ransomed host we see,
> As numberless as—'

Well, what do you say? Shall we heave ahead for the place where Uncle Sam's birds are goin' to nest—his two-legged birds, I mean?"

They walked up the beach a little way, then turned inland, climbed a dune covered with beachgrass and emerged upon the flat meadows which would soon be the flying field. They walked about among the sheds, the frames of the barracks, and inspected the office building from outside. There were gangs of workmen, carpenters, plumbers and shovelers, but almost no uniforms. Barbara was disappointed.

"But there ARE soldiers here," she declared. "Mamma said there were, officer soldiers, you know."

"I cal'late there ain't very many yet," explained her companion. "Only the few that's in charge, I guess likely. By and by there'll be enough, officers and men both, but now there's only carpenters and such."

"But there are SOME officer ones—" insisted Babbie. "I wonder— Oh, see, Uncle Jed, through that window—see, aren't those soldiers? They've got on soldier clothes."

Jed presumed likely that they were. Barbara nodded, sagely. "And they're officers, too," she said, "I'm sure they are because they're in the office. Do they call them officers because they work in offices, Uncle Jed?"

After an hour's walking about they went back to the place where they had left the boat and Jed set about making the chowder. Barbara watched him build the fire and open the clams, but then, growing tired of sitting still, she was seized with an idea.

"Uncle Jed," she asked, "can't you whittle me a shingle boat? You know you did once at our beach at home. And there's the cunningest little pond to sail it on. Mamma would let me sail it there, I know, 'cause it isn't a bit deep. You come and see, Uncle Jed."

The "pond" was a puddle, perhaps twenty feet across, left by the outgoing tide. Its greatest depth was not more than a foot. Jed absent-mindedly declared the pond to be safe enough but that he could not make a shingle boat, not having the necessary shingle.

"Would you if you had one?" persisted the young lady.

"Eh? . . . Oh, yes, sartin, I guess so."

"All right. Here is one. I picked it up on top of that little hill. I guess it blew there. It's blowing ever so much harder up there than it is here on the beach."

The shingle boat being hurriedly made, its owner begged for a paper sail. "The other one you made me had a paper sail, Uncle Jed."

Jed pleaded that he had no paper. "There's some wrapped 'round the lunch," he said, "but it's all butter and such. 'Twouldn't be any good for a sail. Er—er—don't you think we'd better put off makin' the sail till we get home or—or somewheres? This chowder is sort of on my conscience this minute."

Babbie evidently did not think so. She went away on an exploring expedition. In a few minutes she returned, a sheet of paper in her hand.

"It was blowing around just where I found the shingle," she declared. "It's a real nice place to find things, up on that hill place, Uncle Jed."

Jed took the paper, looked at it absently—he had taken off his coat during the fire-building and his glasses were presumably in the coat pocket—and then hastily doubled it across, thrust the mast of the "shingle boat" through it at top and bottom, and handed the craft to his small companion.

"There!" he observed; "there she is, launched, rigged and all but christened. Call her the—the 'Geranium'—the 'Sunflower'—what's the name of that doll baby of yours? Oh, yes, the 'Petunia.' Call her that and set her afloat."

But Barbara shook her head.

"I think," she said, "if you don't mind, Uncle Jed, I shall call this one 'Ruth,' that's Mamma's name, you know. The other one you made me was named for Petunia, and we wouldn't want to name 'em ALL for her. It might make her too—too— Oh, what ARE those things you make, Uncle Jed? In the shop, I mean."

"Eh? Windmills?"

"No. The others—those you tell the wind with. I know—vanes. It might make Petunia too vain. That's what Mamma said I mustn't be when I had my new coat, the one with the fur, you know."

She trotted off. Jed busied himself with the chowder. A few minutes later a voice behind him said: "Hi, there!" He turned to see a broad-shouldered stranger, evidently a carpenter or workman of some sort, standing at the top of the sand dune and looking down at him with marked interest.

"Hi, there!" repeated the stranger.

Jed nodded; his attention was centered on the chowder. "How d'ye do?" he observed, politely. "Nice day, ain't it? . . . Hum. . . . About five minutes more."

The workman strode down the bank.

"Say," he demanded, "have you seen anything of a plan?"

"Eh? . . . Hum. . . . Two plates and two spoons . . . and two tumblers. . . ."

"Hey! Wake up! Have you seen anything of a plan, I ask you?"

"Eh? . . . A plan? . . . No, I guess not. . . . No, I ain't. . . . What is it?"

"What IS it? How do you know you ain't seen it if you don't know what it is?"

"Eh? . . . I don't, I guess likely."

"Say, you're a queer duck, it strikes me. What are you up to? What are you doin' here, anyway?"

Jed took the cover from the kettle and stirred the fragrant, bubbling mass with a long-handled spoon.

"About done," he mused, slowly. "Just . . . about . . . done. Give her two minutes more for luck and then. . . ."

But his visitor was becoming impatient. "Are you deaf or are you tryin' to get my goat?" he demanded. "Because if you are you're pretty close to doin' it, I'll tell you that. You answer when I speak to you; understand? What are you doin' here?"

His tone was so loud and emphatic that even Mr. Winslow could not help but hear and understand. He looked up, vaguely troubled.

"I—I hope you'll excuse me, Mister," he stammered. "I'm afraid I haven't been payin' attention the way I'd ought to. You see, I'm makin' a chowder here and it's just about got to the place where you can't—"

"Look here, you," began his questioner, but he was interrupted in his turn. Over the edge of the bank came a young man in the khaki uniform of the United States Army. He was an officer, a second lieutenant, and a very young and very new second lieutenant at that. His face was white and he seemed much agitated.

"What's the matter here?" he demanded. Then, seeing Jed for the first time, he asked: "Who is this man and what is he doing here?"

"That's just what I was askin' him, sir," blustered the workman. "I found him here with this fire goin' and I asked him who he was and what he was doin'. I asked him first if he'd seen the plan—"

"Had he?" broke in the young officer, eagerly. Then, addressing Jed, he said: "Have you seen anything of the plan?"

Jed slowly shook his head. "I don't know's I know what you mean by a plan," he explained. "I ain't been here very long. I just— My soul and body!"

He snatched the kettle from the fire, took off the cover, sniffed anxiously, and then added, with a sigh of relief, "Whew! I declare I thought I smelt it burnin'. Saved it just in time. Whew!"

The lieutenant looked at Jed and then at the workman. The latter shook his head.

"Don't ask me, sir," he said. "That's the way he's been actin' ever since I struck here. Either he's batty or else he's pretendin' to be, one or the other. Look here, Rube!" he roared at the top of his lungs, "can the cheap talk and answer the lieutenant's questions or you'll get into trouble. D'ye hear?"

Jed looked up at him. "I'm pretty nigh sure I should hear if you whispered a little louder," he said, gently.

The young officer drew himself up. "That's enough of this," he ordered. "A plan has been lost here on this reservation, a valuable plan, a drawing of—well, a drawing that has to do with the laying out of this camp and which might be of value to the enemy if he could get it. It was on my table in the office less than an hour ago. Now it is missing. What we are asking you is whether or not you have seen anything of it. Have you?"

Jed shook his head. "I don't think I have," he replied.

"You don't think? Don't you know? What is the matter with you? Is it impossible for you to answer yes or no to a question?"

"Um—why, yes, I cal'late 'tis—to some questions."

"Well, by George! You're fresh enough."

"Now—now, if you please, I wasn't intendin' to be fresh. I just—"

"Well, you are. Who is this fellow? How does he happen to be here? Does any one know?"

Jed's first interrogator, the big workman, being the only one present beside the speaker and the object of the question, took it upon himself to answer.

"I don't know who he is," he said. "And he won't tell why he's here. Looks mighty suspicious to me. Shouldn't wonder if he was a German spy. They're all around everywheres, so the papers say."

This speech had a curious effect. The stoop in the Winslow shoulders disappeared. Jed's tall form straightened. When he spoke it was in a tone even more quiet and deliberate than usual, but there could be no shadow of a doubt that he meant what he said.

"Excuse me, Mister," he drawled, "but there's one or two names that just now I can't allow anybody to call me. 'German' is one and 'spy' is another. And you put 'em both together. I guess likely you was only foolin', wasn't you?"

The workman looked surprised. Then he laughed. "Shall I call a guard, sir?" he asked, addressing the lieutenant. "Better have him searched, I should say. Nine chances to one he's got the plan in his pocket."

The officer—he was very young—hesitated. Jed, who had not taken his eyes from the face of the man who had called him a German spy, spoke again.

"You haven't answered me yet," he drawled. "You was only foolin' when you said that, wasn't you?"

The lieutenant, who may have felt that he had suddenly become a negligible factor in the situation, essayed to take command of it.

"Shut up," he ordered, addressing Winslow. Then to the other, "Yes, call a guard. We'll see if we can't get a straight answer from this fellow. Hurry up."

The workman turned to obey. But, to his surprise, his path was blocked by Jed, who quietly stepped in front of him.

"I guess likely, if you wasn't foolin', you'd better take back what you called me," said Jed.

They looked at each other. The workman was tall and strong, but Jed, now that he was standing erect, was a little taller. His hands, which hung at his sides, were big and his arms long. And in his mild blue eye there was a look of unshakable determination. The workman saw that look and stood still.

"Hurry up!" repeated the lieutenant.

Just how the situation might have ended is uncertain. How it did end was in an unexpected manner. From the rear of the trio, from the top of the sandy ridge separating the beach from the meadow, a new voice made itself heard.

"Well, Rayburn, what's the trouble?" it asked.

The lieutenant turned briskly, so, too, did Mr. Winslow and his vis-a-vis. Standing at the top of the ridge was another officer. He was standing there looking down upon them and, although he was not smiling, Jed somehow conceived the idea that he was much amused about something. Now he descended the ridge and walked toward the group by the fire.

"Well, Rayburn, what is it?" he asked again.

The lieutenant saluted.

"Why—why, Major Grover," he stammered, "we—that is I found this man here on the Government property and—and he won't explain what he's doing here. I—I asked him if he had seen anything of the plan and he won't answer. I was just going to put him under arrest as—as a suspicious person when you came."

Major Grover turned and inspected Jed, and Jed, for his part, inspected the major. He saw a well set-up man of perhaps thirty-five, dark-haired, brown-eyed and with a closely clipped mustache above a pleasant mouth and a firm chin. The inspection lasted a minute or more. Then the major said:

"So you're a suspicious character, are you?"

Jed's hand moved across his chin in the gesture habitual with him.

"I never knew it afore," he drawled. "A suspicious character is an important one, ain't it? I—er—I'm flattered."

"Humph! Well, you realize it now, I suppose?"

"Cal'late I'll have to, long's your—er—chummie there says it's so."

The expression of horror upon Lieutenant Rayburn's face at hearing himself referred to as "chummie" to his superior officer was worth seeing.

"Oh, I say, sir!" he explained. The major paid no attention.

"What were you and this man," indicating the big carpenter, "bristling up to each other for?" he inquired.

"Well, this guy he—" began the workman. Major Grover motioned him to be quiet.

"I asked the other fellow," he said. Jed rubbed his chin once more.

"He said I was a German spy," he replied.

"Are you?"

"No." The answer was prompt enough and emphatic enough. Major Grover tugged at the corner of his mustache.

"Well, I—I admit you don't look it," he observed, dryly. "What's your name and who are you?"

Jed told his name, his place of residence and his business.

"Is there any one about here who knows you, who could prove you were who you say you are?"

Mr. Winslow considered. "Ye-es," he drawled. "Ye-es, I guess so. 'Thoph Mullett and 'Bial Hardy and Georgie T. Nickerson and Squealer Wixon, they're all carpenterin' over here and they're from Orham and know me. Then there's Bluey Batcheldor and Emulous Baker and 'Gawpy'—I mean Freddie G.—and—"

"There, there! That's quite sufficient, thank you. Do you know any of those men?" he asked, turning to the workman.

"Yes, sir, I guess I do."

"Very well. Go up and bring two of them here; not more than two, understand."

Jed's accuser departed. Major Grover resumed his catechizing.

"What were you doing here?" he asked.

"Eh? Me? Oh, I was just picnicin', as you might say, along with a little girl, daughter of a neighbor of mine. She wanted to see where the soldiers was goin' to fly, so I borrowed Perez Ryder's power dory and we came over. 'Twas gettin' along dinner time and I built a fire so as to cook. . . . My soul!" with a gasp of consternation, "I forgot all about that chowder. And now it's got stone cold. Yes, sir!" dropping on his knees and removing the cover of the kettle, "stone cold or next door to it. Ain't that a shame!"

Lieutenant Rayburn snorted in disgust. His superior officer, however, merely smiled.

"Never mind the chowder just now," he said. "So you came over here for a picnic, did you? Little late for picnics, isnt it?"

"Yes—ye-es," drawled Jed, "'tis kind of late, but 'twas a nice, moderate day and Babbie she wanted to come, so—"

"Babbie? That's the little girl? . . . Oh," with a nod, "I remember now. I saw a man with a little girl wandering about among the buildings a little while ago. Was that you?"

"Ye-es, yes, that was me. . . . Tut, tut, tut! I'll have to warm this chowder all up again now. That's too bad!"

Voices from behind the ridge announced the coming of the carpenter and the two "identifiers." The latter, Mr. Emulous Baker and Mr. "Squealer" Wixon, were on the broad grin.

"Yup, that's him," announced Mr. Wixon. "Hello, Shavin's! Got you took up for a German spy, have they? That's a good one! haw, haw!"

"Do you know him?" asked the major.

"Know him?" Mr. Wixon guffawed again. "Known him all my life. He lives over to Orham. Makes windmills and whirlagigs and such for young-ones to play with. HE ain't any spy. His name's Jed Winslow, but we always call him 'Shavin's,' 'count of his whittlin' up so much good wood, you understand. Ain't that so, Shavin's? Haw, haw!"

Jed regarded Mr. Wixon mournfully.

"Um-hm," he admitted. "I guess likely you're right, Squealer."

"I bet you! There's only one Shavin's in Orham."

Jed sighed. "There's consider'ble many squealers," he drawled; "some in sties and some runnin' loose."

Major Grover, who had appeared to enjoy this dialogue, interrupted it now.

"That would seem to settle the spy question," he said. "You may go, all three of you," he added, turning to the carpenters. They departed, Jed's particular enemy muttering to himself and Mr. Wixon laughing uproariously. The major once more addressed Jed.

"Where is the little girl you were with?" he asked.

"Eh? Oh, she's over yonder just 'round the p'int, sailin' a shingle boat I made her. Shall I call her?"

"No, it isn't necessary. Mr. Winslow, I'm sorry to have put you to all this trouble and to have cooled your—er—chowder. There is no regulation against visitors to our reservation here just now, although there will be, of course, later on. There is a rule against building fires on the beach, but you broke that in ignorance, I'm sure. The reason why you have been cross-questioned to-day is a special one. A construction plan has been lost, as Lieutenant Rayburn here informed you. It was on his desk in the office and it has disappeared. It may have been stolen, of course, or, as both windows were open, it may have blown away. You are sure you haven't seen anything of it? Haven't seen any papers blowing about?"

"I'm sure it didn't blow away, sir," put in the lieutenant. "I'm positive it was stolen. You see—"

He did not finish his sentence. The expression upon Jed's face caused him to pause. Mr. Winslow's mouth and eyes were opening wider and wider.

"Sho!" muttered Jed. "Sho, now! . . . 'Tain't possible that . . . I snum if . . . Sho!"

"Well, what is it?" demanded both officers, practically in concert.

Jed did not reply. Instead he turned his head, put both hands to his mouth and shouted "Babbie!" through them at the top of his lungs. The third shout brought a faint, "Yes, Uncle Jed, I'm coming."

"What are you calling her for?" asked Lieutenant Rayburn, forgetting the presence of his superior officer in his anxious impatience. Jed did not answer. He was kneeling beside his jacket, which he had thrown upon the sand when he landed, and was fumbling in the pockets. "Dear me! dear me!" he was muttering. "I'm sartin they must be here. I KNOW I put 'em here because . . . OW!"

He was kneeling and holding the coat with one hand while he fumbled in the pockets with the other. Unconsciously he had leaned backward until he sat upon his heels. Now, with an odd expression of mingled pain and relief, he reached into the hip pocket of his trousers and produced a pair of spectacles. He smiled his slow, fleeting smile.

"There!" he observed, "I found 'em my way—backwards. Anybody else would have found 'em by looking for 'em; I lost 'em lookin' for 'em and found 'em by sittin' on 'em.... Oh, here you are, Babbie! Sakes alive, you're sort of dampish."

She was all of that. She had come running in answer to his call and had the shingle boat hugged close to her. The water from it had trickled down the front of her dress. Her shoes and stockings were splashed with wet sand.

"Is dinner ready, Uncle Jed?" she asked, eagerly. Then becoming aware that the two strange gentlemen standing by the fire were really and truly "officer ones," she looked wide-eyed up at them and uttered an involuntary "Oh!"

"Babbie," said Jed, "let me see that boat of yours a minute, will you?"

Babbie obediently handed it over. Jed inspected it through his spectacles. Then he pulled the paper sail from the sharpened stick—the mast—unfolded it, looked at it, and then extended it at arm's length toward Major Grover.

"That's your plan thing, ain't it?" he asked, calmly.

Both officers reached for the paper, but the younger, remembering in time, drew back. The other took it, gave it a quick glance, and then turned again to Mr. Winslow.

"Where did you get this?" he asked, crisply.

Jed shook his head.

"She gave it to me, this little girl here," he explained. She wanted a sail for that shingle craft I whittled out for her. Course if I'd had on my specs I presume likely I'd have noticed that 'twas an out of the common sort of paper, but—I was wearin' 'em in my pants pocket just then."

"Where did you get it?" demanded Rayburn, addressing Barbara. The child looked frightened. Major Grover smiled reassuringly at her and she stammered a rather faint reply.

"I found it blowing around up on the little hill there," she said, pointing. "It was blowing real hard and I had to run to catch it before it got to the edge of the water. I'm—I—I'm sorry I gave it to Uncle Jed for a sail. I didn't know—and—and he didn't either," she added, loyally.

"That's all right, my dear. Of course you didn't know. Well, Rayburn," turning to the lieutenant, "there's your plan. You see it did blow away, after all. I think you owe this young lady thanks that it is not out in mid-channel by this time. Take it back to the office and see if the holes in it have spoiled its usefulness to any extent."

The lieutenant, very red in the face, departed, bearing his precious plan. Jed heaved a sigh of relief.

"There!" he exclaimed, "now I presume likely I can attend to my chowder."

"The important things of life, eh?" queried Major Grover.

"Um-hm. I don't know's there's anything much more important than eatin'. It's a kind of expensive habit, but an awful hard one to swear off of. . . . Hum. . . . Speakin' of important things, was that plan of yours very important, Mr.—I mean Major?"

"Rather—yes."

"Sho! . . . And I stuck it on a stick and set it afloat on a shingle. I cal'late if Sam Hunniwell knew of that he'd say 'twas characteristic. . . . Hum. . . . Sho! . . . I read once about a feller that found where the great seal of England was hid and he used it to crack nuts with. I guess likely that feller must have been my great, great, great granddad."

Major Grover looked surprised.

"I've read that story," he said, "but I can't remember where."

Jed was stirring his chowder. "Eh?" he said, absently. "Where? Oh, 'twas in—the—er—'Prince and the Pauper,' you know. Mark Twain wrote it."

"That's so; I remember now. So you've read 'The Prince and the Pauper'?"

"Um-hm. Read about everything Mark Twain ever wrote, I shouldn't wonder."

"Do you read a good deal?"

"Some. . . . There! Now we'll call that chowder done for the second time, I guess. Set down and pass your plate, Babbie. You'll set down and have a bite with us, won't you, Mr.—Major—I snum I've forgot your name. You mustn't mind; I forget my own sometimes."

"Grover. I am a major in the Engineers, stationed here for the present to look after this construction work. No, thank you, I should like to stay, but I must go back to my office."

"Dear, dear! That's too bad. Babbie and I would like first-rate to have you stay. Wouldn't we, Babbie?"

Barbara nodded.

"Yes, sir," she said. "And the chowder will be awf'ly good. Uncle Jed's chowders always are."

"I'm sure of it." Major Grover's look of surprise was more evident than ever as he gazed first at Barbara and then at Mr. Winslow. His next question was addressed to the latter.

"So you are this young lady's uncle?" he inquired. It was Barbara who answered.

"Not my really uncle," she announced. "He's just my make-believe uncle. He says he's my step-uncle 'cause he comes to our back steps so much. But he's almost better than a real uncle," she declared, emphatically.

The major laughed heartily and said he was sure of it. He seemed to find the pair hugely entertaining.

"Well, good-by," he said. "I hope you and your uncle will visit us again soon. And I hope next time no one will take him for a spy."

Jed looked mournfully at the fire. "I've been took for a fool often enough," he observed, "but a spy is a consider'ble worse guess."

Grover looked at him. "I'm not so sure," he said. "I imagine both guesses would be equally bad. Well, good-by. Don't forget to come again."

"Thank you, thank you. And when you're over to Orham drop in some day and see Babbie and me. Anybody—the constable or anybody—will tell you where I live."

Their visitor laughed, thanked him, and hurried away. Said Barbara between spoonfuls:

"He's a real nice officer one, isn't he, Uncle Jed? Petunia and I like him."

During the rest of the afternoon they walked along the beach, picked up shells, inspected "horse-foot" crabs, jelly fish and "sand collars," and enjoyed themselves so thoroughly that it was after four when they started for home. The early October dusk settled down as they entered the winding channel between the sand islands and the stretches of beaches. Barbara, wrapped in an old coat of Captain Perez's, which, smelling strongly of fish, had been found in a locker, seemed to be thinking very hard and, for a wonder, saying little. At last she broke the silence.

"That Mr. Major officer man was 'stonished when I called you 'Uncle Jed,'" she observed. "Why, do you s'pose?"

Jed whistled a few bars and peered over the side at the seaweed marking the border of the narrow, shallow channel.

"I cal'late," he drawled, after a moment, "that he hadn't noticed how much we look alike."

It was Barbara's turn to be astonished.

"But we DON'T look alike, Uncle Jed," she declared. "Not a single bit."

Jed nodded. "No-o," he admitted. "I presume that's why he didn't notice it."

This explanation, which other people might have found somewhat unsatisfactory, appeared to satisfy Miss Armstrong; at any rate she accepted it without comment. There was another pause in the conversation. Then she said:

"I don't know, after all, as I ought to call you 'Uncle Jed,' Uncle Jed."

"Eh? Why not, for the land sakes?"

"'Cause uncles make people cry in our family. I heard Mamma crying last night, after she thought I was asleep. And I know she was crying about Uncle Charlie. She cried when they took him away, you know, and now she cries when he's coming home again. She cried awf'ly when they took him away."

"Oh, she did, eh?"

"Yes. He used to live with Mamma and me at our house in Middleford. He's awful nice, Uncle Charlie is, and Petunia and I were very fond of him. And then they took him away and we haven't seen him since."

"He's been sick, maybe."

"Perhaps so. But he must be well again now cause he's coming home; Mamma said so."

"Um-hm. Well, I guess that was it. Probably he had to go to the— the hospital or somewhere and your ma has been worried about him. He's had an operation maybe. Lots of folks have operations nowadays; it's got to be the fashion, seems so."

The child reflected.

"Do they have to have policemen come to take you to the hospital?" she asked.

"Eh? . . . Policemen?"

"Yes. 'Twas two big policemen took Uncle Charlie away the first time. We were having supper, Mamma and he and I, and Nora went to the door when the bell rang and the big policemen came and Uncle Charlie went away with them. And Mamma cried so. And she wouldn't tell me a bit about. . . . Oh! OH! I've told about the policemen! Mamma said I mustn't ever, EVER tell anybody that. And—and I did! I DID!"

Aghast at her own depravity, she began to sob. Jed tried to comfort her and succeeded, after a fashion, at least she stopped crying, although she was silent most of the way home. And Jed himself was silent also. He shared her feeling of guilt. He felt that he had been told something which neither he nor any outsider should have heard, and his sensitive spirit found little consolation in the fact that the hearing of it had come through no fault of his. Besides, he was not so sure that he had been faultless. He had permitted the child's disclosures to go on when, perhaps, he should have stopped them. By the time the "Araminta's" nose slid up on the sloping beach at the foot of the bluff before the Winslow place she held two conscience-stricken culprits instead of one.

And if Ruth Armstrong slept but little that night, as her daughter said had been the case the night before, she was not the only wakeful person in that part of Orham. She would have been surprised if she had known that her eccentric neighbor and landlord was also lying awake and that his thoughts were of her and her trouble. For Jed, although he had heard but the barest fragment of the story of "Uncle Charlie," a mere hint dropped from the lips of a child who did not understand the meaning of what she said, had heard enough to make plain to him that the secret which the young widow was hiding from the world was a secret involving sorrow and heartbreak for herself and shame and disgrace for others. The details he did not know, nor did he wish to know them; he was entirely devoid of that sort of curiosity. Possession of the little knowledge which had been given him, or, rather, had been thrust upon him, and which Gabe Bearse would have considered a gossip treasure trove, a promise of greater treasures to be diligently mined, to Jed was a miserable, culpable thing, like the custody of stolen property. He felt wicked and mean, as if he had been caught peeping under a window shade.

CHAPTER X

That night came a sudden shift in the weather and when morning broke the sky was gray and overcast and the wind blew raw and penetrating from the northeast. Jed, at work in his stock room sorting a variegated shipment of mills and vanes which were to go to a winter resort on the west coast of Florida, was, as he might have expressed it, down at the mouth. He still felt the sense of guilt of the night before, but with it he felt a redoubled realization of his own incompetence. When he had surmised his neighbor and tenant to be in trouble he had felt a strong desire to help her; now that surmise had changed to certainty his desire to help was stronger than ever. He pitied her from the bottom of his heart; she seemed so alone in the world and so young. She needed a sympathetic counselor and advisor. But he could not advise or help because neither he nor any one else in Orham was supposed to know of her trouble and its nature. Even if she knew that he knew, would she accept the counsel of Shavings Winslow? Hardly! No sensible person would. How the townsfolk would laugh if they knew he had even so much as dreamed of offering it.

He was too downcast even to sing one of his lugubrious hymns or to whistle. Instead he looked at the letter pinned on a beam beside him and dragged from the various piles one half-dozen crow vanes, one half-dozen gull vanes, one dozen medium-sized mills, one dozen small mills, three sailors, etc., etc., as set forth upon that order. One of the crows fell to the floor and he accidently stepped upon it and snapped its head off. He was gazing solemnly down at the wreck when the door behind him opened and a strong blast of damp, cold wind blew in. He turned and found that Mrs. Armstrong had opened the door. She entered and closed it behind her.

"Good morning," she said.

Jed was surprised to see her at such an early hour; also just at that time her sudden appearance was like a sort of miracle, as if the thoughts in his brain had taken shape, had materialized. For a moment he could not regain presence of mind sufficient to return her greeting. Then, noticing the broken vane on the floor, she exclaimed:

"Oh, you have had an accident. Isn't that too bad! When did it happen?"

He looked down at the decapitated crow and touched one of the pieces with the toe of his boot.

"Just this minute," he answered. "I stepped on it and away she went. Did a pretty neat, clean job, didn't I? . . . Um-hm. . . . I wonder if anybody stepped on MY head 'twould break like that. Probably not; the wood in it is too green, I cal'late."

She smiled, but she made no comment on this characteristic bit of speculation. Instead she asked: "Mr. Winslow, are you very busy this morning? Is your work too important to spare me just a few minutes?"

Jed looked surprised; he smiled his one-sided smile.

"No, ma'am," he drawled. "I've been pretty busy but 'twan't about anything important. I presume likely," he added, "there ain't anybody in Ostable County that can be so busy as I can be doin' nothin' important."

"And you can spare a few minutes? I—I want to talk to you very much. I won't be long, really."

He regarded her intently. Then he walked toward the door leading to the little workroom. "Come right in here, ma'am," he said, gravely; adding, after they had entered the other apartment, "Take that chair. I'll sit over here on the box."

He pulled forward the box and turned to find her still standing.

"Do sit down," he urged. "That chair ain't very comfortable, I know. Perhaps I'd better get you another one from my sittin'-room in yonder."

He was on his way to carry out the suggestion, but she interrupted him. "Oh, no," she said. "This one will be perfectly comfortable, I'm sure, only—"

"Yes? Is there somethin' the matter with it?"

"Not the matter with it, exactly, but it seems to be—occupied."

Jed stepped forward and peered over the workbench at the chair. Its seat was piled high with small pasteboard boxes containing hardware-screws, tacks and metal washers—which he used in his mill and vane-making.

"Sho!" he exclaimed. "Hum! Does seem to be taken, as you say. I recollect now; a lot of that stuff came in by express day before yesterday afternoon and I piled it up there while I was unpackin' it. Here!" apparently addressing the hardware, "you get out of that. That seat's reserved."

He stretched a long arm over the workbench, seized the chair by the back and tipped it forward. The pasteboard boxes went to the floor in a clattering rush. One containing washers broke open and the little metal rings rolled everywhere. Mr. Winslow did not seem to mind.

"There!" he exclaimed, with evident satisfaction; "sit right down, ma'am."

The lady sat as requested, her feet amid the hardware boxes and her hands upon the bench before her. She was evidently very nervous, for her fingers gripped each other tightly. And, when she next spoke, she did not look at her companion.

"Mr. Winslow," she began, "I—I believe—that is, Babbie tells me that— that last evening, when you and she were on your way back here in the boat, she said something—she told you something concerning our—my—family affairs which—which—"

She faltered, seeming to find it hard to continue. Jed did not wait. He was by this time at least as nervous as she was and considerably more distressed and embarrassed. He rose from the box and extended a protesting hand.

"Now, now, ma'am," he begged. "Now, Mrs. Armstrong, please— please don't say any more. It ain't necessary, honest it ain't. She— she—that child she didn't tell me much of anything anyhow, and she didn't mean to tell that. And if you knew how ashamed and—and mean I've felt ever since to think I let myself hear that much! I hope—I do hope you don't think I tried to get her to tell me anything. I do hope you don't think that."

His agitation was so acute and so obvious that she looked at him in wonder for a moment. Then she hastened to reassure him.

"Don't distress yourself, Mr. Winslow," she said, smiling sadly. "I haven't known you very long but I have already learned enough about you to know that you are an honorable man. If I did not know that I shouldn't be here now. It is true that I did not mean for you or any one here in Orham to learn of my—of our trouble, and if Babbie had not told you so much I probably should never have spoken to you about it. The poor child's conscience troubled her so last evening that she came crying to me and confessed, and it is because I gathered from her that she had told enough to make you at least guess the truth that I am here now. I prefer that you should hear the story just as it is from me, rather than imagine something which might be worse. Don't you see?"

Jed saw, but he was still very much perturbed.

"Now, now, Mrs. Armstrong," he begged, "don't tell me anything, please don't. I laid awake about all night thinkin' what I'd ought to do, whether I'd ought to tell you what Babbie said, or just not trouble you at all and try to forget I ever heard it. That's what I decided finally, to forget it; and I will—I vow and declare I will! Don't you tell me anything, and let me forget this. Now please."

But she shook her head. "Things like that are not so easily forgotten," she said; "even when one tries as hard to forget as I am sure you would, Mr. Winslow. No, I want to tell you; I really do. Please don't say any more. Let me go on. . . . Oh," with a sudden burst of feeling "can't you see that I must talk with SOMEONE—I MUST?"

Her clasped fingers tightened and the tears sprang to her eyes. Poor Jed's distress was greater than ever.

"Now—now, Mrs. Armstrong," he stammered, "all I meant to say was that you mustn't feel you've got to tell me. Course if you want to, that's different altogether. What I'm tryin' to say," he added, with a desperate attempt to make his meaning perfectly clear, "is not to pay any attention to ME at all but do just what YOU want to, that's all."

Even on the verge of tears as she was, she could not forbear smiling a little at this proclamation of complete self-effacement. "I fear I must pay some attention to you," she said, "if I am to confide in you and—and perhaps ask your help, your advice, afterwards. I have reached a point when I must ask some one's advice; I have thought myself into a maze and I don't know what to do—I don't know WHAT to do. I have no near relatives, no friends here in Orham—"

Jed held up a protesting hand.

"Excuse me, Mrs. Armstrong," he stammered; "I don't know as you recollect, probably it might not have meant as much to you as it did to me; but a spell ago you said somethin' about countin' me as a friend."

"I know I did. And I meant it. You have been very kind, and Barbara is so fond of you. . . . Well, perhaps you can advise me, at least you can suggest—or—or—help me to think. Will you?"

Jed passed his hand across his chin. It was obvious that her asking his counsel was simply a last resort, a desperate, forlorn hope. She had no real confidence in his ability to help. He would have been the last to blame her for this; her estimate of his capabilities was like his own, that was all.

"W-e-e-ll," he observed, slowly, "as to givin' my advice, when a man's asked to give away somethin' that's worth nothin' the least he can do is say yes and try to look generous, I cal'late. If I can advise you any, why, I'll feel proud, of course."

"Thank you. Mr. Winslow, for the past two years or more I have been in great trouble. I have a brother—but you knew that; Babbie told you."

"Um-hm. The one she calls 'Uncle Charlie'?"

"Yes. He is—he is serving his sentence in the Connecticut State Prison."

Jed leaned back upon the box. His head struck smartly against the edge of the bandsaw bench, but he did not seem to be aware of the fact.

"My Lord above!" he gasped.

"Yes, it is true. Surely you must have guessed something of that sort, after Babbie's story of the policemen."

"I—I—well, I did sort of—of presume likely he must have got into some sort of—of difficulty, but I never thought 'twas bad as that. . . . Dear me! . . . Dear me!"

"My brother is younger than I; he is scarcely twenty-three years old. He and I are orphans. Our home was in Wisconsin. Father was killed in a railway accident and Mother and my brother Charles and I were left with very little money. We were in a university town and Mother took a few students as lodgers. Doctor Armstrong was one; I met him there, and before he left the medical college we were engaged to be married. Charlie was only a boy then, of course. Mother died three years later. Meanwhile Seymour—Doctor Armstrong—had located in Middleford, Connecticut, and was practicing medicine there. He came on, we were married, and I returned to Middleford with him. We had been married but a few years when he died—of pneumonia. That was the year after Babbie was born. Charles remained in Wisconsin, boarding with a cousin of Mother's, and, after he graduated from high school, entered one of the banks in the town. He was very successful there and the bank people liked him. After Seymour—my husband—died, he came East to see me at Middleford. One of Doctor Armstrong's patients, a bond broker in New Haven, took a fancy to him, or we thought he did, and offered him a position. He accepted, gave up his place at the bank in Wisconsin, and took charge of this man's Middleford office, making his home with Babbie and me. He was young, too young I think now, to have such a responsible position, but every one said he had a remarkably keen business mind and that his future was certain to be brilliant. And then—"

She paused. It was evident that the hard part of her story was coming. After a moment she went on.

"Charlie was popular with the young people there in Middleford. He was always a favorite, at home, at school, everywhere. Mother idolized him while she lived, so did I, so did Babbie. He was fond of society and the set he was friendly with was made up, for the most part, of older men with much more money than he. He was proud, he would not accept favors without repaying them, he liked a good time, perhaps he was a little fast; not dissipated—I should have known if he were that—but—careless—and what you men call a 'good fellow.' At any rate, he—"

Again she paused. Jed, sitting on the box, clasping his knee between his hands, waited anxiously for her to continue.

"Of course you can guess what happened," she said, sadly, after a moment. "It was the old story, that is all. Charlie was living beyond his means, got into debt and speculated in stocks, hoping to make money enough to pay those debts. The stocks went down and— and—well, he took money belonging to his employer to protect his purchases."

She waited, perhaps expecting her companion to make some comment. He did not and again she spoke.

"I know he meant only to borrow it," she declared. "I KNOW it. He isn't bad, Mr. Winslow; I know him better than any one and he ISN'T bad. If he had only come to me when he got into the trouble! If he had only confided in me! But he was proud and—and he didn't. . . . Well, I won't tell you how his—his fault was discovered; it would take a long time and it isn't worth while. They arrested him, he was tried and—and sent to prison for two years."

For the first time since she began her story Jed uttered a word.

"Sho!" he exclaimed. "Sho, sho! Dear me! The poor young feller!"

She looked up at him quickly. "Thank you," she said, gratefully. "Yes, he was sent to prison. He was calm and resigned and very brave about it, but to me it was a dreadful shock. You see, he had taken so little money, not much over two thousand dollars. We could have borrowed it, I'm sure; he and I could have worked out the debt together. We could have done it; I would have worked at anything, no matter how hard, rather than have my brother branded all his life with the disgrace of having been in prison. But the man for whom he had worked was furiously angry at what he called Charlie's ingratitude; he would teach the young thief a lesson, he said. Our lawyer went to him; I went to him and begged him not to press the case. Of course Charlie didn't know of my going; he never would have permitted it if he had. But I went and begged and pleaded. It did no good. Why, even the judge at the trial, when he charged the jury, spoke of the defendant's youth and previous good character. . . ."

She covered her eyes with her hand. Poor Jed's face was a picture of distress.

"Now—now, Mrs. Armstrong," he urged, "don't, please don't. I—I wouldn't tell me any more about it, if I was you. Of course I'm— I'm proud to think you believed I was worth while tellin' it to and all that, but—you mustn't. You'll make yourself sick, you know. Just don't tell any more, please."

She took her hand away and looked at him bravely.

"There isn't any more to tell," she said. "I have told you this because I realized that Barbara had told you enough to make you imagine everything that was bad concerning my brother. And he is not bad, Mr. Winslow. He did a wrong thing, but I know—I KNOW he did not mean deliberately to steal. If that man he worked for had been—if he had been— But there, he was what he was. He said thieves should be punished, and if they were punished when they were young, so much the better, because it might be a warning and keep them honest as they grew older. He told me that, Mr. Winslow, when I pleaded with him not to make Charles' disgrace public and not to wreck the boy's life. That was what he told me then. And they say," she added, bitterly, "that he prides himself upon being a staunch supporter of the church."

Jed let go of his knee with one hand in order to rub his chin.

"I have queer notions, I cal'late," he drawled. "If they wasn't queer they wouldn't be mine, I suppose. If I was—er—as you might say, first mate of all creation I'd put some church folks in jail and a good many jail folks in church. Seems's if the swap would be a help to both sides. . . . I—I hope you don't think I'm—er— unfeelin', jokin', when you're in such worry and trouble," he added, anxiously. "I didn't mean it."

His anxiety was wasted. She had heard neither his first remark nor the apology for it. Her thoughts had been far from the windmill shop and its proprietor. Now, apparently awakening to present realities, she rose and turned toward the door.

"That was all," she said, wearily. "You know the whole truth now, Mr. Winslow. Of course you will not speak of it to any one else." Then, noticing the hurt look upon his face, she added, "Forgive me. I know you will not. If I had not known it I should not have confided in you. Thank you for listening so patiently."

She was going, but he touched her arm.

"Excuse me, Mrs. Armstrong," he faltered, "but—but wasn't there somethin' else? Somethin' you wanted to ask my advice about—or— or— somethin'?"

She smiled faintly. "Yes, there was," she admitted. "But I don't know that it is worth while troubling you, after all. It is not likely that you can help me. I don't see how any one can."

"Probably you're right. I—I ain't liable to be much help to anybody. But I'm awful willin' to try. And sometimes, you know— sometimes surprisin' things happen. 'Twas a—a mouse, or a ground mole, wasn't it, that helped the lion in the story book out of the scrape? . . . Not that I don't look more like a—er—giraffe than I do like a mouse," he added.

Mrs. Armstrong turned and looked at him once more. "You're very kind," she said. "And I know you mean what you say. . . . Why, yes, I'll tell you the rest. Perhaps," with the slight smile, "you CAN advise me, Mr. Winslow. You see—well, you see, my brother will be freed very shortly. I have received word that he is to be pardoned, his sentence is to be shortened because of what they call his good conduct. He will be free—and then? What shall he do then? What shall we all do? That is my problem."

She went on to explain. This was the situation: Her own income was barely sufficient for Barbara and herself to live, in the frugal way they were living, in a country town like Orham. That was why she had decided to remain there. No one in the village knew her story or the story of her brother's disgrace. But now, almost any day, her brother might be discharged from prison. He would be without employment and without a home. She would so gladly offer him a home with her—they could manage to live, to exist in some way, she said—but she knew he would not be content to have her support him. There was no chance of employment in Orham; he would therefore be forced to go elsewhere, to go wandering about looking for work. And that she could not bear to think of.

"You see," she said, "I—I feel as if I were the only helper and— well— guardian the poor boy has. I can imagine," smiling wanly, "how he would scorn the idea of his needing a guardian, but I feel as if it were my duty to be with him, to stand by him when every one else has deserted him. Besides," after an instant's hesitation, "I feel—I suppose it is unreasonable, but I feel as if I had neglected my duty before; as if perhaps I had not watched him as carefully as I should, or encouraged him to confide in me; I can't help feeling that perhaps if I had been more careful in this way the dreadful thing might not have happened. . . . Oh," she added, turning away again, "I don't know why I am telling all these things to you, I'm sure. They can't interest you much, and the telling isn't likely to profit either of us greatly. But I am so alone, and I have brooded over my troubles so much. As I said I have felt as if I must talk with some one. But there—good morning, Mr. Winslow."

"Just a minute, please, Mrs. Armstrong; just a minute. Hasn't your brother got any friends in Middleford who could help him get some work—a job—you know what I mean? Seems as if he must have, or you must have."

"Oh, we have, I suppose. We had some good friends there, as well as others whom we thought were friends. But—but I think we both had rather die than go back there; I am sure I should. Think what it would mean to both of us."

Jed understood. She might have been surprised to realize how clearly he understood. She was proud, and it was plain to see that she had been very proud of her brother. And Middleford had been her home where she and her husband had spent their few precious years together, where her child was born, where, after her brother came, she had watched his rise to success and the apparent assurance of a brilliant future. She had begun to be happy once more. Then came the crash, and shame and disgrace instead of pride and confidence. Jed's imagination, the imagination which was quite beyond the comprehension of those who called him the town crank, grasped it all—or, at least, all its essentials. He nodded slowly.

"I see," he said. "Yes, yes, I see. . . . Hum."

"Of course, any one must see. And to go away, to some city or town where we are not known—where could we go? What should we live on? And yet we can't stay here; there is nothing for Charles to do."

"Um. . . . He was a—what did you say his trade was?"

"He was a bond broker, a kind of banker."

"Eh? . . . A kind of banker. . . . Sho! Did he work in a bank?"

"Why, yes, I told you he did, in Wisconsin, where he and I used to live."

"Hum. . . . Pretty smart at it, too, seems to me you said he was?"

"Yes, very capable indeed."

"I want to know. . . . Hum. . . . Sho!"

He muttered one or two more disjointed exclamations and then ceased to speak altogether, staring abstractedly at a crack in the floor. All at once he began to hum a hymn. Mrs. Armstrong, whose nerves were close to the breaking point, lost patience.

"Good morning, Mr. Winslow," she said, and opened the door to the outer shop. This time Jed did not detain her. Instead he stared dreamily at the floor, apparently quite unconscious of her or his surroundings.

"Eh?" he drawled. "Oh, yes, good mornin',—good mornin'. . . . Hum. . . .

> 'There is a fountain filled with blood
> Drawn from Emmanuel's veins,
> And sinners plunged de de de de
> De de di dew dum de.'"

His visitor closed the door. Jed still sat there gazing at vacancy and droning, dolefully.

CHAPTER XI

For nearly an hour he sat there, scarcely changing his position, and only varying his musical program by whistling hymns instead of singing them. Once, hearing a step in the yard, he looked through the window and saw Gabriel Bearse walking toward the gate from the direction of the shop door instead of in the opposite direction. Evidently he had at first intended to call and then had changed his mind. Mr. Winslow was duly grateful to whoever or whatever had inspired the change. He had no desire to receive a visit from "Gab" Bearse, at this time least of all.

Later on he heard another step, and, again glancing through the window, saw Seth Wingate, the vegetable and fruit peddler, walking from the door to the gate, just as Mr. Bearse had done. Apparently Seth had changed his mind also. Jed thought this rather odd, but again he was grateful. He was thinking hard and was quite willing not to be disturbed.

But the disturbing came ten minutes after Mr. Wingate's departure and came in the nature of a very distinct disturbance. There was a series of thunderous knocks on the front door, that door was thrown violently open, and, before the startled maker of mills could do much more than rise to his feet, the door to the workroom was pulled open also. Captain Hunniwell's bulk filled the opening. Captain Sam was red-faced and seemed excited.

"Well, by the gracious king," he roared, "you're here, anyhow! What else is the matter with you?"

Jed, who, after recognizing his visitor, had seated himself once more, looked up and nodded.

"Hello, Sam," he observed. "Say, I was just thinkin' about you. That's kind of funny, ain't it?"

"Funny! Just thinkin' about me! Well, I've been thinkin' about you, I tell you that: Have you been in this shop all the forenoon?"

"Eh? . . . Why, yes. . . . Sartin. . . . I've been right here."

"You HAVE? Gracious king! Then why in the Old Harry have you got that sign nailed on your front door out here tellin' all hands you're out for the day and for 'em to ask for you up at Abijah Thompson's?"

Jed looked much surprised. His hand moved slowly across his chin.

"Sho!" he drawled. "Sho! Has that sign been hangin' there all this forenoon?"

"Don't ask me. I guess it has from what I've heard. Anyhow it's there now. And WHAT'S it there for? That's what I want to know."

Jed's face was very solemn, but there was a faint twinkle in his eye. "That explains about Seth Wingate," he mused. "Yes, and Gab Bearse too. . . . Hum. . . . The Lord was better to me than I deserved. They say He takes care of children and drunken men and— er—the critters that most folks think belong to my lodge. . . . Hum. . . . To think I forgot to take that sign down! Sho!"

"Forgot to take it down! What in everlastin' blazes did you ever put it up for?"

Jed explained why the placard had been prepared and affixed to the door. "I only meant it for yesterday, though," he added. "I'd intended takin' it down this mornin'."

Captain Sam put back his head and laughed until the shop echoed.

"Ho, ho, ho!" he roared. "And you mean to tell me that you put it up there because you was goin' cruisin' to the aviation camp and you didn't want callers disturbin' Mrs. Armstrong?"

His friend nodded. "Um-hm," he admitted. "I sent 'em to 'Bije's because he was as far off as anybody I could think of. Pretty good idea, wasn't it?"

The captain grinned. "Great!" he declared. "Fine! Wonderful! You wait till 'Bije comes to tell you how fine 'twas. He's in bed, laid up with neuralgia, and Emma J., his wife, says that every hour or less yesterday there was somebody bangin' at their door asking about you. Every time they banged she says that 'Bije, his nerves bein' on edge the way they are, would pretty nigh jump the quilts up to the ceilin' and himself along with 'em. And his remarks got more lit up every jump. About five o'clock when somebody came poundin' he let out a roar you could hear a mile. 'Tell 'em Shavin's Winslow's gone to the devil,' he bellowed, 'and that I say they can go there too.' And then Emma J. opened the door and 'twan't anybody askin' about you at all; 'twas the Baptist minister come callin'. I was drivin' past there just now and Emma J. came out to tell me about it. She wanted to know if you'd gone clear crazy instead of part way. I told her I didn't know, but I'd make it my business to find out. Tut, tut, tut! You are a wonder, Jed."

Jed did not dispute the truth of this statement. He looked troubled, however. "Sho!" he said; "I'm sorry if I plagued 'Bijah that way. If I'd known he was sick I wouldn't have done it. I never once thought so many folks as one every hour would want to see me this time of year. Dear me! I'm sorry about 'Bije. Maybe I'd better go down and kind of explain it to him."

Captain Sam chuckled. "I wouldn't," he said. "If I was you I'd explain over the long distance telephone. But, anyhow, I wouldn't worry much. I cal'late Emma J. exaggerated affairs some. Probably, if the truth was known, you'd find not more than four folks came there lookin' for you yesterday. Don't worry, Jed."

Jed did not answer. The word "worry" had reminded him of his other visitor that morning. He looked so serious that his friend repeated his adjuration.

"Don't worry, I tell you," he said, again. "'Tisn't worth it."

"All right, I won't. . . . I won't. . . . Sam, I was thinkin' about you afore you came in. You remember I told you that?"

"I remember. What have you got on your mind? Any more money kickin' around this glory-hole that you want me to put to your account?"

"Eh? . . . Oh, yes, I believe there is some somewheres. Seems to me I put about a hundred and ten dollars, checks and bills and such, away day before yesterday for you to take when you came. Maybe I'll remember where I put it before you go. But 'twan't about that I was thinkin'. Sam, how is Barzilla Small's boy, Lute, gettin' along in Gus Howes' job at the bank?"

Captain Sam snorted disgust.

"Gettin' along!" he repeated. "He's gettin' along the way a squid swims, and that's backwards. And, if you asked me, I'd say the longer he stayed the further back he'd get."

"Sho! then he did turn out to be a leak instead of an able seaman, eh?"

"A leak! Gracious king! He's like a torpedo blow-up under the engine-room. The bank'll sink if he stays aboard another month, I do believe. And yet," he added, with a shake of the head, "I don't see but he'll have to stay; there ain't another available candidate for the job in sight. I 'phoned up to Boston and some of our friends are lookin' around up there, but so far they haven't had any success. This war is makin' young men scarce, that is young men that are good for much. Pretty soon it'll get so that a healthy young feller who ain't in uniform will feel about as much out of place as a hog in a synagogue. Yes, sir! Ho, ho!"

He laughed in huge enjoyment of his own joke. Jed stared dreamily at the adjusting screw on the handsaw. His hands clasped his knee, his foot was lifted from the floor and began to swing back and forth.

"Well," queried his friend, "what have you got on your mind? Out with it."

"Eh? . . . On my mind?"

"Yes. When I see you begin to shut yourself together in the middle like a jackknife and start swinging that number eleven of yours I know you're thinkin' hard about somethin' or other. What is it this time?"

"Um . . . well . . . er . . . Sam, if you saw a chance to get a real smart young feller in Lute's place in the bank you'd take him, wouldn't you?"

"Would I? Would a cat eat lobster? Only show him to me, that's all!"

"Um-hm. . . . Now of course you know I wouldn't do anything to hurt Lute. Not for the world I wouldn't. It's only if you ARE goin' to let him go—"

"IF I am. Either he'll have to let go or the bank will, one or t'other. United we sink, divided one of us may float, that's the way I look at it. Lute'll stay till we can locate somebody else to take his job, and no longer."

"Ya-as. . . . Um-hm. . . . Well, I tell you, Sam: Don't you get anybody else till you and I have another talk. It may be possible that I could find you just the sort of young man you're lookin' for."

"Eh? YOU can find me one? YOU can? What are you givin' me, Jed? Who is the young man; you?"

Jed gravely shook his head. "No-o," he drawled. "I hate to disappoint you, Sam, but it ain't me. It's another—er—smart, lively young feller. He ain't quite so old as I am; there's a little matter of twenty odd years between us, I believe, but otherwise than that he's all right. And he knows the bankin' trade, so I'm told."

"Gracious king! Who is he? Where is he?"

"That I can't tell you just yet. But maybe I can by and by."

"Tell me now."

"No-o. No, I just heard about him and it was told to me in secret. All I can say is don't get anybody to fill Lute Small's place till you and I have another talk."

Captain Sam stared keenly into his friend's face. Jed bore the scrutiny calmly; in fact he didn't seem to be aware of it. The captain gave it up.

"All right," he said. "No use tryin' to pump you, I know that. When you make up your mind to keep your mouth shut a feller couldn't open it with a cold chisel. I presume likely you'll tell in your own good time. Now if you'll scratch around and find those checks and things you want me to deposit for you I'll take 'em and be goin'. I'm in a little bit of a hurry this mornin'."

Jed "scratched around," finally locating the checks and bills in the coffee pot on the shelf in his little kitchen.

"There!" he exclaimed, with satisfaction, "I knew I put 'em somewheres where they'd be safe and where I couldn't forget 'em."

"Where you couldn't forget 'em! Why, you did forget 'em, didn't you?"

"Um . . . yes . . . I cal'late I did this mornin', but that's because I didn't make any coffee for breakfast. If I'd made coffee same as I usually do I'd have found 'em."

"Why didn't you make coffee this mornin'?"

Jed's eye twinkled.

"W-e-e-ll," he drawled, "to be honest with you, Sam, 'twas because I couldn't find the coffee pot. After I took it down to put this money in it I put it back on a different shelf. I just found it now by accident."

As the captain was leaving Jed asked one more question. "Sam," he asked, "about this bank job now? If you had a chance to get a bright, smart young man with experience in bank work, you'd hire him, wouldn't you?"

Captain Hunniwell's answer was emphatic.

"You bet I would!" he declared. "If I liked his looks and his references were good I'd hire him in two minutes. And salary, any reasonable salary, wouldn't part us, either. . . . Eh? What makes you look like that?"

For Jed's expression had changed; his hand moved across his chin.

"Eh—er—references?" he repeated.

"Why, why, of course. I'd want references from the folks he'd worked for, statin' that he was honest and capable and all that. With those I'd hire him in two minutes, as I said. You fetch him along and see. So long, Jed. See you later."

He hustled out, stopping to tear from the outer door the placard directing callers to call at Abijah Thompson's. Jed returned to his box and sat down once more to ponder. In his innocence it had not occurred to him that references would be required.

That evening, about nine, he crossed the yard and knocked at the back door of the little house. Mrs. Armstrong answered the knock; Barbara, of course, was in bed and asleep. Ruth was surprised to see her landlord at that, for him, late hour. Also, remembering the unceremonious way in which he had permitted her to depart at the end of their interview that forenoon, she was not as cordial as usual. She had made him her confidant, why she scarcely knew; then, after expressing great interest and sympathy, he had suddenly seemed to lose interest in the whole matter. She was acquainted with his eccentricities and fits of absent-mindedness, but nevertheless she had been hurt and offended. She told herself that she should have expected nothing more from "Shavings" Winslow, the person about whom two-thirds of Orham joked and told stories, but the fact remained that she was disappointed. And she was angry, not so much with him perhaps, as with herself. WHY had she been so foolish as to tell any one of their humiliation?

So when Jed appeared at the back door she received him rather coldly. He was quite conscious of the change in temperature, but he made no comment and offered no explanation. Instead he told his story, the story of his interview with Captain Hunniwell. As he told it her face showed at first interest, then hope, and at the last radiant excitement. She clasped her hands and leaned toward him, her eyes shining.

"Oh, Mr. Winslow," she cried, breathlessly, "do you mean it? Do you really believe Captain Hunniwell will give my brother a position in his bank?"

Jed nodded slowly. "Yes," he said, "I think likely he might. Course 'twouldn't be any great of a place, not at first—nor ever, I cal'late, so far as that goes. 'Tain't a very big bank and wages ain't—"

But she interrupted. "But that doesn't make any difference," she cried. "Don't you see it doesn't! The salary and all that won't count—now. It will be a start for Charles, an opportunity for him to feel that he is a man again, doing a man's work, an honest man's work. And he will be here where I can be with him, where we can be together, where it won't be so hard for us to be poor and where there will be no one who knows us, who knows our story. Oh, Mr. Winslow, is it really true? If it is, how—how can we ever thank you? How can I ever show you how grateful I feel?"

Her cheeks were flushed, her lips parted and joy shone in her eager eyes. Her voice broke a little as she uttered the words. Jed looked at her and then quickly looked away.

"I—I—don't talk so, Mrs. Armstrong," he pleaded, hastily. "It— it ain't anything, it ain't really. It just—"

"Not anything? Not anything to find my brother the opportunity he and I have been praying for? To give me the opportunity of having him with me? Isn't that anything? It is everything. Oh, Mr. Winslow, if you can do this for us—"

"Shsh! Sshh! Now, Mrs. Armstrong, please. You mustn't say I'm doin' it for you. I'm the one that just happened to think of it, that's all. You could have done it just as well, if you'd thought of it."

"Perhaps," with a doubtful smile, "but I should never have thought of it. You did because you were thinking for me—for my brother and me. And—and I thought you didn't care."

"Eh? . . . Didn't care?"

"Yes. When I left you at the shop this morning after our talk. You were so—so odd. You didn't speak, or offer to advise me as I had asked you to; you didn't even say good-by. You just sat there and let me go. And I didn't understand and—"

Jed put up a hand. His face was a picture of distress.

"Dear, dear, dear!" he exclaimed. "Did I do that? I don't remember it, but of course I did if you say so. Now what on earth possessed me to? . . . Eh?" as the idea occurred to him. "Tell me, was I singin'?"

"Why, yes, you were. That is, you were—were—"

"Makin' a noise as if I'd swallowed a hymn book and one of the tunes was chokin' me to death? Um-hm, that's the way I sing. And I was singin' when you left me, eh? That means I was thinkin' about somethin'. I told Babbie once, and it's the truth, that thinkin' was a big job with me and when I did it I had to drop everything else, come up into the wind like a schooner, you know, and just lay to and think. . . . Oh, I remember now! You said somethin' about your brother's workin' in a bank and that set me thinkin' that Sam must be needin' somebody by this time in Lute Small's place."

"You didn't know he needed any one?"

"No-o, not exactly; but I knew Lute, and that amounted to the same thing. Mrs. Armstrong, I do hope you'll forgive me for—for singin' and—and all the rest of my foolish actions."

"Forgive you! Will you forgive me for misjudging you?"

"Land sakes, don't talk that way. But there's one thing I haven't said yet and you may not like it. I guess you and your brother'll have to go to Sam and tell him the whole story."

Her expression changed. "The whole story?" she repeated. "Why, what do you mean? Tell him that Charles has been in—in prison? You don't mean THAT?"

"Um-hm," gravely; "I'm afraid I do. It looks to me as if it was the only way."

"But we can't! Oh, Mr. Winslow, we can't do that."

"I know 'twill be awful hard for you. But, when I talked to Sam about my havin' a possible candidate for the bank place, the very last thing he said was that he'd be glad to see him providin' his references was all right. I give you my word I'd never thought of references, not till then."

"But if we tell him—tell him everything, we shall only make matters worse, shan't we? Of course he won't give him the position then."

"There's a chance he won't, that's true. But Sam Hunniwell's a fine feller, there ain't any better, and he likes you and—well, he and I have been cruisin' in company for a long spell. Maybe he'll give your brother a chance to make good. I hope he will."

"You only hope? I thought you said you believed."

"Well, I do, but of course it ain't sartin. I wish 'twas."

She was silent. Jed, watching her, saw the last traces of happiness and elation fade from her face and disappointment and discouragement come back to take their places. He pitied her, and he yearned to help her. At last he could stand it no longer.

"Now, Mrs. Armstrong," he pleaded, "of course—"

She interrupted.

"No," she said, as if coming to a final decision and speaking that decision aloud: "No, I can't do it."

"Eh? Can't do—what?"

"I can't have Captain Hunniwell know of our trouble. I came here to Orham, where no one knew me, to avoid that very thing. At home there in Middleford I felt as if every person I met was staring at me and saying, 'Her brother is in prison.' I was afraid to have Babbie play with the other children. I was—but there, I won't talk about it. I can't. And I cannot have it begin again here. I'll go away first. We will all go away, out West, anywhere—anywhere where we can be—clean—and like other people."

Jed was conscious of a cold sensation, like the touch of an icicle, up and down his spine. Going away! She and Babbie going away! In his mind's eye he saw a vision of the little house closed once more and shuttered tight as it used to be. He gasped.

"Now, now, Mrs. Armstrong," he faltered. "Don't talk about goin' away. It—it isn't needful for you to do anything like that. Of course it ain't. You—you mustn't. I—we can't spare you."

She drew a long breath. "I would go to the other end of the world," she said, "rather than tell Captain Hunniwell the truth about my brother. I told you because Babbie had told you so much already.... Oh," turning swiftly toward him, "YOU won't tell Captain Hunniwell, will you?"

Before he could answer she stretched out her hand. "Oh, please forgive me," she cried. "I am not myself. I am almost crazy, I think. And when you first told me about the position in the bank I was so happy. Oh, Mr. Winslow, isn't there SOME way by which Charles could have that chance? Couldn't—couldn't he get it and— and work there for—for a year perhaps, until they all saw what a splendid fellow he was, and THEN tell them—if it seemed necessary? They would know him then, and like him; they couldn't help it, every one likes him."

She brushed the tears from her eyes. Poor Jed, miserable and most unreasonably conscience-stricken, writhed in his chair. "I—I don't know," he faltered. "I declare I don't see how. Er—er— Out in that bank where he used to work, that Wisconsin bank, he— you said he did first-rate there?"

She started. "Yes, yes," she cried, eagerly. "Oh, he was splendid there! And the man who was the head of that bank when Charles was there is an old friend of ours, of the family; he has retired now but he would help us if he could, I know. I believe... I wonder if... Mr. Winslow, I can't tell any one in Orham of our disgrace and I can't bear to give up that opportunity for my brother. Will you leave it to me for a little while? Will you let me think it over?"

Of course Jed said he would and went back to his little room over the shop. As he was leaving she put out her hand and said, with impulsive earnestness:

"Thank you, Mr. Winslow. Whatever comes of this, or if nothing comes of it, I can never thank you enough for your great kindness."

Jed gingerly shook the extended hand and fled, his face scarlet.

During the following week, although he saw his neighbors each day, and several times a day, Mrs. Armstrong did not mention her brother or the chance of his employment in the Orham bank. Jed, very much surprised at her silence, was tempted to ask what her decision was, or even if she had arrived at one. On one occasion he threw out a broad hint, but the hint was not taken, instead the lady changed the subject; in fact, it seemed to him that she made it a point of avoiding that subject and was anxious that he should avoid it, also. He was sure she had not abandoned the idea which, at first, had so excited her interest and raised her hopes. She seemed to him to be still under a strong nervous strain, to speak and act as if under repressed excitement; but she had asked him to leave the affair to her, to let her think it over, so of course he could do or say nothing until she had spoken. But he wondered and speculated a good deal and was vaguely troubled. When Captain Sam Hunniwell called he did not again refer to his possible candidate for the position now held by Luther Small. And, singularly enough, the captain himself did not mention the subject.

But one morning almost two weeks after Jed's discussion with the young widow she and Captain Hunniwell came into the windmill shop together. Mrs. Armstrong's air of excitement was very much in evidence. Her cheeks were red, her eyes sparkled, her manner animated. Her landlord had never seen her look so young, or, for that matter, so happy.

Captain Sam began the conversation. He, too, seemed to be in high good humor.

"Well, Jedidah Wilfred Shavin's'," he observed, facetiously, "what do you suppose I've got up my sleeve this mornin'?"

Jed laid down the chisel he was sharpening.

"Your arms, I presume likely," he drawled.

"Yes, I've got my arms and there's a fist at the end of each one of 'em. Any more—er—flippity answers like that one and you're liable to think you're struck by lightnin'. This lady and I have got news for you. Do you know what 'tis?"

Jed looked at Mrs. Armstrong and then at the speaker.

"No-o," he said, slowly.

"Well, to begin with it's this: Lute Small is leavin' the Orham National a week from next Saturday by a vote of eight to one. The directors and the cashier and I are the eight and he's the one. Ho, ho! And who do you suppose comes aboard on the next Monday mornin' to take over what Lute has left of the job? Eh? Who? Why, your own candidate, that's who."

Jed started. Again he looked at Mrs. Armstrong and, as if in answer to that look, she spoke.

"Yes, Mr. Winslow," she said, quickly, "my brother is coming to Orham and Captain Hunniwell has given him the position. It is really you to whom he owes it all. You thought of it and spoke to the captain and to me."

"But why in time," demanded Captain Sam, "didn't you tell me right out that 'twas Mrs. Armstrong's brother you had in mind? Gracious king! if I'd known that I'd have had Lute out a fortni't sooner."

Jed made no reply to this. He was still staring at the lady.

"But—but—" he faltered, "did you—have you—"

He stopped in the middle of a word. Ruth was standing behind the captain and he saw the frightened look in her eyes and the swift movement of her finger to her lips.

"Oh, yes," she said. "I—I have. I told Captain Hunniwell of Charlie's experience in the bank in Wisconsin. He has written there and the answer is quite satisfactory, or so he seems to think."

"Couldn't be better," declared Captain Sam. "Here's the letter from the man that used to be the bank president out there. Read it, Jed, if you want to."

Jed took the letter and, with a hand which shook a little, adjusted his glasses and read. It was merely a note, brief and to the point. It stated simply that while Charles Phillips had been in the employ of their institution as messenger, bookkeeper and assistant teller, he had been found honest, competent, ambitious and thoroughly satisfactory.

"And what more do I want than that?" demanded the captain. "Anybody who can climb up that way afore he's twenty-five will do well enough for yours truly. Course he and I haven't met yet, but his sister and I've met, and I'm not worryin' but what I'll like the rest of the family. Besides," he added, with a combination laugh and groan, "it's a case of desperation with us up at the bank. We've got to have somebody to plug that leak you was talkin' about, Jed, and we've got to have 'em immediate, right off quick, at once, or a little sooner. It's a providence, your brother is to us, Mrs. Armstrong," he declared; "a special providence and no mistake."

He hurried off a moment later, affirming that he was late at the bank already.

"Course the cashier's there and the rest of the help," he added, "but it takes all hands and the cat to keep Lute from puttin' the kindlin' in the safe and lightin' up the stove with ten dollar bills. So long."

After he had gone Jed turned to his remaining visitor. His voice shook a little as he spoke.

"You haven't told him!" he faltered, reproachfully. "You—you haven't told him!"

She shook her head. "I couldn't—I couldn't," she declared. "DON'T look at me like that. Please don't! I know it is wrong. I feel like a criminal; I feel wicked. But," defiantly, "I should feel more wicked if I had told him and my brother had lost the only opportunity that might have come to him. He WILL make good, Mr. Winslow. I KNOW he will. He will make them respect him and like him. They can't help it. See!" she cried, her excitement and agitation growing; "see how Mr. Reed, the bank president there at home, the one who wrote that letter, see what he did for Charles! He knows, too; he knows the whole story. I—I wrote to him. I wrote that very night when you told me, Mr. Winslow. I explained everything, I begged him—he is an old, old friend of our family— to do this thing for our sakes. You see, it wasn't asking him to lie, or to do anything wrong. It was just that he tell of Charles and his ability and character as he knew them. It wasn't wrong, was it?"

Jed did not answer.

"If it was," she declared, "I can't help it. I would do it again— for the same reason—to save him and his future, to save us all. I can't help what you think of me. It doesn't matter. All that does matter is that you keep silent and let my brother have his chance."

Jed, leaning forward in his chair by the workbench, put his hand to his forehead.

"Don't—don't talk so, Mrs. Armstrong," he begged. "You know—you know I don't think anything you've done is wrong. I ain't got the right to think any such thing as that. And as for keepin' still— why, I—I did hope you wouldn't feel 'twas necessary to ask that."

"I don't—I don't. I know you and I trust you. You are the only person in Orham whom I have trusted. You know that."

"Why, yes—why, yes, I do know it and—and I'm ever so much obliged to you. More obliged than I can tell you, I am. Now—now would you mind tellin' me just one thing more? About this Mr. What's- his-name out West in the bank there—this Mr. Reed—did he write you he thought 'twas all right for him to send Sam the—the kind of letter he did send him, the one givin' your brother such a good reference?"

The color rose in her face and she hesitated before replying.

Shavings: A Novel | 145

"No," she confessed, after a moment. "He did not write me that he thought it right to give Captain Hunniwell such a reference. In fact he wrote that he thought it all wrong, deceitful, bordering on the dishonest. He much preferred having Charles go to the captain and tell the whole truth. On the other hand, however, he said he realized that that might mean the end of the opportunity here and perhaps public scandal and gossip by which we all might suffer. And he said he had absolute confidence that Charles was not a criminal by intent, and he felt quite sure that he would never go wrong again. If he were still in active business, he said, he should not hesitate to employ him. Therefore, although he still believed the other course safer and better, he would, if Captain Hunniwell wrote, answer as I had asked. And he did answer in that way. So, you see," she cried, eagerly, "HE believes in Charles, just as I do. And just as you will when you know, Mr. Winslow. Oh, WON'T you try to believe now?"

A harder-hearted man than Jed Winslow would have found it difficult to refuse such a plea made in such a way by such a woman. And Jed's heart was anything but hard.

"Now, now, Mrs. Armstrong," he stammered, "you don't have to ask me that. Course I believe in the poor young chap. And—and I guess likely everything's goin' to come out all right. That Mr. What's-his-name—er—Wright—no, Reed—I got read and write mixed up, I guess—he's a business man and he'd ought to know about such things better'n I do. I don't doubt it'll come out fine and we won't worry any more about it."

"And we will still be friends? You know, Mr. Winslow, you are the only real friend I have in Orham. And you have been so loyal."

Jed flushed with pleasure.

"I—I told you once," he said, "that my friends generally called me 'Jed.'"

She laughed. "Very well, I'll call you 'Jed,'" she said. "But turn about is fair play and you must call me 'Ruth.' Will you? Oh, there's Babbie calling me. Thank you again, for Charles' sake and my own. Good morning—Jed."

"Er—er—good mornin', Mrs. Armstrong."

"What?"

"Er—I mean Mrs. Ruth."

The most of that forenoon, that is the hour or so remaining, was spent by Mr. Winslow in sitting by the workbench and idly scratching upon a board with the point of the chisel. Sometimes his scratches were meaningless, sometimes they spelled a name, a name which he seemed to enjoy spelling.

But at intervals during that day, and on other days which followed, he was conscious of an uneasy feeling, a feeling almost of guilt coupled with a dim foreboding.

Ruth Armstrong had called him a friend and loyal. But had he been as loyal to an older friend, a friend he had known all his life? Had he been loyal to Captain Sam Hunniwell?

That was the feeling of guilt. The foreboding was not as definite, but it was always with him; he could not shake it off. All his life he had dealt truthfully with the world, had not lied, or evaded, or compromised. Now he had permitted himself to become a silent partner in such a compromise. And some day, somehow, trouble was coming because of it.

CHAPTER XII

Before the end of another week Charles Phillips came to Orham. It was Ruth who told Jed the news. She came into the windmill shop and, standing beside the bench where he was at work, she said: "Mr. Winslow, I have something to tell you."

Jed put down the pencil and sheet of paper upon which he had been drawing new patterns for the "gull vane" which was to move its wings when the wind blew. This great invention had not progressed very far toward practical perfection. Its inventor had been busy with other things and had of late rather lost interest in it. But Barbara's interest had not flagged and to please her Jed had promised to think a little more about it during the next day or so.

"But can't you make it flap its wings, Uncle Jed?" the child had asked.

Jed rubbed his chin. "W-e-e-ll," he drawled, "I don't know. I thought I could, but now I ain't so sure. I could make 'em whirl 'round and 'round like a mill or a set of sailor paddles, but to make 'em flap is different. They've got to be put on strong enough so they won't flop off. You see," he added, solemnly, "if they kept floppin' off they wouldn't keep flappin' on. There's all the difference in the world between a flap and flop."

He was trying to reconcile that difference when Ruth entered the shop. He looked up at her absently. "Mr. Winslow," she began again, "I—"

His reproachful look made her pause and smile slightly in spite of herself.

"I'm sorry," she said. "Well, then—Jed—I have something to tell you. My brother will be here to-morrow."

Jed had been expecting to hear this very thing almost any day, but he was a little startled nevertheless.

"Sho!" he exclaimed. "You don't tell me!"

"Yes. He is coming on the evening train to-morrow. I had word from him this morning."

Jed's hand moved to his chin. "Hum . . ." he mused. "I guess likely you'll be pretty glad to see him."

"I shall be at least that," with a little break in her voice. "You can imagine what his coming will mean to me. No, I suppose you can't imagine it; no one can."

Jed did not say whether he imagined it or not.

"I—I'm real glad for you, Mrs. Ruth," he declared. "Mrs. Ruth" was as near as he ever came to fulfilling their agreement concerning names.

"I'm sure you are. And for my brother's sake and my own I am very grateful to you. Mr. Winslow—Jed, I mean—you have done so much for us already; will you do one thing more?"

Jed's answer was given with no trace of his customary hesitation. "Yes," he said.

"This is really for me, perhaps, more than for Charles—or at least as much."

Again there was no hesitation in the Winslow reply.

"That won't make it any harder," he observed, gravely.

"Thank you. It is just this: I have decided not to tell my brother that I have told you of his—his trouble, of his having been—where he has been, or anything about it. He knows I have not told Captain Hunniwell; I'm sure he will take it for granted that I have told no one. I think it will be so much easier for the poor boy if he can come here to Orham and think that no one knows. And no one does know but you. You understand, don't you?" she added, earnestly.

He looked a little troubled, but he nodded.

"Yes," he said, slowly. "I understand, I cal'late."

"I'm sure you do. Of course, if he should ask me point-blank if I had told any one, I should answer truthfully, tell him that I had told you and explain why I did it. And some day I shall tell him whether he asks or not. But when he first comes here I want him to be—to be—well, as nearly happy as is possible under the circumstances. I want him to meet the people here without the feeling that they know he has been—a convict, any of them. And so, unless he asks, I shall not tell him that even you know; and I am sure you will understand and not—not—"

"Not say anything when he's around that might let the cat out of the bag. Yes, yes, I see. Well, I'll be careful; you can count on me, Mrs. Ruth."

She looked down into his homely, earnest face. "I do," she said, simply, and went out of the room. For several minutes after she had gone Jed sat there gazing after her. Then he sighed, picked up his pencil and turned again to the drawing of the gull.

And the following evening young Phillips came. Jed, looking from his shop window, saw the depot-wagon draw up at the gate. Barbara was the first to alight. Philander Hardy came around to the back of the vehicle and would have assisted her, but she jumped down without his assistance. Then came Ruth and, after her, a slim young fellow carrying a traveling bag. It was dusk and Jed could not see his face plainly, but he fancied that he noticed a resemblance to his sister in the way he walked and the carriage of his head. The two went into the little house together and Jed returned to his lonely supper. He was a trifle blue that evening, although he probably would not have confessed it. Least of all would he have confessed the reason, which was that he was just a little jealous. He did not grudge his tenant her happiness in her brother's return, but he could not help feeling that from that time on she would not be as intimate and confidential with him, Jed Winslow, as she had been. After this it would be to this brother of hers that she would turn for help and advice. Well, of course, that was what she should do, what any one of sense would do, but Jed was uncomfortable all the same. Also, because he was himself, he felt a sense of guilty remorse at being uncomfortable.

The next morning he was presented to the new arrival. It was Barbara who made the presentation. She came skipping into the windmill shop leading the young man by the hand.

"Uncle Jed," she said, "this is my Uncle Charlie. He's been away and he's come back and he's going to work here always and live in the bank. No, I mean he's going to work in the bank always and live— No, I don't, but you know what I do mean, don't you, Uncle Jed?"

Charles Phillips smiled. "If he does he must be a mind-reader, Babbie," he said. Then, extending his hand, he added: "Glad to know you, Mr. Winslow. I've heard a lot about you from Babbie and Sis."

Jed might have replied that he had heard a lot about him also, but he did not. Instead he said "How d'ye do," shook the proffered hand, and looked the speaker over. What he saw impressed him favorably. Phillips was a good-looking young fellow, with a pleasant smile, a taking manner and a pair of dark eyes which reminded Mr. Winslow of his sister's. It was easy to believe Ruth's statement that he had been a popular favorite among their acquaintances in Middleford; he was the sort the average person would like at once, the sort which men become interested in and women spoil.

He was rather quiet during this first call. Babbie did two-thirds of the talking. She felt it her duty as an older inhabitant to display "Uncle Jed" and his creations for her relative's benefit. Vanes, sailors, ships and mills were pointed out and commented upon.

"He makes every one, Uncle Charlie," she declared solemnly. "He's made every one that's here and—oh, lots and lots more. He made the big mill that's up in our garret— You haven't seen it yet, Uncle Charlie; it's going to be out on our lawn next spring—and he gave it to me for a—for a— What kind of a present was that mill you gave me, Uncle Jed, that time when Mamma and Petunia and I were going back to Mrs. Smalley's because we thought you didn't want us to have the house any longer?"

Jed looked puzzled.

"Eh?" he queried. "What kind of a present? I don't know's I understand what you mean."

"I mean what kind of a present was it. It wasn't a Christmas present or a birthday present or anything like that, but it must be SOME kind of one. What kind of present would you call it, Uncle Jed?"

Jed rubbed his chin.

"W-e-e-ll," he drawled, "I guess likely you might call it a forget- me-not present, if you had to call it anything."

Barbara pondered.

"A—a forget-me-not is a kind of flower, isn't it?" she asked.

"Um-hm."

"But this is a windmill. How can you make a flower out of a windmill, Uncle Jed?"

Jed rubbed his chin. "Well, that's a question," he admitted. "But you can make flour IN a windmill, 'cause I've seen it done."

More pondering on the young lady's part. Then she gave it up.

"You mustn't mind if you don't understand him, Uncle Charlie," she said, in her most confidential and grown-up manner. "He says lots of things Petunia and I don't understand at all, but he's awful nice, just the same. Mamma says he's choking—no, I mean joking when he talks that way and that we'll understand the jokes lots better when we're older. SHE understands them almost always," she added proudly.

Phillips laughed. Jed's slow smile appeared and vanished. "Looks as if facin' my jokes was no child's play, don't it," he observed. "Well, I will give in that gettin' any fun out of 'em is a man's size job."

On the following Monday the young man took up his duties in the bank. Captain Hunniwell interviewed him, liked him, and hired him all in the same forenoon. By the end of the first week of their association as employer and employee the captain liked him still better. He dropped in at the windmill shop to crow over the fact.

"He takes hold same as an old-time first mate used to take hold of a green crew," he declared. "He had his job jumpin' to the whistle before the second day was over. I declare I hardly dast to wake up mornin's for fear I'll find out our havin' such a smart feller is only a dream and that the livin' calamity is Lute Small. And to think," he added, "that you knew about him for the land knows how long and would only hint instead of tellin'. I don't know as you'd have told yet if his sister hadn't told first. Eh? Would you?"

Jed deliberately picked a loose bristle from his paint brush.

"Maybe not," he admitted.

"Gracious king! Well, WHY not?"

"Oh, I don't know. I'm kind of—er—funny that way. Like to take my own time, I guess likely. Maybe you've noticed it, Sam."

"Eh? MAYBE I've noticed it? A blind cripple that was born deef and dumb would have noticed that the first time he ran across you. What on earth are you doin' to that paint brush; tryin' to mesmerize it?"

His friend, who had been staring mournfully at the brush, now laid it down.

"I was tryin' to decide," he drawled, "whether it needed hair tonic or a wig. So you like this Charlie Phillips, do you?"

"Sartin sure I do! And the customers like him, too. Why, old Melissa Busteed was in yesterday and he waited on her for half an hour, seemed so, and when the agony was over neither one of 'em had got mad enough so anybody outside the buildin' would notice it. And that's a miracle that ain't happened in that bank for more'n ONE year. Why, I understand Melissa went down street tellin' all hands what a fine young man we'd got workin' for us.... Here, what are you laughin' at?"

The word was ill-chosen; Jed seldom laughed, but he had smiled slightly and the captain noticed it.

"What are you grinnin' at?" he repeated.

Jed's hand moved across his chin.

"Gab Bearse was in a spell ago," he replied, "and he was tellin' about what Melissa said."

"Well, she said what I just said she said, didn't she?"

Mr. Winslow nodded. "Um-hm," he admitted, "she said—er—all of that."

"All of it? Was there some more?"

"'Cordin' to Gabe there was. 'Cordin' to him she said . . . she said . . . er . . . Hum! this brush ain't much better'n the other. Seem to be comin' down with the mange, both of 'em."

"Gracious king! Consarn the paint brushes! Tell me what Melissa said."

"Oh, yes, yes. . . . Well, 'cordin' to Gabe she said 'twas a comfort to know there was a place in this town where an unprotected female could go and not be insulted."

Captain Sam's laugh could have been heard across the road.

"Ho, ho!" he roared. "An unprotected female, eh? 'Cordin' to my notion it's the male that needs protection when Melissa's around. I've seen Lute Small standin' in the teller's cage, tongue-tied and with the sweat standin' on his forehead, while Melissa gave him her candid opinion of anybody that would vote to allow alcohol to be sold by doctors in this town. And 'twas ten minutes of twelve Saturday mornin', too, and there was eight men waitin' their turn in line, and nary one of them or Lute either had the spunk to ask Melissa to hurry. Ho, ho! 'unprotected female' is good!"

He had his laugh out and then added: "But there's no doubt that Charlie's goin' to be popular with the women. Why, even Maud seems to take a shine to him. Said she was surprised to have me show such good judgment. Course she didn't really mean she was surprised," he hastened to explain, evidently fearing that even an old friend like Jed might think he was criticizing his idolized daughter. "She was just teasin' her old dad, that's all. But I could see that Charlie kind of pleased her. Well, he pleases me and he pleases the cashier and the directors. We agree, all of us, that we're mighty lucky. I gave you some of the credit for gettin' him for us, Jed," he added magnanimously. "You don't really deserve much, because you hung back so and wouldn't tell his name, but I gave it to you just the same. What's a little credit between friends, eh? That's what Bluey Batcheldor said the other day when he came in and wanted to borrow a hundred dollars on his personal note. Ho! ho!"

Captain Sam's glowing opinion of his paragon was soon echoed by the majority of Orham's population. Charlie Phillips, although quiet and inclined to keep to himself, was liked by almost every one. In the bank and out of it he was polite, considerate and always agreeable. During these first days Jed fancied that he detected in the young man a certain alert dread, a sense of being on guard, a reserve in the presence of strangers, but he was not sure that this was anything more than fancy, a fancy inspired by the fact that he knew the boy's secret and was on the lookout for something of the sort. At all events no one else appeared to notice it and it became more and more evident that Charlie, as nine-tenths of Orham called him within a fortnight, was destined to be the favorite here that, according to his sister, he had been everywhere else.

Of course there were a few who did not, or would not, like him. Luther Small, the deposed bank clerk, was bitter in his sneers and caustic in his comments. However, as Lute loudly declared that he was just going to quit anyhow, that he wouldn't have worked for old Hunniwell another week if he was paid a million a minute for it, his hatred of his successor seemed rather unaccountable. Barzilla Small, Luther's fond parent, also professed intense dislike for the man now filling his son's position in the bank. "I don't know how 'tis," affirmed Barzilla, "but the fust time I see that young upstart I says to myself: 'Young feller, you ain't my kind.'" This remark being repeated to Captain Sam, the latter observed: 'That's gospel truth and thank the Lord for it.'"

Another person who refused to accept Phillips favorably was Phineas Babbitt. Phineas's bitterness was not the sort to sweeten over night. He disliked the new bank clerk and he told Jed Winslow why. They met at the post office—Phineas had not visited the windmill shop since the day when he received the telegram notifying him of his son's enlistment—and some one of the group waiting for the mail had happened to speak of Charlie Phillips. "He's a nice obligin' young chap," said the speaker, Captain Jeremiah Burgess. "I like him fust-rate; everybody does, I guess."

Mr. Babbitt, standing apart from the group, his bristling chin beard moving as he chewed his eleven o'clock allowance of "Sailor's Sweetheart," turned and snarled over his shoulder.

"I don't," he snapped.

His tone was so sharp and his utterance so unexpected that Captain Jerry jumped.

"Land of Goshen! You bark like a dog with a sore throat," he exclaimed. "Why don't you like him?"

"'Cause I don't, that's all."

"That ain't much of a reason, seems to me. What have you got against him, Phin? You don't know anything to his discredit, do you?"

"Never you mind whether I do or not."

Captain Jerry grunted but seemed disinclined to press the point further. Every one was surprised therefore when Jed Winslow moved across to where Phineas was standing, and looking mildly down at the little man, asked: "Do you know anything against him, Phin?"

"None of your business. What are you buttin' in for, Shavin's?"

"I ain't. I just asked you, that's all. DO you know anything against Charlie Phillips?"

"None of your business, I tell you."

"I know it ain't. But do you, Phin?"

Each repetition of the question had been made in the same mild, monotonous drawl. Captain Jerry and the other loungers burst into a laugh. Mr. Babbitt's always simmering temper boiled over.

"No, I don't," he shouted. "But I don't know anything in his favor, neither. He's a pet of Sam Hunniwell and that's enough for me. Sam Hunniwell and every one of his chums can go to the devil. Every one of 'em; do you understand that, Jed Winslow?"

Jed rubbed his chin. The solemn expression of his face did not change an atom. "Thank you, Phin," he drawled. "When I'm ready to start I'll get you to give me a letter of introduction."

Jed had been fearful that her brother's coming might lessen the intimate quality of Ruth Armstrong's friendship with and dependence upon him. He soon discovered, to his delight, that these fears were groundless. He found that the very fact that Ruth had made him her sole confidant provided a common bond which brought them closer together. Ruth's pride in her brother's success at the bank and in the encomiums of the townsfolk had to find expression somewhere. She could express them to her landlord and she did. Almost every day she dropped in at the windmill shop for a moment's call and chat, the subject of that chat always, of course, the same.

"I told you he would succeed," she declared, her eyes shining and her face alight. "I told you so, Jed. And he has. Mr. Barber, the cashier, told me yesterday that Charles was the best man they had had in the bank for years. And every time I meet Captain Hunniwell he stops to shake hands and congratulates me on having such a brother. And they like him, not only because he is successful in the bank, but for himself; so many people have told me so. Why, for the first time since we came to Orham I begin to feel as if I were becoming acquainted, making friends."

Jed nodded. "He's a nice young chap," he said, quietly.

"Of course he is.... You mustn't mind my shameless family boasting," she added, with a little laugh. "It is only because I am so proud of him, and so glad—so glad for us all."

Jed did not mind. It is doubtful if at that moment he was aware of what she was saying. He was thinking how her brother's coming had improved her, how well she was looking, how much more color there was in her cheeks, and how good it was to hear her laugh once more. The windmill shop was a different place when she came. It was a lucky day for him when the Powlesses frightened him into letting Barbara and her mother move into the old house for a month's trial.

Of course he did not express these thoughts aloud, in fact he expressed nothing whatever. He thought and thought and, after a time, gradually became aware that there was absolute silence in the shop. He looked at his caller and found that she was regarding him intently, a twinkle in her eye and an amused expression about her mouth. He started and awoke from his day-dream.

"Eh?" he exclaimed. "Yes—yes, I guess so."

She shook her head.

"You do?" she said. "Why, I thought your opinion was exactly the opposite."

"Eh? Oh, yes, so 'tis, so 'tis."

"Of course. And just what did you say about it?"

Jed was confused. He swallowed hard, hesitated, swallowed again and stammered: "I— Why, I—that is—you see—"

She laughed merrily. "You are a very poor pretender, Jed," she declared. "Confess, you haven't the least idea what opinion I mean."

"Well—well, to be right down honest, I—I don't know's I have, Mrs. Ruth."

"Of course, you haven't. There isn't any opinion. You have been sitting there for the last five minutes, staring straight at me and picking that paint brush to pieces. I doubt if you even knew I was here."

"Eh? Oh, yes, I know that, I know that all right. Tut! tut!" inspecting the damaged brush. "That's a nice mess, ain't it? Now what do you suppose I did that for? I'm scared to death, when I have one of those go-to-sleeptic fits, that I'll pick my head to pieces. Not that that would be as big a loss as a good paint brush," he added, reflectively.

His visitor smiled. "I think it would," she said. "Neither Babbie nor I could afford to lose that head; it and its owner have been too thoughtful and kind. But tell me, what WERE you thinking about just then?"

The question appeared to embarrass Mr. Winslow a good deal. He colored, fidgeted and stammered. "Nothin', nothin' of any account," he faltered. "My—er—my brain was takin' a walk around my attic, I cal'late. There's plenty of room up there for a tramp."

"No, tell me; I want to know." Her expression changed and she added: "You weren't thinking of—of Charles'—his trouble at Middleford? You don't still think me wrong in not telling Captain Hunniwell?"

"Eh? . . . Oh, no, no. I wasn't thinkin' that at all."

"But you don't answer my question. Well, never mind. I am really almost happy for the first time in ever so long and I mean to remain so if I can. I am glad I did not tell—glad. And you must agree with me, Mr. Winslow—Jed, I mean—or I shall not run in so often to talk in this confidential way."

"Eh? Not run in? Godfreys, Mrs. Ruth, don't talk so! Excuse my strong language, but you scared me, talkin' about not runnin' in."

"You deserve to be scared, just a little, for criticizing me in your thoughts. Oh, don't think me frivolous," she pleaded, with another swift change. "I realize it was all wrong. And some time, by and by, after Charles has firmly established himself, after they really know him, I shall go to the bank people, or he will go to them, and tell the whole story. By that time I'm sure—I'm sure they will forgive us both. Don't you think so?"

Jed would have forgiven her anything. He nodded.

"Sartin sure they will," he said. Then, asking a question that had been in his thoughts for some time, he said: "How does your brother feel about it himself, Mrs. Ruth?"

"At first he thought he should tell everything. He did not want to take the position under false pretenses, he said. But when I explained how he might lose this opportunity and what an opportunity it might be for us all he agreed that perhaps it was best to wait. And I am sure it is best, Jed. But then, I mean to put the whole dreadful business from my mind, if I can, and be happy with my little girl and my brother. And I am happy; I feel almost like a girl myself. So you mustn't remind me, Jed, and you mustn't criticize me, even though you and I both know you are right. You are my only confidant, you know, and I don't know what in the world I should do without you, so try to bear with me, if you can."

Jed observed that he guessed likely there wouldn't be much trouble at his end of the line, providing she could manage to worry along with a feller that went to sleep sittin' up, and in the daytime, like an owl. After she had gone, however, he again relapsed into slumber, and his dreams, judging by his expression, must have been pleasant.

That afternoon he had an unexpected visit. He had just finished washing his dinner dishes and he and Babbie were in the outer shop together, when the visitor came. Jed was droning "Old Hundred" with improvisations of his own, the said improvising having the effect of slowing down the already extremely deliberate anthem until the result compared to the original was for speed, as an oyster scow compared to an electric launch. This musical crawl he used as an accompaniment to the sorting and piling of various parts of an order just received from a Southern resort. Barbara was helping him, at least she called her activities "helping." When Jed had finished counting a pile of vanes or mill parts she counted them to make sure. Usually her count and his did not agree, so both counted again, getting in each other's way and, as Mr. Winslow expressed it, having a good time generally. And this remark, intended to be facetious, was after all pretty close to the literal truth. Certainly Babbie was enjoying herself, and Jed, where an impatient man would have been frantic, was enjoying her enjoyment. Petunia, perched in lopsided fashion on a heap of mill-sides was, apparently, superintending.

"There!" declared Jed, stacking a dozen sailors beside a dozen of what the order called "birdhouses medium knocked down." "There! that's the livin' last one, I do believe. Hi hum! Now we've got to box 'em, haven't we? ... Ye-es, yes, yes, yes.... Hum...."

"'Di—de—di—de—di—de....'"

"Where's that hammer? Oh, yes, here 'tis."

"'Di—de—di—de—'

"Now where on earth have I put that pencil, Babbie? Have I swallowed it? DON'T tell me you've seen me swallow it, 'cause that flavor of lead-pencil never did agree with me."

The child burst into a trill of laughter.

"Why, Uncle Jed," she exclaimed, "there it is, behind your ear."

"Is it? Sho, so 'tis! Now that proves the instinct of dumb animals, don't it? That lead-pencil knew enough to realize that my ear was so big that anything short of a cord-wood stick could hide behind it. Tut, tut! Surprisin', surprisin'!"

"But, Uncle Jed, a pencil isn't an animal."

"Eh? Ain't it? Seemed to me I'd read somethin' about the ragin' lead-pencil seekin' whom it might devour. But maybe that was a— er—lion or a clam or somethin'."

Babbie looked at him in puzzled fashion for a moment. Then she sagely shook her head and declared: "Uncle Jed, I think you are perfectly scru-she-aking. Petunia and I are convulshed. We—" she stopped, listened, and then announced: "Uncle Jed, I THINK somebody came up the walk."

The thought received confirmation immediately in the form of a knock at the door. Jed looked over his spectacles.

"Hum," he mused, sadly, "there's no peace for the wicked, Babbie. No sooner get one order all fixed and out of the way than along comes a customer and you have to get another one ready. If I'd known 'twas goin' to be like this I'd never have gone into business, would you? But maybe 'tain't a customer, maybe it's Cap'n Sam or Gabe Bearse or somebody. . . . They wouldn't knock, though, 'tain't likely; anyhow Gabe wouldn't. . . . Come in," he called, as the knock was repeated.

The person who entered the shop was a tall man in uniform. The afternoon was cloudy and the outer shop, piled high with stock and lumber, was shadowy. The man in uniform looked at Jed and Barbara and they looked at him. He spoke first.

"Pardon me," he said, "but is your name Winslow?"

Jed nodded. "Yes, sir," he replied, deliberately. "I guess likely 'tis."

"I have come here to see if you could let me have—"

Babbie interrupted him. Forgetting her manners in the excitement of the discovery which had just flashed upon her, she uttered an exclamation.

"Oh, Uncle Jed!" she exclaimed.

Jed, startled, turned toward her.

"Yes?" he asked, hastily. "What's the matter?"

"Don't you know? He—he's the nice officer one."

"Eh? The nice what? What are you talkin' about, Babbie?"

Babbie, now somewhat abashed and ashamed of her involuntary outburst, turned red and hesitated.

"I mean," she stammered, "I mean he—he's the—officer one that— that was nice to us that day."

"That day? What day? . . . Just excuse the little girl, won't you?" he added, apologetically, turning to the caller. "She's made a mistake; she thinks she knows you, I guess."

"But I DO, Uncle Jed. Don't you remember? Over at the flying place?"

The officer himself took a step forward.

"Why, of course," he said, pleasantly. "She is quite right. I thought your faces were familiar. You and she were over at the camp that day when one of our construction plans was lost. She found it for us. And Lieutenant Rayburn and I have been grateful many times since," he added.

Jed recognized him then.

"Well, I snum!" he exclaimed. "Of course! Sartin! If it hadn't been for you I'd have lost my life and Babbie'd have lost her clam chowder. That carpenter feller would have had me hung for a spy in ten minutes more. I'm real glad to see you, Colonel—Colonel Wood. That's your name, if I recollect right."

"Not exactly. My name is Grover, and I'm not a colonel, worse luck, only a major."

"Sho! Grover, eh? Now how in the nation did I get it Wood? Oh, yes, I cal'late 'twas mixin' up groves and woods. Tut, tut! Wonder I didn't call you 'Pines' or 'Bushes' or somethin'. . . . But there, sit down, sit down. I'm awful glad you dropped in. I'd about given up hopin' you would."

He brought forward a chair, unceremoniously dumping two stacks of carefully sorted and counted vanes and sailors from its seat to the floor prior to doing so. Major Grover declined to sit.

"I should like to, but I mustn't," he said. "And I shouldn't claim credit for deliberately making you a social call. I came—that is, I was sent here on a matter of—er—well, first aid to the injured. I came to see if you would lend me a crank."

Jed looked at him. "A—a what?" he asked.

"A crank, a crank for my car. I motored over from the camp and stopped at the telegraph office. When I came out my car refused to go; the self-starter appears to have gone on a strike. I had left my crank at the camp and my only hope seemed to be to buy or borrow one somewhere. I asked the two or three fellows standing about the telegraph office where I might be likely to find one. No one seemed to know, but just then the old grouch—excuse me, person who keeps the hardware store came along."

"Eh? Phin Babbitt? Little man with the stub of a paint brush growin' on his chin?"

"Yes, that's the one. I asked him where I should be likely to find a crank. He said if I came across to this shop I ought to find one."

"He did, eh? . . . Hum!"

"Yes, he did. So I came."

"Hum!"

This observation being neither satisfying nor particularly illuminating, Major Grover waited for something more explicit. He waited in vain; Mr. Winslow, his eyes fixed upon the toe of his visitor's military boot, appeared to be mesmerized.

"So I came," repeated the major, after an interval.

"Eh? . . . Oh, yes, yes. So you did, so you did. . . . Hum!"

He rose and, walking to the window, peeped about the edge of the shade across and down the road in the direction of the telegraph office.

"Phineas," he drawled, musingly, "and Squealer and Lute Small and Bluey. Hu-u-m! . . . Yes, yes."

He turned away from the window and began intoning a hymn. Major Grover seemed to be divided between a desire to laugh and a tendency toward losing patience.

"Well," he queried, after another interval, "about that crank? Have you one I might borrow? It may not fit, probably won't, but I should like to try it."

Jed sighed. "There's a crank here," he drawled, "but it wouldn't be much use around automobiles, I'm afraid. I'm it."

"What? I don't understand."

"I say I'm it. My pet name around Orham is town crank. That's why Phineas sent you to my shop. He said you OUGHT to find a crank here. He was right, I'm 'most generally in."

This statement was made quietly, deliberately and with no trace of resentment. Having made it, the speaker began picking up the vanes and sailors he had spilled when he proffered his visitor the chair. Major Grover colored, and frowned.

"Do you mean to tell me," he demanded, "that that fellow sent me over here because—because—"

"Because I'm town crank? Ye-es, that's what I mean."

"Indeed! That is his idea of a joke, is it?"

"Seems to be. He's an awful comical critter, Phin Babbitt is—in his own way."

"Well, it's not my way. He sends me over here to make an ass of myself and insult you—"

"Now, now, Major, excuse me. Phin didn't have any idea that you'd insult me. You see," with the fleeting smile, "he wouldn't believe anybody could do that."

Grover turned sharply to the door. Mr. Winslow spoke his name.

"Er—Major Grover," he said, gently, "I wouldn't."

The major paused. "Wouldn't what?" he demanded.

"Go over there and tell Phin and the rest what you think of 'em. If 'twould do 'em any good I'd say, 'For mercy sakes, go!' But 'twouldn't; they wouldn't believe it."

Grover's lips tightened.

"Telling it might do ME some good," he observed, significantly.

"Yes, I know. But maybe we might get the same good or more in a different way.... Hum!... What—er—brand of automobile is yours?"

The major told him. Jed nodded.

"Hum... yes," he drawled. "I see.... I see."

Grover laughed. "I'll be hanged if I do!" he observed.

"Eh!... Well, I tell you; you sit down and let Babbie talk Petunia to you a minute or two. I'll be right back."

He hurried into the back shop, closing the door after him. A moment later Grover caught a glimpse of him crossing the back yard and disappearing over the edge of the bluff.

"Where in the world has the fellow gone?" he soliloquized aloud, amused although impatient. Barbara took it upon herself to answer. Uncle Jed had left the caller in her charge and she felt her responsibilities.

"He's gone down the shore path," she said. "I don't know where else he's gone, but it's all right, anyway."

"Oh, is it? You seem quite sure of it, young lady."

"I am. Everything Uncle Jed does is right. Sometimes you don't think so at first, but it turns out that way. Mamma says he is petunia—no, I mean peculiar but—but very—re-li-a-ble," the last word conquered after a visible struggle. "She says if you do what he tells you to you will be 'most always glad. I think 'always' without any 'most,'" she added.

Major Grover laughed. "That's a reputation for infallibility worth having," he observed.

Barbara did not know what he meant but she had no intention of betraying that fact.

"Yes," she agreed. A moment later she suggested: "Don't you think you'd better sit down? He told you to, you know."

"Great Scott, so he did! I must obey orders, mustn't I? But he told you to talk—something or other to me, I think. What was it?"

"He told me to talk Petunia to you. There she is—up there."

The major regarded Petunia, who was seated upon the heap of millsides, in a most haphazard and dissipated attitude.

"She is my oldest daughter," continued Barbara. "She's very advanced for her years."

"Dear me!"

"Yes. And . . . oh, here comes Mamma!"

Mrs. Armstrong entered the shop. The major rose. Barbara did the honors.

"I was just going to come in, Mamma," she explained, "but Uncle Jed asked me to stay and talk to Mr.—I mean Major—Grover till he came back. He's gone out, but he won't be long. Mamma, this is Mr. Major Grover, the one who kept Uncle Jed from being spied, over at the flying place that day when I found the plan paper and he made a shingle boat sail out of it."

Ruth came forward. She had been walking along the edge of the bluff, looking out over the tumbled gray and white water, and the late October wind had tossed her hair and brought the color to her cheeks. She put out her hand.

"Oh, yes," she said. "How do you do, Major Grover? I have heard a great deal about you since the day of Babbie's picnic. I'm sure I owe you an apology for the trouble my small daughter must have caused that day."

She and the major shook hands. The latter expressed himself as being very glad to meet Mrs. Armstrong. He looked as if he meant it.

"And no apologies are due, not from your side at least," he declared. "If it had not been for your little girl our missing plan might have been missing yet."

Fifteen minutes elapsed before the owner of the windmill shop returned. When he did come hurrying up the bluff and in at the back door, heated and out of breath, no one seemed to have missed him greatly. Major Grover, who might reasonably have been expected to show some irritation at his long wait, appeared quite oblivious of the fact that he had waited at all. He and Barbara were seated side by side upon a packing case, while Ruth occupied the chair. When Jed came panting in it was Babbie who greeted him.

"Oh, Uncle Jed!" she exclaimed, "you just ought to have been here. Mr.—I mean Major Grover has been telling Mamma and me about going up in a—in a diggible balloon. It was awf'ly interesting. Wasn't it, Mamma?"

Her mother laughingly agreed that it was. Jed, whose hands were full, deposited his burden upon another packing case. The said burden consisted of no less than three motor car cranks. Grover regarded them with surprise.

"Where in the world did you get those?" he demanded. "The last I saw of you you were disappearing over that bank, apparently headed out to sea. Do you dig those things up on the flats hereabouts, like clams?"

Jed rubbed his chin. "Not's I know of," he replied. "I borrowed these down at Joshua Rogers' garage."

"Rogers' garage?" repeated Grover. "That isn't near here, is it?"

"It is an eighth of a mile from here," declared Ruth. "And not down by the beach, either. What do you mean, Jed?"

Jed was standing by the front window, peeping out. "Um-hm," he said, musingly, "they're still there, the whole lot of 'em, waitin' for you to come out, Major. . . . Hum . . . dear, dear! And they're all doubled up now laughin' ahead of time. . . . Dear, dear! this is a world of disappointment, sure enough."

"What ARE you talking about?" demanded Major Grover.

"JED!" exclaimed Ruth.

Barbara said nothing. She was accustomed to her Uncle Jed's vagaries and knew that, in his own good time, an explanation would be forthcoming. It came now.

"Why, you see," said Jed, "Phin Babbitt and the rest sendin' you over here to find a crank was their little joke. They're enjoyin' it now. The one thing needed to make 'em happy for life is to see you come out of here empty-handed and so b'ilin' mad that you froth over. If you come out smilin' and with what you came after, why— why, then the cream of their joke has turned a little sour, as you might say. See?"

Grover laughed. "Yes, I see that plain enough," he agreed. "And I'm certainly obliged to you. I owed those fellows one. But what I don't see is how you got those cranks by going down to the seashore."

"W-e-e-ll, if I'd gone straight up the road to Rogers's our jokin' friends would have known that's where the cranks came from. I wanted 'em to think they came from right here. So I went over the bank back of the shop, where they couldn't see me, along the beach till I got abreast of Joshua's and then up across lots. I came back the way I went. I hope those things 'll fit, Major. One of 'em will, I guess likely."

The major laughed again. "I certainly am obliged to you, Mr. Winslow," he said. "And I must say you took a lot of trouble on my account."

Jed sighed, although there was a little twinkle in his eye.

"'Twan't altogether on your account," he drawled. "I owed 'em one, same as you did. I was the crank they sent you to."

Their visitor bade Barbara and her mother good afternoon, gathered up his cranks and turned to the door.

"I'll step over and start the car," he said. "Then I'll come back and return these things."

Jed shook his head. "I wouldn't," he said. "You may stop again before you get back to Bayport. Rogers is in no hurry for 'em, he said so. You take 'em along and fetch 'em in next time you're over. I want you to call again anyhow and these cranks 'll make a good excuse for doin' it," he added.

"Oh, I see. Yes, so they will. With that understanding I'll take them along. Thanks again and good afternoon."

He hastened across the street. The two in the shop watched from the window until the car started and moved out of sight. The group by the telegraph office seemed excited about something; they laughed no longer and there was considerable noisy argument.

Jed's lip twitched. "'The best laid plans of mice—and skunks,'" he quoted, solemnly. "Hm! . . . That Major Grover seems like a good sort of chap."

"I think he's awful nice," declared Babbie.

Ruth said nothing.

CHAPTER XIII

October passed and November came. The very last of the summer cottages were closed. Orham settled down for its regular winter hibernation. This year it was a bit less of a nap than usual because of the activity at the aviation camp at East Harniss. The swarm of carpenters, plumbers and mechanics was larger than ever there now and the buildings were hastening toward completion, for the first allotment of aviators, soldiers and recruits was due to arrive in March. Major Grover was a busy and a worried man, but he usually found time to drop in at the windmill shop for a moment or two on each of his brief motor trips to Orham. Sometimes he found Jed alone, more often Barbara was there also, and, semi-occasionally, Ruth. The major and Charles Phillips met and appeared to like each other. Charles was still on the rising tide of local popularity. Even Gabe Bearse had a good word to say for him among the many which he said concerning him. Phineas Babbitt, however, continued to express dislike, or, at the most, indifference.

"I'm too old a bird," declared the vindictive little hardware dealer, "to bow down afore a slick tongue and a good-lookin' figgerhead. He's one of Sam Hunniwell's pets and that's enough for me. Anybody that ties up to Sam Hunniwell must have a rotten plank in 'em somewheres; give it time and 'twill come out."

Charles and Jed Winslow were by this time good friends. The young man usually spent at least a few minutes of each day chatting with his eccentric neighbor. They were becoming more intimate, at times almost confidential, although Phillips, like every other friend or acquaintance of "Shavings" Winslow, was inclined to patronize or condescend a bit in his relations with the latter. No one took the windmill maker altogether seriously, not even Ruth Armstrong, although she perhaps came nearest to doing so. Charles would drop in at the shop of a morning, in the interval between breakfast and bank opening, and, perching on a pile of stock, or the workbench, would discuss various things. He and Jed were alike in one characteristic—each had the habit of absent-mindedness and lapsing into silence in the middle of a conversation. Jed's lapses, of course, were likely to occur in the middle of a sentence, even in the middle of a word; with the younger man the symptoms were not so acute.

"Well, Charlie," observed Mr. Winslow, on one occasion, a raw November morning of the week before Thanksgiving, "how's the bank gettin' along?"

Charles was a bit more silent that morning than he had been of late. He appeared to be somewhat reflective, even somber. Jed, on the lookout for just such symptoms, was trying to cheer him up.

"Oh, all right enough, I guess," was the reply.

"Like your work as well as ever, don't you?"

"Yes—oh, yes, I like it, what there is of it. It isn't what you'd call strenuous."

"No, I presume likely not, but I shouldn't wonder if they gave you somethin' more responsible some of these days. They know you're up to doin' it; Cap'n Sam's told me so more'n once."

Here occurred one of the lapses just mentioned. Phillips said nothing for a minute or more. Then he asked: "What sort of a man is Captain Hunniwell?"

"Eh? What sort of a man? You ought to know him yourself pretty well by this time. You see more of him every day than I do."

"I don't mean as a business man or anything like that. I mean what sort of man is he—er—inside? Is he always as good-natured as he seems? How is he around his own house? With his daughter—or—or things like that? You've known him all your life, you know, and I haven't."

"Um—ye-es—yes, I've known Sam for a good many years. He's square all through, Sam is. Honest as the day is long and—"

Charles stirred uneasily. "I know that, of course," he interrupted. "I wasn't questioning his honesty."

Jed's tender conscience registered a pang. The reference to honesty had not been made with any ulterior motive.

"Sartin, sartin," he said; "I know you wasn't, Charlie, course I know that. You wanted to know what sort of a man Sam was in his family and such, I judge. Well, he's a mighty good father—almost too good, I suppose likely some folks would say. He just bows down and worships that daughter of his. Anything Maud wants that he can give her she can have. And she wants a good deal, I will give in," he added, with his quiet drawl.

His caller did not speak. Jed whistled a few mournful bars and sharpened a chisel on an oilstone.

"If John D. Vanderbilt should come around courtin' Maud," he went on, after a moment, "I don't know as Sam would cal'late he was good enough for her. Anyhow he'd feel that 'twas her that was doin' the favor, not John D.... And I guess he'd be right; I don't know any Vanderbilts, but I've known Maud since she was a baby. She's a—"

He paused, inspecting a nick in the chisel edge. Again Phillips shifted in his seat on the edge of the workbench.

"Well?" he asked.

"Eh?" Jed looked up in mild inquiry. "What is it?" he said.

"That's what I want to know—what is it? You were talking about Maud Hunniwell. You said you had known her since she was a baby and that she was—something or other; that was as far as you got."

"Sho!... Hum.... Oh, yes, yes; I was goin' to say she was a mighty nice girl, as nice as she is good-lookin' and lively. There's a dozen young chaps in this county crazy about her this minute, but there ain't any one of 'em good enough for her.... Hello, you goin' so soon? 'Tisn't half-past nine yet, is it?"

Phillips did not answer. His somber expression was still in evidence. Jed would have liked to cheer him up, but he did not know how. However he made an attempt by changing the subject.

"How is Babbie this mornin'?" he asked.

"She's as lively as a cricket, of course. And full of excitement. She's going to school next Monday, you know. You'll rather miss her about the shop here, won't you?"

"Miss her! My land of Goshen! I shouldn't be surprised if I follered her to school myself, like Mary's little lamb. Miss her! Don't talk!"

"Well, so long.... What is it?"

"Eh?"

"What is it you want to say? You look as if you wanted to say something."

"Do I?... Hum.... Oh, 'twasn't anything special.... How's—er—how's your sister this mornin'?"

"Oh, she's well. I haven't seen her so well since—that is, for a long time. You've made a great hit with Sis, Jed," he added, with a laugh. "She can't say enough good things about you. Says you are her one dependable in Orham, or something like that."

Jed's face turned a bright red. "Oh, sho, sho!" he protested, "she mustn't talk that way. I haven't done anything."

"She says you have. Well, by-by."

He went away. It was some time before Jed resumed his chisel-sharpening.

Later, when he came to reflect upon his conversation with young Phillips there were one or two things about it which puzzled him. They were still puzzling him when Maud Hunniwell came into the shop. Maud, in a new fall suit, hat and fur, was a picture, a fact of which she was as well aware as the next person. Jed, as always, was very glad to see her.

"Well, well!" he exclaimed. "Talk about angels and—and they fly in, so to speak. Real glad to see you, Maud. Sit down, sit down. There's a chair 'round here somewheres. Now where—? Oh, yes, I'm sittin' in it. Hum! That's one of the reasons why I didn't see it, I presume likely. You take it and I'll fetch another from the kitchen. No, I won't, I'll sit on the bench. . . . Hum . . . has your pa got any money left in that bank of his?"

Miss Hunniwell was, naturally, surprised at the question.

"Why, I hope so," she said. "Did you think he hadn't?"

"W-e-e-ll, I didn't know. That dress of yours, and that new bonnet, must have used up consider'ble, to say nothin' of that woodchuck you've got 'round your neck. 'Tis a woodchuck, ain't it?" he added, solemnly.

"Woodchuck! Well, I like that! If you knew what a silver fox costs and how long I had to coax before I got this one you would be more careful in your language," she declared, with a toss of her head.

Jed sighed. "That's the trouble with me," he observed. "I never know enough to pick out the right things—or folks—to be careful with. If I set out to be real toady and humble to what I think is a peacock it generally turns out to be a Shanghai rooster. And the same when it's t'other way about. It's a great gift to be able to tell the real—er—what is it?—gold foxes from the woodchucks in this life. I ain't got it and that's one of the two hundred thousand reasons why I ain't rich."

He began to hum one of his doleful melodies. Maud laughed.

"Mercy, what a long sermon!" she exclaimed. "No wonder you sing a hymn after it."

Jed sniffed. "Um . . . ye-es," he drawled. "If I was more worldly-minded I'd take up a collection, probably. Well, how's all the United States Army; the gold lace part of it, I mean?"

His visitor laughed again. "Those that I know seem to be very well and happy," she replied.

"Um...yes...sartin. They'd be happy, naturally. How could they help it, under the circumstances?"

He began picking over an assortment of small hardware, varying his musical accompaniment by whistling instead of singing. His visitor looked at him rather oddly.

"Jed," she observed, "you're changed."

Changed? I ain't changed my clothes, if that's what you mean. Course if I'd know I was goin' to have bankers' daughters with gold—er—muskrats 'round their necks come to see me I'd have dressed up."

"Oh, I don't mean your clothes. I mean you—yourself—you've changed."

"I've changed! How, for mercy sakes?"

"Oh, lots of ways. You pay the ladies compliments now. You wouldn't have done that a year ago."

"Eh? Pay compliments? I'm afraid you're mistaken. Your pa says I'm so absent-minded and forgetful that I don't pay some of my bills till the folks I owe 'em to make proclamations they're goin' to sue me; and other bills I pay two or three times over."

"Don't try to escape by dodging the subject. You HAVE changed in the last few months. I think," holding the tail of the silver fox before her face and regarding him over it, "I think you must be in love."

"Eh?" Jed looked positively frightened. "In love!"

"Yes. You're blushing now."

"Now, now, Maud, that ain't—that's sunburn."

"No, it's not sunburn. Who is it, Jed?" mischievously. "Is it the pretty widow? Is it Mrs. Armstrong?"

A good handful of the hardware fell to the floor. Jed thankfully scrambled down to pick it up. Miss Hunniwell, expressing contrition at being indirectly responsible for the mishap, offered to help him. He declined, of course, but in the little argument which followed the dangerous and embarrassing topic was forgotten. It was not until she was about to leave the shop that Maud again mentioned the Armstrong name. And then, oddly enough, it was she, not Mr. Winslow, who showed embarrassment.

"Jed," she said, "what do you suppose I came here for this morning?"

Jed's reply was surprisingly prompt.

"To show your new rig-out, of course," he said. "'Vanity of vanities, all is vanity.' There, NOW I can take up a collection, can't I?"

His visitor pouted. "If you do I shan't put anything in the box," she declared. "The idea of thinking that I came here just to show off my new things. I've a good mind not to invite you at all now."

She doubtless expected apologies and questions as to what invitation was meant. They might have been forthcoming had not the windmill maker been engaged just at that moment in gazing abstractedly at the door of the little stove which heated, or was intended to heat, the workshop. He did not appear to have heard her remark, so the young lady repeated it. Still he paid no attention. Miss Maud, having inherited a goodly share of the Hunniwell disposition, demanded an explanation.

"What in the world is the matter with you?" she asked. "Why are you staring at that stove?"

Jed started and came to life. "Eh?" he exclaimed. "Oh, I was thinkin' what an everlastin' nuisance 'twas—the stove, I mean. It needs more wood about every five minutes in the day, seems to— needs it now, that's what made me think of it. I was just wonderin' if 'twouldn't be a good notion to set it up out in the yard."

"Out in the yard? Put the stove out in the yard? For goodness' sake, what for?"

Jed clasped his knee in his hand and swung his foot back and forth.

"Oh" he drawled, "if 'twas out in the yard I shouldn't know whether it needed wood or not, so 'twouldn't be all the time botherin' me."

However, he rose and replenished the stove. Miss Hunniwell laughed. Then she said: "Jed, you don't deserve it, because you didn't hear me when I first dropped the hint, but I came here with an invitation for you. Pa and I expect you to eat your Thanksgiving dinner with us."

If she had asked him to eat it in jail Jed could not have been more disturbed.

"Now—now, Maud," he stammered, "I—I'm ever so much obliged to you, but I—I don't see how—"

"Nonsense! I see how perfectly well. You always act just this way whenever I invite you to anything. You're not afraid of Pa or me, are you?"

"W-e-e-ll, well, I ain't afraid of your Pa 's I know of, but of course, when such a fascinatin' young woman as you comes along, all rigged up to kill, why, it's natural that an old single relic like me should get kind of nervous."

Maud clasped her hands. "Oh," she cried, "there's another compliment! You HAVE changed, Jed. I'm going to ask Father what it means."

This time Jed was really alarmed. "Now, now, now," he protested, "don't go tell your Pa yarns about me. He'll come in here and pester me to death. You know what a tease he is when he gets started. Don't, Maud, don't."

She looked hugely delighted at the prospect. Her eyes sparkled with mischief. "I certainly shall tell him," she declared, "unless you promise to eat with us on Thanksgiving Day. Oh, come along, don't be so silly. You've eaten at our house hundreds of times."

This was a slight exaggeration. Jed had eaten there possibly five times in the last five years. He hesitated.

"Ain't goin' to be any other company, is there?" he asked, after a moment. It was now that Maud showed her first symptoms of embarrassment.

"Why," she said, twirling the fox tail and looking at the floor, "there may be one or two more. I thought—I mean Pa and I thought perhaps we might invite Mrs. Armstrong and Babbie. You know them, Jed, so they won't be like strangers. And Pa thinks Mrs. Armstrong is a very nice lady, a real addition to the town; I've heard him say so often," she added, earnestly.

Jed was silent. She looked up at him from under the brim of the new hat.

"You wouldn't mind them, Jed, would you?" she asked. "They wouldn't be like strangers, you know."

Jed rubbed his chin. "I—I don't know's I would," he mused, "always providin' they didn't mind me. But I don't cal'late Mrs. Ruth—Mrs. Armstrong, I mean—would want to leave Charlie to home alone on Thanksgivin' Day. If she took Babbie, you know, there wouldn't be anybody left to keep him company."

Miss Hunniwell twirled the fox tail in an opposite direction. "Oh, of course," she said, with elaborate carelessness, "we should invite Mrs. Armstrong's brother if we invited her. Of course we should HAVE to do that."

Jed nodded, but he made no comment. His visitor watched him from beneath the hat brim.

"You—you haven't any objection to Mr. Phillips, have you?" she queried.

"Eh? Objections? To Charlie? Oh, no, no."

"You like him, don't you? Father likes him very much."

"Yes, indeed; like him fust-rate. All hands like Charlie, the women-folks especially."

There was a perceptible interval before Miss Hunniwell spoke again. "What do you mean by that?" she asked.

"Eh? Oh, nothin', except that, accordin' to your dad, he's a 'specially good hand at waitin' on the women and girls up at the bank, polite and nice to 'em, you know. He's even made a hit with old Melissy Busteed, and it takes a regular feller to do that."

He would not promise to appear at the Hunniwell home on Thanksgiving, but he did agree to think it over. Maud had to be content with that. However, she declared that she should take his acceptance for granted.

"We shall set a place for you," she said. "Of course you'll come. It will be such a nice party, you and Pa and Mrs. Armstrong and I and little Babbie. Oh, we'll have great fun, see if we don't."

"And Charlie; you're leavin' out Charlie," Jed reminded her.

"Oh, yes, so I was. Well, I suppose he'll come, too. Good-by."

She skipped away, waving him a farewell with the tail of the silver fox. Jed, gazing after her, rubbed his chin reflectively.

His indecision concerning the acceptance of the Hunniwell invitation lasted until the day before Thanksgiving. Then Barbara added her persuasions to those of Captain Sam and his daughter and he gave in.

"If you don't go, Uncle Jed," asserted Babbie, "we're all goin' to be awfully disappointed, 'specially me and Petunia—and Mamma—and Uncle Charlie."

"Oh, then the rest of you folks won't care, I presume likely?"

Babbie thought it over. "Why, there aren't any more of us," she said. "Oh, I see! You're joking again, aren't you, Uncle Jed? 'Most everybody I know laughs when they make jokes, but you don't, you look as if you were going to cry. That's why I don't laugh sometimes right off," she explained, politely. "If you was really feeling so bad it wouldn't be nice to laugh, you know."

Jed laughed then, himself. "So Petunia would feel bad if I didn't go to Sam's, would she?" he inquired.

"Yes," solemnly. "She told me she shouldn't eat one single thing if you didn't go. She's a very high-strung child."

That settled it. Jed argued that Petunia must on no account be strung higher than she was and consented to dine at the Hunniwells'.

The day before Thanksgiving brought another visitor to the windmill shop, one as welcome as he was unexpected. Jed, hearing the door to the stock room open, shouted "Come in" from his seat at the workbench in the inner room. When his summons was obeyed he looked up to see a khaki-clad figure advancing with extended hand.

"Why, hello, Major!" he exclaimed. "I'm real glad to— Eh, 'tain't Major Grover, is it? Who— Why, Leander Babbitt! Well, well, well!"

Young Babbitt was straight and square-shouldered and brown. Military training and life at Camp Devens had wrought the miracle in his case which it works in so many. Jed found it hard to recognize the stoop-shouldered son of the hardware dealer in the spruce young soldier before him. When he complimented Leander upon the improvement the latter disclaimed any credit.

"Thank the drill master second and yourself first, Jed," he said. "They'll make a man of a fellow up there at Ayer if he'll give 'em half a chance. Probably I shouldn't have had the chance if it hadn't been for you. You were the one who really put me up to enlisting."

Jed refused to listen. "Can't make a man out of a punkinhead," he asserted. "If you hadn't had the right stuff in you, Leander, drill masters nor nobody else could have fetched it out. How do you like belongin' to Uncle Sam?"

Young Babbitt liked it and said so. "I feel as if I were doing something at last," he said; "as if I was part of the biggest thing in the world. Course I'm only a mighty little part, but, after all, it's something."

Jed nodded, gravely. "You bet it's somethin'," he argued. "It's a lot, a whole lot. I only wish I was standin' alongside of you in the ranks, Leander. . . . I'd be a sight, though, wouldn't I?" he added, his lip twitching in the fleeting smile. "What do you think the Commodore, or General, or whoever 'tis bosses things at the camp, would say when he saw me? He'd think the flagpole had grown feet, and was walkin' round, I cal'late."

He asked his young friend what reception he met with upon his return home. Leander smiled ruefully.

"My step-mother seemed glad enough to see me," he said. "She and I had some long talks on the subject and I think she doesn't blame me much for going into the service. I told her the whole story and, down in her heart, I believe she thinks I did right."

Jed nodded. "Don't see how she could help it," he said. "How does your dad take it?"

Leander hesitated. "Well," he said, "you know Father. He doesn't change his mind easily. He and I didn't get as close together as I wish we could. And it wasn't my fault that we didn't," he added, earnestly.

Jed understood. He had known Phineas Babbitt for many years and he knew the little man's hard, implacable disposition and the violence of his prejudices.

"Um-hm," he said. "All the same, Leander, I believe your father thinks more of you than he does of anything else on earth."

"I shouldn't wonder if you was right, Jed. But on the other hand I'm afraid he and I will never be the same after I come back from the war—always providing I do come back, of course."

"Sshh, sshh! Don't talk that way. Course you'll come back."

"You never can tell. However, if I knew I wasn't going to, it wouldn't make any difference in my feelings about going. I'm glad I enlisted and I'm mighty thankful to you for backing me up in it. I shan't forget it, Jed."

"Sho, sho! It's easy to tell other folks what to do. That's how the Kaiser earns his salary; only he gives advice to the Almighty, and I ain't got as far along as that yet."

They discussed the war in general and by sections. Just before he left, young Babbitt said:

"Jed, there is one thing that worries me a little in connection with Father. He was bitter against the war before we went into it and before he and Cap'n Sam Hunniwell had their string of rows. Since then and since I enlisted he has been worse than ever. The things he says against the government and against the country make ME want to lick him—and I'm his own son. I am really scared for fear he'll get himself jailed for being a traitor or something of that sort."

Mr. Winslow asked if Phineas' feeling against Captain Hunniwell had softened at all. Leander's reply was a vigorous negative.

"Not a bit," he declared. "He hates the cap'n worse than ever, if that's possible, and he'll do him some bad turn some day, if he can, I'm afraid. You must think it's queer my speaking this way of my own father," he added. "Well, I don't to any one else. Somehow a fellow always feels as if he could say just what he thinks to you, Jed Winslow. I feel that way, anyhow."

He and Jed shook hands at the door in the early November twilight. Leander was to eat his Thanksgiving dinner at home and then leave for camp on the afternoon train.

"Well, good-by," he said.

Jed seemed loath to relinquish the handclasp.

"Oh, don't say good-by; it's just 'See you later,'" he replied.

Leander smiled. "Of course. Well, then, see you later, Jed. We'll write once in a while; eh?"

Jed promised. The young fellow strode off into the dusk. Somehow, with his square shoulders and his tanned, resolute country face, he seemed to typify Young America setting cheerfully forth to face— anything—that Honor and Decency may still be more than empty words in this world of ours.

CHAPTER XIV

The Hunniwell Thanksgiving dinner was an entire success. Even Captain Sam himself was forced to admit it, although he professed to do so with reluctance.

"Yes," he said, with an elaborate wink in the direction of his guests, "it's a pretty good dinner, considerin' everything. Of course 'tain't what a feller used to get down at Sam Coy's eatin'- house on Atlantic Avenue, but it's pretty good—as I say, when everything's considered."

His daughter was highly indignant. "Do you mean to say that this dinner isn't as good as those you used to get at that Boston restaurant, Pa?" she demanded. "Don't you dare say such a thing."

Her father tugged at his beard and looked tremendously solemn.

"Well," he observed, "as a boy I was brought up to always speak the truth and I've tried to live up to my early trainin'. Speakin' as a truthful man, then, I'm obliged to say that this dinner ain't like those I used to get at Sam Coy's."

Ruth put in a word. "Well, then, Captain Hunniwell," she said, "I think the restaurant you refer to must be one of the best in the world."

Before the captain could reply, Maud did it for him.

"Mrs. Armstrong," she cautioned, "you mustn't take my father too seriously. He dearly loves to catch people with what he hopes is a joke. For a minute he caught even me this time, but I see through him now. He didn't say the dinner at his precious restaurant was BETTER than this one, he said it wasn't like it, that's all. Which is probably true," she added, with withering scorn. "But what I should like to know is what he means by his 'everything considered.'"

Her father's gravity was unshaken. "Well," he said, "all I meant was that this was a pretty good dinner, considerin' who was responsible for gettin' it up."

"I see, I see. Mrs. Ellis, our housekeeper, and I are responsible, Mrs. Armstrong, so you understand now who he is shooting at. Very well, Pa," she added, calmly, "the rest of us will have our dessert now. You can get yours at Sam Coy's."

The dessert was mince pie and a Boston frozen pudding, the latter an especial favorite of Captain Sam's. He capitulated at once.

"'Kamerad! Kamerad!'" he cried, holding up both hands. "That's what the Germans say when they surrender, ain't it? I give in, Maud. You can shoot me against a stone wall, if you want to, only give me my frozen puddin' first. It ain't so much that I like the puddin'," he explained to Mrs. Armstrong, "but I never can make out whether it's flavored with tansy or spearmint. Maud won't tell me, but I know it's somethin' old-fashioned and reminds me of my grandmother; or, maybe, it's my grandfather; come to think, I guess likely 'tis."

Ruth grasped his meaning later when she tasted the pudding and found it flavored with New England rum.

After dinner they adjourned to the parlor. Maud, being coaxed by her adoring father, played the piano. Then she sang. Then they all sang, all except Jed and the captain, that is. The latter declared that his voice had mildewed in the damp weather they had been having lately, and Jed excused himself on the ground that he had been warned not to sing because it was not healthy.

Barbara was surprised and shocked.

"Why, Uncle Jed!" she cried. "You sing EVER so much. I heard you singing this morning."

Jed nodded. "Ye-es," he drawled, "but I was alone then and I'm liable to take chances with my own health. Bluey Batcheldor was in the shop last week, though, when I was tunin' up and it disagreed with HIM."

"I don't believe it, Uncle Jed," with righteous indignation. "How do you know it did?"

"'Cause he said so. He listened a spell, and then said I made him sick, so I took his word for it."

Captain Sam laughed uproariously. "You must be pretty bad then, Jed," he declared. "Anybody who disagrees with Bluey Batcheldor must be pretty nigh the limit."

Jed nodded. "Um-hm," he said, reflectively, "pretty nigh, but not quite. Always seemed to me the real limit was anybody who agreed with him."

So Jed, with Babbie on his knee, sat in the corner of the bay window looking out on the street, while Mrs. Armstrong and her brother and Miss Hunniwell played and sang and the captain applauded vigorously and loudly demanded more. After a time Ruth left the group at the piano and joined Jed and her daughter by the window. Captain Hunniwell came a few minutes later.

"Make a good-lookin' couple, don't they?" he whispered, bending down, and with a jerk of his head in the direction of the musicians. "Your brother's a fine-lookin' young chap, Mrs. Armstrong. And he acts as well as he looks. Don't know when I've taken such a shine to a young feller as I have to him. Yes, ma'am, they make a good-lookin' couple, even if one of 'em is my daughter."

The speech was made without the slightest thought or suggestion of anything but delighted admiration and parental affection. Nevertheless, Ruth, to whom it was made, started slightly, and, turning, regarded the pair at the piano. Maud was fingering the pages of a book of college songs and looking smilingly up into the face of Charles Phillips, who was looking down into hers. There was, apparently, nothing in the picture—a pretty one, by the way— to cause Mrs. Armstrong to gaze so fixedly or to bring the slight frown to her forehead. After a moment she turned toward Jed Winslow. Their eyes met and in his she saw the same startled hint of wonder, of possible trouble, she knew he must see in hers. Then they both looked away.

Captain Hunniwell prated proudly on, chanting praises of his daughter's capabilities and talents, as he did to any one who would listen, and varying the monotony with occasional references to the wonderful manner in which young Phillips had "taken hold" at the bank. Ruth nodded and murmured something from time to time, but to any one less engrossed by his subject than the captain it would have been evident she was paying little attention. Jed, who was being entertained by Babbie and Petunia, was absently pretending to be much interested in a fairy story which the former was improvising—she called the process "making up as I go along"—for his benefit. Suddenly he leaned forward and spoke.

"Sam," he said, "there's somebody comin' up the walk. I didn't get a good sight of him, but it ain't anybody that lives here in Orham regular."

"Eh? That so?" demanded the captain. "How do you know 'tain't if you didn't see him?"

"'Cause he's comin' to the front door," replied Mr. Winslow, with unanswerable logic. "There he is now, comin' out from astern of that lilac bush. Soldier, ain't he?"

It was Ruth Armstrong who first recognized the visitor. "Why," she exclaimed, "it is Major Grover, isn't it?"

The major it was, and a moment later Captain Hunniwell ushered him into the room. He had come to Orham on an errand, he explained, and had stopped at the windmill shop to see Mr. Winslow. Finding the latter out, he had taken the liberty of following him to the Hunniwell home.

"I'm going to stay but a moment, Captain Hunniwell," he went on. "I wanted to talk with Winslow on a—well, on a business matter. Of course I won't do it now but perhaps we can arrange a time convenient for us both when I can."

"Don't cal'late there'll be much trouble about that," observed the captain, with a chuckle. "Jed generally has time convenient for 'most everybody; eh, Jed?"

Jed nodded. "Um-hm," he drawled, "for everybody but Gab Bearse."

"So you and Jed are goin' to talk business, eh?" queried Captain Sam, much amused at the idea. "Figgerin' to have him rig up windmills to drive those flyin' machines of yours, Major?"

"Not exactly. My business was of another kind, and probably not very important, at that. I shall probably be over here again on Monday, Winslow. Can you see me then?"

Jed rubbed his chin. "Ye-es," he said, "I'll be on private exhibition to my friends all day. And children half price," he added, giving Babbie a hug. "But say, Major, how in the world did you locate me to-day? How did you know I was over here to Sam's? I never told you I was comin', I'll swear to that."

For some reason or other Major Grover seemed just a little embarrassed.

"Why no," he said, stammering a trifle, "you didn't tell me, but some one did. Now, who—"

"I think I told you, Major," put in Ruth Armstrong. "Last evening, when you called to—to return Charlie's umbrella. I told you we were to dine here to-day and that Jed—Mr. Winslow—was to dine with us. Don't you remember?"

Grover remembered perfectly then, of course. He hastened to explain that, having borrowed the umbrella of Charles Phillips the previous week, he had dropped in on his next visit to Orham to return it.

Jed grunted.

"Humph!" he said, "you never came to see me last night. When you was as close aboard as next door seems's if you might."

The major laughed. "Well, you'll have to admit that I came to-day," he said.

"Yes," put in Captain Sam, "and, now you are here, you're goin' to stay a spell. Oh, yes, you are, too. Uncle Sam don't need you so hard that he can't let you have an hour or so off on Thanksgiving Day. Maud, why in time didn't we think to have Major Grover here for dinner along with the rest of the folks? Say, couldn't you eat a plate of frozen puddin' right this minute? We've got some on hand that tastes of my grandfather, and we want to get rid of it."

Their caller laughingly declined the frozen pudding, but he was prevailed upon to remain and hear Miss Hunniwell play. So Maud played and Charles turned the music for her, and Major Grover listened and talked with Ruth Armstrong in the intervals between selections. And Jed and Barbara chatted and Captain Sam beamed good humor upon every one. It was a very pleasant, happy afternoon. War and suffering and heartache and trouble seemed a long, long way off.

On the way back to the shop in the chill November dusk Grover told Jed a little of what he had called to discuss with him. If Jed's mind had been of the super-critical type it might have deemed the subject of scarcely sufficient importance to warrant the major's pursuing him to the Hunniwells'. It was simply the subject of Phineas Babbitt and the latter's anti-war utterances and surmised disloyalty.

"You see," explained Grover, "some one evidently has reported the old chap to the authorities as a suspicious person. The government, I imagine, isn't keen on sending a special investigator down here, so they have asked me to look into the matter. I don't know much about Babbitt, but I thought you might. Is he disloyal, do you think?"

Jed hesitated. Things the hardware dealer had said had been reported to him, of course; but gossip—particularly the Bearse brand of gossip—was not the most reliable of evidence. Then he remembered his own recent conversation with Leander and the latter's expressed fear that his father might get into trouble. Jed determined, for the son's sake, not to bring that trouble nearer.

"Well, Major," he answered, "I shouldn't want to say that he was. Phineas talks awful foolish sometimes, but I shouldn't wonder if that was his hot head and bull temper as much as anything else. As to whether he's anything more than foolish or not, course I couldn't say sartin, but I don't think he's too desperate to be runnin' loose. I cal'late he won't put any bombs underneath the town hall or anything of that sort. Phin and his kind remind me some of that new kind of balloon you was tellin' me they'd probably have over to your camp when 'twas done, that—er—er—dirigible; wasn't that what you called it?"

"Yes. But why does Babbitt remind you of a dirigible balloon? I don't see the connection."

"Don't you? Well, seems's if I did. Phin fills himself up with the gas he gets from his Anarchist papers and magazines—the 'rich man's war' and all the rest of it—and goes up in the air and when he's up in the air he's kind of hard to handle. That's what you told me about the balloon, if I recollect."

Grover laughed heartily. "Then the best thing to do is to keep him on the ground, I should say," he observed.

Jed rubbed his chin. "Um-hm," he drawled, "but shuttin' off his gas supply might help some. I don't think I'd worry about him much, if I was you."

They separated at the front gate before the shop, where the rows of empty posts, from which the mills and vanes had all been removed, stood as gaunt reminders of the vanished summer. Major Grover refused Jed's invitation to come in and have a smoke.

"No, thank you," he said, "not this evening. I'll wait here a moment and say good-night to the Armstrongs and Phillips and then I must be on my way to the camp.... Why, what's the matter? Anything wrong?"

His companion was searching in his various pockets. The search completed, he proceeded to look himself over, so to speak, taking off his hat and looking at that, lifting a hand and then a foot and looking at them, and all with a puzzled, far-away expression. When Grover repeated his question he seemed to hear it for the first time and then not very clearly.

"Eh?" he drawled. "Oh, why—er—yes, there IS somethin' wrong. That is to say, there ain't, and that's the wrong part of it. I don't seem to have forgotten anything, that's the trouble."

His friend burst out laughing.

"I should scarcely call that a trouble," he said.

"Shouldn't you? No, I presume likely you wouldn't. But I never go anywhere without forgettin' somethin', forgettin' to say somethin' or do somethin' or bring somethin'. Never did in all my life. Now here I am home again and I can't remember that I've forgot a single thing. . . . Hum. . . . Well, I declare! I wonder what it means. Maybe, it's a sign somethin's goin' to happen."

He said good night absent-mindedly. Grover laughed and walked away to meet Ruth and her brother, who, with Barbara dancing ahead, were coming along the sidewalk. He had gone but a little way when he heard Mr. Winslow shouting his name.

"Major!" shouted Jed. "Major Grover! It's all right, Major, I feel better now. I've found it. 'Twas the key. I left it in the front door lock here when I went away this mornin'. I guess there's nothin' unnatural about me, after all; guess nothin's goin' to happen."

But something did and almost immediately. Jed, entering the outer shop, closed the door and blundered on through that apartment and the little shop adjoining until he came to his living-room beyond. Then he fumbled about in the darkness for a lamp and matchbox. He found the latter first, on the table where the lamp should have been. Lighting one of the matches, he then found the lamp on a chair directly in front of the door, where he had put it before going away that morning, his idea in so doing being that it would thus be easier to locate when he returned at night. Thanking his lucky stars that he had not upset both chair and lamp in his prowlings, Mr. Winslow lighted the latter. Then, with it in his hand, he turned, to see the very man he and Major Grover had just been discussing seated in the rocker in the corner of the room and glaring at him malevolently.

Naturally, Jed was surprised. Naturally, also, being himself, he showed his surprise in his own peculiar way. He did not start violently, nor utter an exclamation. Instead he stood stock still, returning Phineas Babbitt's glare with a steady, unwinking gaze.

It was the hardware dealer who spoke first. And that, by the way, was precisely what he had not meant to do.

"Yes," he observed, with caustic sarcasm, "it's me. You needn't stand there blinkin' like a fool any longer, Shavin's. It's me."

Jed set the lamp upon the table. He drew a long breath, apparently of relief.

"Why, so 'tis," he said, solemnly. "When I first saw you sittin' there, Phin, I had a suspicion 'twas you, but the longer I looked the more I thought 'twas the President come to call. Do you know," he added, confidentially, "if you didn't have any whiskers and he looked like you you'd be the very image of him."

This interesting piece of information was not received with enthusiasm. Mr. Babbitt's sense of humor was not acutely developed.

"Never mind the funny business, Shavin's," he snapped. "I didn't come here to be funny to-night. Do you know why I came here to talk to you?"

Jed pulled forward a chair and sat down.

"I presume likely you came here because you found the door unlocked, Phin," he said.

"I didn't say HOW I came to come, but WHY I came. I knew where you was this afternoon. I see you when you left there and I had a good mind to cross over and say what I had to say before the whole crew, Sam Hunniwell, and his stuck-up rattle-head of a daughter, and that Armstrong bunch that think themselves so uppish, and all of 'em."

Mr. Winslow stirred uneasily in his chair. "Now, Phin," he protested, "seems to me—"

But Babbitt was too excited to heed. His little eyes snapped and his bristling beard quivered.

"You hold your horses, Shavin's," he ordered. "I didn't come here to listen to you. I came because I had somethin' to say and when I've said it I'm goin' and goin' quick. My boy's been home. You knew that, I suppose, didn't you?"

Jed nodded. "Yes," he said, "I knew Leander'd come home for Thanksgivin'."

"Oh, you did! He came here to this shop to see you, maybe? Humph! I'll bet he did, the poor fool!"

Again Jed shifted his position. His hands clasped about his knee and his foot lifted from the floor.

"There, there, Phin," he said gently; "after all, he's your only son, you know."

"I know it. But he's a fool just the same."

"Now, Phin! The boy'll be goin' to war pretty soon, you know, and—"

Babbitt sprang to his feet. His chin trembled so that he could scarcely speak.

"Shut up!" he snarled. "Don't let me hear you say that again, Jed Winslow. Who sent him to war? Who filled his head full of rubbish about patriotism, and duty to the country, and all the rest of the rotten Wall Street stuff? Who put my boy up to enlistin', Jed Winslow?"

Jed's foot swung slowly back and forth.

"Well, Phin," he drawled, "to be real honest, I think he put himself up to it."

"You're a liar. YOU did it."

Jed sighed. "Did Leander tell you I did?" he asked.

"No," mockingly, "Leander didn't tell me. You and Sam Hunniwell and the rest of the gang have fixed him so he don't come to his father to tell things any longer. But he told his step-mother this very mornin' and she told me. You was the one that advised him to enlist, he said. Good Lord; think of it! He don't go to his own father for advice; he goes to the town jackass instead, the critter that spends his time whittlin' out young-one's playthings. My Lord A'mighty!"

He spat on the floor to emphasize his disgust. There was an interval of silence before Jed answered.

"Well, Phin," he said, slowly, "you're right, in a way. Leander and I have always been pretty good friends and he's been in the habit of droppin' in here to talk things over with me. When he came to me to ask what he ought to do about enlistin', asked what I'd do if I was he, I told him; that's all there was to it."

Babbitt extended a shaking forefinger.

"Yes, and you told him to go to war. Don't lie out of it now; you know you did."

"Um . . . yes . . . I did."

"You did? You DID? And you have the cheek to own up to it right afore my face."

Jed's hand stroked his chin. "W-e-e-ll," he drawled, "you just ordered me not to lie out of it, you know. Leander asked me right up and down if I wouldn't enlist if I was in his position. Naturally, I said I would."

"Yes, you did. And you knew all the time how I felt about it, you SNEAK."

Jed's foot slowly sank to the floor and just as slowly he hoisted himself from the chair.

"Phin," he said, with deliberate mildness, "is there anything else you'd like to ask me? 'Cause if there isn't, maybe you'd better run along."

"You sneakin' coward!"

"Er—er—now—now, Phin, you didn't understand. I said 'ask' me, not 'call' me."

"No, I didn't come here to ask you anything. I came here and waited here so's to be able to tell you somethin'. And that is that I know now that you're responsible for my son—my only boy, the boy I'd depended on—and—and—"

The fierce little man was, for the moment, close to breaking down. Jed's heart softened; he felt almost conscience-stricken.

"I'm sorry for you, Phineas," he said. "I know how hard it must be for you. Leander realized it, too. He—"

"Shut up! Shavin's, you listen to me. I don't forget. All my life I've never forgot. And I ain't never missed gettin' square. I can wait, just as I waited here in the dark over an hour so's to say this to you. I'll get square with you just as I'll get square with Sam Hunniwell. . . . That's all. . . . That's all. . . . DAMN YOU!"

He stamped from the room and Jed heard him stumbling through the littered darkness of the shops on his way to the front door, kicking at the obstacles he tripped over and swearing and sobbing as he went. It was ridiculous enough, of course, but Jed did not feel like smiling. The bitterness of the little man's final curse was not humorous. Neither was the heartbreak in his tone when he spoke of his boy. Jed felt no self-reproach; he had advised Leander just as he might have advised his own son had his life been like other men's lives, normal men who had married and possessed sons. He had no sympathy for Phineas Babbitt's vindictive hatred of all those more fortunate than he or who opposed him, or for his silly and selfish ideas concerning the war. But he did pity him; he pitied him profoundly.

Babbitt had left the front door open in his emotional departure and Jed followed to close it. Before doing so he stepped out into the yard.

It was pitch dark now and still. He could hear the footsteps of his recent visitor pounding up the road, and the splashy grumble of the surf on the bar was unusually audible. He stood for a moment looking up at the black sky, with the few stars shining between the cloud blotches. Then he turned and looked at the little house next door.

The windows of the sitting-room were alight and the shades drawn. At one window he saw Charles Phillips' silhouette; he was reading, apparently. Across the other shade Ruth's dainty profile came and went. Jed looked and looked. He saw her turn and speak to some one. Then another shadow crossed the window, the shadow of Major Grover. Evidently the major had not gone home at once as he had told Jed he intended doing, plainly he had been persuaded to enter the Armstrong house and make Charlie and his sister a short call. This was Jed's estimate of the situation, his sole speculation concerning it and its probabilities.

And yet Mr. Gabe Bearse, had he seen the major's shadow upon the Armstrong window curtain, might have speculated much.

CHAPTER XV

The pity which Jed felt for Phineas Babbitt caused him to keep silent concerning his Thanksgiving evening interview with the hardware dealer. At first he was inclined to tell Major Grover of Babbitt's expressions concerning the war and his son's enlistment. After reflection, however, he decided not to do so. The Winslow charity was wide enough to cover a multitude of other people's sins and it covered those of Phineas. The latter was to be pitied; as to fearing him, as a consequence of his threat to "get square," Jed never thought of such a thing. If he felt any anxiety at all in the matter it was a trifling uneasiness because his friends, the Hunniwells and the Armstrongs, were included in the threat. But he was inclined to consider Mr. Babbitt's wrath as he had once estimated the speech of a certain Ostable candidate for political office, to be "like a tumbler of plain sody water, mostly fizz and froth and nothin' very substantial or fillin'." He did not tell Grover of the interview in the shop; he told no one, not even Ruth Armstrong.

The—to him, at least—delightful friendship and intimacy between himself and his friends and tenants continued. He and Charlie Phillips came to know each other better and better. Charles was now almost as confidential concerning his personal affairs as his sister had been and continued to be.

"It's surprising how I come in here and tell you all my private business, Jed," he said, laughing. "I don't go about shouting my joys and troubles in everybody's ear like this. Why do I do it to you?"

Jed stopped a dismal whistle in the middle of a bar.

"W-e-e-ll," he drawled, "I don't know. When I was a young-one I used to like to holler out back of Uncle Laban Ryder's barn so's to hear the echo. When you say so and so, Charlie, I generally agree with you. Maybe you come here to get an echo; eh?"

Phillips laughed. "You're not fair to yourself," he said. "I generally find when the echo in here says no after I've said yes it pays me to pay attention to it. Sis says the same thing about you, Jed."

Jed made no comment, but his eyes shone. Charles went on.

"Don't you get tired of hearing the story of my life?" he asked. "I—"

He stopped short and the smile faded from his lips. Jed knew why. The story of his life was just what he had not told, what he could not tell.

As January slid icily into February Mr. Gabriel Bearse became an unusually busy person. There were so many things to talk about. Among these was one morsel which Gabe rolled succulently beneath his tongue. Charles Phillips, "'cordin' to everybody's tell," was keeping company with Maud Hunniwell.

"There ain't no doubt of it," declared Mr. Bearse. "All hands is talkin' about it. Looks's if Cap'n Sam would have a son-in-law on his hands pretty soon. How do you cal'late he'd like the idea, Shavin's?"

Jed squinted along the edge of the board he was planing. He made no reply. Gabe tried again.

"How do you cal'late Cap'n Sam'll like the notion of his pet daughter takin' up with another man?" he queried. Jed was still mute. His caller lost patience.

"Say, what ails you?" he demanded. "Can't you say nothin'?"

Mr. Winslow put down the board and took up another.

"Ye-es," he drawled.

"Then why don't you, for thunder sakes?"

"Eh? . . . Um. . . Oh, I did."

"Did what?"

"Say nothin'."

"Oh, you divilish idiot! Stop tryin' to be funny. I asked you how you thought Cap'n Sam would take the notion of Maud's havin' a steady beau? She's had a good many after her, but looks as if she was stuck on this one for keeps."

Jed sighed and looked over his spectacles at Mr. Bearse. The latter grew uneasy under the scrutiny.

"What in time are you lookin' at me like that for?" he asked, pettishly.

The windmill maker sighed again. "Why—er—Gab," he drawled, "I was just thinkin' likely YOU might be stuck for keeps."

"Eh? Stuck? What are you talkin' about?"

"Stuck on that box you're sittin' on. I had the glue pot standin' on that box just afore you came in and . . . er . . . it leaks consider'ble."

Mr. Bearse raspingly separated his nether garment from the top of the box and departed, expressing profane opinions. Jed's lips twitched for an instant, then he puckered them and began to whistle.

But, although he had refused to discuss the matter with Gabriel Bearse, he realized that there was a strong element of probability in the latter's surmise. It certainly did look as if the spoiled daughter of Orham's bank president had lost her heart to her father's newest employee. Maud had had many admirers; some very earnest and lovelorn swains had hopefully climbed the Hunniwell front steps only to sorrowfully descend them again. Miss Melissa Busteed and other local scandal scavengers had tartly classified the young lady as the "worst little flirt on the whole Cape," which was not true. But Maud was pretty and vivacious and she was not averse to the society and adoration of the male sex in general, although she had never until now shown symptoms of preference for an individual. But Charlie Phillips had come and seen and, judging by appearances, conquered.

Since the Thanksgiving dinner the young man had been a frequent visitor at the Hunniwell home. Maud was musical, she played well and had a pleasing voice. Charles' baritone was unusually good. So on many evenings Captain Sam's front parlor rang with melody, while the captain smoked in the big rocker and listened admiringly and gazed dotingly. At the moving-picture theater on Wednesday and Saturday evenings Orham nudged and winked when two Hunniwells and a Phillips came down the aisle. Even at the Congregational church, where Maud sang in the choir, the young bank clerk was beginning to be a fairly constant attendant. Captain Eri Hedge declared that that settled it.

"When a young feller who ain't been to meetin' for land knows how long," observed Captain Eri, "all of a sudden begins showin' up every Sunday reg'lar as clockwork, you can make up your mind it's owin' to one of two reasons—either he's got religion or a girl. In this case there ain't any revival in town, so—"

And the captain waved his hand.

Jed was not blind and he had seen, perhaps sooner than any one else, the possibilities in the case. And what he saw distressed him greatly. Captain Sam Hunniwell was his life-long friend. Maud had been his pet since her babyhood; she and he had had many confidential chats together, over troubles at school, over petty disagreements with her father, over all sorts of minor troubles and joys. Captain Sam had mentioned to him, more than once, the probability of his daughter's falling in love and marrying some time or other, but they both had treated the idea as vague and far off, almost as a joke.

And now it was no longer far off, the falling in love at least. And as for its being a joke—Jed shuddered at the thought. He was very fond of Charlie Phillips; he had made up his mind at first to like him because he was Ruth's brother, but now he liked him for himself. And, had things been other than as they were, he could think of no one to whom he had rather see Maud Hunniwell married. In fact, had Captain Hunniwell known the young man's record, of his slip and its punishment, Jed would have been quite content to see the latter become Maud's husband. A term in prison, especially when, as in this case, he believed it to be an unwarranted punishment, would have counted for nothing in the unworldly mind of the windmill maker. But Captain Sam did not know. He was tremendously proud of his daughter; in his estimation no man would have been quite good enough for her. What would he say when he learned? What would Maud say when she learned? for it was almost certain that Charles had not told her. These were some of the questions which weighed upon the simple soul of Jedidah Edgar Wilfred Winslow.

And heavier still there weighed the thought of Ruth Armstrong. He had given her his word not to mention her brother's secret to a soul, not even to him. And yet, some day or other, as sure and certain as the daily flowing and ebbing of the tides, that secret would become known. Some day Captain Sam Hunniwell would learn it; some day Maud would learn it. Better, far better, that they learned it before marriage, or even before the public announcement of their engagement—always provided there was to be such an engagement. In fact, were it not for Ruth herself, no consideration for Charles' feelings would have prevented Jed's taking the matter up with the young man and warning him that, unless he made a clean breast to the captain and Maud, he—Jed— would do it for him. The happiness of two such friends should not be jeopardized if he could prevent it.

But there was Ruth. She, not her brother, was primarily responsible for obtaining for him the bank position and obtaining it under fake pretenses. And she, according to her own confession to Jed, had urged upon Charles the importance of telling no one. Jed himself would have known nothing, would have had only a vague, indefinite suspicion, had she not taken him into her confidence. And to him that confidence was precious, sacred. If Charlie's secret became known, it was not he alone who would suffer; Ruth, too, would be disgraced. She and Babbie might have to leave Orham, might have to go out of his life forever.

No wonder that, as the days passed, and Gabe Bearse's comments and those of Captain Eri Hedge were echoed and reasserted by the majority of Orham tongues, Jed Winslow's worry and foreboding increased. He watched Charlie Phillips go whistling out of the yard after supper, and sighed as he saw him turn up the road in the direction of the Hunniwell home. He watched Maud's face when he met her and, although the young lady was in better spirits and prettier than he had ever seen her, these very facts made him miserable, because he accepted them as proofs that the situation was as he feared. He watched Ruth's face also and there, too, he saw, or fancied that he saw, a growing anxiety. She had been very well; her spirits, like Maud's, had been light; she had seemed younger and so much happier than when he and she first met. The little Winslow house was no longer so quiet, with no sound of voices except those of Barbara and her mother. There were Red Cross sewing meetings there occasionally, and callers came. Major Grover was one of the latter. The major's errands in Orham were more numerous than they had been, and his trips thither much more frequent, in consequence. And whenever he came he made it a point to drop in, usually at the windmill shop first, and then upon Babbie at the house. Sometimes he brought her home from school in his car. He told Jed that he had taken a great fancy to the little girl and could not bear to miss an opportunity of seeing her. Which statement Jed, of course, accepted wholeheartedly.

But Jed was sure that Ruth had been anxious and troubled of late and he believed the reason to be that which troubled him. He hoped she might speak to him concerning her brother. He would have liked to broach the subject himself, but feared she might consider him interfering.

One day—it was in late February, the ground was covered with snow and a keen wind was blowing in over a sea gray-green and splashed thickly with white—Jed was busy at his turning lathe when Charlie came into the shop. Business at the bank was not heavy in mid- winter and, although it was but little after three, the young man was through work for the day. He hoisted himself to his accustomed seat on the edge of the workbench and sat there, swinging his feet and watching his companion turn out the heads and trunks of a batch of wooden sailors. He was unusually silent, for him, merely nodding in response to Jed's cheerful "Hello!" and speaking but a few words in reply to a question concerning the weather. Jed, absorbed in his work and droning a hymn, apparently forgot all about his caller.

Suddenly the latter spoke.

"Jed," he said, "when you are undecided about doing or not doing a thing, how do you settle it?"

Jed looked up over his spectacles.

"Eh?" he asked. "What's that?"

"I say when you have a decision to make and your mind is about fifty-fifty on the subject, how do you decide?"

Jed's answer was absently given. "W-e-e-ll," he drawled, "I generally—er—don't."

"But suppose the time comes when you have to, what then?"

"Eh? . . . Oh, then, if 'tain't very important I usually leave it to Isaiah."

"Isaiah? Isaiah who?"

"I don't know his last name, but he's got a whole lot of first ones. That's him, up on that shelf."

He pointed to a much battered wooden figure attached to the edge of the shelf upon the wall. The figure was that of a little man holding a set of mill arms in front of him. The said mill arms were painted a robin's-egg blue, and one was tipped with black.

"That's Isaiah," continued Jed. "Hum . . . yes . . . that's him. He was the first one of his kind of contraption that I ever made and, bein' as he seemed to bring me luck, I've kept him. He's settled a good many questions for me, Isaiah has."

"Why do you call him Isaiah?"

"Eh? Oh, that's just his to-day's name. I called him Isaiah just now 'cause that was the first of the prophet names I could think of. Next time he's just as liable to be Hosea or Ezekiel or Samuel or Jeremiah. He prophesies just as well under any one of 'em, don't seem to be particular."

Charles smiled slightly—he did not appear to be in a laughing mood—and then asked: "You say he settles questions for you? How?"

"How? . . . Oh. . . . Well, you notice one end of that whirligig arm he's got is smudged with black?"

"Yes."

"That's Hosea's indicator. Suppose I've got somethin' on—on what complimentary folks like you would call my mind. Suppose, same as 'twas yesterday mornin', I was tryin' to decide whether or not I'd have a piece of steak for supper. I gave—er—Elisha's whirlagig here a spin and when the black end stopped 'twas p'intin' straight up. That meant yes. If it had p'inted down, 'twould have meant no."

"Suppose it had pointed across—half way between yes and no?"

"That would have meant that—er—what's-his-name—er—Deuteronomy there didn't know any more than I did about it."

Shavings: A Novel | 193

This time Phillips did laugh. "So you had the steak," he observed.

Jed's lip twitched. "I bought it," he drawled. "I got so far all accordin' to prophecy. And I put it on a plate out in the back room where 'twas cold, intendin' to cook it when supper time came."

"Well, didn't you?"

"No-o; you see, 'twas otherwise provided. That everlastin' Cherub tomcat of Taylor's must have sneaked in with the boy when he brought the order from the store. When I shut the steak up in the back room I—er—er—hum...."

"You did what?"

"Eh? ... Oh, I shut the cat up with it. I guess likely that's the end of the yarn, ain't it?"

"Pretty nearly, I should say. What did you do to the cat?"

"Hum.... Why, I let him go. He's a good enough cat, 'cordin' to his lights, I guess. It must have been a treat to him; I doubt if he gets much steak at home.... Well, do you want to give Isaiah a whirl on that decision you say you've got to make?"

Charles gave him a quick glance. "I didn't say I had one to make," he replied. "I asked how you settled such a question, that's all."

"Um. . . . I see. . . . I see. Well, the prophet's at your disposal. Help yourself."

The young fellow shook his head. "I'm afraid it wouldn't be very satisfactory," he said. "He might say no when I wanted him to say yes, you see."

"Um-hm. . . . He's liable to do that. When he does it to me I keep on spinnin' him till we agree, that's all."

Phillips made no comment on this illuminating statement and there was another interval of silence, broken only by the hum and rasp of the turning lathe. Then he spoke again.

"Jed," he said, "seriously now, when a big question comes up to you, and you've got to answer it one way or the other, how do you settle with yourself which way to answer?"

Jed sighed. "That's easy, Charlie," he declared. "There don't any big questions ever come up to me. I ain't the kind of feller the big things come to."

Charles grunted, impatiently. "Oh, well, admitting all that," he said, "you must have to face questions that are big to you, that seem big, anyhow."

Jed could not help wincing, just a little. The matter-of-fact way in which his companion accepted the estimate of his insignificance was humiliating. Jed did not blame him, it was true, of course, but the truth hurt—a little. He was ashamed of himself for feeling the hurt.

"Oh," he drawled, "I do have some things—little no-account things—to decide every once in a while. Sometimes they bother me, too— although they probably wouldn't anybody with a head instead of a Hubbard squash on his shoulders. The only way I can decide 'em is to set down and open court, put 'em on trial, as you might say."

"What do you mean?"

"Why, I call in witnesses for both sides, seems so. Here's the reasons why I ought to tell; here's the reasons why I shouldn't. I—"

"Tell? Ought to TELL? What makes you say that? What have YOU got to tell?"

He was glaring at the windmill maker with frightened eyes. Jed knew as well as if it had been painted on the shop wall before him the question in the boy's mind, the momentous decision he was trying to make. And he pitied him from the bottom of his heart.

"Tell?" he repeated. "Did I say tell? Well, if I did 'twas just a—er—figger of speech, as the book fellers talk about. But the only way to decide a thing, as it seems to me, is to try and figger out what's the RIGHT of it, and then do that."

Phillips looked gloomily at the floor. "And that's such an easy job," he observed, with sarcasm.

"The figgerin' or the doin'?"

"Oh, the doing; the figuring is usually easy enough—too easy. But the doing is different. The average fellow is afraid. I don't suppose you would be, Jed. I can imagine you doing almost anything if you thought it was right, and hang the consequences."

Jed looked aghast. "Who? Me?" he queried. "Good land of love, don't talk that way, Charlie! I'm the scarest critter that lives and the weakest-kneed, too, 'most generally. But—but, all the same, I do believe the best thing, and the easiest in the end, not only for you—or me—but for all hands, is to take the bull by the horns and heave the critter, if you can. There may be an awful big trouble, but big or little it'll be over and done with. THAT bull won't be hangin' around all your life and sneakin' up astern to get you—and those you—er—care for. . . . Mercy me, how I do preach! They'll be callin' me to the Baptist pulpit, if I don't look out. I understand they're candidatin'."

His friend drew a long breath. "There is a poem that I used to read, or hear some one read," he observed, "that fills the bill for any one with your point of view, I should say. Something about a fellow's not being afraid to put all his money on one horse, or the last card—about his not deserving anything if he isn't afraid to risk everything. Wish I could remember it."

Jed looked up from the lathe.

"'He either fears his fate too much,
Or his deserts are small,
Who dares not put it to the touch
To win or lose it all.'

That's somethin' like it, ain't it, Charlie?" he asked.

Phillips was amazed. "Well, I declare, Winslow," he exclaimed, "you beat me! I can't place you at all. Whoever would have accused you of reading poetry—and quoting it."

Jed rubbed his chin. "I don't know much, of course," he said, "but there's consider'ble many poetry books up to the library and I like to read 'em sometimes. You're liable to run across a—er—poem— well, like this one, for instance—that kind of gets hold of you. It fills the bill, you might say, as nothin' else does. There's another one that's better still. About—

'Once to every man and nation
Comes the moment to decide.

Do you know that one?"

His visitor did not answer. After a moment he swung himself from the workbench and turned toward the door.

"'He either fears his fate too much,'" he quoted, gloomily. "Humph! I wonder if it ever occurred to that chap that there might be certain kinds of fate that COULDN'T be feared too much? . . . Well, so long, Jed. Ah hum, you don't know where I can get hold of some money, do you?"

Jed was surprised. "Humph!" he grunted. "I should say you HAD hold of money two-thirds of every day. Feller that works in a bank is supposed to handle some cash."

"Yes, of course," with an impatient laugh, "but that is somebody else's money, not mine. I want to get some of my own."

"Sho! . . . Well, I cal'late I could let you have ten or twenty dollars right now, if that would be any help to you."

"It wouldn't; thank you just the same. If it was five hundred instead of ten, why—perhaps I shouldn't say no."

Jed was startled.

"Five hundred?" he repeated. "Five hundred dollars? Do you need all that so very bad, Charlie?"

Phillips, his foot upon the threshold of the outer shop, turned and looked at him.

"The way I feel now I'd do almost anything to get it," he said, and went out.

Jed told no one of this conversation, although his friend's parting remark troubled and puzzled him. In fact it troubled him so much that at a subsequent meeting with Charles he hinted to the latter that he should be glad to lend the five hundred himself.

"I ought to have that and some more in the bank," he said. "Sam would know whether I had or not. . . . Eh? Why, and you would, too, of course. I forgot you know as much about folks' bank accounts as anybody. . . . More'n some of 'em do themselves, bashfulness stoppin' me from namin' any names," he added.

Charles looked at him. "Do you mean to tell me, Jed Winslow," he said, "that you would lend me five hundred dollars without any security or without knowing in the least what I wanted it for?"

"Why—why, of course. 'Twouldn't be any of my business what you wanted it for, would it?"

"Humph! Have you done much lending of that kind?"

"Eh? . . . Um. . . . Well, I used to do consider'ble, but Sam he kind of put his foot down and said I shouldn't do any more. But I don't HAVE to mind him, you know, although I generally do because it's easier—and less noisy," he added, with a twinkle in his eye.

"Well, you ought to mind him; he's dead right, of course. You're a good fellow, Jed, but you need a guardian."

Jed shook his head sadly. "I hate to be so unpolite as to call your attention to it," he drawled, "but I've heard somethin' like that afore. Up to now I ain't found any guardian that needs me, that's the trouble. And if I want to lend you five hundred dollars, Charlie, I'm goin' to. Oh, I'm a divil of a feller when I set out to be, desperate and reckless, I am."

Shavings: A Novel | 197

Charlie laughed, but he put his hand on Jed's shoulder, "You're a brick, I know that," he said, "and I'm a million times obliged to you. But I was only joking; I don't need any five hundred."

"Eh? . . . You don't? . . . Why, you said—"

"Oh, I—er—need some new clothes and things and I was talking foolishness, that's all. Don't you worry about me, Jed; I'm all right."

But Jed did worry, a little, although his worry concerning the young man's need of money was so far overshadowed by the anxiety caused by his falling in love with Maud Hunniwell that it was almost forgotten. That situation was still as tense as ever. Two-thirds of Orham, so it seemed to Jed, was talking about it, wondering when the engagement would be announced and speculating, as Gabe Bearse had done, on Captain Sam's reception of the news. The principals, Maud and Charles, did not speak of it, of course— neither did the captain or Ruth Armstrong. Jed expected Ruth to speak; he was certain she understood the situation and realized its danger; she appeared to him anxious and very nervous. It was to him, and to him alone—her brother excepted—she could speak, but the days passed and she did not. And it was Captain Hunniwell who spoke first.

CHAPTER XVI

Captain Sam entered the windmill shop about two o'clock one windy afternoon in the first week of March. He was wearing a heavy fur overcoat and a motoring cap. He pulled off the coat, threw it over a pile of boards and sat down.

"Whew!" he exclaimed. "It's blowing hard enough to start the bark on a log."

Jed looked up.

"Did you say log or dog?" he asked, solemnly.

The captain grinned. "I said log," he answered. "This gale of wind would blow a dog away, bark and all. Whew! I'm all out of breath. It's some consider'ble of a drive over from Wapatomac. Comin' across that stretch of marsh road by West Ostable I didn't know but the little flivver would turn herself into a flyin'- machine and go up."

Jed stopped in the middle of the first note of a hymn.

"What in the world sent you autoin' way over to Wapatomac and back this day?" he asked.

His friend bit the end from a cigar. "Oh, diggin' up the root of all evil," he said. "I had to collect a note that was due over there."

"Humph! I don't know much about such things, but I never mistrusted 'twas necessary for you to go cruisin' like that to collect notes. Seems consider'ble like sendin' the skipper up town to buy onions for the cook. Couldn't the—the feller that owed the money send you a check?"

Captain Sam chuckled. "He could, I cal'late, but he wouldn't," he observed. "'Twas old Sylvester Sage, up to South Wapatomac, the 'cranberry king' they call him up there. He owns cranberry bogs from one end of the Cape to the other. You've heard of him, of course."

Jed rubbed his chin. "Maybe so," he drawled, "but if I have I've forgot him. The only sage I recollect is the sage tea Mother used to make me take when I had a cold sometimes. I COULDN'T forget that."

"Well, everybody but you has heard of old Sylvester. He's the biggest crank on earth."

"Hum-m. Seems 's if he and I ought to know each other. . . . But maybe he's a different kind of crank; eh?"

"He's all kinds. One of his notions is that he won't pay bills by check, if he can possibly help it. He'll travel fifty miles to pay money for a thing sooner than send a check for it. He had this note—fourteen hundred dollars 'twas—comin' due at our bank to-day and he'd sent word if we wanted the cash we must send for it 'cause his lumbago was too bad for him to travel. I wanted to see him anyhow, about a little matter of a political appointment up his way, so I decided to take the car and go myself. Well, I've just got back and I had a windy v'yage, too. And cold, don't talk!"

"Um . . . yes. . . . Get your money, did you?"

"Yes, I got it. It's in my overcoat pocket now. I thought one spell I wasn't goin' to get it, for the old feller was mad about some one of his cranberry buyers failin' up on him and he was as cross-grained as a scrub oak root. He and I had a regular row over the matter of politics I went there to see him about 'special. I told him what he was and he told me where I could go. That's how we parted. Then I came home."

"Hum. . . . You'd have had a warmer trip if you'd gone where he sent you, I presume likely. . . . Um. . . . Yes, yes. . . .

'There's a place in this chorus
For you and for me,
And the theme of it ever
And always shall be:
Hallelujah, 'tis do-ne!
I believe. . . .'

Hum! . . . I thought that paint can was full and there ain't more'n a half pint in it. I must have drunk it in my sleep, I guess. Do I look green around the mouth, Sam?"

It was just before Captain Sam's departure that he spoke of his daughter and young Phillips. He mentioned them in a most casual fashion, as he was putting on his coat to go, but Jed had a feeling that his friend had stopped at the windmill shop on purpose to discuss that very subject and that all the detail of his Wapatomac trip had been in the nature of a subterfuge to conceal this fact.

"Oh," said the captain, with somewhat elaborate carelessness, as he struggled into the heavy coat, "I don't know as I told you that the directors voted to raise Charlie's salary. Um-hm, at last Saturday's meetin' they did it. 'Twas unanimous, too. He's as smart as a whip, that young chap. We all think a heap of him."

Jed nodded, but made no comment. The captain fidgeted with a button of his coat. He turned toward the door, stopped, cleared his throat, hesitated, and then turned back again.

"Jed," he said, "has—has it seemed to you that—that he—that Charlie was—maybe—comin' to think consider'ble of—of my daughter—of Maud?"

Jed looked up, caught his eye, and looked down again. Captain Sam sighed.

"I see," he said. "You don't need to answer. I presume likely the whole town has been talkin' about it for land knows how long. It's generally the folks at home that don't notice till the last gun fires. Of course I knew he was comin' to the house a good deal and that he and Maud seemed to like each other's society, and all that. But it never struck me that—that it meant anything serious, you know—anything—anything—well, you know what I mean, Jed."

"Yes. Yes, Sam, I suppose I do."

"Yes. Well, I—I don't know why it never struck me, either. If Georgianna—if my wife had been alive, she'd have noticed, I'll bet, but I didn't. 'Twas only last evenin'; when he came to get her to go to the pictures, that it came across me, you might say, like—like a wet, cold rope's end' slappin' me in the face. I give you my word, Jed, I—I kind of shivered all over. She means—she means somethin' to me, that little girl and—and—"

He seemed to find it hard to go on. Jed leaned forward.

"I know, Sam, I know," he said. His friend nodded.

"I know you do, Jed," he said. "I don't think there's anybody else knows so well. I'm glad I've got you to talk to. I cal'late, though," he added, with a short laugh, "if some folks knew I came here to—to talk over my private affairs they'd think I was goin' soft in the head."

Jed smiled, and there was no resentment in the smile.

"They'd locate the softness in t'other head of the two, Sam," he suggested.

"I don't care where they locate it. I can talk to you about things I never mention to other folks. Guess it must be because you—you— well, I don't know, but it's so, anyhow. . . . Well, to go ahead, after the young folks had gone I sat there alone in the parlor, in the dark, tryin' to think it out. The housekeeper had gone over to her brother's, so I had the place to myself. I thought and thought and the harder I thought the lonesomer the rest of my life began to look. And yet—and yet I kept tellin' myself how selfish and foolish that was. I knew 'twas a dead sartinty she'd be gettin' married some time. You and I have laughed about it and joked about it time and again. And I've joked about it with her, too. But— but jokin's one thing and this was another.... Whew!"

He drew a hand across his forehead. Jed did not speak. After a moment the captain went on.

"Well," he said, "when she got home, and after he'd gone, I got Maud to sit on my knee, same as she's done ever since she was a little girl, and she and I had a talk. I kind of led up to the subject, as you might say, and by and by we—well, we talked it out pretty straight. She thinks an awful sight of him, Jed. There ain't any doubt about that, she as much as told me in those words, and more than told me in other ways. And he's the only one she's ever cared two straws for, she told me that. And—and—well, I think she thinks he cares for her that way, too, although of course she didn't say so. But he hasn't spoken to her yet. I don't know, but—but it seemed to me, maybe, that he might be waitin' to speak to me first. I'm his—er—boss, you know, and perhaps he may feel a little—little under obligations to me in a business way and that might make it harder for him to speak. Don't it seem to you maybe that might be it, Jed?"

Poor Jed hesitated. Then he stammered that he shouldn't be surprised. Captain Sam sighed.

"Well," he said, "if that's it, it does him credit, anyhow. I ain't goin' to be selfish in this thing, Jed. If she's goin' to have a husband—and she is, of course—I cal'late I'd rather 'twas Charlie than anybody else I've ever run across. He's smart and he'll climb pretty high, I cal'late. Our little single-sticked bankin' craft ain't goin' to be big enough for him to sail in very long. I can see that already. He'll be navigatin' a clipper one of these days. Well, that's the way I'd want it. I'm pretty ambitious for that girl of mine and I shouldn't be satisfied short of a top-notcher. And he's a GOOD feller, Jed; a straight, clean, honest and above-board young chap. That's the best of it, after all, ain't it?"

Jed's reply was almost a groan, but his friend did not notice. He put on his overcoat and turned to go.

"So, there you are," he said. "I had to talk to somebody, had to get it off my chest, and, as I just said, it seems to be easier to talk such things to you than anybody else. Now if any of the town gas engines—Gab Bearse or anybody else—comes cruisin' in here heavin' overboard questions about how I like the notion of Maud and Charlie takin' up with each other, you can tell 'em I'm tickled to death. That won't be all lie, neither. I can't say I'm happy, exactly, but Maud is and I'm goin' to make-believe be, for her sake. So long."

He went out. Jed put his elbows on the workbench and covered his face with his hands. He was still in that position when Ruth Armstrong came in. He rose hastily, but she motioned him to sit again.

"Jed," she said, "Captain Hunniwell was just here with you; I saw him go. Tell me, what was he talking about?"

Jed was confused. "Why—why, Mrs. Ruth," he stammered, "he was just talkin' about—about a note he'd been collectin', and—and such."

"Wasn't he speaking of his daughter—and—and my brother?"

This time Jed actually gasped. Ruth drew a long breath. "I knew it," she said.

"But—but, for mercy sakes, HOW did you know? Did he—?"

"No, he didn't see me at all. I was watching him from the window. But I saw his face and—" with a sudden gesture of desperation, "Oh, it wasn't that at all, Jed. It was my guilty conscience, I guess. I've been expecting him to speak to you—or me—have been dreading it every day—and now somehow I knew he had spoken. I KNEW it. What did he say, Jed?"

Jed told the substance of what Captain Sam had said. She listened. When he finished her eyes were wet.

"Oh, it is dreadful," she moaned. "I—I was so hoping she might not care for Charlie. But she does—of course she does. She couldn't help it," with a sudden odd little flash of loyalty.

Jed rubbed his chin in desperation.

"And—and Charlie?" he asked, anxiously. "Does he—"

"Yes, yes, I'm sure he does. He has never told me so, never in so many words, but I can see. I know him better than any one else in the world and I can see. I saw first, I think, on Thanksgiving Day; at least that is when I first began to suspect—to fear."

Jed nodded. "When they was at the piano together that time and Sam said somethin' about their bein' a fine-lookin' couple?" he said.

"Why, yes, that was it. Are you a mind reader, Jed?"

"No-o, I guess not. But I saw you lookin' kind of surprised and—er—well, scared for a minute. I was feelin' the same way just then, so it didn't need any mind reader to guess what had scared you."

"I see. But, oh, Jed, it is dreadful! What SHALL we do? What will become of us all? And now, when I—I had just begun to be happy, really happy."

She caught her breath in a sob. Jed instinctively stretched out his hand.

"But there," she went on, hurriedly wiping her eyes, "I mustn't do this. This is no time for me to think of myself. Jed, this mustn't go any further. He must not ask her to marry him; he must not think of such a thing."

Jed sadly shook his head. "I'm afraid you're right," he said. "Not as things are now he surely mustn't. But—but, Mrs. Ruth—"

"Oh, don't!" impatiently. "Don't use that silly 'Mrs.' any longer. Aren't you the—the best friend I have in the world? Do call me Ruth."

If she had been looking at his face just then she might have seen—things. But she was not looking. There was an interval of silence before he spoke.

"Well, then—er—Ruth—" he faltered.

"That's right. Go on."

"I was just goin' to ask you if you thought Charlie was cal'latin' to ask her. I ain't so sure that he is."

He told of Charles' recent visit to the windmill shop and the young man's query concerning the making of a decision. She listened anxiously.

"But don't you think that means that he was wondering whether or not he should ask her?" she said.

"No. That is, I don't think it's sartin sure it means that. I rather had the notion it might mean he was figgerin' whether or not to go straight to Sam and make a clean breast of it."

"You mean tell—tell everything?"

"Yes, all about the—the business at Middleford. I do honestly believe that's what the boy's got on his mind to do. It ain't very surprisin' that he backs and fills some before that mind's made up. See what it might mean to him: it might mean the loss of his prospects here and his place in the bank and, more'n everything else, losin' Maud. It's some decision to make. If I had to make it I— Well, I don't know."

She put her hand to her eyes. "The POOR boy," she said, under her breath. "But, Jed, DO you think that is the decision he referred to? And why hasn't he said a word to me, his own sister, about it? I'm sure he loves me."

"Sartin he does, and that's just it, as I see it. It ain't his own hopes and prospects alone that are all wrapped up in this thing, it's yours—and

Babbie's. He's troubled about what'll happen to you. That's why he hasn't asked your advice, I believe."

They were both silent for a moment. Then she said, pleadingly, "Oh, Jed, it is up to you and me, isn't it? What shall we do?"

It was the "we" in this sentence which thrilled. If she had bade him put his neck in front of the handsaw just then Jed would have obeyed, and smilingly have pulled the lever which set the machine in motion. But the question, nevertheless, was a staggerer.

"W-e-e-ll," he admitted, "I—I hardly know what to say, I will give in. To be right down honest—and the Lord knows I hate to say it— it wouldn't do for a minute to let those two young folks get engaged—to say nothin' of gettin' married—with this thing between 'em. It wouldn't be fair to her, nor to Sam—no, nor to him or you, either. You see that, don't you?" he begged. "You know I don't say it for any reason but just—just for the best interests of all hands. You know that, don't you—Ruth?"

"Of course, of course. But what then?"

"I don't really know what then. Seems to me the very first thing would be for you to speak to him, put the question right up to him, same as he's been puttin' it to himself all this time. Get him to talk it over with you. And then—well, then—"

"Yes?"

"Oh, I don't know! I declare I don't."

"Suppose he tells me he means to marry her in spite of everything? Suppose he won't listen to me at all?"

That possibility had been in Jed's mind from the beginning, but he refused to consider it.

"He will listen," he declared, stoutly. "He always has, hasn't he?"

"Yes, yes, I suppose he has. He listened to me when I persuaded him that coming here and hiding all—all that happened was the right thing to do. And now see what has come of it! And it is all my fault. Oh, I have been so selfish!"

"Sshh! sshh! You ain't; you couldn't be if you tried. And, besides, I was as much to blame as you. I agreed that 'twas the best thing to do."

"Oh," reproachfully, "how can you say that? You know you were opposed to it always. You only say it because you think it will comfort me. It isn't true."

"Eh? Now—now, don't talk so. Please don't. If you keep on talkin' that way I'll do somethin' desperate, start to make a johnny cake out of sawdust, same as I did yesterday mornin', or somethin' else crazy."

"Jed!"

"It's true, that about the johnny cake. I came pretty nigh doin' that very thing. I bought a five-pound bag of corn meal yesterday and fetched it home from the store all done up in a nice neat bundle. Comin' through the shop here I had it under my arm, and— hum—er—well, to anybody else it couldn't have happened, but, bein' Jed Shavin's Winslow, I was luggin' the thing with the top of the bag underneath. I got about abreast of the lathe there when the string came off and in less'n two thirds of a shake all I had under my arm was the bag; the meal was on the floor—what wasn't in my coat pocket and stuck to my clothes and so on. I fetched the water bucket and started to salvage what I could of the cargo. Pretty soon I had, as nigh as I could reckon it, about fourteen pound out of the five scooped up and in the bucket. I begun to think the miracle of loaves and fishes was comin' to pass again. I was some shy on fish, but I was makin' up on loaves. Then I sort of looked matters over and found what I had in the bucket was about one pound of meal to seven of sawdust. Then I gave it up. Seemed to me the stuff might be more fillin' than nourishin'."

Ruth smiled faintly. Then she shook her head.

"Oh, Jed," she said, "you're as transparent as a windowpane. Thank you, though. If anything could cheer me up and help me to forget I think you could."

Jed looked repentant. "I'd no business to tell you all that rigamarole," he said. "I'm sorry. I'm always doin' the wrong thing, seems so. But," he added, earnestly, "I don't want you to worry too much about your brother—er—Ruth. It's goin' to come out all right, I know it. God won't let it come out any other way."

She had never heard him speak in just that way before and she looked at him in surprise.

"And yet God permits many things that seem entirely wrong to us humans," she said.

"I know. Things like the Kaiser, for instance. Well, never mind; this one's goin' to come out all right. I feel it in my bones. And," with a return of his whimsical drawl, "I may be short on brains, but a blind man could see they never skimped me when they passed out the bones."

She looked at him a moment. Then, suddenly leaning forward, she put her hand upon his big red one as it lay upon the bench.

"Jed," she said, earnestly, "what should I do without you? You are my one present help in time of trouble. I wonder if you know what you have come to mean to me."

It was an impulsive speech, made from the heart, and without thought of phrasing or that any meaning other than that intended could be read into it. A moment later, and without waiting for an answer, she hurried from the shop.

"I must go," she said. "I shall think over your advice, Jed, and I will let you know what I decide to do. Thank you ever and ever so much."

Jed scarcely heard her. After she had gone, he sat perfectly still by the bench for a long period, gazing absently at the bare wall of the shop and thinking strange thoughts. After a time he rose and, walking into the little sitting-room, sat down beside the ugly little oak writing table he had bought at a second-hand sale and opened the upper drawer.

Weeks before, Ruth, yielding to Babbie's urgent appeal, had accompanied the latter to the studio of the local photographer and there they had been photographed, together, and separately. The results, although not artistic triumphs, being most inexpensive, had been rather successful as likenesses. Babbie had come trotting in to show Jed the proofs. A day or so later he found one of the said proofs on the shop floor where the little girl had dropped it. It happened to be a photograph of Ruth, sitting alone.

And then Jed Winslow did what was perhaps the first dishonest thing he had ever done. He put that proof in the drawer of the oak writing table and said nothing of his having found it. Later he made a wooden frame for it and covered it with glass. It faded and turned black as all proofs do, but still Jed kept it in the drawer and often, very often, opened that drawer and looked at it. Now he looked at it for a long, long time and when he rose to go back to the shop there was in his mind, along with the dream that had been there for days and weeks, for the first time the faintest dawning of a hope. Ruth's impulsive speech, hastily and unthinkingly made, was repeating itself over and over in his brain. "I wonder if you know what you have come to mean to me?" What had he come to mean to her?

An hour later, as he sat at his bench, Captain Hunniwell came banging in once more. But this time the captain looked troubled.

"Jed," he asked, anxiously, "have you found anything here since I went out?"

Jed looked up.

"Eh?" he asked, absently. "Found? What have you found, Sam?"

"I? I haven't found anything. I've lost four hundred dollars, though. You haven't found it, have you?"

Still Jed did not appear to comprehend. He had been wandering the rose-bordered paths of fairyland and was not eager to come back to earth.

"Eh?" he drawled. "You've—what?"

His friend's peppery temper broke loose.

"For thunder sakes wake up!" he roared. "I tell you I've lost four hundred dollars of the fourteen hundred I told you I collected from Sylvester Sage over to Wapatomac this mornin'. I had three packages of bills, two of five hundred dollars each and one of four hundred. The two five hundred packages were in the inside pocket of my overcoat where I put 'em. But the four hundred one's gone. What I want to know is, did it drop out when I took off my coat here in the shop? Do you get that through your head, finally?"

It had gotten through. Jed now looked as troubled as his friend. He rose hastily and went over to the pile of boards upon which Captain Sam had thrown his coat upon entering the shop on his previous visit that day. Together they searched, painstakingly and at length. The captain was the first to give up.

"'Tain't here," he snapped. "I didn't think 'twas. Where in time is it? That's what I want to know."

Jed rubbed his chin.

"Are you sure you had it when you left Wapatomac?" he asked.

"Sure? No, I ain't sure of anything. But I'd have sworn I did. The money was on the table along with my hat and gloves. I picked it up and shoved it in my overcoat pocket. And that was a darned careless place to put it, too," he added, testily. "I'd have given any feller that worked for me the devil for doin' such a thing."

Jed nodded, sympathetically. "But you might have left it there to Sylvester's," he said. "Have you thought of telephonin' to find out?"

"Have I thought? Tut, tut, tut! Do you think I've got a head like a six-year-old young-one—or you? Course I've thought—and 'phoned, too. But it didn't do me any good. Sylvester's house is shut up and the old man's gone to Boston, so the postmaster told me when I 'phoned and asked him. Won't be back for a couple of days, anyhow. I remember he told me he was goin'!"

"Sho, sho! that's too bad."

"Bad enough, but I don't think it makes any real difference. I swear I had that money when I left Sage's. I came in here and then I went straight to the bank."

"And after you got there?"

"Oh, when I got there I found no less than three men, not countin' old Mrs. Emmeline Bartlett, in my room waitin' to see me. Nellie Hall—my typewriter, you know—she knew where I'd been and what a crank old Sage is and she says: 'Did you get the money, Cap'n?' And I says: 'Yes, it's in my overcoat pocket this minute.' Then I hurried in to 'tend to the folks that was waitin' for me. 'Twas an hour later afore I went to my coat to get the cash. Then, as I say, all I could find was the two five hundred packages. The four hundred one was gone."

"Sho, sho! Tut, tut, tut! Where did you put the coat when you took it off?"

"On the hook in the clothes closet where I always put it."

"Hum-m! And—er—when you told Nellie about it did you speak loud?"

"Loud? No louder'n I ever do."

"Well—er—that ain't a—er—whisper, Sam, exactly."

"Don't make any difference. There wasn't anybody outside the railin' that minute to hear if I'd bellered like a bull of Bashan. There was nobody in the bank, I tell you, except the three men and old Aunt Emmeline and they were waitin' in my private room. And except for Nellie and Eddie Ellis, the messenger, and Charlie Phillips, there wan't a soul around, as it happened. The money hasn't been stolen; I lost it somewheres—but where? Well, I can't stop here any longer. I'm goin' back to the bank to have another hunt."

He banged out again. Fortunately he did not look at his friend's face before he went. For that face had a singular expression upon it. Jed sat heavily down in the chair by the bench. A vivid recollection of a recent remark made in that very shop had suddenly come to him. Charlie Phillips had made it in answer to a question of his own. Charlie had declared that he would do almost anything to get five hundred dollars.

CHAPTER XVII

The next morning found Jed heavy-eyed and without appetite, going through the form of preparing breakfast. All night, with the exception of an hour or two, he had tossed on his bed alternately fearing the worst and telling himself that his fears were groundless. Of course Charlie Phillips had not stolen the four hundred dollars. Had not he, Jed Winslow, loudly proclaimed to Ruth Armstrong that he knew her brother to be a fine young man, one who had been imprudent, it is true, but much more sinned against than sinning and who would henceforth, so he was willing to swear, be absolutely upright and honest? Of course the fact that a sum of money was missing from the Orham National Bank, where Phillips was employed, did not necessarily imply that the latter had taken it.

Not necessarily, that was true; but Charlie had, in Jed's presence, expressed himself as needing money, a sum approximately that which was missing; and he had added that he would do almost anything to get it. And—there was no use telling oneself that the fact had no bearing on the case, because it would bear heavily with any unprejudiced person—Charlie's record was against him. Jed loyally told himself over and over again that the boy was innocent, he KNEW he was innocent. But— The dreadful "but" came back again and again to torment him.

All that day he went about in an alternate state of dread and hope. Hope that the missing four hundred might be found, dread of—many possibilities. Twice he stopped at the bank to ask Captain Sam concerning it. The second time the captain was a trifle impatient.

"Gracious king, Jed," he snapped. "What's the matter with you? 'Tain't a million. This institution'll probably keep afloat even if it never turns up. And 'twill turn up sooner or later; it's bound to. There's a chance that I left it at old Sage's. Soon's the old cuss gets back and I can catch him by telephone I'll find out. Meanwhile I ain't worryin' and I don't know why you should. The main thing is not to let anybody know anything's missin'. Once let the news get out 'twill grow to a hundred thousand afore night. There'll be a run on us if Gab Bearse or Melissa Busteed get goin' with their throttles open. So don't you whisper a word to anybody, Jed. We'll find it pretty soon."

And Jed did not whisper a word. But he anxiously watched the inmates of the little house, watched Charles' face when he came home after working hours, watched the face of his sister as she went forth on a marketing expedition, even scrutinized Babbie's laughing countenance as she came dancing into the shop, swinging Petunia by one arm. And it was from Babbie he first learned that, in spite of all Captain Hunniwell's precautions, some one had dropped a hint. It may as well be recorded here that the identity of that some one was never clearly established. There were suspicions, centering about the bank messenger, but he stoutly denied having told a living soul.

Barbara, who was on her way home from school, and had rescued the long-suffering Petunia from the front fence where she had been left suspended on a picket to await her parent's return, was bubbling over with news and giggles.

"Oh, Uncle Jed," she demanded, jumping up to perch panting upon a stack of the front elevations of birdhouses, "isn't Mr. Gabe Bearse awfully funny?"

Jed sighed. "Yes," he said, "Gabe's as funny as a jumpin' toothache."

The young lady regarded him doubtfully. "I see," she said, after a moment, "you're joking again. I wish you'd tell me when you're going to do it, so Petunia and I would know for sure."

"All right, I'll try not to forget to remember. But how did you guess I was jokin' this time?"

"'Cause you just had to be. A jumping toothache isn't funny. I had one once and it made me almost sick."

"Um-hm. W-e-e-ll, Gabe Bearse makes 'most everybody sick. What set you thinkin' about him?"

"'Cause I just met him on the way home and he acted so funny. First he gave me a stick of candy."

Mr. Winslow leaned back in his chair.

"What?" he cried. "He gave you a stick of candy? GAVE it to you?"

"Yes. He said: 'Here, little girl, don't you like candy?' And when I said I did he gave me a stick, the striped peppermint kind it was. I'd have saved a bite for you, Uncle Jed, only I and the rest ate it all before I remembered. I'm awfully sorry."

"That's all right. Striped candy don't agree with me very well, anyway; I'm liable to swallow the stripes crossways, I guess likely. But tell me, did Gabe look wild or out of his head when he gave it to you?"

"Why, no. He just looked—oh—oh, you know, Uncle Jed—MYSter'ous—that's how he looked, MYSter'ous."

"Hum! Well, I'm glad to know he wan't crazy. I've known him a good many years and this is the first time I ever knew him to GIVE anybody anything worth while. When I went to school with him he gave me the measles, I remember, but even then they was only imitation—the German kind. And now he's givin' away candy: Tut, tut! No wonder he looked—what was it?—mysterious. . . . Hum. . . . Well, he wanted somethin' for it, didn't he? What was it?"

"Why, he just wanted to know if I'd heard Uncle Charlie say anything about a lot of money being gone up to the bank. He said he had heard it was ever and ever so much—a hundred hundred dollars—or a thousand dollars, or something—I don't precactly remember, but it was a great, big lot. And he wanted to know if Uncle Charlie had said how much it was and what had become of it and—and everything. When I said Uncle Charlie hadn't said a word he looked so sort of disappointed and funny that it made me laugh."

It did not make Jed laugh. The thought that the knowledge of the missing money had leaked out and was being industriously spread abroad by Bearse and his like was very disquieting. He watched Phillips more closely than before. He watched Ruth, and, before another day had passed, he had devised a wonderful plan, a plan to be carried out in case of alarming eventualities.

On the afternoon of the third day he sat before his workbench, his knee clasped between his hands, his foot swinging, and his thoughts busy with the situation in all its alarming phases. It had been bad enough before this new development, bad enough when the always present danger of Phillips' secret being discovered had become complicated by his falling in love with his employer's daughter. But now— Suppose the boy had stolen the money? Suppose he was being blackmailed by some one whom he must pay or face exposure? Jed had read of such things; they happened often enough in novels.

He did not hear the door of the outer shop open. A month or more ago he had removed the bell from the door. His excuse for so doing had been characteristic.

"I can't stand the wear and tear on my morals," he told Ruth. "I ain't sold anything, except through the mail, since the winter really set in. And yet every time that bell rings I find myself jumpin' up and runnin' to wait on a customer. When it turns out to be Gabe Bearse or somebody like him I swear, and swearin' to me is like whiskey to some folks—comfortin' but demoralizin'."

So the bell having been removed, Jed did not hear the person who came into and through the outer shop. The first sign of that person's presence which reached his ears was an unpleasant chuckle. He turned, to see Mr. Phineas Babbitt standing in the doorway of the inner room. And—this was the most annoying and disturbing fact connected with the sight—the hardware dealer was not scowling, he was laughing. The Winslow foot fell to the floor with a thump and its owner sat up straight.

"He, he, he!" chuckled Phineas. Jed regarded him silently. Babbitt's chuckle subsided into a grin. Then he spoke.

"Well," he observed, with sarcastic politeness, "how's the great Shavin's Jedidah, the famous inventor of whirlagigs? He, he, he!"

Jed slowly shook his head. "Phin," he said, "either you wear rubbers or I'm gettin' deaf, one or the other. How in the world did you get in here this time without my hearin' you?"

Phineas ignored the question. He asked one of his own. "How's the only original high and mighty patriot this afternoon?" he sneered.

The Winslow hand caressed the Winslow chin.

"If you mean me, Phin," drawled Jed, "I'm able to sit up and take nourishment, thank you. I judge you must be kind of ailin', though. Take a seat, won't you?"

"No, I won't. I've got other fish to fry, bigger fish than you, at that"

"Um-hm. Well, they wouldn't have to be sperm whales to beat me, Phin. Be kind of hard to fry 'em if they was too big, wouldn't it?"

"They're goin' to fry, you hear me. Yes, and they're goin' to sizzle. He, he, he!"

Mr. Winslow sadly shook his head. "You must be awful sick, Phin," he drawled. "That's the third or fourth time you've laughed since you came in here."

His visitor stopped chuckling and scowled instead. Jed beamed gratification.

"That's it," he said. "Now you look more natural. Feelin' a little better ... eh?"

The Babbitt chin beard bristled. Its wearer leaned forward.

"Shut up," he commanded. "I ain't takin' any of your sass this afternoon, Shavin's, and I ain't cal'latin' to waste much time on you, neither. You know where I'm bound now? Well, I'm bound up to the Orham National Bank to call on my dear friend Sam Hunniwell. He, he, he! I've got a little bit of news for him. He's in trouble, they tell me, and I want to help him out. . . . Blast him!"

This time Jed made no reply; but he, too, leaned forward and his gaze was fixed upon the hardware dealer's face. There was an expression upon his own face which, when Phineas saw it, caused the latter to chuckle once more.

"He, he!" he laughed. "What's the matter, Shavin's? You look kind of scared about somethin'. 'Tain't possible you've known all along what I've just found out? I wonder if you have. Have you?"

Still Jed was silent. Babbit grunted.

"It don't make any difference whether you have or not," he said. "But if you ain't I wonder what makes you look so scared. There's nothin' to be scared about, as I see. I'm just cal'latin' to do our dear old chummie, Cap'n Sam, a kindness, that's all. He's lost some money up there to the bank, I understand. Some says it's four thousand dollars and some says it's forty. It don't make any difference, that part don't. Whatever 'tis it's missin' and I'm going to tell him where to find it. That's real good of me, ain't it? Ain't it, Shavin's; eh?"

The little man's malignant spite and evident triumph were actually frightening. And it was quite evident that Jed was frightened. Yet he made an effort not to appear so.

"Yes," he agreed. "Yes, yes, seems 's if 'twas. Er—er— Where is it, Phin?"

Phineas burst out laughing. "'Where is it, Phin?'" he repeated, mockingly. "By godfreys mighty, I believe you do know where 'tis, Shavin's! You ain't gettin' any of it, are you? You ain't dividin' up with the blasted jailbird?"

Jed was very pale. His voice shook as he essayed to speak.

"Wh-what jailbird?" he faltered. "What do you mean? What—what are you talkin' about, Phin?"

"'What are you talkin' about, Phin?' God sakes, hear him, will you! All right, I'll tell you what I'm talkin' about. I'm talkin' about Sam Hunniwell's pet, his new bookkeeper up there to the bank. I'm talkin' about that stuck-up, thievin' hypocrite of a Charlie Phillips, that's who I'm talkin' about.

I called him a jailbird, didn't I? Well, he is. He's served his term in the Connecticut State's prison for stealin'. And I know it."

Jed groaned aloud. Here it was at last. The single hair had parted and the sword had fallen. And now, of all times, now! He made a pitiful attempt at denial.

"It ain't so," he protested.

"Oh, yes, it is so. Six or eight weeks ago—in January 'twas— there was a drummer in my store sellin' a line of tools and he was lookin' out of the window when this Phillips cuss went by with Maud Hunniwell, both of 'em struttin' along as if common folks, honest folks, was dirt under their feet. And when this drummer see 'em he swore right out loud. 'Why,' says he, 'that's Charlie Phillips, of Middleford, ain't it?' 'His name's Phillips and he comes from Connecticut somewheres,' says I. 'I thought he was in state's prison,' says he. 'What do you mean?' says I. And then he told me. 'By godfreys,' says I, 'if you can fix it so's I can prove that's true I'll give you the biggest order you ever got in this store.' ''Twon't be any trouble to prove it,' says he. 'All you've got to do is look up his record in Middleford.' And I've looked it up. Yes, sir-ee, I've looked it up. Ho, ho!"

Jed, white and shaking, made one more attempt.

"It's all a lie," he cried. "Of course it is. Besides, if you knew so much why have you been waitin' all this time before you told it? If you found out all this—this pack of rubbish in January why did you wait till March before you told it? Humph! That's pretty thin, I—"

Phineas interrupted.

"Shut up!" he ordered. "Why did I wait? Well, now, Shavin's, seein' it's you and I love you so, I'll tell you. At first I was for runnin' right out in the street and hollerin' to all hands to come and hear the good news about Sam Hunniwell's pet. And then thinks I: 'Hold on! don't be in any hurry. There's time enough. Just wait and see what happens. A crook that steals once is liable to try it again. Let's wait and see.' And I waited, and— He, he, he!—he has tried it again. Eh, Shavin's?"

Jed was speechless. Babbitt, looking like a triumphantly vicious Bantam rooster, crowed on.

"You don't seem to be quite so sassy and talky as you was when I first came in, Shavin's," he sneered. "Guess likely YOU ain't feelin' well now . . . eh? Do you remember what I told you last time I was in this shop? I told you I'd pay my debts to you and Sam Hunniwell if I waited fifty year. Well, here's Hunniwell's pay comin' to him now. He's praised that Phillips thief from one end of Ostable county to the other, told how smart he was and how honest and good he was till—Lord A'mighty, it's enough to turn a decent man's stomach! And not only that, but here's the feller courtin' his daughter. Oh, ho, ho, ho! that's the best of the whole business. That was another thing made me hang off and wait; I wanted to see how the courtin' came along. And it's come along all right. Everybody's onto 'em, hangin' over each other, and lookin' soft at each other. She's just fairly heavin' herself at his head, all hands says so. There ain't been anybody in this town good enough for her till he showed up. And now it's comin' out that he's a crook and a jailbird! And he'll be jailed for stealin' THIS time, too. Ho, ho!"

He stopped, out of breath, to indulge in another long chuckle. Jed leaned forward.

"What are you talkin' about, Phin?" he demanded. "Even allowin' all this—this rigmarole of yours about—about Middleford business— was true—"

"It is true and you know it is. I believe you've known it all along."

"I say allowin' it is, you haven't any right to say Charlie took this money from the Orham bank. You can't prove any such thing."

"Aw, be still! Prove—prove nothin'. When a cat and a sasser of milk's shut up together and the milk's gone, you don't need proof to know where it's gone, do you? Don't talk to me about proof, Jed Winslow. Put a thief alongside of money and anybody knows what'll happen. Why, YOU know what's happened yourself. You know darn well Charlie Phillips has stole the money that's gone from the bank. Down inside you you're sartin sure of it; and I don't want any better proof of THAT than just your face, Shavin's."

This time Jed did not attempt to contradict. Instead he tried a new hazard.

"Phin," he pleaded, "don't be too hard. Just think of what'll happen if you come out with that—that wild-goose yarn of yours. Think of Maud, poor girl. You haven't got anything against her, have you?"

"Yes, I have. She's stuck-up and nose in the air and looks at me as if I was some sort of—of a bug she wouldn't want to step on for fear of mussin' up her shoes. I never did like her, blast her. But leavin' that all to one side, she's Sam Hunniwell's young-one and that's enough for me."

"But she's his only child, Phin."

"Good enough! I had a boy; he was an only child, too, you'll remember. Where is he now? Out somewheres where he don't belong, fightin' and bein' killed to help Wall Street get rich. And who sent him there? Why, Sam

Hunniwell and his gang. You're one of 'em, Jed Winslow. To hell with you, every one of you, daughters and all hands."

"But, Phin—just a minute. Think of what it'll mean to Charlie, poor young feller. It'll mean—"

"It'll mean ten years this time, and a good job, too. You poor fool, do you think you can talk me out of this? You, you sawdust- head? What do you think I came into your hole here for? I came here so's you'd know what I was goin' to do to your precious chums. I wanted to tell you and have the fun of watchin' you squirm. Well, I'm havin' the fun, plenty of it. Squirm, you Wall Street bloodsucker, squirm."

He fairly stood on tiptoe to scream the last command. To a disinterested observer the scene might have had some elements of farce comedy. Certainly Phineas, his hat fallen off and under foot, his scanty gray hair tousled and his pugnacious chin beard bristling, was funny to look at. And the idea of calling Jed Winslow a "Wall Street bloodsucker" was the cream of burlesque. But to Jed himself it was all tragedy, deep and dreadful. He made one more desperate plea.

"But, Phin," he begged, "think of his—his sister, Charlie's sister. What'll become of her and—and her little girl?"

Phineas snorted. "His sister," he sneered. "All right, I'll think about her all right. She's another stuck-up that don't speak to common folks. Who knows anything about her any more'n they did about him? Better look up her record, I guess. The boy's turned out to be a thief; maybe the sister'll turn out to be—"

"Stop! Be still!"

Jed actually shouted it. Babbitt stopped, principally because the suddenness of the interruption had startled him into doing so. But the pause was only momentary. He stared at the interrupter in enraged amazement for an instant and then demanded: "Stop? Who are you tellin' to stop?"

"You."

"I want to know! Well, I'll stop when I get good and ready and if you don't like it, Shavin's, you can lump it. That Phillips kid has turned out to be a thief and, so far as anybody 'round here knows, his sister may be—"

"Stop!" Again Jed shouted it; and this time he rose to his feet. Phineas glared at him.

"Humph!" he grunted. "You'll make me stop, I presume likely."

"Yes."

"Is that so?"

"Yes, it's got to be so. Look here, Phin, I realize you're mad and don't care much what you say, but there's a limit, you know. It's bad enough to hear you call poor Charlie names, but when you start in on Ruth—on Mrs. Armstrong, I mean—that's too much. You've got to stop."

This speech was made quietly and with all the customary Winslow deliberation and apparent calm, but there was one little slip in it and that slip Babbitt was quick to notice.

"Oh, my!" he sneered. "Ruth's what we call her, eh? Ruth! Got so chummy we call each other by our first names. Ruthie and Jeddie, I presume likely. Aw, haw, haw!"

Jed's pallor was, for the moment, succeeded by a vivid crimson. He stammered. Phineas burst into another scornful laugh.

"Haw, haw, haw!" he crowed. "She lets him call her Ruth. Oh, my Lord A'mighty! Let's Shavin's Winslow call her that. Well, I guess I sized her up all right. She must be about on her brother's level. A thief and—"

"Shut up, Phin!"

"Shut up? YOU tell me to shut up!"

"Yes."

"Well, I won't. Ruth Armstrong! What do I care for—"

The speech was not finished. Jed had taken one long stride to where Babbitt was standing, seized the furious little creature by the right arm with one hand and with the other covered his open mouth, covered not only the mouth, but a large section of face as well.

"You keep quiet, Phin," he drawled. "I want to think."

Phineas struggled frantically. He managed to get one corner of his mouth from behind that mammoth hand.

"Ruth Armstrong!" he screamed. "Ruth Armstrong is—"

The yell died away to a gurgle, pinched short by the Winslow fingers. Then the door leading to the kitchen, the door behind the pair, opened and Ruth Armstrong herself came in. She was pale and she stared with frightened eyes at the little man struggling in the tall one's clutch.

"Oh, Jed," she breathed, "what is it?"

Jed did not reply. Phineas could not.

"Oh, Jed, what is it?" repeated Ruth. "I heard him shouting my name. I was in the yard and I heard it.... Oh, Jed, what IS it?"

Babbitt at last managed to wriggle partially clear. He was crazy with rage, but he was not frightened. Fear of physical violence was not in his make-up; he was no coward.

"I'll tell you what it is," he screamed. "I'll tell you what it is: I've found out about you and that stuck-up crook of a brother of yours. He's a thief. That's what he is, a thief and a jailbird. He stole at Middleford and now he's stole again here. And Jed Winslow and you are—"

He got no further, being once more stoppered like a bottle by the Winslow grip and the Winslow hand. He wriggled and fought, but he was pinned and helpless, hands, feet and vocal organs. Jed did not so much as look at him; he looked only at Ruth.

Her pallor had increased. She was trembling.

"Oh, Jed," she cried, "what does he mean? What does he mean by—by 'again—here'?"

Jed's grip tightened over his captive's mouth.

"He doesn't mean anything," he declared, stoutly. "He don't know what he means."

From behind the smothering fingers came a defiant mumble. Ruth leaned forward.

"Jed," she begged, "does he—does he know about—about—"

Jed nodded. She closed her eyes and swayed slightly, but she did not collapse or give way.

"And he is going to tell?" she whispered.

"And he is going to tell?" she whispered.

A furious mumble from behind the fingers and a venomous flash from the Babbitt eyes were answers sufficient.

"Oh, Jed," she pleaded, "what SHALL we do?"

For the instant a bit of the old Jed came to the surface. His lip twitched grimly as he looked down at the crimson face above his own hand.

"I ain't sartin—yet," he drawled. "How do you start in killin' a—a snappin' turtle? I ain't tackled the job since I was a boy."

Phineas looked as if he could have furnished some points on the subject. His eyes were bulging. Then all three heard the door of the outer shop open.

Ruth looked desperately about her. She hastened to the door by which she had entered. "There's some one coming," she whispered.

Jed glanced over his shoulder. "You go away," he whispered in reply. "Go away, Ruth. Hurry!"

Her hand was on the latch of the door, but before she could open it the other door, that leading from the outer shop, opened and Leonard Grover came in. He stared at the picture before him—at Ruth Armstrong's pale, frightened face, at Babbitt struggling in his captor's clutch, at Jed.

"Why!" he exclaimed. "What is it?"

No one answered. Phineas was the only one who stirred. He seemed anxious to turn the tableau into a moving picture, but his success was limited. The Major turned to Ruth.

"What is it?" he asked again.

She was silent. Grover repeated his question, addressing Jed this time.

"Well?" he asked, sharply. "What is the trouble here? What has that fellow been doing?"

Jed looked down at his wriggling captive. "He's—he's—" he stammered. "Well, you see, Major, he . . . Hum . . . well, I'm afraid I can't tell you."

"You can't tell me! What on earth— Mrs. Armstrong, will you tell me?"

She looked at him appealingly, pitifully, but she shook her head.

"I—I can't," she said.

He looked from one to the other. Then, with a shrug, he turned to the door.

"Pardon me for interrupting," he observed. "Good afternoon."

It was Ruth who detained him. "Oh, please!" she cried, involuntarily. He turned again.

"You wish me to stay?" he asked.

"Oh—oh, I don't know. I—"

She had not finished the sentence; she was falteringly trying to finish it when Mr. Babbitt took the center of the stage. Once more he managed to free himself from Jed's grip and this time he darted across the shop and put the workbench between himself and his enemy.

"I'll tell you what it is," he screamed. "I've found out some things they don't want anybody to know, that's what. I've found out what sort of folks they are, she and her brother. He's a common— Let go of me! By—"

The scream ended in another mumble. Jed had swarmed over the bench and once more pinned him fast.

"You'll have to excuse me, Major," he panted. "I—I can't help it. This feller's got what ailed the parrot—he talks too darn much. He's got to stop! He's GOT to!"

But Grover was paying little attention. He was looking at Ruth.

"Mrs. Armstrong," he asked, "has he been saying—saying things he should not say about you? Is that the trouble?"

She answered without returning his look.

"Yes," she said, almost in a whisper. "About me and—and my— Yes, that was it."

The Major's eyes flashed. "Let go of him, Jed," he commanded. Jed hesitated.

"If I do he'll blow up again," he said.

"Let go of him."

Jed let go. Phineas caught his breath and opened his mouth. Major Grover stepped in front of him and leveled a forefinger straight at the crimson Babbitt nose.

"Stop!" he ordered, sharply.

"Stop? What right have you got to tell me to stop? By—"

"Stop! Listen to me. I don't know what you've been saying about this lady—"

"I ain't been saying anything, except what I know, and that is that—"

"Stop! And I don't care. But I know about you, sir, because it is my business to know. The Government has had its eye on you for some time and it has asked me to look into your record. I have looked into it. You are not a very dangerous person, Mr. Babbitt, but that is because of your lack of ability to harm, not because of any good will on your part toward the United States. You have done all the harm you could, you have talked sedition, you've written and talked against the draft, you have corresponded with German agents in Boston and New York."

"That's a lie."

"No, it's the truth. I have copies of your letters and the Government has the originals. They are not very dangerous, but that is because you are not big enough to be dangerous. The authorities have left you pretty much to my discretion, sir. It rests with me whether to have you taken in charge and held for trial or merely to warn you and watch you. Very well. I warn you now and you may be certain that you are watched. You'll stop your silly, seditious talk at once and you'll write no more letters like those I have seen. If you do it will be a prison term for you as sure as I stand here. Do you understand?"

Apparently Phineas understood. His face was not as red as it had been and there was a different look in his eye. Jed's rough handling had not frightened him, but the Major's cold, incisive tones and the threat of a term in prison had their effect. Nevertheless he could still bluster.

"You can't talk to me that way," he sputtered. "I—I ain't scared of you even if you are all dressed up in fuss and feathers like a hand-organ monkey. This is a free country."

"Yes, it is. For decent people it is absolutely free. The other sort have to be put where they can't interfere with that freedom. Whether you, Babbit, remain free or not depends entirely upon what you do—and say. Is this perfectly clear?"

Phineas did not answer the question directly. For a moment he stood there, his fists clenching and unclenching, and his eyes snapping. Then he turned away.

"All right," he said, sullenly. "I hear what you say. Now I can go, I presume likely—unless you've got some more lyin' and bullyin' to do. Get out of my way, Shavin's, you fool."

But Grover had not finished with him.

"Just a minute," he said. "There is one thing more. I don't know what it is, and I don't wish to know, but evidently you have been saying, or threatening to say, something concerning this lady, Mrs. Armstrong, which should not be said. You are not to mention her name. Do you understand that?"

The little hardware dealer almost jumped from the floor as his rage again got the better of him.

"The blazes I ain't!" he shrieked. "Who says I ain't? Is that any of your business, Mr.—Mr. Brass Monkey? What's you or the United States gov'ment got to say about my mentionin' names? To the devil with the United States and you, too! You hear that?"

Major Grover smiled. "Yes," he said, quietly. "I hear it. So does Mr. Winslow here, and Mrs. Armstrong. They can be called as witnesses if it is necessary. You had better let me finish, Babbitt. As I say, you are not to mention Mrs. Armstrong's name, you are not to repeat or circulate any scandal or story reflecting upon her character—"

"Or her brother's either," put in Jed, eagerly. "Tell him he can't talk against Charlie, either."

"Certainly. You are not to repeat or circulate anything derogatory to the character of either Mrs. Armstrong or Mr. Phillips. In any way derogatory."

Phineas tossed both fists in the air.

"You can't order me around that way," he yelled. "Besides, if you knew what I know about that gang you'd—"

"Hush! I don't want to know anything you know—or pretend to know. As for ordering you about—well, we'll see."

"I tell you you can't. You ain't got the right."

"Perhaps not. But I have the right to use my discretion—my judgment in your case. And my judgment is that if I hear one scandalous story about town reflecting upon the character of Mrs. Armstrong or her brother—yes, or her friends—I shall know who is responsible and I shall have you arrested and held for trial as an enemy of the country. You condemned the United States to the devil only a moment ago in my hearing. Do you think that would help you in court, Babbitt? I don't."

The little man's face was a sight. As Jed said afterward, he looked as if he would have enjoyed biting his way out of the shop.

"Huh!" he snarled; "I see. You're all in together, the whole lot of you. And you, you brass buttons, you're usin' your soldierin' job to keep your friends out of trouble.... Huh! Yes, that's what you're doin'."

The Major's smile was provokingly cool.

"Perhaps I am," he admitted. "But I shouldn't advise you to forget what I have just told you, Babbitt. I mean every word of it."

It was Ruth who spoke next. She uttered a startled exclamation.

"There's some one coming up the walk," she cried. "Listen."

Sure enough, heavy footsteps sounded upon the walk leading from the front gate to the shop. Jed ran to the window.

"It's Sam," he exclaimed. "Good heavens above! It's Sam Hunniwell, of all folks—now!"

Grover looked from one face to the other.

"Is there any particular reason why Captain Hunniwell shouldn't come?" he asked.

Jed and Ruth were silent. Phineas chuckled malevolently. Jed heard the chuckle and spoke.

"'Twas—'twas Cap'n Sam he was goin' to tell," he whispered, pointing at Babbitt. Ruth caught her breath with a frightened gasp.

Grover nodded. "Oh, I see," he said. "Well, I don't think he will. He'll be more—more—careful, I'm sure. Babbitt, remember."

They heard the captain rattle the latch of the front door. Ruth opened the door behind her. "I must go, Jed," she whispered. "I—I can't stay."

The Major turned. "I'll go with you, Mrs. Armstrong," he said. But Jed leaned forward.

"I—I wish you'd stay, Major Grover," he whispered. "I—I'd like to have you stay here just a minute or two."

Grover hesitated. Ruth went out, closing the living-room door after her. A moment later Captain Sam came into the workshop.

"Hello, Jed!" he hailed. "Why, hello, Major! What—" Then for the first time he saw and recognized the third member of the group. He looked at Phineas and the little man looked at him. The looks were studies in expression.

"Humph!" grunted Captain Sam. "What in time—?... Humph!... Well, Phin, you look awful glad to see me, I must say. Gracious king, man, don't glower at me like that! I haven't done anything to you, if you'd only have sense enough to believe it."

Babbitt did not answer. He looked as if he were going to burst. Major Grover was regarding him with a whimsical twinkle in his eye.

"Mr. Babbitt and I have just been discussing some points connected with the war," he observed. "I don't know that we agree, exactly, but we have—well, we have reached an understanding."

The captain was plainly puzzled. "Humph!" he grunted. "You don't say! . . . Well, I— Eh, what is it, Jed?"

If any one had been watching Jed particularly during the recent few minutes they might have observed in his face the dawning of an idea and the changing of that idea into a set purpose. The idea seemed to dawn the moment after he saw Captain Hunniwell coming up the walk. It had become a purpose by the time the captain rattled the latch. While Captain Sam and the major were speaking he had hastened to the old desk standing by the wall and was rummaging in one of the drawers. Now he came forward.

"Sam—" he began, but broke off to address Mr. Babbitt, who was striding toward the door. "Don't go, Phin," he cried. "I'd rather you didn't go just this minute. I'd like to have you stay. Please."

Phineas answered over his shoulder. The answer was a savage snarl and a command for "Shavings" to mind his own business. Grover spoke then.

"Mr. Babbitt," he suggested, "don't you think you had better stay a moment? Mr. Winslow seems to wish it."

Babbitt reached for the handle of the door, but Grover's hand was lightly laid on his shoulder.

"Do stay, Mr. Babbitt," begged the Major, sweetly. "To oblige me, you know."

Phineas swore with such vehemence that the oath might have been heard across the road. What he might have said thereafter is a question. At that moment his attention was caught by something which Jed Winslow had in his hands and he stayed to stare at it. The something was a bundle of crumpled banknotes.

CHAPTER XVIII

Jed came forward, the roll of bills in his hand. He seemed quite oblivious of the Babbitt stare, or, for that matter, of the complete silence which had so suddenly fallen upon the group in the shop. He came forward, smoothing the crumpled notes with fingers which shook a little. He stopped in front of Captain Hunniwell. The captain was gazing at him and at the money. Jed did not meet his friend's eye; he continued to smooth the banknotes. Captain Sam spoke first.

"What's that?" he demanded. "What money's that?"

Jed's fingers moved back and forth across the bills and he answered without looking up. He seemed much embarrassed.

"Sam," he faltered. "Sam—er—you remember you told me you'd—er—lost some money a spell ago? Some—er—money you'd collected over to Wapatomac. You remember that, don't you?"

Captain Sam looked at him in puzzled surprise. "Remember it?" he repeated. "Course I remember it. Gracious king, 'tain't likely I'd forget it, is it?"

Jed nodded. "No-o," he drawled, solemnly. "No, course you couldn't. 'Twas four hundred dollars you was short, wan't it?"

The Captain's puzzled look was still there.

"Yes," he replied. "What of it?"

"Why—why, just this, Sam: I—I want it to be plain, you understand. I want Major Grover and Phineas here to understand the—the whole of it. There's a lot of talk, seems so, around town about money bein' missin' from the bank—"

Captain Sam interrupted. "The deuce there is!" he exclaimed. "That's the first I've heard of any such talk. Who's talkin'?"

"Oh, a—a good many folks, I judge likely. Gabe Bearse asked Babbie about it, and Phin here he—"

"Eh?" The captain turned to face his old enemy. "So you've been talkin', have you?" he asked.

Mr. Babbitt leaned forward. "I ain't begun my talkin' yet, Sam Hunniwell," he snarled. "When I do you'll—"

He stopped. Grover had touched him on the shoulder.

"Sshh!" said the Major quietly. To the absolute amazement of Captain Sam, Phineas subsided. His face was blazing red and he seemed to be boiling inside, but he did not say another word. Jed seized the opportunity to continue.

"I—I just want to get this all plain, Sam," he put in, hastily. "I just want it so all hands'll understand it, that's all. You went over to Sylvester Sage's in Wapatomac and he paid you four hundred dollars. When you got back home here fourteen hundred of it was missin'. No, no, I don't mean that. I mean you couldn't find fourteen hundred—I mean—"

The captain's patience was, as he himself often said, moored with a short cable. The cable parted now.

"Gracious king!" he snapped. "Jed, if that yarn you're tryin' to spin was wound in a ball and a kitten was playin' with it you couldn't be worse snarled up. What he's tryin' to tell you," he explained, turning to Grover, "is that the other day, when I was over to Wapatomac, old Sylvester Sage over there paid me fourteen hundred dollars in cash and when I got back here all I could find was a thousand. That's what you're tryin' to say, ain't it?" turning to Jed once more.

"Yes—yes, that's it, Sam. That's it."

"Course it's it. But what do you want me to say it for? And what are you runnin' around with all that money in your hands for? That's what I want to know."

Jed swallowed hard. "Well, Sam," he stammered, "that—that's what I was goin' to tell you. You see—you see, that's the four hundred you lost. I—I found it."

Major Grover looked surprised. Phineas Babbitt looked more surprised. But, oddly enough, it was Captain Sam Hunniwell who appeared to be most surprised by his friend's statement. The captain seemed absolutely dumbfounded.

"You—you WHAT?" he cried.

Jed smoothed the bills in his hand. "I found it, Sam," he repeated. "Here 'tis—here."

He extended the bundle of banknotes. The captain made no move to take them. Jed held them a little nearer.

"You—you'd better take it, Sam," he urged. "It might get lost again, you know."

Still Captain Sam made no move. He looked from the bills in Jed's hands to Jed's face and back again. The expression on his own face was a strange one.

"You found it," he repeated. "YOU did?"

"Yes—yes, I found it, Sam. Just happened to."

"Where did you find it?"

"Over yonder behind that pile of boards. You know you said the money was in your overcoat pocket and—and when you came in here on your way back from Sylvester's you hove your coat over onto those boards. I presume likely the—the money must have fell out of the pocket then. You see, don't you, Sam?"

The tone in which the question was asked was one, almost, of pleading. He appeared very, very anxious to have the captain "see." But the latter seemed as puzzled as ever.

"Here's the money, Sam," urged Jed. "Take it, won't you?"

Captain Sam took it, but that is all he did. He did not count it or put it in his pocket. He merely took it and looked at the man who had given it to him.

Jed's confusion seemed to increase. "Don't you—don't you think you'd better count it, Sam?" he stammered. "If—if the Major here and Phin see you count it and—and know it's all right, then they'll be able to contradict the stories that's goin' around about so much bein' stolen, you know."

The captain grunted.

"Stolen?" he repeated. "You said folks were talkin' about money bein' lost. Have they been sayin' 'twas stolen?"

It was Grover who answered. "I haven't heard any such rumors," he said. "I believe Lieutenant Rayburn said he heard some idle report about the bank's having lost a sum of money, but there was no hint at dishonesty."

Captain Sam turned to Mr. Babbitt.

"YOU haven't heard any yarns about money bein' stolen at the bank, have you?" he demanded.

Before Phineas could answer Grover's hand again fell lightly on his shoulder.

"I'm sure he hasn't," observed the Major. The captain paid no attention to him.

"Have you?" he repeated, addressing Babbitt.

The little man shook from head to foot. The glare with which he regarded his hated rival might have frightened a timid person. But Captain Sam Hunniwell was distinctly not timid.

"Have you?" he asked, for the third time.

Phineas' mouth opened, but Grover's fingers tightened on his shoulder and what came out of that mouth was merely a savage repetition of his favorite retort, "None of your darned business."

"Yes, 'tis my business," began Captain Sam, but Jed interrupted.

"I don't see as it makes any difference whether he's heard anything or not, Sam," he suggested eagerly. "No matter what he's heard, it ain't so, because there couldn't have been anything stolen. There was only four hundred missin'. I've found that and you've got it back; so that settles it, don't it?"

"It certainly would seem as if it did," observed Grover. "Congratulations, Captain Hunniwell. You're fortunate that so honest a man found the money, I should say."

The captain merely grunted. The odd expression was still on his face. Jed turned to the other two.

"Er—er—Major Grover," he said, "if—if you hear any yarns now about money bein' missin'—or—or stolen you can contradict 'em now, can't you?"

"I certainly can—and will."

"And you'll contradict 'em, too, eh, Phin?"

Babbitt jerked his shoulder from Grover's grasp and strode to the door.

"Let me out of here," he snarled. "I'm goin' home."

No one offered to detain him, but as he threw open the door to the outer shop Leonard Grover followed him.

"Just a moment, Babbitt," he said. "I'll go as far as the gate with you, if you don't mind. Good afternoon, Jed. Good afternoon, Captain, and once more—congratulations.... Here, Babbitt, wait a moment."

Phineas did not wait, but even so his pursuer caught him before he reached the gate. Jed, who had run to the window, saw the Major and the hardware dealer in earnest conversation. The former seemed to be doing most of the talking. Then they separated, Grover remaining by the gate and Phineas striding off in the direction of his shop. He was muttering to himself and his face was working with emotion. Between baffled malice and suppressed hatred he looked almost as if he were going to cry. Even amid his own feelings of thankfulness and relief Jed felt a pang of pity for Phineas Babbitt. The little man was the incarnation of spite and envy and vindictive bitterness, but Jed was sorry for him, just as he would have been sorry for a mosquito which had bitten him. He might be obliged to crush the creature, but he would feel that it was not much to blame for the bite; both it and Phineas could not help being as they were—they were made that way.

He heard an exclamation at his shoulder and turned to find that Captain Sam had also been regarding the parting at the gate.

"Humph!" grunted the captain. "Phin looks as if he'd been eatin' somethin' that didn't set any too good. What's started him to obeyin' orders from that Grover man all to once? I always thought he hated soldierin' worse than a hen hates a swim.... Humph! ... Well, that's the second queerest thing I've run across to-day."

Jed changed the subject, or tried to change it.

"What's the first one, Sam?" he hastened to ask. His friend looked at him for an instant before he answered.

"The first one?" he repeated, slowly. "Well, I'll tell you, Jed. The first one—and the queerest of all—is your findin' that four hundred dollars."

Jed was a good deal taken aback. He had not expected an answer of that kind. His embarrassment and confusion returned.

"Why—why," he stammered, "is—is that funny, Sam? I don't—I don't know's I get what you mean. What's—what is there funny about my findin' that money?"

The captain stepped across the shop, pulled forward a chair and seated himself. Jed watched him anxiously.

"I—I don't see anything very funny about my findin' that money, Sam," he said, again. Captain Sam grunted.

"Don't you?" he asked. "Well, maybe my sense of humor's gettin' cross-eyed or—or somethin'. I did think I could see somethin' funny in it, but most likely I was mistaken. Sit down, Jed, and tell me all about how you found it."

Jed hesitated. His hand moved slowly across his chin.

"Well, now, Sam," he faltered, "there ain't nothin' to tell. I just—er—found it, that's all. . . . Say, you ain't seen that new gull vane of mine lately, have you? I got her so she can flop her wings pretty good now."

"Hang the gull vane! I want to hear how you found that money. Gracious king, man, you don't expect I'm goin' to take the gettin' back of four hundred dollars as cool as if 'twas ten cents, do you? Sit down and tell me about it."

So Jed sat, not with eagerness, but more as if he could think of no excuse for refusing. His companion tilted back in his chair, lit a cigar, and bade him heave ahead.

"Well," began Jed, "I—I—you see, Sam, I happened to look behind that heap of boards there and—"

"What made you think of lookin' behind those boards?"

"Eh? Why, nothin' 'special. I just happened to look. That's where your coat was, you know. So I looked and—and there 'twas."

"I see. There 'twas, eh? Where?"

"Why—why, behind the boards. I told you that, you know."

"Gracious king, course I know! You've told me that no less than ten times. But WHERE was it? On the boards? On the floor?"

"Eh? . . . Oh, . . . oh, seems to me 'twas on the floor."

"Don't you KNOW 'twas on the floor?"

"Why . . . why, yes, sartin."

"Then what made you say 'seems as if' it was there?"

"Oh, . . . oh, I don't know. Land sakes, Sam, what are you askin' me all these questions for?"

"Just for fun, I guess. I'm interested, naturally. Tell me some more. How was the money—all together, or kind of scattered 'round?"

"Eh? . . . Oh, all together."

"Sure of that?"

"Course I'm sure of it. I can see it just as plain as day, now I come to think of it. 'Twas all together, in a heap like."

"Um-hm. The band that was round it had come off, then?"

"Band? What band?"

"Why, the paper band with '$400' on it. That had come off when it fell out of my pocket, I presume likely."

"Yes. . . . Yes, I guess likely it did. Must have. . . . Er— Sam, let me show you that gull vane. I got it so now that—"

"Hold on a minute. I'm mighty interested about your findin' this money. It's so—so sort of unexpected, as you might say. If that band came off it must have broke when the money tumbled down behind the boards. Let's see if it did."

He rose and moved toward the pile of boards. Jed also rose.

"What are you goin' to look for?" he asked, anxiously.

"Why, the paper band with the '$400' on it. I'd like to see if it broke. . . . Humph!" he added, peering down into the dark crevice between the boards and the wall of the shop. "Can't see anything of it, can you?"

Jed, peering solemnly down, shook his head. "No," he said. "I can't see anything of it."

"But it may be there, for all that." He reached down. "Humph!" he exclaimed. "I can't touch bottom. Jed, you've got a longer arm than I have; let's see if you can."

Jed, sprawled upon the heap of lumber, stretched his arm as far as it would go. "Hum," he drawled, "I can't quite make it, Sam. . . . There's a place where she narrows way down here and I can't get my fingers through it."

"Is that so? Then we'd better give up lookin' for the band, I cal'late. Didn't amount to anything, anyhow. Tell me more about what you did when you found the money. You must have been surprised."

"Eh? . . . Land sakes, I was. I don't know's I ever was so surprised in my life. Thinks I, 'Here's Sam's money that's missin' from the bank.' Yes, sir, and 'twas, too."

"Well, I'm much obliged to you, Jed, I surely am. And when you found it— Let's see, you found it this mornin', of course?"

"Eh? Why—why, how—what makes you think I found it this mornin'?"

"Oh, because you must have. 'Cause if you'd found it yesterday or the day before you'd have told me right off."

"Yes—oh, yes, that's so. Yes, I found it this mornin'."

"Hadn't you thought to hunt for it afore?"

"Eh? . . . Land sakes, yes . . . yes, I'd hunted lots of times, but I hadn't found it."

"Hadn't thought to look in that place, eh?"

"That's it. . . . Say, Sam, what—"

"It's lucky you hadn't moved those boards. If you'd shifted them any since I threw my coat on 'em you might not have found it for a month, not till you used up the whole pile. Lucky you looked afore you shifted the lumber."

"Yes . . . yes, that's so. That's a fact. But, Sam, hadn't you better take that money back to the bank? The folks up there don't know it's been found yet. They'll be some surprised, too."

"So they will. All hands'll be surprised. And when I tell 'em how you happened to see that money lyin' in a pile on the floor behind those boards and couldn't scarcely believe your eyes, and couldn't believe 'em until you'd reached down and picked up the money, and counted it— That's about what you did, I presume likely, eh?"

"Yes. . . . Yes, that's just it."

"They'll be surprised then, and no wonder. But they'd be more surprised if I should bring 'em here and show 'em the place where you found it. 'Twould surprise 'most anybody to know that there was a man livin' who could see down a black crack four foot deep and two inches wide and around a corner in that crack and see money lyin' on the floor, and know 'twas money, and then stretch his arm out a couple of foot more and thin his wrist down until it was less than an inch through and pick up that money. That WOULD surprise em. Don't you think 'twould, Jed?"

The color left Jed's face. His mouth fell open and he stared blankly at his friend. The latter chuckled.

"Don't you think 'twould surprise 'em, Jed?" he repeated. "Seems likely as if 'twould. It surprised me all right enough."

The color came surging back. Jed's cheeks flamed. He tried to speak, but what he said was not coherent nor particularly intelligible.

"Now—now—now, Sam," he stammered. "I—I— You don't understand. You ain't got it right. I—I—"

The captain interrupted. "Don't try so hard, Jed," he continued. "Take time to get your steam up. You'll bust a b'iler if you puff that way. Let's see what it is I don't understand. You found this money behind those boards?"

"Eh? Yes . . . yes . . . but—"

"Wait. And you found it this mornin'?"

"Yes . . . yes . . . but, Sam—"

"Hold on. You saw it layin' on the floor at the bottom of that crack?"

"Well—well, I don't know as I saw it exactly, but—but— No, I didn't see it. I—I felt it."

"Oh, you felt it! Thought you said you saw it. Well, you reached down and felt it, then. How did you get your arm stretched out five foot long and three-quarters of an inch thick? Put it under the steam roller, did you?"

Jed swallowed twice before replying. "I—I—" he began. "Well— well, come to think of it, Sam, I—I guess I didn't feel it with my fingers. I—I took a stick. Yes, that was it. I poked in behind there with a stick."

"Oh, you felt it with a stick. And knew 'twas money? Tut, tut! You must have a good sense of touch, Jed, to know bills when you scratch across 'em with the far end of a five foot stick. Pick 'em up with a stick, too, did you?"

Mr. Winslow was speechless. Captain Sam shook his head.

"And that ain't the most astonishin' part either," he observed. "While those bills were in the dark at the bottom of that crack they must have sprouted. They went in there nothin' but tens and twenties. These you just gave me are fives and twos and all sorts. You'd better poke astern of those boards again, Jed. The roots must be down there yet; all you've scratched up are the sprouts."

His only answer was a hopeless groan. Captain Sam rose and, walking over to where his friend sat with his face buried between his hands, laid his own hand on the latter's shoulder.

"There, there, Jed," he said, gently. "I beg your pardon. I'm sorry I stirred you up this way. 'Twas mean of me, I know, but when you commenced givin' me all this rigmarole I couldn't help it. You never was meant for a liar, old man; you make a mighty poor fist at it. What is it all about? What was you tryin' to do it for?"

Another groan. The captain tried again.

"What's the real yarn?" he asked. "What are you actin' this way for? Course I know you never found the money. Is there somebody—"

"No! No, no!" Jed's voice rose almost to a shout. He sprang to his feet and clutched at Captain Sam's coat-sleeve. "No," he shouted. "Course there ain't anybody. Wh-what makes you say such a thing as that? I—I tell you I did find the money. I did—I did."

"Jed! Of course you didn't. I know you didn't. I KNOW. Gracious king, man, be sensible."

"I did! I did! I found it and now I give it back to you. What more do you want, Sam Hunniwell? Ain't that enough?"

"Enough! It's a darned sight too much. I tell you I know you didn't find it."

"But I did."

"Rubbish! In the first place, you and I hunted every inch behind those boards the very day the money was missin', and 'twa'n't there then. And, besides, this isn't the money I lost."

"Well—well, what if 'tain't? I don't care. I—I know 'tain't. I—I spent your money."

"You SPENT it? When? You told me you only found it this mornin'."

"I—I know I did, but 'twan't so. I—I—" Jed was in an agony of alarm and frantic haste. "I found your money two or three days ago. Yes, sir, that's when I found it. . . . Er . . . er . . ."

"Humph! Why didn't you tell me you found it then? If you'd found it what made you keep runnin' into the bank to ask me if I'D found it? Why didn't you give it back to me right off? Oh, don't be so ridiculous, Jed."

"I—I ain't. It's true. I—I didn't give it back to you because— because I—I thought first I'd keep it."

"Keep it? KEEP it? Steal it, do you mean?"

"Yes—yes, that's what I mean. I—I thought first I'd do that and then I got—got kind of sorry and—and scared and I got some more money—and now I'm givin' it back to you. See, don't you, Sam? That's the reason."

Captain Sam shook his head. "So you decided to be a thief, did you, Jed?" he said, slowly. "Well, the average person never'd have guessed you was such a desperate character.... Humph!... Well, well!... What was you goin' to do with the four hundred, provided you had kept it? You spent the money I lost anyway; you said you did. What did you spend it for?"

"Oh—oh, some things I needed."

"Sho! Is that so? What things?"

Jed's shaking hand moved across his chin.

"Oh—I—I forget," he faltered. Then, after a desperate struggle, "I—I—I bought a suit of clothes."

The effort of this confession was a peculiar one. Captain Sam Hunniwell put back his head and roared with laughter. He was still laughing when he picked up his hat and turned to the door. Jed sprang from his seat.

"Eh?... You're not GOIN', are you, Sam?" he cried. The captain, wiping his eyes, turned momentarily.

"Yes, Jed," he said, chokingly, "I'm goin'. Say, if—if you get time some of these days dress up in that four hundred dollar suit you bought and then send me word. I'd like to see it."

He went out. The door of the outer shop slammed. Jed wiped the perspiration from his forehead and groaned helplessly and hopelessly.

The captain had reached the gate when he saw Phillips coming along the road toward him. He waited until the young man arrived.

"Hello, Captain," hailed Charles. "So you decided not to come back to the bank this afternoon, after all?"

His employer nodded. "Yes," he said. "I've been kept away on business. Funny kind of business, too. Say, Charlie," he added, "suppose likely your sister and you would be too busy to see me for a few minutes now? I'd like to see if you've got an answer to a riddle."

"A riddle?"

"Um-hm. I've just had the riddle sprung on me and it's got MY head whirlin' like a bottle in a tide rip. Can I come into your house for a minute and spring it on you?"

The young man looked puzzled, which was not surprising, but his invitation to come into the house was most cordial. They entered by the front door. As they came into the little hall they heard a man's voice in the living-room beyond. It was Major Grover's voice and they heard the major say:

"It doesn't matter at all. Please understand I had no thought of asking. I merely wanted you to feel that what that fellow said had no weight with me whatever, and to assure you that I will make it my business to see that he keeps his mouth shut. As for the other question, Ruth—"

Ruth Armstrong's voice broke in here.

"Oh, please," she begged, "not now. I—I am so sorry I can't tell you everything, but—but it isn't my secret and—and I can't. Perhaps some day— But please believe that I am grateful, very, very grateful. I shall never forget it."

Charlie, with an anxious glance at Captain Hunniwell, cleared his throat loudly. The captain's thoughts, however, were too busy with his "riddle" to pay attention to the voices in the living-room. As he and Phillips entered that apartment Major Grover came into the hall. He seemed a trifle embarrassed, but he nodded to Captain Sam, exchanged greetings with Phillips, and hurried out of the house. They found Ruth standing by the rear window and looking out toward the sea.

The captain plunged at once into his story. He began by asking Mrs. Armstrong if her brother had told her of the missing four hundred dollars. Charles was inclined to be indignant.

"Of course I haven't," he declared. "You asked us all to keep quiet about it and not to tell a soul, and I supposed you meant just that."

"Eh? So I did, Charlie, so I did. Beg your pardon, boy. I might have known you'd keep your hatches closed. Well, here's the yarn, Mrs. Armstrong. It don't make me out any too everlastin' brilliant. A grown man that would shove that amount of money into his overcoat pocket and then go sasshayin' from Wapatomac to Orham ain't the kind I'd recommend to ship as cow steward on a cattle boat, to say nothin' of president of a bank. But confessin's good for the soul, they say, even if it does make a feller feel like a fool, so here goes. I did just that thing."

He went on to tell of his trip to Wapatomac, his interview with Sage, his visit to the windmill shop, his discovery that four hundred of the fourteen hundred had disappeared. Then he told of his attempts to trace it, of Jed's anxious inquiries from day to day, and, finally, of the scene he had just passed through.

"So there you are," he concluded. "I wish to mercy you'd tell me what it all means, for I can't tell myself. If it hadn't been so— so sort of pitiful, and if I hadn't been so puzzled to know what made him do it, I cal'late I'd have laughed myself sick to see poor old Jed tryin' to lie. Why, he ain't got the first notion of how to begin; I don't cal'late he ever told a real, up-and-down lie afore in his life. That was funny enough—but when he began to tell me he was a thief! Gracious king! And all he could think of in the way of an excuse was that he stole the four hundred to buy a suit of clothes with. Ho, ho, ho!"

He roared again. Charlie Phillips laughed also. But his sister did not laugh. She had seated herself in the rocker by the window when the captain began his tale and now she had drawn back into the corner where the shadows were deepest.

"So there you are," said Captain Sam, again. "There's the riddle. Now what's the answer? Why did he do it? Can either of you guess?"

Phillips shook his head. "You have got me," he declared. "And the money he gave you was not the money you lost? You're sure of that?"

"Course I'm sure of it. In the first place I lost a packet of clean tens and twenties; this stuff I've got in my pocket now is all sorts, ones and twos and fives and everything. And in the second place—"

"Pardon me, just a minute, Captain Hunniwell. Where did he get the four hundred to give you, do you think? He hasn't cashed any large checks at the bank within the last day or two, and he would scarcely have so much on hand in his shop."

"Not as much as that—no. Although I've known the absent-minded, careless critter to have over two hundred knockin' around among his tools and chips and glue pots. Probably he had some to start with, and he got the rest by gettin' folks around town and over to Harniss to cash his checks. Anthony Hammond over there asked me a little while ago, when I met him down to the wharf, if I thought Shavin's Winslow was good for a hundred and twenty-five. Said Jed had sent over by the telephone man's auto and asked him to cash a check for that much. Hammond said he thought 'twas queer he hadn't cashed it at our bank; that's why he asked me about it."

"Humph! But why should he give his own money away in that fashion? And confess to stealing and all that stuff? I never heard of such a thing."

"Neither did anybody else. I've known Jed all my life and I never can tell what loony thing he's liable to do next. But this beats all of 'em, I will give in."

"You don't suppose—you don't suppose he is doing it to help you, because you are his friend? Because he is afraid the bank—or you— may get into trouble because of—well, because of having been so careless?"

Captain Sam laughed once more. "No, no," he said. "Gracious king, I hope my reputation's good enough to stand the losin' of four hundred dollars. And Jed knows perfectly well I could put it back myself, if 'twas necessary, without runnin' me into the poorhouse. No, 'tain't for me he's doin' it. I ain't the reason."

"And you're quite sure his story is ALL untrue. You don't imagine that he did find the money, your money, and then, for some reason or other, change it with smaller bills, and—"

"Sshh, sshh, Charlie, don't waste your breath. I told you I KNEW he hadn't found the four hundred dollars I lost, didn't I? Well, I do know it and for the very best of reasons; in fact, my stoppin' into his shop just now was to tell him what I'd heard. You see, Charlie, old Sylvester Sage has got back from Boston and opened up his house again. And he telephoned me at two o'clock to say that the four hundred dollar packet was layin' on his sittin'-room table just where I left it when he and I parted company four days or so ago. That's how I KNOW Jed didn't find it."

From the shadowy corner where Ruth Armstrong sat came a little gasp and an exclamation. Charles whistled.

"Well, by George!" he exclaimed. "That certainly puts a crimp in Jed's confession."

"Sartin sure it does. When Sylvester and I parted we was both pretty hot under the collar, havin' called each other's politics about every mean name we could think of. I grabbed up my gloves, and what I thought was my money from the table and slammed out of the house. Seems all I grabbed was the two five hundred packages; the four hundred one was shoved under some papers and magazines and there it stayed till Sylvester got back from his Boston cruise.

"But that don't answer my riddle," he added, impatiently. "What made Jed act the way he did? Got the answer, Charlie?"

The young man shook his head. "No, by George, I haven't!" he replied.

"How about you, Mrs. Armstrong? Can you help us out?"

Ruth's answer was brief. "No, I'm afraid not," she said. There was a queer note in her voice which caused her brother to glance at her, but Captain Hunniwell did not notice. He turned to go.

"Well," he said, "I wish you'd think it over and see if you can spy land anywheres ahead. I need a pilot. This course is too crooked for me. I'm goin' home to ask Maud; maybe she can see a light. So long."

He went out. When Charles returned, having accompanied his employer as far as the door, he found Ruth standing by her chair and looking at him. A glance at her face caused him to stop short and look at her.

"Why, Ruth," he asked, "what is it?"

She was pale and trembling. There were tears in her eyes.

"Oh, Charlie," she cried, "can't you see? He—he did it for you."

"Did it for me? Did what? Who? What are you talking about, Sis?"

"Jed. Jed Winslow. Don't you see, Charlie? He pretended to have found the money and to have stolen it just to save you. He thought you—he thought you had taken it."

"WHAT? Thought I had taken it? I had? Why in the devil should he think—"

He stopped. When he next spoke it was in a different tone.

"Sis," he asked, slowly, "do you mean that he thought I took this money because he knew I had—had done that thing at Middleford? Does he know—about that?"

The tears were streaming down her cheeks. "Yes, Charlie," she said, "he knows. He found it out, partly by accident, before you came here. And—and think how loyal, how wonderful he has been! It was through him that you got your opportunity there at the bank. And now—now he has done this to save you. Oh, Charlie!"

CHAPTER XIX

The clock in the steeple of the Methodist church boomed eleven times and still the lights shone from the sitting-room windows of the little Winslow house and from those of Jed's living quarters behind his windmill shop. At that time of year and at that time of night there were few windows alight in Orham, and Mr. Gabe Bearse, had he been astir at such an hour, might have wondered why the Armstrongs and "Shavings" were "settin' up." Fortunately for every one except him, Gabe was in bed and asleep, otherwise he might have peeped under Jed's kitchen window shade—he had been accused of doing such things—and had he done so he would have seen Jed and Charlie Phillips in deep and earnest conversation. Neither would have wished to be seen just then; their interview was far too intimate and serious for that.

They had been talking since eight. Charles and his sister had had a long conversation following Captain Hunniwell's visit and then, after a pretense at supper—a pretense made largely on Babbie's account—the young man had come straight to the shop and to Jed. He had found the latter in a state of extreme dejection. He was sitting before the little writing table in his living-room, his elbows on the desk and his head in his hands. The drawer of the table was open and Jed was, apparently, gazing intently at something within. When Phillips entered the room he started, hastily slammed the drawer shut, and raised a pale and distressed face to his visitor.

"Eh?" he exclaimed. "Oh, it's you, Charlie, ain't it? I—I—er— good mornin'. It's—it's a nice day."

Charles smiled slightly and shook his head.

"You're a little mixed on the time, aren't you, Jed?" he observed. "It WAS a nice day, but it is a nice evening now."

"Eh? Is it? Land sakes, I presume likely 'tis. Must be after supper time, I shouldn't wonder."

"Supper time! Why, it's after eight o'clock. Didn't you know it?"

"No-o. No, I guess not. I—I kind of lost run of the time, seems so."

"Haven't you had any supper?"

"No-o. I didn't seem to care about supper, somehow."

"But haven't you eaten anything?"

"No. I did make myself a cup of tea, but twan't what you'd call a success. ... I forgot to put the tea in it.... But it don't make any difference; I ain't hungry—or thirsty, either."

Phillips leaned forward and laid a hand on the older man's shoulder.

"Jed," he said gently, "I know why you're not hungry. Oh, Jed, what in the world made you do it?"

Jed started back so violently that his chair almost upset. He raised a hand with the gesture of one warding off a blow.

"Do?" he gasped. "Do what?"

"Why, what you did about that money that Captain Hunniwell lost. What made you do it, Jed?"

Jed's eyes closed momentarily. Then he opened them and, without looking at his visitor, rose slowly to his feet.

"So Sam told you," he said, with a sigh. "I—I didn't hardly think he'd do that.... Course 'twas all right for him to tell," he added hastily. "I didn't ask him not to, but—but, he and I havin' been—er—chums, as you might say, for so long, I—I sort of thought.... Well, it don't make any difference, I guess. Did he tell your—your sister? Did he tell her how I—how I stole the money?"

Charles shook his head.

"No," he said quietly. "No, he didn't tell either of us that. He told us that you had tried to make him believe you took the money, but that he knew you were not telling the truth. He knew you didn't take it."

"Eh? Now . . . now, Charlie, that ain't so." Jed was even more disturbed and distressed than before. "I—I told Sam I took it and—and kept it. I TOLD him I did. What more does he want? What's he goin' around tellin' folks I didn't for? What—"

"Hush, Jed! He knows you didn't take it. He knew it all the time you were telling him you did. In fact he came into your shop this afternoon to tell you that the Sage man over at Wapatomac had found the four hundred dollars on the table in his sitting-room just where the captain left it. Sage had just 'phoned him that very thing. He would have told you that, but you didn't give him the chance. Jed, I—"

But Jed interrupted. His expression as he listened had been changing like the sky on a windy day in April.

"Here, here!" he cried wildly. "What—what kind of talk's that? Do—do you mean to tell me that Sam Hunniwell never lost that money at all? That all he did was leave it over at Wapatomac?"

"Yes, that's just what I mean."

"Then—then all the time when I was—was givin' him the—the other money and tellin' him how I found it and—and all—he knew—"

"Certainly he knew. I've just told you that he knew."

Jed sat heavily down in the chair once more. He passed his hand slowly across his chin.

"He knew!" he repeated. "He knew! . . ." Then, with a sudden gasp as the full significance of the thought came to him, he cried: "Why, if—if the money wasn't ever lost you couldn't—you—"

Charles shook his head: "No, Jed," he said, "I couldn't have taken it. And I didn't take it."

Jed gasped again. He stretched out a hand imploringly. "Oh, Lord," he exclaimed, "I never meant to say that. I—I—"

"It's all right, Jed. I don't blame you for thinking I might have taken it. Knowing what you did about—well, about my past record, it is not very astonishing that you should think almost anything."

Jed's agonized contrition was acute.

"Don't talk so, Charlie!" he pleaded. "Don't! I—I'd ought to be ashamed of myself. I am—mercy knows I am! But . . . Eh? Why, how did you know I knew about—that?"

"Ruth told me just now. After Captain Hunniwell had gone, she told me the whole thing. About how Babbie let the cat out of the bag and how she told you for fear you might suspect something even worse than the truth; although," he added, "that was quite bad enough. Yes, she told me everything. You've been a brick all through, Jed. And now—"

"Wait, Charlie, wait. I—I don't know what to say to you. I don't know what you must think of me for ever—ever once suspectin' you. If you hadn't said to me only such a little spell ago that you needed money so bad and would do most anything to get five hundred dollars—if you hadn't said that, I don't think the notion would ever have crossed my mind."

Phillips whistled. "Well, by George!" he exclaimed. "I had forgotten that. No wonder you thought I had gone crooked again. Humph! . . . Well, I'll tell you why I wanted that money. You see, I've been trying to pay back to the man in Middleford the money of his which—which I took before. It is two thousand dollars and," with a shrug, "that looks a good deal bigger sum to me now than it used to, you can bet on that. I had a few hundred in a New York savings bank before I—well, before they shut me up. No one knew about it, not even Sis. I didn't tell her because— well, I wish I could say it was because I was intending to use it to pay back what I had taken, but that wasn't the real reason why I kept still about it. To tell you the truth, Jed, I didn't feel— no, I don't feel yet any too forgiving or kindly toward that chap who had me put in prison. I'm not shirking blame; I was a fool and a scamp and all that; but he is—he's a hard man, Jed."

Jed nodded. "Seems to me Ru—your sister said he was a consider'ble of a professor," he observed.

"Professor? Why no, he was a bond broker."

"I mean that he professed religion a good deal. Called himself a Christian and such kind of names."

Phillips smiled bitterly. "If he is a Christian I prefer to be a heathen," he observed.

"Um-hm. Well, maybe he ain't one. You could teach a parrot to holler 'Praise the Lord,' I cal'late, and the more crackers he got by it the louder he'd holler. So you never said anything about the four hundred you had put by, Charlie."

"No. I felt that I had been treated badly and—why, Jed, the man used to urge me to dress better than I could afford, to belong to the most expensive club and all that sort of thing. He knew I was in with a set sporting ten times the money I could muster, and spending it, too, but he seemed to like to have me associate with them. Said it was good for the business."

"Sartin! More crackers for Polly. Go on."

"I intended that he should never have that money, but after I came here, after I had been here for a time, I changed my mind. I saw things in a different light. I wrote him a letter, told him I meant to pay back every cent of the two thousand I had taken and enclosed my check for the seven hundred and fifty I had put by. Since then I have paid him two hundred and fifty more, goodness knows how. I have squeezed every penny from my salary that I could spare. I have paid him half of the two thousand and, if everything had gone on well, some day or other I would have paid the other half."

Jed laid a hand on his companion's knee. "Good boy, Charlie," he said. "And how did the—er—professin' poll parrot act about your payin' it back?"

Charles smiled faintly. "Just before I talked with you that day, Jed," he said, "I received a letter from him stating that he did not feel I was paying as rapidly as I could and that, if he did not receive another five hundred shortly he should feel it his duty to communicate with my present employers. Do you wonder I said I would do almost anything to get the money?"

Jed's hand patted the knee sympathetically.

"Sho, sho, sho!" he exclaimed. "Have you heard from him since?"

"No, I wrote him that I was paying as fast as I could and that if he communicated with my employers that would end any chances of his ever getting more. He hasn't written since; afraid of stopping the golden egg supply, I presume. . . . But there," he added, "that's enough of that. Jed, how could you do it—just for me? Of course I had come to realize that your heart was as big as a bushel basket, and that you and I were friends. But when a fellow gives up four hundred dollars of his own money, and, not only does that, but deliberately confesses himself a thief—when he does that to save some one else who, as he knew, had really been a thief and who he was pretty sure must have stolen again—why, Jed, it is unbelievable. Why did you do it? What can I say to you?"

Jed held up a protesting hand.

"Don't say anything," he stammered. "Don't! It's—it's all foolishness, anyhow."

"Foolishness! It's—oh, I don't know what it is! And to sacrifice your reputation and your character and your friendship with Captain Hunniwell, all for me! I can't understand it."

"Now—now—now, Charlie, don't try to. If I can't understand myself more'n half the time, what's the use of your strainin' your brains? I—I just took a notion, that's all. I—"

"But, Jed, why did you do it—for me? I have heard of men doing such things for—for women, sacrificing themselves to save a woman they were in love with. You read of that in books and—yes, I think I can understand that. But for you to do it—for ME!"

Jed waved both hands this time. "Sshh! sshh!" he cried, in frantic protest. His face was a brilliant crimson and his embarrassment and confusion were so acute as to be laughable, although Phillips was far from laughing. "Sshh, sshh, Charlie," pleaded Jed. "You— you don't know what you're talkin' about. You're makin' an awful fuss about nothin'. Sshh! Yes, you are, too. I didn't have any notion of tellin' Sam I stole that four hundred when I first gave it to him. I was goin' to tell him I found it, that's all. That would keep him bottled up, I figgered, and satisfied and then—then you and I'd have a talk and I'd tell you what I'd done and—well, some day maybe you could pay me back the money; don't you see? I do hope," he added anxiously, "you won't hold it against me, for thinkin' maybe you had taken it. Course I'd ought to have known better. I would have known better if I'd been anybody but Shavin's Winslow. HE ain't responsible."

"Hush, Jed, hush! But why did you say you had—kept it?"

"Eh? Oh, that was Sam's doin's. He commenced to ask questions, and, the first thing I knew, he had me on the spider fryin' over a hot fire. The more I sizzled and sputtered and tried to get out of that spider, the more he poked up the fire. I declare, I never knew lyin' was such a job! When I see how easy and natural it comes to some folks I feel kind of ashamed to think what a poor show I made at it. Well, Sam kept pokin' the fire and heatin' me up till I got desperate and swore I stole the money instead of findin' it. And that was hoppin' out of the fryin' pan INTO the fire," he drawled reflectively.

Charles smiled. "Captain Sam said you told him you took the money to buy a suit of clothes with," he suggested.

"Eh? Did I? Sho! That was a real bright idea of mine, wasn't it? A suit of clothes. Humph! Wonder I didn't say I bought shoe laces or collar buttons or somethin'. . . . Sho! . . . Dear, dear! Well, they say George Washin'ton couldn't tell a lie and I've proved I can't either; only I've tried to tell one and I don't recollect that he ever did that. . . . Humph! . . . A suit of clothes. . . . Four hundred dollars. . . . Solomon in all his glory would have looked like a calico shirt and a pair of overalls alongside of me, eh? . . . Humph!"

Phillips shook his head. "Nevertheless, Jed," he declared, "I can't understand why you did it and I never—never shall forget it. Neither will Ruth. She will tell you so to-morrow."

Jed was frightened. "No, no, no, she mustn't," he cried, quickly. "I—I don't want her to talk about it. I—I don't want anybody to talk about it. Please tell her not to, Charlie! Please! It's— it's all such foolishness anyhow. Let's forget it."

"It isn't the sort of thing one forgets easily. But we won't talk of it any more just now, if that pleases you better. I have some other things to talk about and I must talk about them with some one. I MUST—I've got to."

Jed looked at him. The words reminded him forcibly of Ruth's on that day when she had come to the windmill shop to tell him her brother's story and to discuss the question of his coming to Orham. She, too, had said that she must talk with some one—she MUST.

"Have—you talked 'em over with—with your sister?" he asked.

"Yes. But she and I don't agree completely in the matter. You see, Ruth thinks the world of me, she always did, a great deal more than I deserve, ever have deserved or ever will. And in this matter she thinks first of all of me—what will become of me provided—well, provided things don't go as I should like to have them. That isn't the way I want to face the question. I want to know what is best for every one, for her, for me and—and for some one else—most of all for some one else, I guess," he added.

Jed nodded slowly. "For Maud," he said.

Charles looked at him. "How on earth—?" he demanded. "What in blazes are you—a clairvoyant?"

"No-o. No. But it don't need a spirit medium to see through a window pane, Charlie; that is, the average window pane," he added, with a glance at his own, which were in need of washing just then. "You want to know," he continued, "what you'd ought to do now that will be the right thing, or the nighest to the right thing, for your sister and Babbie and yourself—and Maud."

"Yes, I do. It isn't any new question for me. I've been putting it up to myself for a long time, for months; by, George, it seems years."

"I know. I know. Well, Charlie, I've been puttin' it up to myself, too. Have you got any answer?"

"No, none that exactly suits me. Have you?"

"I don't know's I have—exactly."

"Exactly? Well, have you any, exact or otherwise?"

"Um.... Well, I've got one, but ... but perhaps it ain't an answer. Perhaps it wouldn't do at all. Perhaps ... perhaps ..."

"Never mind the perhapses. What is it?"

"Um.... Suppose we let it wait a little spell and talk the situation over just a little mite. You've been talkin' with your sister, you say, and she don't entirely agree with you."

"No. I say things can't go on as they've been going. They can't."

"Um-hm. Meanin'—what things?"

"Everything. Jed, do you remember that day when you and I had the talk about poetry and all that? When you quoted that poem about a chap's fearing his fate too much? Well, I've been fearing my fate ever since I began to realize what a mess I was getting into here in Orham. When I first came

I saw, of course, that I was skating on thin ice, and it was likely to break under me at any time. I knew perfectly well that some day the Middleford business was bound to come out and that my accepting the bank offer without telling Captain Hunniwell or any one was a mighty risky, not to say mean, business. But Ruth was so very anxious that I should accept and kept begging me not to tell, at least until they had had a chance to learn that I was worth something, that I gave in and . . . I say, Jed," he put in, breaking his own sentence in the middle, "don't think I'm trying to shove the blame over on to Sis. It's not that."

Jed nodded. "Sho, sho, Charlie," he said, "course 'tain't. I understand."

"No, I'll take the blame. I was old enough to have a mind of my own. Well, as I was saying, I realized it all, but I didn't care so much. If the smash did come, I figured, it might not come until I had established myself at the bank, until they might have found me valuable enough to keep on in spite of it. And I worked mighty hard to make them like me. Then—then—well, then Maud and I became friends and—and—oh, confound it, you see what I mean! You must see."

The Winslow knee was clasped between the Winslow hands and the Winslow foot was swinging. Jed nodded again.

"I see, Charlie," he said.

"And—and here I am. The smash has come, in a way, already. Babbitt, so Ruth tells me, knows the whole story and was threatening to tell, but she says Grover assures her that he won't tell, that he, the major, has a club over the old fellow which will prevent his telling. Do you think that's true?"

"I shouldn't be surprised. Major Grover sartinly did seem to put the fear of the Lord into Phin this afternoon. . . . And that's no one-horse miracle," he drawled, "when you consider that all the ministers in Orham haven't been able to do it for forty odd years. . . . Um. . . . Yes, I kind of cal'late Phin'll keep his hatches shut. He may bust his b'iler and blow up with spite, but he won't talk about you, Charlie, I honestly believe. And we can all thank the major for that."

"I shall thank him, for one!"

"Mercy on us! No, no. He doesn't know your story at all. He just thinks Babbitt was circulatin' lies about Ruth—about your sister. You mustn't mention the Middleford—er—mess to Major Grover."

"Humph! Well, unless I'm greatly mistaken, Ruth—"

"Eh? Ruth—what?"

"Oh, nothing. Never mind that now. And allowing that Babbitt will, as you say, keep his mouth shut, admitting that the situation is just what it was before Captain Hunniwell lost the money or Babbitt came into the affair at all, still I've made up my mind that things can't go on as they are. Jed, I—it's a mighty hard thing to say to another man, but—the world—my world—just begins and ends with—with her."

His fists clenched and his jaw set as he said it. Jed bowed his head.

"With Maud, you mean," he said.

"Yes. I—I don't care for anything else or anybody else. . . . Oh, of course I don't mean just that, you know. I do care for Sis and Babbie. But—they're different."

"I understand, Charlie."

"No, you don't. How can you? Nobody can understand, least of all a set old crank like you, Jed, and a confirmed bachelor besides. Beg pardon for contradicting you, but you don't understand, you can't."

Jed gazed soberly at the floor.

"Maybe I can understand a little, Charlie," he drawled gently.

"Well, all right. Let it go at that. The fact is that I'm at a crisis."

"Just a half minute, now. Have you said anything to Maud about—about how you feel?"

"Of course I haven't," indignantly. "How could I, without telling her everything?"

"That's right, that's right. Course you couldn't, and be fair and honorable. . . . Hum. . . . Then you don't know whether or not she—er—feels the same way about—about you?"

Charles hesitated. "No-o," he hesitated. "No, I don't know, of course. But I—I feel—I—"

"You feel that that part of the situation ain't what you'd call hopeless, eh? . . . Um. . . . Well, judgin' from what I've heard, I shouldn't call it that, either. Would it surprise you to know, Charlie, that her dad and I had a little talk on this very subject not so very long ago?"

Evidently it did surprise him. Charles gasped and turned red.

"Captain Hunniwell!" he exclaimed. "Did Captain Hunniwell talk with you about—about Maud and—and me?"

"Yes."

"Well, by George! Then he suspected—he guessed that— That's strange."

Jed relinquished the grip of one hand upon his knee long enough to stroke his chin.

"Um . . . yes," he drawled drily. "It's worse than strange, it's— er— paralyzin'. More clairvoyants in Orham than you thought there was; eh, Charlie?"

"But why should he talk with you on that subject; about anything so— er—personal and confidential as that? With YOU, you know!"

Jed's slow smile drifted into sight and vanished again. He permitted himself the luxury of a retort.

"Well," he observed musingly, "as to that I can't say for certain. Maybe he did it for the same reason you're doin' it now, Charlie."

The young man evidently had not thought of it in just that light. He looked surprised and still more puzzled.

"Why, yes," he admitted. "So I am, of course. And I do talk to you about things I never would think of mentioning to other people. And Ruth says she does. That's queer, too. But we are—er— neighbors of yours and—and tenants, you know. We've known you ever since we came to Orham."

"Ye-es. And Sam's known me ever since I came. Anyhow he talked with me about you and Maud. I don't think I shall be sayin' more'n I ought to if I tell you that he likes you, Charlie."

"Does he?" eagerly. "By George, I'm glad of that! But, oh, well," with a sigh, "he doesn't know. If he did know my record he might not like me so well. And as for my marrying his daughter—good NIGHT!" with hopeless emphasis.

"No, not good night by any means. Maybe it's only good mornin'. Go on and tell me what you mean by bein' at a crisis, as you said a minute ago."

"I mean just that. The time has come when I must speak to Maud. I must find out if—find out how she feels about me. And I can't speak to her, honorably, without telling her everything. And suppose she should care enough for me to—to—suppose she should care in spite of everything, there's her father. She is his only daughter; he worships the ground she steps on. Suppose I tell him I've been," bitterly, "a crook and a jailbird; what will HE think of me—as a son-in-law? And now suppose he was fool enough to consent—which isn't supposable—how could I stay here, working for him, sponging a living from him, with this thing hanging over us all? No, I can't—I can't. Whatever else happens I can't do that. And I can't go on as I am—or I won't. Now what am I going to do?"

He had risen and was pacing the floor. Jed asked a question.

"What does your sister want you to do?" he asked.

"Ruth? Oh, as I told you, she thinks of no one but me. How dreadful it would be for me to tell of my Middleford record! How awful if I lost my position in the bank! Suppose they discharged me and the town learned why! I've tried to make her see that, compared to the question of Maud, nothing else matters at all, but I'm afraid she doesn't see it as I do. She only sees—me."

"Her brother. Um . . . yes, I know."

"Yes. Well, we talked and talked, but we got nowhere. So at last I said I was coming out to thank you for what you did to save me, Jed. I could hardly believe it then; I can scarcely believe it now. It was too much for any man to do for another. And she said to talk the whole puzzle out with you. She seems to have all the confidence on earth in your judgment, Jed. She is as willing to leave a decision to you, apparently, as you profess to be to leave one to your wooden prophet up on the shelf there; what's-his-name—er—Isaiah."

Jed looked greatly pleased, but he shook his head. "I'm afraid her confidence ain't founded on a rock, like the feller's house in the Bible," he drawled. "My decisions are liable to stick half way betwixt and between, same as—er—Jeremiah's do. But," he added, gravely, "I have been thinkin' pretty seriously about you and your particular puzzle, Charlie, and—and I ain't sure that I don't see one way out of the fog. It may be a hard way, and it may turn out wrong, and it may not be anything you'll agree to. But—"

"What is it? If it's anything even half way satisfactory I'll believe you're the wisest man on earth, Jed Winslow."

"Well, if I thought you was liable to believe that I'd tell you to send your believer to the blacksmith's 'cause there was somethin' wrong with it. No, I ain't wise, far from it. But, Charlie, I think you're dead right about what you say concernin' Maud and her father and you. You CAN'T tell her without tellin' him. For your own sake you mustn't tell him without tellin' her. And you shouldn't, as a straight up and down, honorable man keep on workin' for Sam when you ask him, under these circumstances, to give you his daughter. You can't afford to have her say 'yes' because she pities you, nor to have him give in to her because she begs him to. No, you want to be independent, to go to both of 'em and say: 'Here's my story and here am I. You know now what I did and you know, too, what I've been and how I've behaved since I've been with you.' You want to say to Maud: 'Do you care enough for me to marry me in spite of what I've done and where I've been?' And to Sam: 'Providin' your daughter does care for me, I mean to marry her some day or other. And you can't be on his pay roll when you say that, as I see it."

Phillips stopped in his stride.

"You've put it just as it is," he declared emphatically. "There's the situation—what then? For I tell you now, Jed Winslow, I won't give her up until she tells me to."

"Course not, Charlie, course not. But there's one thing more—or two things, rather. There's your sister and Babbie. Suppose you do haul up stakes and quit workin' for Sam at the bank; can they get along without your support? Without the money you earn?"

The young man nodded thoughtfully. "Yes," he replied, "I see no reason why they can't. They did before I came, you know. Ruth has a little money of her own, enough to keep her and Barbara in the way they live here in Orham. She couldn't support me as a loafer, of course, and you can bet I should never let her try, but she could get on quite well without me. . . . Besides, I am not so sure that . . ."

"Eh? What was you goin' to say, Charlie?"

"Oh, nothing, nothing. I have had a feeling, a slight suspicion, recently, that— But never mind that; I have no right to even hint at such a thing. What are you trying to get at, Jed?"

"Get at?"

"Yes. Why did you ask that question about Ruth and Barbara? You don't mean that you see a way out for me, do you?"

"W-e-e-ll, I . . . er . . . I don't cal'late I'd want to go so far as to say that, hardly. No-o, I don't know's it's a way out— quite. But, as I've told you I've been thinkin' about you and Maud a pretty good deal lately and . . . er . . . hum . . ."

"For heaven's sake, hurry up! Don't go to sleep now, man, of all times. Tell me, what do you mean? What can I do?"

Jed's foot dropped to the floor. He sat erect and regarded his companion intently over his spectacles. His face was very grave.

"There's one thing you can do, Charlie," he said.

"What is it? Tell me, quick."

"Just a minute. Doin' it won't mean necessarily that you're out of your worries and troubles. It won't mean that you mustn't make a clean breast of everything to Maud and to Sam. That you must do and I know, from what you've said to me, that you feel you must. And it won't mean that your doin' this thing will necessarily make either Maud or Sam say yes to the question you want to ask 'em. That question they'll answer themselves, of course. But, as I see it, if you do this thing you'll be free and independent, a man doin' a man's job and ready to speak to Sam Hunniwell or anybody else LIKE a man. And that's somethin'."

"Something! By George, it's everything! What is this man's job? Tell me, quick."

And Jed told him.

CHAPTER XX

Mr. Gabe Bearse lost another opportunity the next morning. The late bird misses the early worm and, as Gabriel was still slumbering peacefully at six A. M., he missed seeing Ruth Armstrong and her brother emerge from the door of the Winslow house at that hour and walk to the gate together. Charles was carrying a small traveling bag. Ruth's face was white and her eyes were suspiciously damp, but she was evidently trying hard to appear calm and cheerful. As they stood talking by the gate, Jed Winslow emerged from the windmill shop and, crossing the lawn, joined them.

The three talked for a moment and then Charles held out his hand.

"Well, so long, Jed," he said. "If all goes well I shall be back here to-morrow. Wish me luck."

"I'll be wishin' it for you, Charlie, all day and all night with double time after hours and no allowance for meals," replied Jed earnestly. "You think Sam'll get your note all right?"

"Yes, I shall tuck it under the bank door as I go by. If he should ask what the business was which called me to Boston so suddenly, just dodge the question as well as you can, won't you, Jed?"

"Sartin sure. He'll think he's dealin' with that colored man that sticks his head through the sheet over to the Ostable fair, the one the boys heave baseballs at. No, he won't get anything out of me, Charlie. And the other letter; that'll get to—to her?"

The young man nodded gravely. "I shall mail it at the post-office now," he said. "Don't talk about it, please. Well, Sis, good-by— until to-morrow."

Jed turned his head. When he looked again Phillips was walking rapidly away along the sidewalk. Ruth, leaning over the fence, watched him as long as he was in sight. And Jed watched her anxiously. When she turned he ventured to speak.

"Don't worry," he begged. "Don't. He's doin' the right thing. I know he is."

She wiped her eyes. "Oh, perhaps he is," she said sadly. "I hope he is."

"I know he is. I only wish I could do it, too. . . . I would," he drawled, solemnly, "only for nineteen or twenty reasons, the first one of 'em bein' that they wouldn't let me."

She made no comment on this observation. They walked together back toward the house.

"Jed," she said, after a moment, "it has come at last, hasn't it, the day we have foreseen and that I have dreaded so? Poor Charlie! Think what this means to him."

Jed nodded. "He's puttin' it to the touch, to win or lose it all," he agreed, "same as was in the poem he and I talked about that time. Well, I honestly believe he feels better now that he's made up his mind to do it, better than he has for many a long day."

"Yes, I suppose he does. And he is doing, too, what he has wanted to do ever since he came here. He told me so when he came in from his long interview with you last night. He and I talked until it was almost day and we told each other—many things."

She paused. Jed, looking up, caught her eye. To his surprise she colored and seemed slightly confused.

"He had not said anything before," she went on rather hurriedly, "because he thought I would feel so terribly to have him do it. So I should, and so I do, of course—in one way, but in another I am glad. Glad, and very proud."

"Sartin. He'll make us all proud of him, or I miss my guess. And, as for the rest of it, the big question that counts most of all to him, I hope—yes, I think that's comin' out all right, too. Ruth," he added, "you remember what I told you about Sam's talk with me that afternoon when he came back from Wapatomac. If Maud cares for him as much as all that she ain't goin' to throw him over on account of what happened in Middleford."

"No—no, not if she really cares. But does she care—enough?"

"I hope so. I guess so. But if she doesn't it's better for him to know it, and know it now. . . . Dear, dear!" he added, "how I do fire off opinions, don't I? A body'd think I was loaded up with wisdom same as one of those machine guns is with cartridges. About all I'm loaded with is blanks, I cal'late."

She was not paying attention to this outburst, but, standing with one hand upon the latch of the kitchen door, she seemed to be thinking deeply.

"I think you are right," she said slowly. "Yes, I think you are right. It IS better to know. . . . Jed, suppose—suppose you cared for some one, would the fact that her brother had been in prison make any difference in—in your feeling?"

Jed actually staggered. She was not looking at him, nor did she look at him now.

"Eh?" he cried. "Why—why, Ruth, what—what—?"

She smiled faintly. "And that was a foolish question, too," she said. "Foolish to ask you, of all men. . . . Well, I must go on and get Babbie's breakfast. Poor child, she is going to miss her Uncle Charlie. We shall all miss him. . . . But there, I promised him I would be brave. Good morning, Jed."

"But—but, Ruth, what-what—?"

She had not heard him. The door closed. Jed stood staring at it for some minutes. Then he crossed the lawn to his own little kitchen. The performances he went through during the next hour would have confirmed the opinion of Mr. Bearse and his coterie that "Shavings" Winslow was "next door to loony." He cooked a breakfast, but how he cooked it or of what it consisted he could not have told. The next day he found the stove-lid lifter on a plate in the ice chest. Whatever became of the left-over pork chop which should have been there he had no idea.

Babbie came dancing in at noon on her way home from school. She found her Uncle Jed in a curious mood, a mood which seemed to be a compound of absent-mindedness and silence broken by sudden fits of song and hilarity. He was sitting by the bench when she entered and was holding an oily rag in one hand and a piece of emery paper in the other. He was looking neither at paper nor rag, nor at anything else in particular so far as she could see, and he did not notice her presence at all. Suddenly he began to rub the paper and the rag together and to sing at the top of his voice:

> "'He's my lily of the valley,
> My bright and mornin' star;
> He's the fairest of ten thousand to my soul—Hallelujah!
> He's my di-dum-du-dum-di-dum—
> Di—'"

Barbara burst out laughing. Mr. Winslow's hallelujah chorus stopped in the middle and he turned.

"Eh?" he exclaimed, looking over his spectacles. "Oh, it's you! Sakes alive, child, how do you get around so quiet? Haven't borrowed the cat's feet to walk, on, have you?"

Babbie laughed again and replied that she guessed the cat wouldn't lend her feet.

"She would want 'em herself, prob'ly, Uncle Jed," she added. "Don't you think so?"

Jed appeared to consider.

"Well," he drawled, "she might, I presume likely, be as selfish and unreasonable as all that. But then again she might . . . hum . . . what was it the cat walked on in that story you and I was readin' together a spell ago? That—er—Sure Enough story—you know. By Kipling, 'twas."

"Oh, I know! It wasn't a Sure Enough story; it was a 'Just So' story. And the name of it was 'The Cat Who Walked by His Wild Lone.'"

Jed looked deeply disappointed. "Sho!" he sighed. "I thought 'twas on his wild lone he walked. I was thinkin' that maybe he'd gone walkin' on that for a spell and had lent you his feet. . . . Hum. . . . Dear, dear!

> "'Oh, trust and obey,
> For there's no other way
> To be de-de-de-di-dum—
> But to trust and obey.'"

Here he relapsed into another daydream. After waiting for a moment, Babbie ventured to arouse him.

"Uncle Jed," she asked, "what were you doing with those things in your hand—when I came in, you know? That cloth and that piece of paper. You looked so funny, rubbing them together, that I couldn't help laughing."

Jed regarded her solemnly. "It's emery paper," he said; "like fine sandpaper, you know. And the cloth's got ile in it. I'm cleanin' the rust off this screwdriver. I hadn't used it for more'n a fortni't and it got pretty rusty this damp weather."

The child looked at him wonderingly.

"But, Uncle Jed," she said, "there isn't any screwdriver. Anyhow I don't see any. You were just rubbing the sandpaper and the cloth together and singing. That's why it looked so funny."

Jed inspected first one hand and then the other.

"Hum!" he drawled. "Hu-um! . . . Well, I declare! . . . Now you mention it, there don't seem to be any screwdriver, does there? . . . Here 'tis on the bench. . . . And I was rubbin' the sandpaper with ile, or ilin' the sandpaper with the rag, whichever you like. . . . Hum, ye-es, I should think it might have looked funny. . . . Babbie, if you see me walkin' around without any head some mornin' don't be scared. You'll know that that part of me ain't got out of bed yet, that's all."

Barbara leaned her chin on both small fists and gazed at him. "Uncle Jed," she said, "you've been thinking about something, haven't you?"

"Eh? . . . Why, yes, I—I guess likely maybe I have. How did you know?"

"Oh, 'cause I did. Petunia and I know you ever and ever so well now and we're used to—to the way you do. Mamma says things like forgetting the screwdriver are your ex-eccen-tricks. Is this what you've been thinking about a nice eccen-trick or the other kind?"

Jed slowly shook his head. "I—I don't know," he groaned. "I dasn't believe— There, there! That's enough of my tricks. How's Petunia's hair curlin' this mornin'?"

After the child left him he tried to prepare his dinner, but it was as unsatisfactory a meal as breakfast had been. He couldn't eat, he couldn't work. He could only think, and thinking meant alternate periods of delirious hope and black depression. He sat down before the little table in his living-room and, opening the drawer, saw Ruth Armstrong's pictured face looking up at him.

"Jed! Oh, Jed!"

It was Maud Hunniwell's voice. She had entered the shop and the living-room without his hearing her and now she was standing behind him with her hand upon his shoulder. He started, turned and looked up into her face. And one glance caused him to forget himself and even the pictured face in the drawer for the time and to think only of her.

"Maud!" he exclaimed. "Maud!"

Her hair, usually so carefully arranged, was disordered; her hat was not adjusted at its usual exact angle; and as for the silver fox, it hung limply backside front. Her eyes were red and she held a handkerchief in one hand and a letter in the other.

"Oh, Jed!" she cried.

Jed put out his hands. "There, there, Maud!" he said. "There, there, little girl."

They had been confidants since her babyhood, these two. She came to him now, and putting her head upon his shoulder, burst into a storm of weeping. Jed stroked her hair.

"There, there, Maud," he said gently. "Don't, girlie, don't. It's goin' to be all right, I know it. . . . And so you came to me, did you? I'm awful glad you did, I am so."

"He asked me to come," she sobbed. "He wrote it—in—in the letter."

Jed led her over to a chair. "Sit down, girlie," he said, "and tell me all about it. You got the letter, then?"

She nodded. "Yes," she said, chokingly; "it—it just came. Oh, I am so glad Father did not come home to dinner to-day. He would have—have seen me and—and—oh, why did he do it, Jed? Why?"

Jed shook his head. "He had to do it, Maud," he answered. "He wanted to do the right thing and the honorable thing. And you would rather have had him do that, wouldn't you?"

"Oh—oh, I don't know. But why didn't he come to me and tell me? Why did he go away and—and write me he had gone to enlist? Why didn't he come to me first? Oh. . . . Oh, Jed, how COULD he treat me so?"

She was sobbing again. Jed took her hand and patted it with his own big one.

"Didn't he tell you in the letter why?" he asked.

"Yes—yes, but—"

"Then let me tell you what he told me, Maud. He and I talked for up'ards of three solid hours last night and I cal'late I understood him pretty well when he finished. Now let me tell you what he said to me."

He told her the substance of his long interview with Phillips. He told also of Charles' coming to Orham, of why and how he took the position in the bank, of his other talks with him—Winslow.

"And so," said Jed, in conclusion, "you see, Maud, what a dreadful load the poor young feller's been carryin' ever since he came and especially since he—well, since he found out how much he was carin' for you. Just stop for a minute and think what a load 'twas. His conscience was troublin' him all the time for keepin' the bank job, for sailin' under false colors in your eyes and your dad's. He was workin' and pinchin' to pay the two thousand to the man in Middleford. He had hangin' over him every minute the practical certainty that some day—some day sure—a person was comin' along who knew his story and then the fat would all be in the fire. And when it went into that fire he wouldn't be the only one to be burnt; there would be his sister and Babbie—and you; most of all, you."

She nodded. "Yes, yes, I know," she cried. "But why—oh, why didn't he come to me and tell me? Why did he go without a word? He must have known I would forgive him, no matter what he had done. It wouldn't have made any difference, his having been in—in prison. And now—now he may be—oh, Jed, he may be killed!"

She was sobbing again. Jed patted her hand. "We won't talk about his bein' killed," he said stoutly. "I know he won't be; I feel it in my bones. But, Maud, can't you see why he didn't come and tell you before he went to enlist? Suppose he had. If you care for him so much—as much as I judge you do—"

She interrupted. "Care for him!" she repeated. "Oh, Jed!"

"Yes, yes, dearie, I know. Well, then, carin' for him like that, you'd have told him just what you told me then; that about his havin' done what he did and havin' been where he's been not makin' any difference. And you'd have begged and coaxed him to stay right along in the bank, maybe? Eh?"

"Yes," defiantly. Of course I would. Why not?"

"And your father, would you have told him?"

She hesitated. "I don't know," she said, but with less assurance. "Perhaps so, later on. It had all been kept a secret so far, all the whole dreadful thing, why not a little longer? Besides— besides, Father knows how much Charlie means to me. Father and I had a long talk about him one night and I—I think he knows. And he is very fond of Charlie himself; he has said so so many times. He would have forgiven him, too, if I had asked him. He always does what I ask."

"Yes, ye-es, I cal'late that's so. But, to be real honest now, Maud, would you have been satisfied to have it that way? Would you have felt that it was the honorable thing for Charlie to do? Isn't what he has done better? He's undertakin' the biggest and finest job a man can do in this world to-day, as I see it. It's the job he'd have taken on months ago if he'd felt 'twas right to leave Ruth—Mrs. Armstrong—so soon after—after bein' separated from her so long. He's taken on this big job, this man's job, and he says to you: 'Here I am. You know me now. Do you care for me still? If you do will you wait till I come back?' And to your dad, to Sam, he says: 'I ain't workin' for you now. I ain't on your payroll and so I can speak out free and independent. If your daughter'll have me I mean to marry her some day.' Ain't that the better way, Maud? Ain't that how you'd rather have him feel—and do?"

She sighed and shook her head. "I—I suppose so," she admitted. "Oh, I suppose that you and he are right. In his letter he says just that. Would you like to see it; that part of it, I mean?"

Jed took the crumpled and tear-stained letter from her hand.

"I think I ought to tell you, Maud," he said, "that writin' this was his own idea. It was me that suggested his enlistin', although I found he'd been thinkin' of it all along, but I was for havin' him go and enlist and then come back and tell you and Sam. But he says, 'No. I'll tell her in a letter and then when I come back she'll have had time to think it over. She won't say 'yes' then simply because she pities me or because she doesn't realize what it means. No, I'll write her and then when I come back after enlistin' and go to her for my answer, I'll know it's given deliberate.'"

She nodded. "He says that there," she said chokingly. "But he—he must have known. Oh, Jed, how CAN I let him go—to war?"

That portion of the letter which Jed was permitted to read was straightforward and honest and manly. There were no appeals for pity or sympathy. The writer stated his case and left the rest to her, that was all. And Jed, reading between the lines, respected Charles Phillips more than ever.

He and Maud talked for a long time after that. And, at last, they reached a point which Jed had tried his best to avoid. Maud mentioned it first. She had been speaking of his friendship for her lover and for herself.

"I don't see what we should have done without your help, Jed," she said. "And when I think what you have done for Charlie! Why, yes— and now I know why you pretended to have found the four hundred dollars Father thought he had lost. Pa left it at Wapatomac, after all; you knew that?"

Jed stirred uneasily. He was standing by the window, looking out into the yard.

"Yes, yes," he said hastily, "I know. Don't talk about it, Maud. It makes me feel more like a fool than usual and . . . er . . . don't seem as if that was hardly necessary, does it?"

"But I shall talk about it. When Father came home that night he couldn't talk of anything else. He called it the prize puzzle of the century. You had given him four hundred dollars of your own money and pretended it was his and that you had—had stolen it, Jed. He burst out laughing when he told me that and so did I. The idea of your stealing anything! You!"

Jed smiled, feebly.

"'Twas silly enough, I give in," he admitted. "You see," he added, in an apologetic drawl, "nine-tenths of this town think I'm a prize idiot and sometimes I feel it's my duty to live up—or down—to my reputation. This was one of the times, that's all. I'm awful glad Sam got his own money back, though."

"The money didn't amount to anything. But what you did was the wonderful thing. For now I understand why you did it. You thought—you thought Charlie had taken it to—to pay that horrid man in Middleford. That is what you thought and you—"

Jed broke in. "Don't! Don't put me in mind of it, Maud," he begged. "I'm so ashamed I don't know what to do. You see—you see, Charlie had said how much he needed about that much money and— and so, bein' a—a woodenhead, I naturally—"

"Oh, don't! Please don't! It was wonderful of you, Jed. You not only gave up your own money, but you were willing to sacrifice your good name; to have Father, your best friend, think you a thief. And you did it all to save Charlie from exposure. How could you, Jed?"

Jed didn't answer. He did not appear to have heard her. He was gazing steadily out into the yard.

"How could you, Jed?" repeated Maud. "It was wonderful! I can't understand. I—"

She stopped at the beginning of the sentence. She was standing beside the little writing-table and the drawer was open. She looked down and there, in that drawer, she saw the framed photograph of Ruth Armstrong. She remembered that Jed had been sitting at that desk and gazing down into that drawer when she entered the room. She looked at him now. He was standing by the window peering out into the yard. Ruth had come from the back door of the little Winslow house and was standing on the step looking up the road, evidently waiting for Barbara to come from school. And Jed was watching her. Maud saw the look upon his face—and she understood.

A few moments later she and Ruth met. Maud had tried to avoid that meeting by leaving Jed's premises by the front door, the door of the outer shop. But Ruth had walked to the gate to see if Babbie was coming and, as Maud emerged from the shop, the two women came face to face. For an instant they did not speak. Maud, excited and overwrought by her experience with the letter and her interview with Jed, was still struggling for self-control, and Ruth, knowing that the other must by this time have received that letter and learned her brother's secret, was inclined to be coldly defiant. She was the first to break the silence. She said "Good afternoon" and passed on. But Maud, after another instant of hesitation, turned back.

"Oh, Mrs. Armstrong," she faltered, "may I speak with you just— just for a few minutes?"

And now Ruth hesitated. What was it the girl wished to speak about? If it was to reproach her or her brother, or to demand further explanations or apologies, the interview had far better not take place. She was in no mood to listen to reproaches. Charles was, in her eyes, a martyr and a hero and now, largely because of this girl, he was going away to certain danger, perhaps to death. She had tried, for his sake, not to blame Maud Hunniwell because Charles had fallen in love with her, but she was not, just then, inclined toward extreme forbearance. So she hesitated, and Maud spoke again.

"May I speak with you for just a few minutes?" she pleaded. "I have just got his letter and—oh, may I?"

Ruth silently led the way to the door of the little house.

"Come in," she said.

Together they entered the sitting-room. Ruth asked her caller to be seated, but Maud paid no attention.

"I have just got his letter," she faltered. "I—I wanted you to know—to know that it doesn't make any difference. I—I don't care. If he loves me, and—and he says he does—I don't care for anything else. . . . Oh,' PLEASE be nice to me," she begged, holding out her hands. "You are his sister and—and I love him so! And he is going away from both of us."

So Ruth's coldness melted like a fall of snow in early April, and the April showers followed it. She and Maud wept in each other's arms and were femininely happy accordingly. And for at least a half hour thereafter they discussed the surpassing excellencies of Charlie Phillips, the certainty that Captain Hunniwell would forgive him because he could not help it and a variety of kindred and satisfying subjects. And at last Jed Winslow drifted into the conversation.

"And so you have been talking it over with Jed," observed Ruth. "Isn't it odd how we all go to him when we are in trouble or need advice or anything? I always do and Charlie did, and you say that you do, too."

Maud nodded. "He and I have been what Pa calls 'chummies' ever since I can remember," she said simply.

"I don't know why I feel that I can confide in him to such an extent. Somehow I always have. And, do you know, his advice is almost always good? If I had taken it from the first we might, all of us, have avoided a deal of trouble. I have cause to think of Jed Winslow as something sure and safe and trustworthy. Like a nice, kindly old watch dog, you know. A queer one and a funny one, but awfully nice. Babbie idolizes him."

Maud nodded again. She was regarding her companion with an odd expression.

"And when I think," continued Ruth, "of how he was willing to sacrifice his character and his honor and even to risk losing your father's friendship—how he proclaimed himself a thief to save Charlie! When I think of that I scarcely know whether to laugh or cry. I want to do both, of course. It was perfectly characteristic and perfectly adorable—and so absolutely absurd. I love him for it, and as yet I haven't dared thank him for fear I shall cry again, as I did when Captain Hunniwell told us. Yet, when I think of his declaring he took the money to buy a suit of clothes, I feel like laughing. Oh, he IS a dear, isn't he?"

Now, ordinarily, Maud would have found nothing in this speech to arouse resentment. There was the very slight, and in this case quite unintentional, note of patronage in it that every one used when referring to Jed Winslow. She herself almost invariably used that note when speaking of him or even to him. But now her emotions were so deeply stirred and the memories of her recent interview with Jed, of his understanding and his sympathy, were so vivid. And, too, she had just had that glimpse into his most secret soul. So her tone, as she replied to Ruth's speech, was almost sharp.

"He didn't do it for Charlie," she declared. "That is, of course he did, but that wasn't the real reason."

"Why, what do you mean?"

"Don't you know what I mean? Don't you really know?"

"Why, of course I don't. What ARE you talking about? Didn't do it for Charlie? Didn't say that he was a thief and give your father his own money, do you mean? Do you mean he didn't do that for Charlie?"

"Yes. He did it for you."

"For me? For ME?"

"Yes. . . . Oh, can't you understand? It's absurd and foolish and silly and everything, but I know it's true. Jed Winslow is in love with you, Mrs. Armstrong."

Ruth leaned back in her chair and stared at her as if she thought her insane.

"In love with ME?" she repeated. "Jed Winslow! Maud, don't!"

"It's true, I tell you. I didn't know until just now, although if it had been any one but Jed I should have suspected for some time. But to-day when I went in there I saw him sitting before his desk looking down into an open drawer there. He has your photograph in that drawer. And, later on, when you came out into the yard, I saw him watching you; I saw his face and that was enough. . . . Oh, don't you SEE?" impatiently. "It explains everything. You couldn't understand, nor could I, why he should sacrifice himself so for Charlie. But because Charlie was your brother—that is another thing. Think, just think! You and I would have guessed it before if he had been any one else except just Jed. Yes, he is in love with you. . . . It's crazy and it's ridiculous and—and all that, of course it is. But," with a sudden burst of temper, "if you—if you dare to laugh I'll never speak to you again."

But Ruth was not laughing.

It was a cloudy day and Jed's living-room was almost dark when Ruth entered it. Jed, who had been sitting by the desk, rose when she came in.

"Land sakes, Ruth," he exclaimed, "it's you, ain't it? Let me light a lamp. I was settin' here in the dark like a . . . like a hen gone to roost. . . . Eh? Why, it's 'most supper 'time, ain't it? Didn't realize 'twas so late. I'll have a light for you in a jiffy."

He was on his way to the kitchen, but she stopped him.

"No," she said quickly. "Don't get a light. I'd rather not, please. And sit down again, Jed; just as you were. There, by the desk; that's it. You see," she added, "I—I—well, I have something to tell you, and—and I can tell it better in the dark, I think."

Jed looked at her in surprise. He could not see her face plainly, but she seemed oddly confused and embarrassed.

"Sho!" he drawled. "Well, I'm sure I ain't anxious about the light, myself. You know, I've always had a feelin' that the dark was more becomin' to my style of beauty. Take me about twelve o'clock in a foggy night, in a cellar, with the lamp out, and I look pretty nigh handsome—to a blind man. . . . Um-hm."

She made no comment on this confession. Jed, after waiting an instant for her to speak, ventured a reminder.

"Don't mind my talkin' foolishness," he said, apologetically. "I'm feelin' a little more like myself than I have for—for a week or so, and when I feel that way I'm bound to be foolish. Just gettin' back to nature, as the magazine folks tell about, I cal'late 'tis."

She leaned forward and laid a hand on his sleeve.

"Don't!" she begged. "Don't talk about yourself in that way, Jed. When I think what a friend you have been to me and mine I—I can't bear to hear you say such things. I have never thanked you for what you did to save my brother when you thought he had gone wrong again. I can't thank you now—I can't."

Her voice broke. Jed twisted in his seat.

"Now—now, Ruth," he pleaded, "do let's forget that. I've made a fool of myself a good many times in my life—more gettin' back to nature, you see—but I hope I never made myself out quite such a blitherin' numbskull as I did that time. Don't talk about it, don't. I ain't exactly what you'd call proud of it."

"But I am. And so is Charlie. But I won't talk of it if you prefer I shouldn't. . . . Jed—" she hesitated, faltered, and then began again: "Jed," she said, "I told you when I came in that I had something to tell you. I have. I have told no one else, not even Charlie, because he went away before I was—quite sure. But now I am going to tell you because ever since I came here you have been my father confessor, so to speak. You realize that, don't you?"

Jed rubbed his chin.

"W-e-e-ll," he observed, with great deliberation, "I don't know's I'd go as far as to say that. Babbie and I've agreed that I'm her back-step-uncle, but that's as nigh relation as I've ever dast figure I was to the family."

"Don't joke about it. You know what I mean. Well, Jed, this is what I am going to tell you. It is very personal and very confidential and you must promise not to tell any one yet. Will you?"

"Eh? Why, sartin, of course."

"Yes. I hope you may be glad to hear it. It would make you glad to know that I was happy, wouldn't it?"

For the first time Jed did not answer in the instant. The shadows were deep in the little living-room now, but Ruth felt that he was leaning forward and looking at her.

"Yes," he said, after a moment. "Yes . . . but—I don't know as I know exactly what you mean, do I?"

"You don't—yet. But I hope you will be glad when you do. Jed, you like Major Grover, don't you?"

Jed did not move perceptibly, but she heard his chair creak. He was still leaning forward and she knew his gaze was fixed upon her face.

"Yes," he said very slowly. "I like him first-rate."

"I'm glad. Because—well, because I have come to like him so much. Jed, he—he has asked me to be his wife."

There was absolute stillness in the little room. Then, after what seemed to her several long minutes, he spoke.

"Yes . . . yes, I see . . ." he said. "And you? You've . . ."

"At first I could not answer him. My brother's secret was in the way and I could not tell him that. But last night—or this morning—Charlie and I discussed all our affairs and he gave me permission to tell—Leonard. So when he came to-day I told him. He said it made no difference. And—and I am going to marry him, Jed."

Jed's chair creaked again, but that was the only sound. Ruth waited until she felt that she could wait no longer. Then she stretched out a hand toward him in the dark.

"Oh, Jed," she cried, "aren't you going to say anything to me— anything at all?"

She heard him draw a long breath. Then he spoke.

"Why—why, yes, of course," he said. "I—I—of course I am. I— you kind of got me by surprise, that's all. . . . I hadn't—hadn't expected it, you see."

"I know. Even Charlie was surprised. But you're glad, for my sake, aren't you, Jed?"

"Eh? . . . Yes, oh, yes! I'm—I'm glad."

"I hope you are. If it were not for poor Charlie's going away and the anxiety about him and his problem I should be very happy— happier than I believed I ever could be again. You're glad of that, aren't you, Jed?"

"Eh? . . . Yes, yes, of course. . . ."

"And you will congratulate me? You like Major Grover? Please say you do."

Jed rose slowly from his chair. He passed a hand in dazed fashion across his forehead.

"Yes," he said, again. "The major's a fine man. . . . I do congratulate you, ma'am."

"Oh, Jed! Not that way. As if you meant it."

"Eh? . . . I—I do mean it. . . . I hope—I hope you'll be real happy, both of you, ma'am."

"Oh, not that—Ruth."

"Yes—yes, sartin, of course . . . Ruth, I mean."

Shavings: A Novel | 267

She left him standing by the writing table. After she had gone he sank slowly down into the chair again. Eight o'clock struck and he was still sitting there.... And Fate chose that time to send Captain Sam Hunniwell striding up the walk and storming furiously at the back door.

"Jed!" roared the captain. "Jed Winslow! Jed!"

Jed lifted his head from his hands. He most decidedly did not wish to see Captain Sam or any one else.

"Jed!" roared the captain again.

Jed accepted the inevitable. "Here I am," he groaned, miserably.

The captain did not wait for an invitation to enter. Having ascertained that the owner of the building was within, he pulled the door open and stamped into the kitchen.

"Where are you?" he demanded.

"Here," replied Jed, without moving.

"Here? Where's here? ... Oh, you're in there, are you? Hidin' there in the dark, eh? Afraid to show me your face, I shouldn't wonder. By the gracious king, I should think you would be! What have you got to say to me, eh?"

Apparently Jed had nothing to say. Captain Sam did not wait.

"And you've called yourself my friend!" he sneered savagely. "Friend— you're a healthy friend, Jed Winslow! What have you got to say to me ... eh?"

Jed sighed. "Maybe I'd be better able to say it if I knew what you was talkin' about, Sam," he observed, drearily.

"Know! I guess likely you know all right. And according to her you've known all along. What do you mean by lettin' me take that— that state's prison bird into my bank? And lettin' him associate with my daughter and—and ... Oh, by gracious king! When I think that you knew what he was all along, I—I—"

His anger choked off the rest of the sentence. Jed rubbed his eyes and sat up in his chair. For the first time since the captain's entrance he realized a little of what the latter said. Before that he had been conscious only of his own dull, aching, hopeless misery.

"Hum.... So you've found out, Sam, have you?" he mused.

"Found out! You bet I've found out! I only wish to the Lord I'd found out months ago, that's all."

"Hum.... Charlie didn't tell you?... No-o, no, he couldn't have got back so soon."

"Back be hanged! I don't know whether he's back or not, blast him. But I ain't a fool ALL the time, Jed Winslow, not all the time I ain't. And when I came home tonight and found Maud cryin' to herself and no reason for it, so far as I could see, I set out to learn that reason. And I did learn it. She told me the whole yarn, the whole of it. And I saw the scamp's letter. And I dragged out of her that you—you had known all the time what he was, and had never told me a word.... Oh, how could you, Jed! How could you!"

Jed's voice was a trifle less listless as he answered.

"It was told me in confidence, Sam," he said. "I COULDN'T tell you. And, as time went along and I began to see what a fine boy Charlie really was, I felt sure 'twould all come out right in the end. And it has, as I see it."

"WHAT?"

"Yes, it's come out all right. Charlie's gone to fight, same as every decent young feller wants to do. He thinks the world of Maud and she does of him, but he was honorable enough not to ask her while he worked for you, Sam. He wrote the letter after he'd gone so as to make it easier for her to say no, if she felt like sayin' it. And when he came back from enlistin' he was goin' straight to you to make a clean breast of everything. He's a good boy, Sam. He's had hard luck and he's been in trouble, but he's all right and I know it. And you know it, too, Sam Hunniwell. Down inside you you know it, too. Why, you've told me a hundred times what a fine chap Charlie Phillips was and how much you thought of him, and—"

Captain Hunniwell interrupted. "Shut up!" he commanded. "Don't talk to me that way! Don't you dare to! I did think a lot of him, but that was before I knew what he'd done and where he'd been. Do you cal'late I'll let my daughter marry a man that's been in state's prison?"

"But, Sam, it wan't all his fault, really. And he'll go straight from this on. I know he will."

"Shut up! He can go to the devil from this on, but he shan't take her with him.... Why, Jed, you know what Maud is to me. She's all I've got. She's all I've contrived for and worked for in this world. Think of all the plans I've made for her!"

"I know, Sam, I know; but pretty often our plans don't work out just as we make 'em. Sometimes we have to change 'em—or give 'em up. And you want Maud to be happy."

"Happy! I want to be happy myself, don't I? Do you think I'm goin' to give up all my plans and all my happiness just—just because she wants to make a fool of herself? Give 'em up! It's easy for you to say 'give up.' What do you know about it?"

It was the last straw. Jed sprang to his feet so suddenly that his chair fell to the floor.

"Know about it!" he burst forth, with such fierce indignation that the captain actually gasped in astonishment. "Know about it!" repeated Jed. "What do I know about givin' up my own plans and— and hopes, do you mean? Oh, my Lord above! Ain't I been givin' 'em up and givin' 'em up all my lifelong? When I was a boy didn't I give up the education that might have made me a—a MAN instead of—of a town laughin' stock? While Mother lived was I doin' much but give up myself for her? I ain't sayin' 'twas any more'n right that I should, but I did it, didn't I? And ever since it's been the same way. I tell you, I've come to believe that life for me means one 'give up' after the other and won't mean anything but that till I die. And you—you ask me what I know about it! YOU do!"

Captain Sam was so taken aback that he was almost speechless. In all his long acquaintance with Jed Winslow he had never seen him like this.

"Why—why, Jed!" he stammered. But Jed was not listening. He strode across the room and seized his visitor by the arm.

"You go home, Sam Hunniwell," he ordered. "Go home and think—THINK, I tell you. All your life you've had just what I haven't. You married the girl you wanted and you and she were happy together. You've been looked up to and respected here in Orham; folks never laughed at you or called you 'town crank.' You've got a daughter and she's a good girl. And the man she wants to marry is a good man, and, if you'll give him a chance and he lives through the war he's goin' into, he'll make you proud of him. You go home, Sam Hunniwell! Go home, and thank God you're what you are and AS you are. . . . No, I won't talk! I don't want to talk! . . . Go HOME."

He had been dragging his friend to the door. Now he actually pushed him across the threshold and slammed the door between them.

"Well, for . . . the Lord . . . sakes!" exclaimed Captain Hunniwell.

The scraping of the key in the lock was his only answer.

CHAPTER XXI

A child spends time and thought and energy upon the building of a house of blocks. By the time it is nearing completion it has become to him a very real edifice. Therefore, when it collapses into an ungraceful heap upon the floor it is poor consolation to be reminded that, after all, it was merely a block house and couldn't be expected to stand.

Jed, in his own child-like fashion, had reared his moonshine castle beam by beam. At first he had regarded it as moonshine and had refused to consider the building of it anything but a dangerously pleasant pastime. And then, little by little, as his dreams changed to hopes, it had become more and more real, until, just before the end, it was the foundation upon which his future was to rest. And down it came, and there was his future buried in the ruins.

And it had been all moonshine from the very first. Jed, sitting there alone in his little living-room, could see now that it had been nothing but that. Ruth Armstrong, young, charming, cultured— could she have thought of linking her life with that of Jedidah Edgar Wilfred Winslow, forty-five, "town crank" and builder of windmills? Of course not—and again of course not. Obviously she never had thought of such a thing. She had been grateful, that was all; perhaps she had pitied him just a little and behind her expressions of kindliness and friendship was pity and little else. Moonshine—moonshine—moonshine. And, oh, what a fool he had been! What a poor, silly fool!

So the night passed and morning came and with it a certain degree of bitterly philosophic acceptance of the situation. He WAS a fool; so much was sure. He was of no use in the world, he never had been. People laughed at him and he deserved to be laughed at. He rose from the bed upon which he had thrown himself some time during the early morning hours and, after eating a cold mouthful or two in lieu of breakfast, sat down at his turning lathe. He could make children's whirligigs, that was the measure of his capacity.

All the forenoon the lathe hummed. Several times steps sounded on the front walk and the latch of the shop door rattled, but Jed did not rise from his seat. He had not unlocked that door, he did not mean to for the present. He did not want to wait on customers; he did not want to see callers; he did not want to talk or be talked to. He did not want to think, either, but that he could not help.

And he could not shut out all the callers. One, who came a little after noon, refused to remain shut out. She pounded the door and shouted "Uncle Jed" for some few minutes; then, just as Jed had begun to think she had given up and gone away, he heard a thumping upon the window pane and, looking up, saw her laughing and nodding outside.

"I see you, Uncle Jed," she called. "Let me in, please."

So Jed was obliged to let her in and she entered with a skip and a jump, quite unconscious that her "back-step-uncle" was in any way different, either in feelings or desire for her society, than he had been for months.

"Why did you have the door locked, Uncle Jed?" she demanded. "Did you forget to unlock it?"

Jed, without looking at her, muttered something to the effect that he cal'lated he must have.

"Um-hm," she observed, with a nod of comprehension. "I thought that was it. You did it once before, you know. It was a ex-eccen- trick, leaving it locked was, I guess. Don't you think it was a— a—one of those kind of tricks, Uncle Jed?"

Silence, except for the hum and rasp of the lathe.

"Don't you, Uncle Jed?" repeated Barbara.

"Eh? . . . Oh, yes, I presume likely so."

Babbie, sitting on the lumber pile, kicked her small heels together and regarded him with speculative interest.

"Uncle Jed," she said, after a few moments of silent consideration, "what do you suppose Petunia told me just now?"

No answer.

"What do you suppose Petunia told me?" repeated Babbie. "Something about you 'twas, Uncle Jed."

Still Jed did not reply. His silence was not deliberate; he had been so absorbed in his own pessimistic musings that he had not heard the question, that was all. Barbara tried again.

"She told me she guessed you had been thinking AWF'LY hard about something this time, else you wouldn't have so many eccen-tricks to-day."

Silence yet. Babbie swallowed hard:

"I—I don't think I like eccen-tricks, Uncle Jed," she faltered.

Not a word. Then Jed, stooping to pick up a piece of wood from the pile of cut stock beside the lathe, was conscious of a little sniff. He looked up. His small visitor's lip was quivering and two big tears were just ready to overflow her lower lashes.

"Eh? . . . Mercy sakes alive!" he exclaimed. "Why, what's the matter?"

The lip quivered still more. "I—I don't like to have you not speak to me," sobbed Babbie. "You—you never did it so—so long before."

That appeal was sufficient. Away, for the time, went Jed's pessimism and his hopeless musings. He forgot that he was a fool, the "town crank," and of no use in the world. He forgot his own heartbreak, chagrin and disappointment. A moment later Babbie was on his knee, hiding her emotion in the front of his jacket, and he was trying his best to soothe her with characteristic Winslow nonsense.

"You mustn't mind me, Babbie," he declared. "My—my head ain't workin' just right to-day, seems so. I shouldn't wonder if—if I wound it too tight, or somethin' like that."

Babbie's tear-stained face emerged from the jacket front.

"Wound your HEAD too tight, Uncle Jed?" she cried.

"Ye-es, yes. I was kind of extra absent-minded yesterday and I thought I wound the clock, but I couldn't have done that 'cause the clock's stopped. Yet I know I wound somethin' and it's just as liable to have been my head as anything else. You listen just back of my starboard ear there and see if I'm tickin' reg'lar."

The balance of the conversation between the two was of a distinctly personal nature.

"You see, Uncle Jed," said Barbara, as she jumped from his knee preparatory to running off to school, "I don't like you to do eccen-tricks and not talk to me. I don't like it at all and neither does Petunia. You won't do any more—not for so long at a time, will you, Uncle Jed?"

Jed sighed. "I'll try not to," he said, soberly.

She nodded. "Of course," she observed, "we shan't mind you doing a few, because you can't help that. But you mustn't sit still and not pay attention when we talk for ever and ever so long. I—I don't know precactly what I and Petunia would do if you wouldn't talk to us, Uncle Jed."

"Don't, eh? Humph! I presume likely you'd get along pretty well. I ain't much account."

Barbara looked at him in horrified surprise.

"Oh, Uncle Jed!" she cried, "you mustn't talk so! You MUSTN'T! Why—why, you're the bestest man there is. And there isn't anybody in Orham can make windmills the way you can. I asked Teacher if there was and she said no. So there! And you're a GREAT cons'lation to all our family," she added, solemnly. "We just couldn't ever—EVER do without you."

When the child went Jed did not take the trouble to lock the door after her; consequently his next callers entered without difficulty and came directly to the inner shop. Jed, once more absorbed in gloomy musings—not quite as gloomy, perhaps; somehow the clouds had not descended quite so heavily upon his soul since Babbie's visit—looked up to see there standing behind him Maud Hunniwell and Charlie Phillips.

He sprang to his feet. "Eh?" he cried, delightedly. "Well, well, so you're back, Charlie, safe and sound. Well, well!"

Phillips grasped the hand which Jed had extended and shook it heartily.

"Yes, I'm back," he said.

"Um-hm. . . . And—er—how did you leave Uncle Sam? Old feller's pretty busy these days, 'cordin' to the papers."

"Yes, I imagine he is."

"Um-hm. . . . Well, did you—er—make him happy? Give his army the one thing needful to make it—er—perfect?"

Charlie laughed. "If you mean did I add myself to it," he said, "I did. I am an enlisted man now, Jed. As soon as Von Hindenburg hears that, he'll commit suicide, I'm sure."

Jed insisted on shaking hands with him again. "You're a lucky feller, Charlie," he declared. "I only wish I had your chance. Yes, you're lucky—in a good many ways," with a glance at Maud. "And, speaking of Uncle Sam," he added, "reminds me of—well, of Daddy Sam. How's he behavin' this mornin'? I judge from the fact that you two are together he's a little more rational than he was last night. . . . Eh?"

Phillips looked puzzled, but Maud evidently understood. "Daddy has been very nice to-day," she said, demurely. "Charlie had a long talk with him and—and—"

"And he was mighty fine," declared Phillips with emphasis. "We had a heart to heart talk and I held nothing back. I tell you, Jed, it did me good to speak the truth, whole and nothing but. I told Captain Hunniwell that I didn't deserve his daughter. He agreed with me there, of course."

"Nonsense!" interrupted Maud, with a happy laugh.

"Not a bit of nonsense. We agreed that no one was good enough for you. But I told him I wanted that daughter very much indeed and, provided she was agreeable and was willing to wait until the war was over and I came back; taking it for granted, of course, that I—"

He hesitated, bit his lip and looked apprehensively at Miss Hunniwell. Jed obligingly helped him over the thin ice.

"Provided you come back a major general or—or a commodore or a corporal's guard or somethin'," he observed.

"Yes," gratefully, "that's it. I'm sure to be a high private at least. Well, to cut it short, Jed, I told Captain Hunniwell all my past and my hopes and plans for the future. He was forgiving and forbearing and kinder than I had any right to expect. We understand each other now and he is willing, always provided that Maud is willing, too, to give me my opportunity to make good. That is all any one could ask."

"Yes, I should say 'twas. . . . But Maud, how about her? You had consider'ble of a job makin' her see that you was worth waitin' for, I presume likely, eh?"

Maud laughed and blushed and bade him behave himself. Jed demanded to be told more particulars concerning the enlisting. So Charles told the story of his Boston trip, while Maud looked and listened adoringly, and Jed, watching the young people's happiness, was, for the time, almost happy himself.

When they rose to go Charlie laid a hand on Jed's shoulder.

"I can't tell you," he said, "what a brick you've been through all this. If it hadn't been for you, old man, I don't know how it might have ended. We owe you about everything, Maud and I. You've been a wonder, Jed."

Jed waved a deprecating hand. "Don't talk so, Charlie," he said, gruffly.

"But, I tell you, I—"

"Don't. . . . You see," with a twist of the lip, "it don't do to tell a—a screech owl he's a canary. He's liable to believe it by and by and start singin' in public. . . . Then he finds out he's just a fool owl, and has been all along. Humph! Me a wonder! . . . A blunder, you mean."

Neither of the young people had ever heard him use that tone before. They both cried out in protest.

"Look here, Jed—" began Phillips.

Maud interrupted. "Just a moment, Charlie," she said. "Let me tell him what Father said last night. When he went out he left me crying and so miserable that I wanted to die. He had found Charlie's letter and we—we had had a dreadful scene and he had spoken to me as I had never heard him speak before. And, later, after he came back I was almost afraid to have him come into the room where I was. But he was just as different as could be. He told me he had been thinking the matter over and had decided that, perhaps, he had been unreasonable and silly and cross. Then he said some nice things about Charlie, quite different from what he said at first. And when we had made it all up and I asked him what had changed his mind so he told me it was you, Jed. He said he came to you and you put a flea in his ear. He wouldn't tell me what he meant, but he simply smiled and said you had put a flea in his ear."

Jed, himself, could not help smiling faintly.

"W-e-e-ll," he drawled, "I didn't use any sweet ile on the job, that's sartin. If he said I pounded it in with a club 'twouldn't have been much exaggeration."

"So we owe you that, too," continued Maud. "And, afterwards, when Daddy and I were talking we agreed that you were probably the best man in Orham. There!"

And she stooped impulsively and kissed him.

Jed, very much embarrassed, shook his head. "That—er—insect I put in your pa's ear must have touched both your brains, I cal'late," he drawled. But he was pleased, nevertheless. If he was a fool it was something to have people think him a good sort of fool.

It was almost four o'clock when Jed's next visitor came. He was the one man whom he most dreaded to meet just then. Yet he hid his feelings and rose with hand outstretched.

"Why, good afternoon, Major!" he exclaimed. "Real glad to see you. Sit down."

Grover sat. "Jed," he said, "Ruth tells me that you know of my good fortune. Will you congratulate me?"

Jed's reply was calm and deliberate and he did his best to make it sound whole-hearted and sincere.

"I sartin do," he declared. "Anybody that wouldn't congratulate you on that could swap his head for a billiard ball and make money on the dicker; the ivory he'd get would be better than the bone he gave away. . . . Yes, Major Grover, you're a lucky man."

To save his life he could not entirely keep the shake from his voice as he said it. If Grover noticed it he put it down to the sincerity of the speaker.

"Thank you," he said. "I realize my luck, I assure you. And now, Jed, first of all, let me thank you. Ruth has told me what a loyal friend and counselor you have been to her and she and I both are very, very grateful."

Jed stirred uneasily. "Sho, sho!" he protested. "I haven't done anything. Don't talk about it, please. I—I'd rather you wouldn't."

"Very well, since you wish it, I won't. But she and I will always think of it, you may be sure of that. I dropped in here now just to tell you this and to thank you personally. And I wanted to tell you, too, that I think we need not fear Babbitt's talking too much. Of course it would not make so much difference now if he did; Charlie will be away and doing what all decent people will respect him for doing, and you and I can see that Ruth does not suffer. But I think Babbitt will keep still. I hope I have frightened him; I certainly did my best."

Jed rubbed his chin.

"I'm kind of sorry for Phin," he observed.

"Are you? For heaven's sake, why?"

"Oh, I don't know. When you've been goin' around ever since January loaded up to the muzzle with spite and sure-thing vengeance, same as an old-fashioned horse pistol used to be loaded with powder and ball, it must be kind of hard, just as you're set to pull trigger, to have to quit and swaller the whole charge. Liable to give you dyspepsy, if nothin' worse, I should say."

Grover smiled. "The last time I saw Babbitt he appeared to be nearer apoplexy than dyspepsia," he said.

"Ye-es. Well, I'm sorry for him, I really am. It must be pretty dreadful to be so cross-grained that you can't like even your own self without feelin' lonesome. . . . Yes, that's a bad state of affairs. . . . I don't know but I'd almost rather be 'town crank' than that."

The Major's farewell remark, made as he rose to go, contained an element of mystery.

"I shall have another matter to talk over with you soon, Jed," he said. "But that will come later, when my plans are more complete. Good afternoon and thank you once more. You've been pretty fine through all this secret-keeping business, if you don't mind my saying so. And a mighty true friend. So true," he added, "that I shall, in all probability, ask you to assume another trust for me before long. I can't think of any one else to whom I could so safely leave it. Good-by."

One more visitor came that afternoon. To be exact, he did not come until evening. He opened the outer door very softly and tiptoed into the living-room. Jed was sitting by the little "gas burner" stove, one knee drawn up and his foot swinging. There was a saucepan perched on top of the stove. A small hand lamp on the table furnished the only light. He did not hear the person who entered and when a big hand was laid upon his shoulder he started violently.

"Eh?" he exclaimed, his foot falling with a thump to the floor. "Who? . . . Oh, it's you, ain't it, Sam? . . . Good land, you made me jump! I must be gettin' nervous, I guess."

Captain Sam looked at him in some surprise. "Gracious king, I believe you are," he observed. "I didn't think you had any nerves, Jed. No, nor any temper, either, until last night. You pretty nigh blew me out of water then. Ho, ho!"

Jed was much distressed. "Sho, sho, Sam," he stammered; "I'm awful sorry about that. I—I wasn't feelin' exactly—er—first rate or I wouldn't have talked to you that way. I—I—you know I didn't mean it, don't you, Sam?"

The captain pulled forward a chair and sat down. He chuckled. "Well, I must say it did sound as if you meant it, Jed," he declared. "Yes, sir, I cal'late the average person would have been willin' to risk a small bet—say a couple of million—that you meant it. When you ordered me to go home I just tucked my tail down and went. Yes, sir, if you didn't mean it you had ME fooled. Ho, ho!"

Jed's distress was keener than ever. "Mercy sakes alive!" he cried. "Did I tell you to go home, Sam? Yes, yes, I remember I did. Sho, sho! . . . Well, I'm awful sorry. I hope you'll forgive me. 'Twan't any way for a feller like me to talk—to you."

Captain Sam's big hand fell upon his friend's knee with a stinging slap. "You're wrong there, Jed," he declared, with emphasis. "'Twas just the way for you to talk to me. I needed it; and," with another chuckle, "I got it, too, didn't I? Ho, ho!"

"Sam, I snum, I—"

"Sshh! You're goin' to say you're sorry again; I can see it in your eye. Well, don't you do it. You told me to go home and think, Jed, and those were just the orders I needed. I did go home and I did think. . . . Humph! Thinkin's a kind of upsettin' job sometimes, ain't it, especially when you sit right down and think about yourself, what you are compared to what you think you are. Ever think about yourself that way, Jed?"

It was a moment before Jed answered. Then all he said was, "Yes."

"I mean have you done it lately? Just given yourself right up to doin' it?"

Jed sighed. "Ye-es," he drawled. "I shouldn't wonder if I had, Sam."

"Well, probably 'twan't as disturbin' a job with you as 'twas for me. You didn't have as high a horse to climb down off of. I thought and thought and thought and the more I thought the meaner the way I'd acted and talked to Maud seemed to me. I liked Charlie; I'd gone around this county for months braggin' about what a smart, able chap he was. As I told you once I'd rather have had her marry him than anybody else I know. And I had to give in that the way he'd behaved—his goin' off and enlistin', settlin' that before he asked her or spoke to me, was a square, manly thing to do. The only thing I had against him was that Middleford mess. And I believe he's a GOOD boy in spite of it."

"He is, Sam. That Middleford trouble wan't all his fault, by any means!"

"I know. He told me this mornin'. Well, then, if he and Maud love each other, thinks I, what right have I to say they shan't be happy, especially as they're both willin' to wait? Why should I say he can't at least have his chance to make good? Nigh's I could make out the only reason was my pride and the big plans I'd made for my girl. I came out of my thinkin' spell with my mind made up that what ailed me was selfishness and pride. So I talked it over with her last night and with Charlie to-day. The boy shall have his chance. Both of 'em shall have their chance, Jed. They're happy and—well, I feel consider'ble better myself. All else there is to do is to just hope to the Lord it turns out right."

"That's about all, Sam. And I feel pretty sure it's goin' to."

"Yes, I know you do. Course those big plans of mine that I used to make—her marryin' some rich chap, governor or senator or somethin'—they're all gone overboard. I used to wish and wish for her, like a young-one wishin' on a load of hay, or the first star at night, or somethin'. But if we can't have our wishes, why—why— then we'll do without 'em. Eh?"

Jed rubbed his chin. "Sam," he said, "I've been doin' a little thinkin' myself. . . . Ye-es, consider'ble thinkin'. . . . Fact is, seems now as if I hadn't done anything BUT think since the world was cranked up and started turnin' over. And I guess there's only one answer. When we can't have our wishes then it's up to us to—to—"

"Well, to what?"

"Why, to stick to our jobs and grin, that's about all. 'Tain't much, I know, especially jobs like some of us have, but it's somethin'."

Captain Sam nodded. "It's a good deal, Jed," he declared. "It's some stunt to grin—in these days."

Jed rose slowly to his feet. He threw back his shoulders with the gesture of one determined to rid himself of a burden.

"It is—it is so, Sam," he drawled. "But maybe that makes it a little more worth while. What do you think?"

His friend regarded him thoughtfully. "Jed," he said, "I never saw anybody who had the faculty of seein' straight through to the common sense inside of things the way you have. Maud and I were talkin' about that last night. 'Go home and think and thank God,' you said to me. And that was what I needed to do. 'Enlist and you'll be independent,' you said to Charlie and it set him on the road. 'Stick to your job and grin,' you say now. How do you do it, Jed? Remember one time I told you I couldn't decide whether you was a dum fool or a King Solomon? I know now. Of the two of us I'm nigher to bein' the dum fool; and, by the gracious king, you ARE a King Solomon."

Jed slowly shook his head. "Sam," he said, sadly, "if you knew what I know about me you'd . . . but there, you're talkin' wild. I was cal'latin' to have a cup of tea and you'd better have one, too. I'm heatin' some water on top of the stove now. It must be about ready."

He lifted the saucepan from the top of the "gas burner" and tested the water with his finger.

"Hum," he mused, "it's stone cold. I can't see why it hasn't het faster. I laid a nice fresh fire, too."

He opened the stove door and looked in.

"Hum . . ." he said, again. "Yes, yes . . . I laid it but, I—er— hum . . . I forgot to light it, that's all. Well, that proves I'm King Solomon for sartin. Probably he did things like that every day or so. . . . Give me a match, will you, Sam?"

CHAPTER XXII

It had been a chill morning in early spring when Charlie Phillips went to Boston to enlist. Now it was a balmy evening in August and Jed sat upon a bench by his kitchen door looking out to sea. The breeze was light, barely sufficient to turn the sails of the little mills, again so thickly sprinkled about the front yard, or to cause the wooden sailors to swing their paddles. The August moon was rising gloriously behind the silver bar of the horizon. From the beach below the bluff came the light laughter of a group of summer young folk, strolling from the hotel to the post-office by the shore route.

Babbie, who had received permission to sit up and see the moon rise, was perched upon the other end of the bench, Petunia in her arms. A distant drone, which had been audible for some time, was gradually becoming a steady humming roar. A few moments later and a belated hydro-aeroplane passed across the face of the moon, a dragon-fly silhouette against the shining disk.

"That bumble-bee's gettin' home late," observed Jed. "The rest of the hive up there at East Harniss have gone to roost two or three hours ago. Wonder what kept him out this scandalous hour. Had tire trouble, think?"

Barbara laughed.

"You're joking again, Uncle Jed," she said. "That kind of aeroplane couldn't have any tire trouble, 'cause it hasn't got any tires."

Mr. Winslow appeared to reflect. "That's so," he admitted, "but I don't know as we'd ought to count too much on that. I remember when Gabe Bearse had brain fever."

This was a little deep for Babbie, whose laugh was somewhat uncertain. She changed the subject.

"Oh!" she cried, with a wiggle, "there's a caterpillar right here on this bench with us, Uncle Jed. He's a fuzzy one, too; I can see the fuzz; the moon makes it shiny."

Jed bent over to look. "That?" he said. "That little, tiny one? Land sakes, he ain't big enough to be more than a kitten-pillar. You ain't afraid of him, are you?"

"No-o. No, I guess I'm not. But I shouldn't like to have him walk on me. He'd be so—so ticklesome."

Jed brushed the caterpillar off into the grass.

"There he goes," he said. "I've got to live up to my job as guardian, I expect. Last letter I had from your pa he said he counted on my lookin' out for you and your mamma. If he thought I let ticklesome kitten-pillars come walkin' on you he wouldn't cal'late I amounted to much."

For this was the "trust" to which Major Grover had referred in his conversation with Jed. Later he explained his meaning. He was expecting soon to be called to active service "over there." Before he went he and Ruth were to be married.

"My wife and Barbara will stay here in the old house, Jed," he said, "if you are willing. And I shall leave them in your charge. It's a big trust, for they're pretty precious articles, but they'll be safe with you."

Jed looked at him aghast. "Good land of love!" he cried. "You don't mean it?"

"Of course I mean it. Don't look so frightened, man. It's just what you've been doing ever since they came here, that's all. Ruth says she has been going to you for advice since the beginning. I just want her to keep on doing it."

"But—but, my soul, I—I ain't fit to be anybody's guardian. . . . I—I ought to have somebody guardin' me. Anybody'll tell you that. . . . Besides, I—I don't think—"

"Yes, you do; and you generally think right. Oh, come, don't talk any more about it. It's a bargain, of course. And if there's anything I can do for you on the other side, I'll be only too happy to oblige."

Jed rubbed his chin. "W-e-e-ll," he drawled, "there's one triflin' thing I've been hankerin' to do myself, but I can't, I'm afraid. Maybe you can do it for me."

"All right, what is the trifling thing?"

"Eh? . . . Oh, that—er—-Crown Prince thing. Do him brown, if you get a chance, will you?"

Of course, the guardianship was, in a sense, a joke, but in another it was not. Jed knew that Leonard Grover's leaving his wife and Babbie in his charge was, to a certain extent, a serious trust. And he accepted it as such.

"Has your mamma had any letters from the major the last day or so?" he inquired.

Babbie shook her head. "No," she said, "but she's expecting one every day. And Petunia and I expect one, too, and we're just as excited about it as we can be. A letter like that is most par- particklesome exciting. . . . No, I don't mean particklesome—it was the caterpillar made me think of that. I mean partickle-ar exciting. Don't you think it is, Uncle Jed?"

Captain Sam Hunniwell came strolling around the corner of the shop. Jed greeted him warmly and urged him to sit down. The captain declined.

"Can't stop," he declared. "There's a letter for Maud from Charlie in to-night's mail and I want to take it home to her. Letters like that can't be held up on the way, you know."

Charlie Phillips, too, was in France with his regiment.

"I presume likely you've heard the news from Leander Babbitt, Jed?" asked Captain Sam.

"About his bein' wounded? Yes, Gab flapped in at the shop this afternoon to caw over it. Said the telegram had just come to Phineas. I was hopin' 'twasn't so, but Eri Hedge said he heard it, too. . . . Serious, is it, Sam?"

"They don't say, but I shouldn't wonder. The boy was hit by a shell splinter while doin' his duty with exceptional bravery, so the telegram said. 'Twas from Washin'ton, of course. And there was somethin' in it about his bein' recommended for one of those war crosses."

Jed sat up straight on the bench. "You don't mean it!" he cried. "Well, well, well! Ain't that splendid! I knew he'd do it, too. 'Twas in him, Sam," he added, solemnly, "did I tell you I got a letter from him last week?"

"From Leander?"

"Yes. . . . And before I got it he must have been wounded. . . . Yes, sir, before I got his letter. . . . 'Twas a good letter, Sam, a mighty good letter. Some time I'll read it to you. Not a complaint in it, just cheerfulness, you know, and—and grit and confidence, but no brag."

"I see. Well, Charlie writes the same way."

"Ye-es. They all do, pretty much. Well, how about Phineas? How does the old feller take the news? Have you heard?"

"Why, yes, I've heard. Of course I haven't talked with him. He'd no more speak to me than he would to the Evil One."

Jed's lip twitched. "Why, probably not quite so quick, Sam," he drawled. "Phin ought to be on pretty good terms with the Old Scratch. I've heard him recommend a good many folks to go to him."

"Ho, ho! Yes, that's so. Well, Jim Bailey told me that when Phin had read the telegram he never said a word. Just got up and walked into his back shop. But Jerry Burgess said that, later on, at the post-office somebody said somethin' about how Leander must be a mighty good fighter to be recommended for that cross, and Phineas was openin' his mail box and heard 'em. Jerry says old Phin turned and snapped out over his shoulder: 'Why not? He's my son, ain't he?' So there you are. Maybe that's pride, or cussedness, or both. Anyhow, it's Phin Babbitt."

As the captain was turning to go he asked his friend a question.

"Jed," he asked, "what in the world have you taken your front gate off the hinges for?"

Jed, who had been gazing dreamily out to sea for the past few minutes, started and came to life.

"Eh?" he queried. "Did—did you speak, Sam?"

"Yes, but you haven't yet. I asked you what you took your front gate off the hinges for."

"Oh, I didn't. I took the hinges off the gate."

"Well, it amounts to the same thing. The gate's standin' up alongside the fence. What did you do it for?"

Jed sighed. "It squeaked like time," he drawled, "and I had to stop it."

"So you took the hinges off? Gracious king! Why didn't you ile 'em so they wouldn't squeak?"

"Eh? . . . Oh, I did set out to, but I couldn't find the ile can. The only thing I could find was the screwdriver and at last I came to the conclusion the Almighty must have meant me to use it; so I did. Anyhow, it stopped the squeakin'."

Captain Sam roared delightedly. "That's fine," he declared. "It does me good to have you act that way. You haven't done anything so crazy as that for the last six months. I believe the old Jed Winslow's come back again. That's fine."

Jed smiled his slow smile. "I'm stickin' to my job, Sam," he said.

"And grinnin'. Don't forget to grin, Jed."

"W-e-e-ll, when I stick to MY job, Sam, 'most everybody grins."

Babbie accompanied the captain to the place where the gate had been. Jed, left alone, hummed a hymn. The door of the little house next door opened and Ruth came out into the yard.

"Where is Babbie?" she asked.

"She's just gone as far as the sidewalk with Cap'n Sam Hunniwell," was Jed's reply. "She's all right. Don't worry about her."

Ruth laughed lightly. "I don't," she said. "I know she is all right when she is with you, Jed."

Babbie came dancing back. Somewhere in a distant part of the village a dog was howling dismally.

"What makes that dog bark that way, Uncle Jed?" asked Babbie.

Jed was watching Ruth, who had walked to the edge of the bluff and was looking off over the water, her delicate face and slender figure silver-edged by the moonlight.

"Eh? . . . That dog?" he repeated. "Oh, he's barkin' at the moon, I shouldn't wonder."

"At the moon? Why does he bark at the moon?"

"Oh, he thinks he wants it, I cal'late. Wants it to eat or play with or somethin'. Dogs get funny notions, sometimes."

Babbie laughed. "I, think he's awf'ly silly," she said. "He couldn't have the moon, you know, could he? The moon wasn't made for a dog."

Jed, still gazing at Ruth, drew a long breath.

"That's right," he admitted.

The child listened to the lugubrious canine wails for a moment; then she said thoughtfully: "I feel kind of sorry for this poor dog, though. He sounds as if he wanted the moon just dreadf'ly."

"Um . . . yes . . . I presume likely he thinks he does. But he'll feel better about it by and by. He'll realize that, same as you say, the moon wasn't made for a dog. Just as soon as he comes to that conclusion, he'll be a whole lot better dog. . . . Yes, and a happier one, too," he added, slowly.

Barbara did not speak at once and Jed began to whistle a doleful melody. Then the former declared, with emphasis: "I think SOME dogs are awf'ly nice."

"Um? . . . What? . . . Oh, you do, eh?"

She snuggled close to him on the bench.

"I think you're awf'ly nice, too, Uncle Jed," she confided.

Jed looked down at her over his spectacles.

"Sho! . . . Bow, wow!" he observed.

Babbie burst out laughing. Ruth turned and came toward them over the dew-sprinkled grass.

"What are you laughing at, dear?" she asked.

"Oh, Uncle Jed was so funny. He was barking like a dog."

Ruth smiled. "Perhaps he feels as if he were our watchdog, Babbie," she said. "He guards us as if he were."

Babbie hugged her back-step-uncle's coat sleeve.

"He's a great, big, nice old watchdog," she declared. "We love him, don't we, Mamma?"

Jed turned his head to listen.

"Hum . . ." he drawled. "That dog up town has stopped his howlin'. Perhaps he's beginnin' to realize what a lucky critter he is."

As usual, Babbie was ready with a question.

"Why is he lucky, Uncle Jed?" she asked.

"Why? Oh, well, he . . . he can LOOK at the moon, and that's enough to make any dog thankful."